DEATH CANYON

A JAKE TRENT NOVEL

DAVID RILEY BERTSCH

SCRIBNER
New York   London   Toronto   Sydney   New Delhi

SCRIBNER
A Division of Simon & Schuster, Inc.
1230 Avenue of the Americas
New York, NY 10020

First Scribner hardcover edition August 2013

SCRIBNER and design are registered trademarks of The Gale Group, Inc., used under license by Simon & Schuster, Inc., the publisher of this work.

For information about special discounts for bulk purchases, please contact Simon & Schuster Special Sales at 1-866-506-1949 or business@simonand schuster.com.

The Simon & Schuster Speakers Bureau can bring authors to your live event. For more information or to book an event, contact the Simon & Schuster Speakers Bureau at 1-866-248-3049 or visit our website at www.simonspeakers .com.

Designed by Jill Putorti

Manufactured in the United States of America

10   9   8   7   6   5   4   3   2   1

Library of Congress Cataloging-in-Publication Data is available.

ISBN 978-1-4516-9800-8
ISBN 978-1-4516-9802-2 (ebook)

*This book is dedicated to my
lovely and supportive wife, Katie, and to my family.
Without you, I would never have had the courage to try.*

JACKSON HOLE, WYOMING

One early summer evening, the valley was filled with a hushed rumbling. At first only the wildlife and household pets took notice. It was something almost magnetic, an ethereal reverberation that didn't easily fit into any one sensory category. The elk and bison perceived it at the base of their skulls where their spinal cords met their brains. Their ears perked up in unspoken unison as they looked at the other animals in their herds. *A threat, but what kind of threat?* Their oversized binocular eyes scanned the tree lines and hillsides for predators. *Nothing.*

When the earth moved beneath them again, the shiver was no longer a delicate static. It morphed toward the realm of the physical, corporeal. Pebbles jumped about on the earth like dry corn dumped into a scorching-hot pan.

Its intensity increased rapidly. Almost exponentially. The mammals stamped their feet, their eyes still wandering to find the source of the tumult. The tremors amplified so that humans could detect them, too, and people in town stopped what they were doing, alarmed. They braced themselves for a full-blown quake, eyeing doorjambs and safe spots.

Then, it stopped. The valley was still again. The herds resumed their evening grazing. The townspeople resumed their shopping, headed out to dinner, or went back to work.

But the phenomenon repeated itself the next morning and again a few days later, over and over until the frequency of small tremors called the regional newspapers to attention. The headline in the *Daily* read, "Quakes Felt from Bend, Oregon, to Cedar Breaks, Utah."

Taproom and restaurant conversation convulsed with speculation. *Could this really be it?* Quakes weren't unheard of here, but not like this. Everyone, even regional scientists and universities, began taking notice. Twenty-three occurrences in nine days.

Are we due for the big one?

SNAKE RIVER CANYON, JACKSON HOLE. ONE MONTH LATER.

"What the hell was that?" the first man asked.

His companion shook his head. "'Nother quake maybe."

Once the men were sure their friend was dead, they rigged a ratty climbing rope loose around his ankles so they could pull it off him when they were done. They had no choice but to burn the rope—if someone found it near the body, their plan would fail.

Straining in the dark, they lowered the corpse from the cliff top down to the rapids below. It wasn't easy detecting when the lifeless body hit; they couldn't see more than a few feet ahead, and the force of the current pulled at the rope just as gravity had when they lowered him headfirst down the cliff.

With just a few feet of rope left, they hesitated. Peering over the edge, they stared into an empty, black chasm. One of the men shrugged in the direction of his partner. They shook the rope and no longer felt the weight of the corpse. The man called Ryder turned back toward the car, trembling from the strain. The other man, cloaked in black, pulled up the remainder of the rope.

They made their way back to the car without a word. The man called the Shaman took the driver's seat and stashed the rope under it.

In the passenger seat, a feeling of dense blackness consumed Ryder as the gravity of what he had just done set in. Their task hadn't been easy. Killing a person, no matter the circumstances or the extent of the justification, was a horribly disturbing undertaking.

As the Shaman eased the car onto the dirt road, Ryder started to formulate a thought. The Shaman had doubted Ryder's commitment to the cause not because he didn't trust him but because the Shaman himself appreciated the gravity of the act.

So much was lost in yourself when you took another man's life. Ryder understood that now. A sense of calm washed over him. He looked at the Shaman, whose expression exposed nothing. The man in black had surely done this before.

They drove another mile and pulled over into a clearing to burn the rope. As he watched the embers ascend into the night, Ryder said a prayer to himself. He didn't dare say it aloud.

When they arrived back at their camp, men and women—some fully nude—were already dancing around the fire. With tears in their eyes, they looked up toward the moon with a look of mourning. Their attempt at a chant was cacophonous and incoherent. Very few of them properly spoke the Lakota Sioux language. The chant was called "Mitakuye Oyasin," which means "all my relations."

Its words gave thanks to the animals, plants, earth, and winds one by one. Swaying in the moonlight, the assembled sang:

You are all my relations,
my relatives without whom I would not live.
We are in the circle of life together,
coexisting, codependent, cocreating our destiny.
One not more important than the other.

I

WEST BANK, SNAKE RIVER. TWO DAYS LATER.

The day that would begin the darkest epoch in Jackson Hole's history saw Jake Trent having a personal crisis of his own. He woke up that June morning without any of the rejuvenating energy that should result from a good night's sleep. The previous day's troubles hadn't gone away. Coffee didn't help. It only made him more anxious.

The cause of Jake's irritation was the same issue that had troubled him for months—the increasingly spineless nature of the Jackson Town Council. *Whatever happened to standing up for what you believe in?*

Of course, Jake admitted cooperation and compromise were central to the concepts of democracy, but he ardently felt that such cooperation should take place in a setting free from the temptation of personal gain. Compromise wasn't compromise when there was a reward involved. That was called a bribe.

The issue was land—a very special piece of it. At some point during the council's recent debate, the political forum had become polluted. Poorly disguised buy offs. Misinformation. Jake needed the council members to hear him out. His recommendations were essential if they were to hold on to any hope for a just result. He wasn't so sure they had any such hope. Ears stuffed shut with money, the voting members weren't listening anymore. They were happy to cash in and shut up. Quietly and without remark, Jake's soapbox had been eroded out from under him.

This was Jake's fourth year on the five-member Environmental Review subcommittee of the Jackson Town Council, and he was beginning to think it might be his last. The role was as a citizen appointee, and the job wasn't exactly thrilling—recycling policy, park usage, land impact review—but he liked it. As an ex-lawyer, Jake wasn't afraid of details and fine print, and the gig made him feel connected to his adopted city. He and his fellow committee members could advise and cajole the council, but when it came down to hard decisions, they had to stand back and watch. For years Jake had awaited the dreadful scenario unfolding in front of his eyes now: the greedy overdevelopment of protected land and everyone grabbing for the biggest piece.

The old ranch was beautiful and expansive. Classic Jackson Hole. An eight-hundred-foot-tall butte with magnificent views of the Tetons. Below the hill, a gentle slope continued toward the river. It drained two gin-clear spring creeks, the perfect habitat for spawning trout. Hummocks of cottonwoods provided shade near the creeks and river bottom. Unfortunately, these were all attributes that developers coveted, including the wildlife, fish, and flora. Two hundred and twenty lots were planned.

Two hundred and twenty. They called the proposed neighborhood the Old Teton Dairy Ranch, which to anyone with some knowledge of French meant roughly the Old Breast Milk Ranch. Below that asinine name on the entrance sign, whimsical cursive letters enthusiastically proclaimed: "Taste the Tetons!"

There was no doubt the development would affect the natural environment. Every study showed that. That was what the conservation easement was intended to protect. The easement now in question.

It was a shame. If the protected lands—national parks and forests, riverbanks and mountainsides—were crudely partitioned and sold to the highest bidder, the town would come to regret it.

The United States is still a young nation, Jake thought. *We have the opportunity to learn from the mistakes of the more mature nations,* he had always told others, a distinct advantage. In Jake's mind, the United States was the fortunate youngest sibling of the developed world's family. *By ignoring the repercussions of our historical actions, we'll only destroy ourselves.*

Jake's inability to sway his audience stymied him. He felt, perhaps foolishly, that because of his past accomplishments, his arguments should be afforded some extra consideration. He'd woken up half-seriously asking himself, *Doesn't anybody in this damn town know who I am?*

Jake stood up and paced through his house. He was six feet, six one, maybe. Hair dark and short, with ever more gray around his temples. His body was lean but muscular, evidence of years of aerobic exercise: hiking, trail running, and biking. The push-up/sit-up routine he did every morning kept his upper body defined. His skin was dark now, but this wasn't genetics. He had spent nearly a decade in the high-country sun.

Except for the land issue, Jake was rarely incensed about anything. For the most part, since his move west, he had lived a carefree and happy life. He reminded himself of this fact, and rather than spending all morning wrestling with these questions, he decided to go fishing. He'd had plans to do so anyway—an old acquaintance from back East had asked Jake to take him out while he was in town. But the man had unexpectedly canceled, having been called back home for a pressing work matter. The real world. That was okay. Jake needed some time alone anyway.

The conditions wouldn't be ideal, of course; the water was still high and cold from the melting snow that flushed down the mountainsides each spring. But it was better than spending a sunny Saturday stewing over a righteous cause that was probably doomed anyway.

Jake knew that once he got downstream from the Bald Eagle Creek Bridge, he wasn't likely to encounter any humans for more than twenty-two miles. That suited him just fine. Moose, likely; bald eagles, certainly; bear, possibly—but not humans. Even though the water was moving quickly with spring runoff, which would speed up the boat and shorten the trip, the stretch necessitated an overnight stay. He prepared quickly, packing his hiker/biker two-man tent and a twenty-degree synthetic sleeping bag. A sweatshirt wrapped around an old life vest would serve as a makeshift pillow.

When he was finished gathering what he needed from the house, Jake walked outside and down the worn path, parallel to the stand of lodgepole pines, and through the tall grass and occasional sagebrush.

A pair of eerie eyes, a strikingly mismatched sky-blue and chest-nut-brown duo of orbs, watched him from the tree line. Oblivious to his hidden onlooker, Jake strolled to his boat trailer and stashed his bag in the dry box.

With his target distracted, the animal moved closer, carefully padding through the dry pine needles. Pausing there for a moment, he observed his subject. Clueless. Jake was bent over the gunwale of the boat, shuffling things around. It was the perfect moment for an ambush. The assailant picked up his pace and headed for Jake in an all-out sprint. In seconds, he was within thirty feet.

The footfall startled Jake and he turned to face his attacker.

"Hey! Stop! No!" Jake shouted, but it was too late. *Wham!* The muddy stray leaped up at him, planting his front paws firmly on Jake's groin, tail wagging furiously. Jake stumbled backward, groaning in pain.

The dog skittered away, frightened by the man's outburst.

Jake regained his composure. "Sorry. Shit. It's okay, Chayote, er, whatever the hell your name is." He brushed the mud off his pants and tried to pat the animal on the head. Chayote bounced backward nimbly, avoiding his touch.

The animal slinked away into the woods, his stub tail trying to tuck itself between its legs in embarrassment. Jake shook his head.

The little cattle dog had been hanging around for weeks now, and he was getting friendlier by the day, to Jake's chagrin. At first he would watch Jake from afar and flee the second Jake acknowledged his presence. But by now, the pup was regularly approaching Jake, although he still wouldn't allow Jake to handle him.

He wore no collar, so Jake had started making up names for him: Munson, Sampson, Cutty, but he finally settled on Chayote. Jake didn't know where he'd heard the name; he just liked how it sounded. Plus, the little mottled dog looked and acted like a coyote—athletic and curious and devious. He chuckled to himself at the dog's contrary whims of moxie and reticence.

Approaching his skiff, a sixteen-foot-long flat-bottomed vessel, Jake shook his head again, this time at the craft's grimy floor—evidence of his inability to care for a possession that not only held significant sentimental value but also had provided him with a meager income and purpose during the first years after his relocation to Wyoming.

The boat hadn't been used in months. Checking the tension on the strap, Jake wasn't satisfied that it held the boat securely to the trailer. He removed it and fastened it again, tighter. Then he checked the trailer wheels. A bit wobbly—the trailer was due for two new hubs—but it would be fine for a few more miles.

Jake arrived at the popular put-in across from Charlie's convenience store at 9:15 a.m. Although there weren't many guides launching boats this early in the season, he felt unusually self-conscious to be heading out alone. A solo trip *was* a bit unusual. He figured that it wouldn't go unrecognized, especially with his one-of-a-kind sky-blue skiff and his reputation as a bit of a loner—a reputation he felt unfairly assigned.

Jake couldn't blame the other guides and local fishermen for thinking it strange to float the canyon alone. It was impossible to control the boat and fish at the same time. It was practically a piscine tragedy that he would be back rowing and positioning his skiff simply for his own enjoyment with no anglers standing ready to cast to the trout's likely lies.

Oh well; hopefully nobody is out there today.

As he stepped out to ready the boat, a familiar silver Suburban approached with a drift boat in tow.

So much for solitude.

"Jake, how are you, man? How'd winter treat ya?" Even in June, winter was a not-so-distant memory in the mountains of Wyoming. The driver was shouting over to Jake as he opened the doors for his clients, two well-dressed, portly men who immediately walked off to the Porta Johns. "Hold your breath while you're in there, boys. It's no Four Seasons."

"Not bad, Caddy. Yours?" Jake and the man walked toward each other and shook hands. "Good to see you." Caddy was already tan and leather-skinned despite the early season. Jake thought it must be his permanent skin tone after so many summers.

"Fuckin' Wall Street guys. They'll be a blast. Real exciting folks." The sarcasm was thick. He was pointing toward the toilets and rolling his eyes. "Winter? Shit, too long, man. I need this damn river to clear up so I can make some consistent money." He looked over to see how close his clients were and then spoke in a hushed tone, like what he'd just said wasn't offensive. "We're not gonna catch shit today. Fuckin' first-timers, man! Gonna be a long day!" Caddy put in a bubblegum-sized charge of oily, reddish-black tobacco.

"Well, I have faith in you." Jake gave him a friendly pat on the back.

"What you got going today?" Caddy looked around for Jake's clients. "They in the can?"

"Nada. Just gonna enjoy the day. Going out alone." Jake held eye contact to see how the man would react.

He almost spit out his chew laughing. "Shit, only Jake Trent would come out here in these conditions to 'enjoy the day.'" Caddy collected himself and then let drool what looked like a mugful of tobacco juice into the dust. "Well, you have fun out there. Don't catch 'em all." Caddy rolled his eyes again.

"Will do. Good luck."

Jake tried to let Caddy put in first, but the guide insisted. Jake knew he was trying to kill time—fishing guides sometimes found ways to do this when the fishing was no good.

"Let the water warm up a bit," he was probably telling them. "They ain't been biting till 'bout noon." Probably true, but also convenient for Caddy.

When the boat was launched, Jake headed for a side channel branching away from the main river. He loved to fish the side channels. Dozens of drift boats might float by on the main river, but they were out of sight and mind amid the thick cottonwoods and willows lining the channels. Besides, with this volume of water in the river, the trout wouldn't fight the main river's strong current just to consume the few morsels of food they would make out through the muddy, churning water. Somehow, they always knew the perfect balance between expending energy in the hunt and gaining energy from its spoils. Jake supposed that this idiom applied to all animals, including humans—wasn't it true that no one did anything unless they expected to be rewarded for their work? Maybe that explained the council's behavior.

The fishing in the side channels proved worthwhile. He caught plenty of twelve- to sixteen-inch cutthroats and one large rainbow trout, a nonnative species of West Coast origin that he would keep for the frying pan. While fun to catch, rainbows competed for food and river space with the cutthroats, which were completely unique to the region. Conservationists encouraged the harvest of rainbow trout.

When evening began to settle into the canyon, Jake passed the halfway point of the float and looked for a good campsite. He backed his skiff into a stout and powerful eddy that had formed at the head of an island, and he was reminded again of the force of this river during spring runoff as he struggled to keep the boat parallel to the current lines. If he crossed at the wrong angle, he could capsize.

Jake anchored the boat and tied the bowline to a dead cottonwood where the eddy's current peeled away from the bank. This slack water was littered with debris from the spring runoff—sticks, leaves, and the occasional piece of litter. More interesting to Jake, it also harbored several large shadows, clever fish taking advantage of insects that had been flushed toward them from the main current.

The perfect ratio; little work, big payoff.

When he was sure the skiff was secure, Jake got back into the

14

boat, pulled the fly rod from its sleeve in the gunwale, and stood at the bow's fishing station. He decided to spend just a few moments working the eddy before quitting for the day.

The pale morning duns, a mayfly of the *Ephemerella* genus, had begun their annual emergence early, and the resident fish had taken notice. Jake tied on a #16 comparadun, a close imitation of the frail body silhouette of the mayfly. He worked a chemical into the fly that would allow it to float longer and higher. *Fly-agra*. Always got a laugh from clients. With one false cast, Jake placed the dry fly three feet above the largest of the feeding fish, leaving just enough slack in the leader to allow the fly to float unimpeded into the trout's feeding lane.

The fly drifted toward the fish, which tipped upward and inhaled the fly. Jake laughed with delight. *Early season fish are too easy.* The fish surged, but Jake was able to keep the battle within the boundaries of the eddy, preventing the fish from using the strong current in the middle of the river to free itself from his line. When the trout was within reach, he slid his hand down the transparent leader and into the water, plucking the fly from the fish's mouth. It was a nice fish. Seventeen inches with beautiful deep-red slashes streaking its throat.

It would prove to be Jake's last moment of unhampered happiness for a long time.

After he finished setting up his sleeping quarters, Jake pulled the fire pan from the skiff and walked a short way down the island to prepare dinner, not daring to attract bears or other curious predators to his sleeping area with the scent of food. He seasoned the trout with a mixture of salt, pepper, garlic powder, and dill that he kept with his fishing equipment. He opened the bottle of beer he had brought along, and as evening settled further into the river canyon, the dusky ambiance and alcohol lightened Jake's mood. He smiled when he thought of his earlier frustration with the council. Things moved slowly here, and he needed to be patient and persistent. *Besides,* he thought, *I moved here to escape external pressures. I'm hard enough on myself.*

In reality, the reasons for Jake's relocation to Wyoming changed with his mood. Sometimes it was the noise of the city or the bad air that he said had finally convinced him, and sometimes it was the fast-paced lifestyle.

Eight years ago, Jake was a successful and well-known trial lawyer at Brown and Tallow, a large law firm in Philadelphia. Prior to that he had worked as a prosecutor for the United States Department of Justice in the Office of Special Investigations and then briefly in the City of Philadelphia Special Investigations Office. Jake had been the youngest head of the city's special investigation unit in its history, a fact that once filled him with pride. He eventually left the unit to pursue better pay and security in private practice, but the new job never satisfied him. After a couple of years, he moved west.

The second layer of truth was that he had come to Jackson for a woman. That is to say, he came to live out what he thought was a shared dream with a certain woman. That woman had changed her mind.

Elspet, or Elle, as mostly everyone called her, was a defense attorney like Jake. They had met during a bar association golf outing. Neither hit the ball very well, and this commonality was the first of many that sparked a romance. As with Jake, the stresses of Elle's occupation led her to desire a different life. Childhood visits to the Rockies had planted the seeds in their minds that this region would be an ideal solace from the death, maiming, lying, arguing, and posturing that was inherent to their industry. They dated for only a few months before making plans.

Over late-night glasses of wine in the spring of 2002, the details were ironed out. Jake would make the move first, while Elle wound down her employment. He headed to Jackson in the early summer to look for houses and scout jobs. On impulse and without Elle's knowledge, Jake committed to purchasing an ever-so-slightly run-down bed-and-breakfast on the West Bank of the Snake River, not far from the Idaho border. He figured the property would speak to her the same way it had spoken to him.

Two buildings on the property were in good order, the main house and a smaller guesthouse. Brightly colored wildflowers reached for the sun, complementing the darker cedar structures and patchy snow left in the shadows. The day he first saw it was perfect. Deep-blue skies were broken up only occasionally by pure white puffs of cloud. Walking along the creek frontage, Jake shed his jacket, persuaded by the midday warmth. He wandered the property for over an hour, watching trout sip blue-winged olive mayflies from the glassy surface of the spring.

When Jake returned and told Elle the news, he was met with disbelief. The Jackson Hole dream was a tangible aspiration only to him. To Elle, the notion of "leaving it all behind" was a fantasy, a mental escape.

How would we make enough money? How could we raise kids there, alone in the middle of nowhere? How would we make friends? Why would you do this without asking me?

Before Jake knew it, he was driving across the dusty Midwest alone, turning the stereo up too loud and smoking the cigarettes he hadn't touched since law school.

For the first few months in Jackson, Jake did not operate the bed-and-breakfast. He didn't work at all, for that matter. He was in a slump and surviving only on savings.

Fishing every day, he spent his nights alone in the guesthouse. The hobby kept him content—entertained, perhaps, if not blissful. After all, fly-fishing was ingrained in him. Ever since he'd learned the sport in the halcyon limestone creeks of central Pennsylvania. It was something he took for granted to some extent, yet relied on with an equal or greater weight. It was the most unchanging part of him.

Jake had aspired to become a guide for many years, and his now uncertain future provided the ideal opportunity for a man to chase his dreams. As he familiarized himself with the area's rivers, he began to feel better with each passing day.

Although part of him was recovering quickly from heartbreak, Jake remained in the guesthouse. Optimistically speaking, he felt that sleeping in the main house should wait until Elle joined him— if she ever did. They talked from time to time; she was always in a halfhearted relationship, yearning for something more exciting. Even worse, she would tease Jake with the possibility of a reunion. Eventually he stopped taking her calls.

Fortunately there were distractions. The busy years of his legal career had left Jake comparatively rusty, unfamiliar with the vagaries that allowed an accomplished angler to outproduce the average angler. Trout Run, the creek on his property, reestablished his prowess and, perhaps more important, kept Jake from sitting alone and thinking too much about the past. In a few short months, Jake became a fish bum.

Jake's ambition and his finances necessitated a change. He started working on the river. A small white-water outfit in town had decided to expand and its owner was willing to hire inexperienced guides, if only for their affordability. Jake took the owner, Steve, and retail shop manager, Brent, out on a float trip, and luckily the fishing had been excellent. He was hired halfway through the trip. He knew it was the hungry fish as much as it was his skills at the oars, but no matter.

Jake learned quickly. Within three seasons, he was one of the most sought-after guides in the valley, not only because of his unnatural ability to get his clients onto fish but also because of his growing knowledge of the area.

Whereas many guides gave little thought to anything beyond fishing, Jake became a student of geology, biology, and philosophy. During the slow times in the midafternoon or at lunch, he shared the little-known details of how the volcano that constituted Yellowstone National Park had smeared below the Snake River Valley—or, more accurately, how the tectonic plate on which the Snake River Valley rested had slid above the volcanic hot spot that now sat beneath Yellowstone. In some incomprehensible length of time, the geothermic features that composed Yellowstone would sit somewhere to the north in Canada. That is, if the world's largest volcano had not already erupted and destroyed the entire continent. Jake often left out the latter part, particularly if there were children in the boat.

Jake liked to say his new career had saved his life. During his second season, he grew more ambitious and hired a new friend, J.P., to polish up and operate the old bed-and-breakfast. A consummate Renaissance man, J.P. was an experienced chef and handyman, if a bit rough around the edges. Most important, Jake could afford him. As the majority of his compensation package, J.P. rested his pop-up camper near the firewood pile on the property's southern boundary. He slept in the camper on all but the coldest winter nights, when he would borrow an unoccupied guest room or crash on Jake's small couch in the rare event that the main house was full of guests. He never slept in the beds of the guest rooms because he was too lazy to refresh the linens. He simply brought in his sleeping bag and pad and lay down next to the bed.

The arrangement worked. Jake could afford the mortgage and J.P.'s wages. The business stayed afloat. Jake's accountant handled the financials and doled out a check when there was profit, but it was never much.

In addition to starting up a new business, he'd become involved in conservation causes around town. To that end, he began his modest foray into politics by way of the town council.

Before he knew it, eight years had passed.

Jake finished his beer, extinguished the fire, and cleaned up his camp kitchen. The air was getting chilly, so he changed his clothes quickly and stuffed himself inside the thick sleeping bag. Sleep came more easily for Jake when he was in the wilderness. There was no television, radio, or other distractions to keep him up. Going to bed early meant waking up early and that made him feel healthy and productive. *Yep,* Jake thought as he drifted off to sleep, *a simple life is a better life.* The escape to the river was just what he needed to cope with the headache of taking on the Jackson Town Council.

At some point during the night Jake awoke to a large mammal huffing and bustling in the willows outside the tent. He instinctively grabbed the small knife that he kept on his belt, but as his brain cleared away the fog of slumber, he realized that this was a useless defense. In the event that a bear had become interested in him, his one-and-a-half-inch blade would irritate the beast about as much as acupuncture therapy. He breathed a sigh of relief when the animal revealed itself by moonlight silhouette as a bull moose. A moment later, the animal moved off into the night.

2

JACKSON. THE SAME EVENING.

Twenty miles upriver, an unusual mix of chaos and grief had settled into the valley. Rumors had been circulating all day that two
people had died in the wilderness. A third was in critical condition
at St. John's hospital. By midafternoon, the chief of police had
confirmed the deaths to the media. One victim dead from an avalanche, one dead and one in critical condition from a bear attack.
The news spread like wildfire.

Both incidents took place in the Teton mountains, a rugged and
beautiful range that attracted tourists and adventurers from all
corners of the world. Like many sites of extreme natural beauty,
the range could be deadly. Its rocky cliffs, cold water, predators,
and ever-changing weather had claimed dozens of lives since the
national park was established there in 1929. And this was just
when the park started keeping formal records. Prior to 1929, the

massif was said to have claimed the lives of scores of settlers and frontiersmen.

Stories of old accidents still circulated in local folklore. Some were verifiable; some not. Signal Mountain, a popular tourist outlook in the central part of the park, took its name from one such incident. According to the tale, in 1887 a hunting party had split up and searched for the body—dead or alive—of a compatriot. Before they set out, the group agreed to start a fire on the peak when the missing person was found so that the remaining members of the search party would know their search had been completed. The signal fire was eventually lit when a lifeless body was discovered pinned against a deadfall in the Snake River, his appearance nearly unrecognizable from the wear of the water. The mountain was his only lasting monument.

On this June day, Park Ranger Noelle Klimpton had found the body. Hours later, she was driving her green government-issued pickup down highway 89 toward Jackson to give a statement to the police on her grim discovery. The National Park Service had already taken her statement. Now it was the cops' turn. Her mind skipped through her jumbled recollections, and when it settled on the most ghastly images from that morning, she shuddered. It was warm outside, but she had to close the windows to keep from getting the chills.

Noelle would've liked to stop thinking about it, but she knew it was important to be able to recount the details to the authorities. Keep it fresh. To that end, she recited the known facts: a bear, most likely a black bear, had attacked a couple just below the receding snow line up near Gosling Lake. There was blood, and lots of it.

That part was easy to remember. The time her watch showed when she found the body wouldn't be so easy. *Maybe 10:23 a.m.?* Nor would it be easy to recall the description of the men who led her to the scene. These were the sorts of things that she figured the police would want to know. *Medium build, both with down vests. Young. No, I didn't get their contact information. It was stupid, I know.*

Noelle, an athletic and slender five foot six, didn't have a hint of excess weight to be found. Her body and her dark eyes and hair complemented a wide, white smile. The contrast was striking in the summer when her skin was bronzed by the sun.

But Noelle's stunning physique belied a solitary nature. She spent much of her time alone. Her routines were solitary: solo skiing in the winter and trail running in the summer. At thirty-four, she had all but given up on the pretty notion of sharing her life with someone. Instead, she filled her time with work and sport, two things that had never let her down. She was good at both—well respected within the park service and known throughout the valley as an accomplished athlete. Noelle's social separation was not a result of any personal shortcoming. People loved to be around her, and men found her irresistible. Her isolation was pure preference.

What appeared to some as standoffishness wasn't motivated by arrogance or ego. Her trouble was trusting others: *Who can you truly rely on but yourself?*

She knew it was a stark, maybe cliché, take on the world, but she couldn't deny its truth. In the past, when she had dedicated herself to a man—changing her own life, compromising for *his* happiness—she found that she only lost herself and gained little in return. With female friends it was the same.

Five years back, she'd been engaged to a banker from New York, but Noelle just couldn't go through with it. She'd felt imprisoned, tied down by his expectations. To him she was a wild western filly waiting to be broken. Rather than spend her life as a suburban housewife, she left. There was still too much to explore, both within her and in the outside world. So she joined the National Park Service.

That morning Noelle had felt as she always did, at ease, content, but not particularly energized. She walked to work out of habit, and barely took notice when she arrived, as she had the previous day, and the day before. She had fallen into a comfortable but mundane routine.

Now she was sitting anxiously in her truck, wondering what she was going to tell the cops and picturing the disturbing scene of attack. She felt a new brand of excitement, like adventure was coming her way. The attack had taken at least one innocent life, and this was a tragedy, Noelle knew, but she felt more alive than she had in years. She hoped these feelings weren't overly disrespectful to the dead.

Noelle focused again on how to tell her story to the police.

"I woke up and the sun started to heat the chilly, dry mountain air."

This doesn't have to be literary.

"I was led to the scene shortly after I started work this morning, and no, I didn't get the name or card of the person who led me there, thank you for asking."

Noelle's morning patrol had been interrupted when two young men waved her down as she swung her vehicle in a three-point turn in the Death Canyon parking lot—a popular trailhead in the southwestern part of the park. Putting the truck into park, she went out to see what the fuss was about.

The men were out of breath, and from their faces Noelle knew immediately they had seen something grim. This was not a twisted ankle. She stayed calm. The men motioned for her to follow them to a corner of the parking lot and up the hill.

As they hurried up the trail toward the overlook, the younger of the two, gasping, explained the situation as best he could. He and his friend had been day hiking when they encountered the injured couple. He didn't speak in any real detail. He said they immediately turned and ran to get help before they could assess the gravity of the injuries. But it was bad. Both men looked as if they'd seen a ghost.

Wilderness first aid guidelines dictated that one of the men should have stayed behind to tend to the victims, but Noelle decided it wasn't the time to chide the hikers. Instead, she radioed the park paramedics and told them to send an ambulance to the trailhead and to be on standby for a Life Flight.

When Noelle arrived at the overlook, she gasped and cupped her hand over her mouth. One man and one woman lay facedown on the ground, motionless.

Christ.

Noelle suddenly felt overwhelmed and alone. Like she was lost at sea. Desperate. A feeling of vertigo washed over her. The woods were quiet but she felt the lodgepole pines watching her, taunting. *She's gonna puke! She can't handle it!*

The hikers were still with her, but they only looked on silently as if to say, "Do *something*! Hurry!" Her hands were going numb and her mouth was dry.

What if the bear is still here?

Blood covered the victims' bodies, and sticks and leaves adhered to their skin. Their congealed blood acted like craft glue, decorating them with the forest floor's detritus.

Was that a noise behind me?

Noelle wiped her hand down her face trying to regain focus. *Get to it!* Adrenaline started to kick in and her training finally took over. She hurried toward the bodies. As she got closer, she saw that each body was riddled with puncture wounds, concentrated around the chest. The hikers asked if they could help, but Noelle waved them off.

First, she checked for the female victim's pulse. A faint but steady rhythm. Noelle wrapped a sweatshirt around the woman's upper torso, pressuring the wounds to mitigate her blood loss. Then she moved to the other victim. No pulse. A goner. His head and face looked like a boxer after rounds of brutal fighting.

Somewhere behind the bruises and cuts was the still vivid face of a horror-struck man. Noelle forced herself to look away. She pressed the button on the handset of her radio clipped to her jacket and asked for the status of the paramedics. Dispatch assured Noelle it wouldn't be more than an hour. *Two hours total to St. John's? That's too long!* She pressed the button again and told them no, a helicopter would be necessary for transport. The woman wouldn't last two more hours. She would bleed out in the ambulance, if she even made it that far.

Noelle sent the hikers back down the trailhead; there was nothing they could do here. She checked again on the woman, who seemed to be more or less stable though still losing blood. Her breaths were shallow and raspy. With nothing else to do, Noelle packed the man's sweatshirt around his wounds to curtail the bleeding. Then she performed chest compressions for thirty-five minutes, hoping he might revive. When the rescue team finally arrived, the paramedics took over and quickly pronounced him dead. There had been no saving him, they said.

26

Just as Noelle feared, the female victim was at serious risk of bleeding to death. The paramedics asked Noelle to radio the chopper and explain their location to the pilot.

Death Canyon, up by Gosling Lake. A hundred yards above the clearing with the wildflowers.

A few moments later, dispatch radioed back, saying that the pilot intended to land on any flat area of land he could find in the large, sloping meadow that lay west and uphill of Gosling Lake. The thick forests on the lower slopes of the trail made landing impossible. Noelle looked toward the area the chopper was targeting. Getting the surviving victim to the meadow required a hike of nearly a half mile on windy, steep switchbacks.

Rather than assist the paramedics, Noelle was ordered to return to the trailhead and inform hikers that the Death Canyon trail network, including the Gosling Lake loop, was closed due to a dangerous animal in the area. It was not very likely that any more hikers would be in danger from the bear, but keeping park visitors away from pools of blood and pieces of shredded clothing seemed wise.

As Noelle pulled into police headquarters, she expected a sad scene. This close-knit community was always deeply affected by tragedy. Inside, it was worse than she imagined. A distraught family was being consoled in the waiting area. Behind the reception desk, officers buzzed around the cubicles, looking sweaty and exhausted. The station looked like a war room.

"Ms. Klimpton?" The question brought Noelle back to reality. She nodded. "Could you follow me?"

Here goes.

The young man sitting at the reception desk shoved his stool under the counter and moved briskly through the crowd, guiding her toward the back of the station. She knew she'd met the man before, but she couldn't recall when.

"You can have a seat in here," he said, showing her into what appeared to be a small interrogation room. "Terrell will be with you shortly to take your report." He hurried back to the chaos.

"Wait! What's going on?" Noelle yelled after him. He turned.

"You haven't heard? Maelstrom Couloir slid this afternoon."

"What? Was anyone on it?" Noelle asked.

"Two skiers. One guy is all right. A little bruised up and in shock, that's all. They just found the other. Eight feet under. Didn't have a chance."

Before Noelle could say another word, the officer turned around and left. The door swung shut behind him.

An avalanche on Maelstrom in June?

Sure, it was possible—it was always possible. But by early summer the snowpack in the mountains was consolidated and bonded by freeze-thaw cycles and unlikely to fail. This time of year, backcountry skiers generally enjoyed safe snow conditions and bright sunshine.

Maelstrom Couloir was a popular out-of-bounds run beyond the south boundary of the Jackson Hole Mountain Resort. It was nonetheless easily accessible from the top of the resort's tram. In the spring and early summer, dedicated skiers took the 9 a.m. tram to the summit and boot-packed the mile or so to the top of Tomahawk Peak, where they accessed the couloir—a narrow, rock-lined, and steep chute of snow. Dropping precipitously off the side of Tomahawk Peak, Maelstrom ended above a wide-open alpine bowl. Although the temperatures were rising into the low sixties during the day, the high elevation and substantial snowpack kept skiers busy into early July.

These two hadn't been so lucky.

There was a knock on the door and the chief of police, Roger Terrell, rushed inside. He stood five foot ten with a solid build and big forearms. Noelle knew him rather well. When she moved to the area years ago, she initially pursued a job with the department but she didn't make it past the second interview.

She couldn't blame Terrell. He was well liked and considered fair and honest around town. It was her own past that had come back and haunted her. She had disclosed to the police department that she had once been arrested at a protest. The arrest had only resulted in a charge of breaching the peace, but the department was not impressed. Dismissed from consideration for any job at the department, Noelle *had* managed to form a friendly relationship with Roger Terrell. In a town so small, holding grudges doesn't get you far. He was the one who suggested Noelle take the park service job she now believed to be much better than working for the police department.

"Been a while." Terrell didn't make eye contact. He was too preoccupied. "Nice to see you, despite the circumstances."

"What the hell happened today?" Noelle blurted out.

"Today," Terrell recited as if he was also reminding himself, "a European couple was attacked by a bear while hiking in Death Canyon. Man died in the attack and the woman is still alive. Sometime after this attack, an avalanche near the ski area killed one skier and it injured another—"

She cut him off. "Stop talking like a robot! I mean, an avalanche in June . . ."

"Sure. Wet slide. Snow was soaked with moisture from the heat of the day and simply became too dense to support itself. I mean, hell, you know better than I do. All that 'extreme' stuff you do."

29

She ignored the compliment. *Or was it a dig?*

She said, "Wouldn't *these* guys know that too? Besides, it wasn't that warm today. Doesn't make sense." The last sentiment was made to herself.

The chief finally made solid eye contact. "Doesn't need to make sense to you. They made a bad decision, Noelle, I don't know. Nature's a bitch. Maybe it was a cool day for a slide to occur, but it did happen. Family won't take any comfort in that. Not to mention the victim."

"Is that who was in the waiting area when I came in, the family?" Noelle asked. "Why are they here?"

"No. That's the survivor's family. The DOA is from Colorado and we're still trying to contact his family. Other family is here because his mother says she can't enter a hospital without having an anxiety attack. She says they have nowhere else to go but my police station." Terrell's voice dripped with sarcasm.

"Which one caused the slide?" She sensed she was pushing the chief with this question.

"Are you taking my statement, or am I taking yours?" Noelle didn't respond, so the chief continued. "It looks like the second skier, the survivor, did. He must've broken it free a few turns into the top of the couloir. The first skier was found at the bottom of the chute, approaching the run-out."

Noelle interrupted again. "Why wouldn't the first skier have caused the avalanche?"

"Just luck," Roger answered. "The first guy apparently didn't hit the trigger spot. That's what Max tells me."

Max was the valley's avalanche forecaster.

The concept of a trigger point was a new demon to the avalanche scene. In the past, it was assumed that if a slope was going to slide, it would probably do so wherever a person went on the slope. But now, avalanche experts suspected that snow stability varied drastically from point to point, even on one slope. This idea had called into question the reliability of shovel tests and the Rutschblock test, which used a sample cross section of one small area of snow to predict the stability of the snow slope-wide. The uncomfortable truth was that no current tests did an adequate job of predicting snow stability. Unless the skier dug a snow pit to test every point on her planned line, she could never be sure.

The chief moved farther into the small room and took a seat. "I understand your curiosity, Noelle, but let's get going. I've got a busy night ahead of me."

Noelle wanted more information, but gave in. She didn't envy his position on this night. "What do you want to know?"

"Just a brief summary. When you're finished I'll have you write a more detailed report and leave it at the desk."

"Okay. First off, you should know that I've never witnessed the aftermath of an animal attack like this before. I've only done nonvenomous snakebites before today. To be honest, I was a little overwhelmed. My memory might not be as detailed as you'd like, but I'll do my best."

"I know you will." The chief was urging her along.

She continued. "Well, I was patrolling the southern end of the park for general reasons—wildlife traffic jams, sick animals, traffic violations, whatever. I drove up the road to the summer parking for the Death Canyon trailhead. As I started to turn my truck around, a couple of men waved me down."

"Did you get their names?" Terrell looked up from his notepad.

"Sorry. The paramedics probably did."

Good recovery, Noelle thought. It seemed to placate the chief.

Noelle related the remainder of the story as best she could. She wasn't a trained detective after all.

"Okay. Fill this out." He handed her a one-page report with carbon copies in pink and yellow attached to the back. Chief Terrell went back to the war room.

Noelle had trouble concentrating on her statement with the distraught family so nearby. Trying her best to ignore the noise, she went to task. She knew the chief was interested in the details of the injuries, and she was curious about these things as well. Though Noelle had never witnessed a bear attack, what she saw that morning suggested something unthinkably brutal. One detail stuck in her mind—the deep puncture wounds. It appeared as if the bear had decided unequivocally to kill.

Noelle drove out of town toward the small 1940s cabin that the park service provided as part of her compensation. She pulled into the gravel drive and looked at her diminutive home standing there in the pines. It looked more lonesome than usual.

I really need to spruce this place up.

On the way home from the station, the excitement of the day had almost led her to stop at a bar that she hadn't been to in years. See some old friends, be social. Maybe meet a guy. Instead, she convinced herself that she needed sleep and passed the tavern with only slight hesitation.

Noelle's cabin was on a slope at the western end of the "hole" that gave the area its name. A hole, unlike a valley or a canyon, is bordered by mountains on all sides. A valley features two low-elevation "ends," while the mountains define its sides.

Jackson Hole wasn't so convenient. On the western edge rose

the famous Teton Range and to the east the Gros Ventres. Up north, just above Jackson Lake, sat the Yellowstone Plateau. Down south, where water drains from the hole by way of the Snake River, was the path of least resistance out of the depression, but several parallel mountain ranges still ensured that the region remained isolated. Jackson "Hole" was virtually cut off from the outside world.

As means of transportation improved, Jackson Hole became more accessible, both by high mountain passes that allowed automobiles to travel into the valley and more recently by air.

Its geography helped maintain Jackson Hole's reputation as the last of the old west. Visitors are alerted to this unique designation by a campy wooden sign as they enter from the west via Teton Pass. In recent years, more access meant more people. More second homes. More businesses. A change that many locals resented.

Though Noelle enjoyed the isolation that the hole provided, she could have used some company tonight. She picked up her cell phone and flipped through her contacts, but there was nobody to call. Instead, she put a pot of tea on the small double-burner gas stove that rested in the corner of the cabin. Someone had long ago designated this crook as the kitchen, and Noelle had no reason to argue.

Putting water on the stove reminded Noelle how hungry she was. During the busy day, she had somehow forgotten to eat.

She rummaged through the cupboards. There wasn't much—a few boxes of rice and some macaroni and cheese. She didn't have any butter, so the rice was her only choice. She put it on the stove, added water and some spices. It wasn't much, but at least it smelled good.

While the rice cooked, Noelle grabbed her laptop and headed for the front porch. Her curiosity about the attack had not subsided. After checking her park service email, where two emails from well-meaning coworkers offered company if she needed to "talk" about her day, she went to Google and entered "bear attacks." Wireless Internet access was one of the few amenities that her cabin provided.

The teapot whistled as the search results began to populate the screen. Noelle set the computer on the wooden porch floor and dashed inside. She turned off the burner and bent down below the sink for a mug. Her dorm-style refrigerator sat next to the sink. She opened it and grabbed a beer. Tea could wait.

Sipping the beer, Noelle walked back to the porch and her laptop. It was getting chilly. Although it was June, Noelle knew that summer was a month away in this part of northwestern Wyoming. There were goose bumps on her suntanned arms.

The search results came back just as she expected. At the top of her screen, links for amateur videos purporting to depict bears attacking humans. "Real," "crazy," and "vicious" exclaimed the descriptions. She took a long pull of beer and clicked on one of them, but closed it out almost immediately. Disgusting.

She had witnessed only the aftermath of a bear attack today and it had sickened her. Although she was curious, the footage was too much. Who the hell would put up videos of killing and maiming just for entertainment? What a strange, cannibalistic world.

Below the videos were links explaining the causes of bear attacks and techniques to protect oneself in the event of an attack. Noelle had bear training, but a refresher never hurt. The articles Noelle opened explained that grizzlies are most likely to attack when they feel that their young are at risk. Bears will often charge their victims to scare them off rather than to injure them. This tactic is known as a "false" or "bluff" charge and usually serves the bear's purposes effectively, causing the intruder to retreat.

In the case that the bear perceived a continuing threat, she would follow through with her attack. The sources confirmed what Noelle suspected, that an attack meant to deter a human from harming a cub usually led to scratching injuries. In the event that the bear did bite, it was most likely to bite at the head and neck of the victim. In most cases, the bear left the victim alone once the victim was unconscious or playing dead. There was no mention of bite wounds to the chest. She clicked back to the search results.

One headline stuck out from the other results.

"Killer Canadian Black Bears."

Noelle clicked the link. The article was old—from the mid-nineties. She skimmed it and then read it more thoroughly. The article described a phenomenon in eastern Canada where black bears stalked and killed humans. In most cases the bears consumed the humans entirely, but there were occurrences where a body, or remnants thereof, were found. In these cases, the victims, whether dead or alive, were often catastrophically injured. *Bite wounds.* This behavior seemed just like what happened to the victims today. The article said that black bear attacks were more likely to be of a predatory nature than defensive, in contrast to grizzly attacks.

Maybe the bear was scared off from its food before it was able to eat?

The Canadian incidents intrigued her, but Noelle decided that she didn't know enough about bear attacks in general or the specifics of the attack earlier that day to make any determination. She did have a friend who might, however. A man who spent all his waking hours studying bears. Noelle made a mental note to call him.

She checked a few more bear websites. The most consistent theme was that bears were unpredictable. Like all wild animals, it was impossible to explain every single one of their behaviors.

The rice was ready. *Finally.* Noelle brought it out to the porch. The taste left room for improvement, but the warmth was pleasing. As she ate, Noelle looked out into the empty alpine surroundings and listened to the sounds of nighttime in Jackson Hole. She put her bowl down on the porch's wooden floor and sipped her beer. It tasted better than the rice. Feeling chillier, Noelle put the beer down and went inside to grab another layer of clothes.

As she walked inside, she took careful steps to avoid tripping on any of the discarded clothes and outdoor gear that littered the floor. *So much for keeping a clean house.* In her bedroom she set her computer on the stack of two milk crates that served as her bedside table and sat down on the bed. Feeling her energy drop precipitously, Noelle lay down and closed her eyes for a moment. She fell asleep almost instantly.

Outside the cabin, the smells from Noelle's cooking permeated through the cold valley air. They weren't strong—no human would have noticed—but the foraging animal lifted its heavy head into the breeze and searched for the source of the smell. When it found the scent trail, it followed its nose through the darkness, salivating.

Noelle was startled from her sleep by heavy breathing. She popped out of bed, sleepy brain confused by the sound, and threw the lights on. At the window was a shape, obscured by the condensation of its own breath. Noelle's heart was thumping. She squinted to try to make out the animal's features between hazy breaths, then stepped back, toward the middle of the shaky old cabin.

The beast clobbered the window with a swipe of its paw. The

glass creaked but held. Through the paw print in the condensation she could see the face of the bear, its lips curled, inhaling through its nose. Hungry.

The bear growled and swiped again, harder this time. The glass cracked but didn't shatter. He was just testing it.

Noelle stumbled back again. She found herself at the front door now, wondering whether she should bolt for her vehicle. It was risky. The bear was letting out frustrated groans and mews through curled lips, revealing his two-inch-long canines. He rolled his huge head slowly back and forth.

Stay put until it comes through, and then head for the truck, she thought. *It will take him a minute to get back out of the cabin. He's more interested in the food than me anyway.*

Her keys were in hand. The animal swiped again. Noelle opened the front door a crack and looked toward the car. It was pitch-black outside. Uninviting.

What if there's another bear? Not likely, but Noelle's rapidly firing synapses weren't working in the realm of logic. Her fear was overwhelming her, and she knew she had to try to stay calm. The bear grunted and snorted, pushing against the frame of the window. Claws twice as long as its teeth.

Noelle flashed on the outside lights and searched the driveway for movement. Nothing. A clear route to her truck. She took a deep breath and glanced at the rear window one last time.

The condensation was gone. No sign of the bear.

She closed the door and approached the window slowly, listening. It was quiet.

Noelle put her face to the window and peered into the backyard, awash with yellow from the floodlights. The bear was gone.

The lights must have spooked him. Noelle ran out onto the

porch, grabbed her rice bowl and beer, and brought them inside. *That was stupid.* She shut the door behind her and locked it.

Her heart rate returned to normal after a few minutes and she got back in bed, but not before placing a can of bear spray on the milk crates.

Noelle stripped off her clothes and tossed her undergarments under the sleeping bags so they would be warm from her body heat in the morning. She tucked herself into a fetal ball and remained that way until she stopped shivering.

A few minutes later she mustered up the courage to stick her arm out of her cocoon to set tomorrow's alarm. She set the clock for 6:00 a.m. to give her enough time to jog to the public campsite nearby and take a shower before her 7:00 a.m. patrol began. After that, if she had time she might just return to the scene of the attack at the mouth of Death Canyon to look around. Noelle lay in bed for hours before sleep finally found her.

3

GRAND TETON NATIONAL PARK. THE NEXT MORNING.

Noelle awoke to cold and fog. She was tempted to remain in bed until the bright sun warmed her cabin and the outside air. She felt sure that her superiors at the park would forgive her absence.

But as her senses returned, her curiosity about the prior day's attack came with them. She also felt a strange guilt as she realized that she was more excited to start her patrol than she had been in quite a while. Like the amateur videographers on the Internet, Noelle was somehow intrigued by death and danger. It wasn't the first time she noticed this trait in herself.

It was as if the prospect of danger carried alongside it the potential and even necessity for acts of great significance to take place. Noelle secretly coveted the opportunity to become a hero. *Or at least to make a difference when the stakes are high.* Noelle wished the tragic event had never occurred, but she nevertheless was enthralled with the prospect of being involved in major events.

Dragging herself out of bed, Noelle put on her running shoes and stretched. She stepped out the door and started jogging, taking bouncy steps down the short staircase off the porch. As she ran, she thought about how nice it would be if there were someone waiting at the cabin with a pot of coffee ready when she returned. Someone to romp around with under the sleeping bags. To help turn her cold, taut skin into one big, warm, soft pleasure receptor. Then maybe she wouldn't have to rely on danger and tragedy to break the monotony of daily life.

Noelle made it to the showers in good time. The facility was empty. Its tile floors cold. *Summer can't come soon enough.* She disrobed hastily, positioned her body under the flow of hot water, and stayed there for a long time.

While showering, she thought of the day ahead. She knew a group of Yellowstone bear experts were en route to the ranger station in Moose Junction, where they would be briefed on yesterday's attack. That was standard protocol after any bear incident. They would then be deployed to capture or kill the culprit.

The most valuable protection from bears in the parks was the bears' own natural instincts. Most fled when faced with close-range human interaction. There were times, however, when these instincts were overruled by other considerations in the bears' mind, namely self-defense, starvation, or protection of young.

For the most part, bears feared humans unless they became used to their presence. Unfortunately, the convergence of humans and bears in both Yellowstone National Park and Grand Teton National Park occasionally led to that very phenomenon. That is, bears—usually pursuing an unnatural food source such as a camper's cooler or garbage—sometimes came to realize that humans posed no real threat to them. These semidomesticated bears were dangerous because they felt comfortable among humans and understood themselves to be the dominant species. If they wanted food from a tent, car, or Dumpster, why not take it?

In the course of a food raid, park visitors became collateral damage. It was the job of the bear team to remove or destroy these problem bears.

After her morning ritual, Noelle headed south on the park road toward the Death Canyon trailhead. On the way her supervisor radioed her and requested that she escort the bear team to the site of the attack, which pleased Noelle's growing curiosity.

The bumpy road to the summer trailhead was worse than usual at this time of year. The park had decided to open the road early. May had been warm, relatively speaking, and the snow had melted in all but the shadiest areas below 8,500 feet. In most years, the road wouldn't be open for another three weeks.

Noelle had often wondered about the canyon's uninviting name. There was quite a bit of folklore explaining it, but never one settled-upon tale. Now the name Death Canyon seemed grimly and permanently justified.

According to one story, livestock men used the canyon to enter and exit Jackson Hole in the 1800s. Because of the length of the passage, the men were required to spend the night near the top of the Teton crest in Death Canyon.

One summer night, a group of men with livestock in tow arrived at the top of the canyon to find that another outfit was already occupying the pasture. There wasn't room for both. The first party unkindly suggested that the new arrivals head back into Jackson Hole. This didn't go over well with the latecomers, so instead of leaving in peace, they slaughtered the competing livestock at the top of the canyon. The water that flows through the canyon ran red, temporarily staining the rocks that formed its streambed. According to some variations of the story, a few of the cowboys themselves were killed in the gunfire. From there, it didn't take a very creative man to dub the place Death Canyon.

An alternative story was that Death Canyon was given its name merely because the terrain was such that it was hard to travel through and survive.

Again, one could not dispute the logic—the steep canyon was bordered by sheer cliffs on both sides for the majority of its climb up the Tetons. The canyon floor was lined with large boulders that had broken away from the canyon walls or were deposited as the result of glacial movement.

In many spots throughout the Death Canyon hike, which had become popular for ambitious day hikers, it resembled a scrambling climb more than a walk in the woods.

Maybe in a hundred years they'll be talking about the bear attack when they mention Death Canyon, Noelle mused morbidly.

She arrived at the trailhead, parked, and watched as the bear team assembled their weapons. There were thirteen of them in all. They brought specialized rifles outfitted with laser sights and tranquilizer darts. In case something went wrong, they also carried traditional large-caliber weapons, 7 millimeters with 185-grain ammunition. A large barrel was welded to the flatbed of one of the trucks. On its side were a few stickers that read: "Beware! DANGEROUS ANIMAL!" This meant that the bear's life might be spared if they found it—a thought that pleased Noelle, despite the gruesome attack and her own nighttime visitor.

At least they haven't made a final decision on the bear's fate. It isn't on death row yet. But, this had been an especially vicious encounter. Lots of people in combination with a dangerous animal would mean a high probability of future attacks, and relocated bears often found their way back to their original home, despite the efforts of the team. If the team thought it could find its way back, they would kill it for sure.

"Hi, Ms. Klimpton?" a graying man asked as she approached the tailgate of a truck where several men were preparing for the trek. "I'm Nat Passa, chief of the bear police." He smiled. "And this is my sorry excuse for a team."

"Just Noelle, please." She greeted the burly looking team one by one but quickly forgot their names, as she assumed they did hers.

"We requested your presence so that you could direct us to the scene of yesterday's incident." Nat spoke formally but jovially. Like a captain addressing his lieutenant after hours. Noelle didn't know whether she should be offended at the man's lively tone in light of the circumstances, or to enjoy the masculine charm he emanated. She decided on the latter.

Everybody copes with things differently . . .

Noelle led the team up the trail and chatted intermittently with them. Nat reassured her that the bear team's success rate was not high enough that she should be concerned for the bear just yet. "These guys can't even shoot a basketball," he quipped.

The trail steepened and the crew quieted down, breathing hard. Noelle wasn't put off; she was used to this type of workout. Still curious, she explained the strange nature of the wounds but Nat Passa didn't seem concerned. "Wild animals are inherently unpredictable," he said twice during the short conversation. Big, booming football coach voice.

Finally, Gosling Lake came into view. "This is it. Right below where the snow starts, above the overlook."

A day later, the scene was incredibly peaceful and benign. Nature had already forgotten about the horrific occurrence.

Nat caught his breath and looked toward her. "Noelle, we appreciate your help. We're gonna spend a few minutes here looking for tracks or any other indication of where the bear might be. Then, unless we have clear tracks to follow, we'll simply walk the area in a predetermined pattern and hope to intercept the animal."

"You're of course welcome to come along. With their firepower"—Nat motioned toward his team, taking a deep breath—"and my experience"—he winked—"capturing this bear shouldn't be an exceedingly dangerous task."

"Thanks, but I'd better get back to work."

"Okay," Nat said. "Then farewell. Don't stay in the area. We don't want to flush an irritated bear out toward you, or tranquilize you accidentally." Nat smiled at her one last time.

"No problem," she lied. She did plan to stay in the area.

The team soon headed into the woods. Noelle lingered, walking a zigzag route through the area where the hikers had shown her the victims. She looked closely at the ground, hoping to find fur or some other evidence.

It didn't take long.

Noelle found something that would answer her doubts about the attack. Glinting in the sun, there was a clean ivory object. She almost yelled out. Almost alerted the bear team as to what she'd found. Instead, she put the inch-long bear tooth in the cargo pocket of her park-issued pants and started back down the trail and away from the scene. After all, there was a killer bear in the area.

4

SNAKE RIVER CANYON. THE SAME MORNING.

Jake awoke, dressed in a high-loft fleece and an old pair of insulated jeans, and then took some water from a nearby creek. He put the water on a small camp stove and boiled it for coffee. His breath formed dense, nearly opaque clouds in the cold morning air.

While he waited for the water, he walked the perimeter of his camp looking for the tracks of the moose that visited him the night before and found them easily. They were six inches long and four inches wide. In the damp sand on the river's edge, the animal's tracks were deep and well defined.

Back in camp, Jake spooned four tablespoons of powdered coffee mix into his blue camp mug and, using two thick willow branches to lift the coffeepot from the burner, carefully poured water over the powder. The coffee was too hot to gulp, so Jake sipped what he could tolerate, and it warmed him up. The taste of the coffee reminded him of past camping trips with his father. In all of Jake's years in the wilderness with his dad, the man had always used the same Maxwell House French Vanilla Café instant coffee. It came in a red-and-white rectangular tin with a plastic top. Jake smiled. Sometimes the simplest things brought comfort.

The water level in the Snake River had dropped considerably overnight. Rocks in the riverbed that were submerged when Jake went to sleep were now dry. Since the flow was controlled by a hydroelectric dam many miles upriver, this wasn't unusual. Most western rivers were dammed.

Any sudden change in the water level usually put the fish down. Off the bite. Fishing the Snake shortly after a change in water volume rarely proved to be a worthy endeavor, if the angler was of the type that allowed his catch rate to determine his success.

The idea behind water management was to prevent the reservoirs from totally overflowing during spring runoff while stockpiling the maximum amount of water to be used for irrigation and energy later in the summer. Little consideration was given to how these decisions affected trout or trout fishermen.

Jake had planned on fishing for an hour before continuing downriver, but he changed his plans when he saw that the water level had dropped so much. The fishing wouldn't be any good now.

Instead, he tied on a large rubber-legged nymph that was intended to imitate the large salmonflies that thrived in this section of the river. He fished the first two pools of the small tributary where he had taken the water for his morning coffee. Here, the water volume was unaffected by the dam's release—this stream ran unimpeded from the mountaintops until it reached the Snake.

He landed one cutthroat in each of the pools. Both fish violently attacked the fly. Jake always loved the eagerness with which trout ate these larger fly patterns. Again, he knew that their ferocity resulted from that cardinal equation of trout fishing—that a trout will expend calories only if the expected return is sensible. In this case, the fish had determined that the caloric value of a meaty stone fly nymph warranted an aggressive effort to ensure that the morsel wasn't consumed by a competing trout or left to drift downriver, untouched. The fish shot from their resting positions like cannonballs.

Back East, trout fishing was a far more refined affair. The trout there were consistently difficult—they saw many times more imitations in their lives because of the higher ratio of angler per fish. In order to survive, these trout became very adept at distinguishing artificial flies from their natural counterparts.

On top of that, pollution and low water quality meant that eastern insects were less healthy and thus grew on average to a much smaller size. The fish in turn reacted less enthusiastically to their presence and were less healthy themselves.

Another good reason to be in Wyoming.

After he was through fishing, Jake packed up his camp and freed the boat from its moorings. Before he could get into the boat, he pushed it farther into the water. The receding water level had left the skiff partially beached in the sand.

Jake sat down at the rowing station and pulled the oars hard to get to the main channel. The sun was warm on his face. Downstream, the broken water sparkled brightly. Summer was coming. He pushed the boat forward.

In most cases, guides back rowed with the bow facing downstream so they could provide their anglers with the opportunity to cover the water thoroughly. By slowing the boat down with backstrokes, the guide gave the fishermen the most possible time to cast to the places where trout lived.

If the guide didn't slow the boat, the current would push the boat too quickly and the fishermen wouldn't cover the water well. Still, most anglers simply picked what they thought would have been a likely spot "back home" and beat that spot to a froth with repeated casts rather than covering the water as the guide suggested. The worst clients never hit *any* likely spots. They seemed capable of casting toward only two locations: about ten feet out from the bank, where the current was too strong to hold fish, or straight into the bank side bushes. These anglers never placed a fly in that magic two-foot corridor just off the bank that held 90 percent of the river's feeding fish.

The occasional pleasure of fishing with a good fisherman is what kept the full-time guide sane. Competent casters would toss the fly in the gentle water adjacent to the bank, allow the fly to act naturally and look appetizing, and if there was no result, cast again, slightly downstream, as the boat moved in that direction. They always anticipated the fish-holding lies as the boat approached them and they were never caught flinging the fly desperately back upstream to hit a spot that held a fish as the boat moved inevitably farther away. Jake enjoyed rowing for such fishermen more than he did fishing himself.

An old fly-fishing adage applied to Jake nicely: When a person first starts casting flies he wants to catch a lot of fish. Then, when he has proven to himself that he can catch lots of fish, the man desires trophy fish. After he has caught enough large fish to satisfy himself, he decides to pursue fish under certain difficult conditions. The fourth phase begins when the man wants to go fishing because he truly and thoroughly enjoys the experience. At this point, fly-fishing ceases to be an addiction and becomes a part of the man's life.

Jake had reached this point sometime shortly after his move to Wyoming. He still dabbled in the earlier stages of the sport from time to time, but he was just as likely to be found watching fish rise to consume natural insects as actively pursuing a fish. It was no longer the take, the surging and acrobatic fight, or the pictures of trophy fish that enthralled him.

Jake still believed it was a noble and spiritual pursuit. Fishing rewarded the most humble, observant, and dedicated participants, and for this reason it was inherently fair. There were no rewards in the sport of fly-fishing for those with flashy egos or aggressive personalities. If a man rushed into a stream ignorantly and cast his fly at a feeding fish while prematurely feeling sure of his success, he was certain to fail. In fly-fishing, the patient and quietly confident man always won. Those who did the work, remained humble to nature's complexities, and observed their surroundings caught plenty of fish.

This theory for success, however, was not applicable to life in general. Lawyering, for example, often rewarded the aggressive and the pushy. Business, too. An inflated sense of self could fool others into believing you were the best around. Politics. It was all the same.

It was ironic to Jake that while it was possible to convince other humans using puffery and haughtiness, you could not convince a simpleminded fish this way. There was no bullshitting a trout.

Too many people worked and lived in worlds where they never moved beyond the first or second phase of the hierarchy. That is to say, they wanted only lots of things or big things. They never got to the point where they enjoyed their life's work as an experience, because to them the experience itself was only a means to an end—a way to get many, big things.

As he approached a tricky section of river, Jake broke from this train of thought. He shielded his eyes with his right hand and looked for the safest route through the small rapids. On river left, there was a tree matted with debris jutting into the current. Water siphoned through its branches at a furious pace.

When the Snake's currents were high with runoff, they deposited debris—logs, branches, occasional litter—that was exposed only when the water dropped. The river changed constantly.

Jake slid the skiff past the deadfall just a few yards from the debris. The sun's glare subsided as the boat came parallel with the debris, and he finally got a good view of the tree.

For a split second, Jake thought it was just a tangle of colorful fabric washed downstream from a flooded neighborhood or blown off a clothesline. Then it became disturbingly clear; there was a form filling the clothes. A man's body was stuck in the deadfall, half-submerged and bouncing about in the undulating current.

Shit! River rocks scratched against the hull as Jake pulled the boat against the near bank below the deadfall. He dropped anchor and splashed into the water, hurrying upstream. There was really no chance the man could be alive. He had probably been there for hours, or even days. It would be a miracle to survive a swim in the cold, turbulent water.

Jake fought the current until he got to the tree and the man suspended in its snare. The large, thick trunk spanned the thirty or forty feet between the bank where Jake stood and the man's body. The victim's head was underwater. He was dead.

Jake stood and caught his breath, thinking. Rather than leaving the body, he decided to retrieve it himself. This kind of thing wasn't totally foreign to him. He had seen worse as an investigator.

The log was wide and flat on top, but Jake knew it would be slick. If he slipped off, the cold, churning water would cause hypothermia. In this isolated setting, hypothermia meant death. Jake waded back to his boat to see what he might be able to use to his advantage. He opened the compartment under the front seat and found his bowline. He looped it over his shoulder, then grabbed a life jacket.

His plan was to make his way to the body inch by inch, straddling the log. Then he would attach the rope to the body and return to the riverbank, where he would try to pull the body from the tangle. This way he could avoid struggling with the body on the slick log, where the consequences of a mistake were graver.

Jake reached the body with relative ease, despite the frigid water splashing over him. He regretted not packing additional clothes for the trip. It was going to be a cold couple of hours to the takeout.

He tied the rope around the man and headed toward shore, but he didn't have enough slack to make it back. He would have to pull the body out while sitting on top of the log. He looked at the cold, deep water below him.

Not good.

Jake intertwined his feet in the water underneath the dead tree on which he sat, securing himself. He tugged on the rope. No luck. The heavy current had pinned the body with incredible force. It wouldn't budge. Finally, after a herculean pull, the body came free.

In a split second, the rope was tearing away from Jake with tremendous power. It was swept underneath the log, and the man's body acted like an underwater sail—its crescent-bent broadside harnessing the full force of the river's current.

Jake groaned.

The force was going to pull him in unless he let go, so he risked the loss of the body and dropped the rope underwater and below the tree. A second later the rope resurfaced downstream. Jake lunged for it. The weight of the body was still there.

As the rope became taut, Jake understood his new quandary. The force of the river's current was pushing against the dead man's chest. His body was facing Jake and bent into an unnatural U shape, like in an exorcism movie. It nearly tore Jake from his perch above the water. The direct connection—now unimpeded by the log—was more powerful than ever. The strength of the river threatened to pluck his arms from their sockets.

Then he had an idea. The tree had no bark. Indeed, it was glass smooth. With all his remaining strength, Jake pulled the rope to gain enough slack to plunge it back underwater and around the tree. It took three attempts, but he succeeded in replacing the rope back into its original position. He sat on the rope and rested. His arms had gone numb.

He pulled the body several yards closer to him using the device. In the event that he lost his grip, he would have an opportunity to grab it again before it was pulled out of his reach and downstream.

Then Jake made his way to shore, pushing the loop of rope ahead of him on the tree trunk and then moving himself forward, inch by inch. In a few moments, he was standing in the shallow water at the river's edge.

In the quieter current, Jake dragged the body onto the bank and into the boat. He looked him over. Pricey fishing gear. This wasn't surprising—the Snake was a popular trout river. Jake guessed the man was probably a tourist rather than a local, as his clothing looked new.

In fact, he thought, *this stuff is spotless.* The man wore a sky-blue button-down shirt made by a ubiquitous manufacturer and expensive, unmarred waders.

Jake unclipped the suspenders of the man's waders and checked his jeans pockets for identification. Finding nothing, Jake searched the man's vest. The pockets were mostly empty. No ID. Nothing but a limited selection of terminal tackle—a small fly box with a half dozen fly patterns, one spool of the clear leader material that fly fishermen called tippet, and a pair of nail clippers for snipping and retying line. Even Jake, who was known in the valley as a fisherman who could find success with almost any fly, thought the dead man's tackle selection was dreadfully thin.

In addition to not having a wallet, the man didn't carry a Wyoming fishing license on his person. This struck Jake as odd. The man had obviously spared no expense in outfitting himself for his fishing trip, but no license.

What is he doing out here? Why was a tourist fishing this water alone under such dangerous conditions? No local fly shop would recommend that anyone wade in the river at this point in the season. The water was dangerously high, even in light of the overnight volume drop. It was a difficult river to wade even in low water.

The accident could have been avoided with just a *little* common sense. Then again, here Jake was, on a solo float trip, wet and cold from retrieving a dead body in a precarious spot.

Jake rowed through the deep canyon walls that defined the lateral boundaries of the river. He had taken off his waders to cover the face of the corpse and sat freezing. The wind was blowing briskly through his quick-dry pants.

At least I don't have to look at that face anymore. He figured that was more important than staying warm.

Jake had the stern pointed downstream, rowing powerfully, so that he could reach the takeout as soon as possible and hand the body over to the cops. As he rowed, he wondered what the man's story was, why he was here, what his life was like, how his death had come to pass.

Then he busied his mind with morbid humor, playing on the joke about cemeteries his old man used to tell in the car: *Jake, look at that quiet, gated neighborhood! People are dying to get in.*

He imagined Caddy: "How was your day, man?"

"Not bad, picked up a client as it turns out. He was dying to go fishing, so I let him on. Real quiet guy."

"Shit, well, at least he wasn't rattling off boring stories of his own business prowess," Caddy would say, unhampered by the fact that his own clients were within earshot.

Jake knew dozens of jokes aimed at river guides or their clients, and this situation begged for one more. *Tell you about my favorite client? Sure, the guy was great, never tangled his line, didn't break a rod, and didn't ask stupid questions like, "At what elevation do elk turn into moose?"*

Jake felt only a slight remorse for his thoughts; they kept his mind off the cold.

When he finally arrived at the takeout, Jake was relieved to see his small SUV and trailer. His detail-obsessed nature had never allowed him to get over the nagging fear that his vehicle would not be waiting for him. Before he put in on any float, he asked himself the same few questions over and over again: *Did I call the shuttle driver to make arrangements? Did I tell the driver the correct take-out? Did I put the keys in the gas cap? Did I leave money for the driver?* Over and over again. A mild case of OCD, probably.

Jake's cell phone had died and he was anxious to get to the

police station. For the first time in several years, his nerves caused him to have some difficulty backing the trailer down the boat ramp. When he finally maneuvered the trailer into place, he pulled the parking brake hard and got out.

Then he pondered the traveling arrangements for the corpse. *Should I tether the man to the boat in some way or put him in the car?* He regretted not buying a pickup. If he had, he could put the body in the bed and avoid having to make the drive with a dead man as passenger.

Jake decided that because of the rough surface of the long dirt road between the takeout and the highway, it would be best to put the man in the SUV somewhere. The trailer had no real suspension system to speak of, and he wanted to avoid damage to the corpse—for the man's family and to preserve the body for evidence. The fact that he moved the body would irritate the police enough. He felt certain that either the police department or the man's family would request an autopsy, given the circumstances.

Too bad autopsies almost never provide the family with the answers they want. More often than not, they simply exposed unpleasant truths about the deceased. This was particularly true with this type of mysterious death. At best, the family might discover a hidden drug or alcohol problem. At worst, they might find out that he had killed himself. Death, anyway, was like an unreviewable play in sports—it may have been wrong and unfair, but there was simply no possible way to make it right. The decision would stand.

When he slid the body into the hatchback of his vehicle, Jake noticed for the first time that the man's ankles were bruised. *Must've happened on the riverbed while trying to jam his feet into the rocks to get footing. Scary way to go.*

5

JACKSON POLICE HEADQUARTERS. LATER THAT DAY.

"Tell me you have good news," the chief said tiredly. It was midafternoon. The inside of the station had calmed considerably since the night before. Terrell ignored Jake's outstretched hand. The chief and Jake knew each other well; they were both involved in the town's tiny political community. Jake didn't totally understand the snub but assumed it was related to the Old Teton Dairy Ranch proposal. Jake knew Terrell felt that what was good for the economy was good for the town.

"Well, the best news I can offer is that I don't recognize the dead guy I found this morning in the Snake. I don't think he's a local."

"Don't pull my chain, Jake. Do you have any flippin' idea what I have been dealing with for the last thirty-six hours?" The chief had barely avoided using profane language in front of a woman, his secretary. A cardinal rule of his.

"Sorry, Chief. He's in my truck. Looks like a drowning. What happened here—rodeo parking overflowed again?" Jake could tell immediately that Terrell was in no mood to joke. He followed the chief, who walked briskly back toward his office.

"You really haven't heard? Jesus, Jake. Two wilderness fatalities yesterday. It's been chaos. You know this town as well as anyone. People are putting those Nepalese prayer flags up everywhere. Really freaking out. One vic was a well-liked local. A lot of answers are expected from us and the park service. Answers we don't have. We've been running at full speed since the first accident."

"What happened?" Jake asked as the chief collapsed in the chair behind his desk.

"Avalanche on Maelstrom—massive wet slide, like a cement factory overflowed. Killed one, the local guy. Before that, a European couple got friendly with a bear near the Gosling Lake overlook. One dead. Fucking insanity." The chief shook his head. They were beyond earshot of the secretary and Terrell was talking like a city cop.

Curious, Jake ignored the matter of the body in his trunk for the time being. "They get the bear yet?"

"No, but a team from Yellowstone is up there as we speak. Haven't heard anything. Tell me your story, Trent, you're not the type to drop in for a chat." The chief was frantically searching for something on his desk among hundreds of sheets of yellow notebook paper.

"What were his injuries—the victim, I mean? Has the coroner figured anything out?"

The chief sighed loudly. "Cause of death has not technically been determined, but the man had serious head trauma and several deep bite wounds to his chest. What does that say to you, Einstein?"

"Scalp probably bitten or punctured . . ." Jake knew this was common with bear attacks. One annoying remnant of Jake's past was that he was hopelessly curious about deaths and disappearances.

"No, scalp intact." He looked up at Jake and sighed. "It seemed more like a blunt force injury resulting from a paw swat rather than a bite. A park ranger, Noelle Klimpton, said it looked like he had been pummeled by a boxer."

"Was the bear still around the scene, or are you working by process of elimination?" Jake didn't intend to sound rude, but the chief stopped perusing and looked up.

"Jake, we are all happy you're here and contributing to our community," Terrell said facetiously, "but you can leave your big-city, Mr. District Attorney suspicions at home. We can handle the investigation."

Jake tilted his head back. He'd overstepped. It was time to move on. "You'd better follow me outside, Rog."

"You've got to be shitting me," he said, standing up, and the two walked out to the parking lot.

"Dammit!" the chief shouted as he peered into the back of Jake's SUV. Despite, or perhaps because of, the grave circumstances, the chief seemed to abruptly change moods, looking as if he was going to start laughing.

"Unbelievable!" Sure enough, he smiled in disbelief. "Well, looks like I've gotta take your statement. Then you can take him over to St. John's. The coroner will relieve you of your . . . err . . . cargo. No place to put him here, and I don't think people would react well if I sat him down in the waiting area." The chief laughed. He sounded like a man on his way to having a nervous breakdown.

*   *   *

After taking Jake's statement, the chief walked him back to the parking lot.

"Be discreet," he whispered as Jake got into his truck.

"Of course," Jake said.

As if I'm going to take him to Ripley's Believe It or Not!

Jake checked his mirror before he backed up and then angled it down to make sure that no part of the man's body was visible through the rear windshield of the car. He backed out of the police station's parking lot and headed toward St. John's.

Only in Wyoming would an officer of the law ask a civilian to transport a corpse.

Jake arrived at the hospital to find a man in a long, white coat waving him down. Obviously, Chief Terrell hadn't forgotten to call. When Jake approached the garage door that the coroner pointed to, the man slid a key card through an electronic box in the cement wall. The garage door rose. Jake entered and parked in a spot near a set of double doors.

"Mr. Trent, I presume?" The coroner had a hollow and high-pitched voice, almost flutelike.

"Call me Jake. And you are?"

"Smith," the man responded.

"Nice to meet you, Mr. Smith," Jake said as the man grabbed his hand and shook firmly. *No surprise, he has cold hands,* Jake thought. He wiped his palm off on his jeans.

"Just Smith, actually." He smiled patronizingly and led Jake through the double doors. "If you don't mind, you can help me load the deceased onto a gurney."

The two men pushed the gurney out to Jake's tailgate. Smith

pressed a lever and lowered the surface so it was level with the bumper. They slid the body out and onto the gurney. It was starting to smell. The transfer from the cold river to warmer air must have started the decomposition process. Jake followed Smith inside past two water fountains and through a single door without any windows.

This morgue was smaller than the typical city morgue—just eight large silver drawers. Most cities had ten times that capacity. No matter how often Jake had visited a morgue in the past, he never got used to it. Although he knew the aroma here was only a result of the sanitizing and preservation solutions used by the coroners, it still turned his stomach.

"Are the two bodies from yesterday here?" Jake asked, curious.

Smith looked at him as if to gauge his trustworthiness. "One is, the French guy that the bear got to. Other one is gone. The family of the guy who was killed in the avalanche had his body shipped back to Colorado for the funeral services."

As he spoke, the coroner was looking at the dead fisherman's ankles. "What do you make of that?" Jake asked.

"Hard to say, really. Could've been irritated by the wool in his socks. This certainly isn't what killed him." Smith chuckled.

Sweet guy.

Jake was tempted to ask to see the body of the man who had been killed by the bear, but he refrained. He bid Smith good-bye and drove off, mulling the strange day.

If the coroner, the park, and the police said bear attack, Jake would believe them. It was strange though. Three violent deaths, two days, one small town. These were the sorts of things that got his wheels turning. Patterns. Coincidence. Things that usually led to something bigger.

Dusk nudged away the warmth and light of the sun while Jake pulled into the driveway that led to the main house on his property. He marveled at the beauty of the land in the fleeting sunlight. As always, he slowed down to appreciate the place he called home.

Chayote ran beside the SUV, jumping up and down next to the driver's side window. His stubby tail was wagging insistently, and his half-blue, half-white left eye accentuated the crazed, happy look on his face.

As he pulled into the small gravel parking area at the end of the road, Jake could see J.P. perched on top of the wood pile next to his camper smoking a cigarette. The wood was drying out now from the weeks of early summer sun and it was highly flammable. *Smart.*

He laughed aloud at his friend, who was wearing an obnoxious-looking cowboy hat and sitting with his knees to his chest and his arms wrapped around his shins, looking like a devious child.

"Hey, partner! I got locked out! Stupid dog was waiting for you to come home," J.P. shouted, motioning to Chayote, who was now lying in a playful sphinxlike pose at the edge of the drive. His blue-merle coat offered great camouflage. When Jake shot the mutt a look, it ran off into the woods.

Jake waved and started to walk toward J.P., wondering how he had managed to get locked out of both houses and his own camper.

"I never even knew this thing had a lock, to be honest," J.P. said as he threw a handful of dry pine needles in the direction of his camper. "I decided to make a spare set of keys to put under this hidey-rock thing I saw on TV last night. It blends right in with nature, man. Au naturel. So, anyway, I collected all our originals and went inside to get the business credit card and somehow managed to lock everything in the main house. I tore apart my camper to find another set with no luck. Walked out and slammed the door. That must have forced the lock closed from the inside.

"I figured if we had that fake rock, man, we would never get locked out again." He smiled knowingly. J.P. was not as dumb as he sometimes seemed.

Jake marveled at J.P.'s logic and laughed because there was really no business credit card at all, there was only a debit card in J.P.'s name that drew from Jake's personal account. It was in the kitchen of the main house for emergencies.

In the past such emergencies included: J.P. needing to rent a snowmobile because a winter storm had dumped a ton of snow and J.P. was "so over" skiing at the crowded resort, and a night in a suite at the Four Seasons because J.P. had to convince a woman that he was a famous jazz musician traveling the country.

"Let's get inside, it's getting chilly," Jake suggested. They headed into the main house.

While Jake started a fire in the fireplace, J.P. ran his hands under warm tap water. After a few moments of that, he dried them off on his shirt, walked to the fridge, and grabbed an ice-cold bottle of beer.

He pulled his sweatshirt sleeve over his hand to insulate it from the cold bottle. Jake gave him a dubious look.

"Could use a glass, you know."

"What? You want a brew, man?" he shouted into the den, where the fire was now blazing.

"No thanks," Jake responded. The morgue had put him in no mood to consume anything.

"Did you hear that Marcus Jane bit the dust?" he asked Jake.

Before Jake could answer, his friend spoke again. "Crazy; he was a hell of a skier. Careful, too. Not one of those over-the-top, extreme guys; he just liked to go out and have a good time. Enjoy nature, you know? I've skied with Marcus plenty of times when he walked away from a tasty-looking slope because things just didn't feel right.

"I guess all the preparation in the world can't prevent every accident," J.P. concluded.

"I didn't know him," Jake said, stoking the fire.

"No offense, but Marcus wasn't exactly part of your crowd." Jake laughed. J.P. imagined himself much younger than Jake, while in reality the two were only three years apart.

"Who'd he ski with? Who was he with yesterday?"

"That skinny Ricker kid who lives south of town. The idiot that nearly killed himself up on Jackalope Couloir two winters ago. Had to get airlifted out because he wanted to impress some girl. Don't know his first name. Same one that was arrested in that wolf hunt protest. Remember that?"

Jake remembered the name now. When there was still some question as to whether a wolf hunt would be allowed in Idaho, Ricker had protested and displayed some threatening signs outside public buildings. The one that made the local paper said, "Hey IFG, How would you like it if we shot *you* for feeding *yourself*!" (*IFG* being Idaho Fish and Game.)

When Ricker was arrested for not having a permit to demonstrate, he had threatened the police and spit on them. That makes the paper in Jackson.

The sign reflected the boiling disagreement over a proper solution to livestock predation by wolves. Ranchers lobbied the Idaho government to open a hunting season on wolves to reduce the numbers. Many disagreed, Jake included. But he knew the ranchers had a valid argument too. Wolf numbers were increasing, and ranchers were losing thousands a year in dead stock.

The dispute was resolved in favor of the ranchers. There would be a short hunting season for wolves. Jake didn't mind the decision, really. Perhaps it wasn't the business of Yankees and California hippie kids to decide the fate of those who made their living from this land.

"And Ricker survived?" Jake asked.

"Sure did. One lucky bastard, man. He already made a statement to the press last night. It made it into the *Daily* today. Kind of disrespectful if you ask me." J.P. was nothing if not well informed on gossip.

"What did he say?"

"You'll have to check the paper for the exact quote, but something along the lines of 'If you play with fire, you'll eventually get burned.'" J.P. shook his head.

"Yeah, sounds pretty inappropriate in the wake of a friend's death," Jake said.

"I don't think the two were that close, though," J.P. said, and then changed the subject: "Hey, do you mind if I sleep in here tonight, man? I'll call the lock guy in the morning."

"Of course not." There weren't any guests in the main house tonight. June was always slow. By the end of the month, some tourists would filter into the valley as school ended, but July and August were the high season in Jackson Hole.

Jake said good night to his friend and walked back to the guest-house. It was situated east of the main house, and so as he walked toward the front door, he could see the profile of the ridgeline that resembled a sleeping Indian chief. The sky was fading into night, but Jake could still make out the outline of the chief's nose and forehead. The cliff bands dotted with snow gave the viewer the impression that the chief was wearing a headdress. Often, a pink haze hung above the skyward-facing man as the sun set behind the Tetons on the other side of the valley.

He went through the back door of the guesthouse as he always did, so he had an excuse to check out the stream that ran behind the old building. Although he couldn't see them in the evening's fading light, he could hear some fish still feeding.

Jake set his keys, wallet, and cell phone on the small table he kept by the back door. He walked into the little, drab room where he tied flies, built fly rods, and tinkered with his fishing equipment. He turned on the radio.

The sun was nearly gone and it was now cool in the house, but Jake preferred not to turn on the baseboard heaters unless it was absolutely necessary. He crossed the hall to take a hot shower. He could faintly hear a news report about the slide and a warning to backcountry skiers to thoroughly assess the snow conditions.

Nobody is actually going to heed the weatherman's advice and collect snowpack data before a ski trip in June.

The odds were too far in favor of the skier. The avalanche was a freak event.

After his shower, Jake put on a pair of fleece pants that he had owned since he was a teenager and a long-sleeved shirt. He returned to his tying room and looked through the plastic shelves of drawers that held hundreds of different fly patterns.

Every summer, Jake would leave dozens of flies on the overhanging trees on the river's edge. A few would even be left in the lips of trout that were strong enough to break the leader that connected the man to the fish and some were mangled by the small pinlike teeth of the cutthroats.

In the spring, Jake would spend a few weeks replenishing his stock. There were certain patterns he preferred to tie, and generally these were larger and more colorful. He didn't look forward to tying tiny, drab flecks of fish food and thus did so only when it was necessitated by the fishing conditions.

Fortunately for Jake, Snake River cutthroats were a particularly aggressive species and they favored large, gaudy patterns. Folks often referred to the personality of the local fish by proclaiming "they think they're smallmouth bass!" Hyperbolic, sure, but Jake sometimes thought it was an understatement. More like snook, Jackson Hole's resident trout spent their summer days lying against the bank waiting to ambush their prey. They were more like the mammalian predators in the region, gutsy and vicious, than they were like the shy, wary, and effeminate trout of fly-fishing lore. Oftentimes, a fly that landed harshly on the water, drawing attention to itself, was more effective than a "traditional" presentation, where the fly landed softly and quietly.

He looked through the bins of flies for something that was in low supply and that he enjoyed to tie. He was low on a dry fly pattern called a Fat Albert and scribbled that name down on a scrap of paper. Then he scrawled the word "dozen" in parentheses next to it. Jake kept inventory of the flies he tied so that he was never without one he needed. He grimaced when he looked at his own sloppy handwriting—the result of years of dictation recorders and secretarial assistance.

The Fat Albert was a silly-looking thing. Tied with foam and bulky like its name implied, with rubber daddy-longlegs appendages hanging from the hook. It imitated no bug actually found in nature. It was intended to look too good for a hungry fish to pass up. An old mentor of Jake's had once said that casting a dry fly to a hungry fish was like rolling a liquor bottle into a jail cell. This was especially the case with Snake River fine-spotted cutthroat trout.

It was a strange result of spending too much time with his finned friends, but Jake could see why certain flies looked more edible than others to fish. The Fat Albert was a very edible-looking fly.

Fly tying calmed Jake. It was demanding enough that his mind didn't wander to the nether regions of anxiety, but still dull enough that it never seemed like work. He felt about fly tying what others felt about practicing yoga or listening to jazz. As he trimmed and tied and knotted, he turned up the radio in the small room.

Ugh, political talk radio. The worst.

Jake completed his second Fat Albert and placed it in the section labeled "foam dry flies," in the third compartment from the back, with its brethren of similar flies. His mind wandered back to the three recent tragedies in Jackson Hole. If he were investigating these deaths in Philadelphia, how would he think the problem through?

Back when it was his job to investigate such things for a living, he would start with some premise—the beginning of a narrative—and work from there. Some said his methods relied too much on inference and imagination, that he wrote a script in his own head and then forced the facts to fit the story.

What his critics didn't expect was that he actually had a knack for thinking like a criminal. His wary mind had prevented several would-be crimes: conspiracies, murders, and acts of terror.

The Zoering-Blotzheim case was a shining example. Dr. Adalwullf "Shadow Wolf" Zoering was an eighty-eight-year-old scientist and Nazi who had lived illegally in the United States from 1990 to 2000. Jake and his unit began monitoring Zoering in the mid-nineties because the U.S. government suspected he was financially backing terrorist attacks against Israel and the United States.

It was what the unit called a "hands off" mission. No contact, only surveillance.

Zoering caught wind of the investigation and fled to France, where he quickly turned himself in and pled guilty to war crimes charges stemming from his participation in World War II concentration camps. He died in a Parisian prison eight days after sentencing.

It didn't quite add up to Jake.

Regardless, he was ordered to fly to France and assist the French authorities with closing the case. Jake stopped in D.C. instead, missing his connecting flight to Paris. He was concerned by some questions: *How did Zoering know we were after him? Why did the case wind down so quietly and conveniently?*

Jake spent that evening contacting everyone with knowledge of the Zoering investigation. Finally at midnight, a lead. The home phone number for Agent Carpenter, an FBI liaison, had been disconnected. His superiors reported that he had missed work for the last three days with the flu.

Bingo. Jake spent the night investigating the agent.

As the sun rose, Jake apprehended Carpenter, who was armed with eighty pounds of C-4 and headed to the district's busiest subway station. Zoering had fled to distract them.

After a few years, his success as an investigator was no longer arguable, and his critics gave up. Jake still neglected to mention to anyone that he actually often created elaborate journals containing nicknames, predictions, and motives. He charted out crime sprees as if they were choose-your-own-ending children's books. All before any hard evidence was found. It almost always worked.

The first assumption here would be that the deaths were not

coincidental. From there, he could rule out natural death since nature acted only on coincidence, unless you believed in divine intervention. Jake did not.

Even in a large city like Philadelphia, three accidental deaths in such a short period of time would catch the attention of law enforcement. Move the location of the event to a low-population area like Jackson Hole and it stuck out like a sore thumb.

So, when one assumes that the deaths are related, the next logical assumption is that the victims must have something in common.

In an urban area, this often meant the victims were all members of a certain gang, drug cartel, or crime family. As far as Jake knew, these types of groups were all but nonexistent in the valley. Besides, he knew that at least one victim was a European tourist and the river victim hadn't yet been reported missing.

Two of the victims were not even from the area.

But then the local skier? The pattern doesn't hold.

He shook his head and continued to tie; he was probably getting ahead of himself.

Still, Jake was intrigued by the possibility that these deaths were well-disguised crimes. Three in two days seemed too unlikely.

Jake finished one final fly and put it in its bin. He didn't finish the dozen flies that he'd set as a goal, but he was exhausted from his camping trip and his mind was wandering to places that were both silly and dangerous.

He walked up the creaky, cold wooden stairs to his loft bedroom.

As he lay in bed trying to calm his mind, he remembered that he had to present an argument in opposition to the development program that had been recently proposed for Jackson Hole.

Shit! He'd intended to work on it tonight.

As one of two attorneys involved with the town council, he was often asked to speak when the council was faced with thorny legal matters. He didn't mind. This time, he felt strongly about the issue and looked forward to preparing his argument tomorrow.

The developer, Parrana and Sons, was a conglomerate operating out of Idaho Falls. In an unexpected move, they had recently purchased the Willow Ranch south of town for $100 million. The proposed Old Teton Dairy Ranch. They were now disputing the legitimacy of a conservation easement on the property so they could develop the land.

Conservation easements were a popular legal mechanism in the area. They lasted perpetually and placed restrictions on the future use of the land. In this case, a valid conservation easement would have effectively prohibited the developer from building the condominiums it desired.

The original owner's son, now ninety-two and living at *his* son's house in Richmond, Virginia, attested by phone to Jake that his father had in fact recorded the easement some eighty years ago. He had no paper records.

All the owners since the original owner had believed the easement was valid, too. But Teton County was still in the process of filing its land records in a computer database, and this old record had no backup. The easement had no concrete documentation. Nobody knew whether the easement had once been filed and then lost, or was never properly filed to begin with. Nobody knew anything.

The developer, predicting a hostile response from the town, decided to offer to resolve the dispute by paying an extra sum of money, to be used for conservation efforts, to the township. The township was considering whether they should accept what, to Jake, sounded a lot like a bribe.

Unfortunately, it looked like the money had charmed the majority of the council. But there was one last step: pursuant to the town's bylaws, there would have to be an opportunity for proponents from each side to present their arguments at a public hearing. Jake had been asked to present the opposition's opinion on the matter.

It was now completely dark outside Jake's bedroom window. After reviewing the facts in his head, he was no longer particularly anxious about the speech. His mind finally and subconsciously decided to take its rest.

Then Jake's eyes flashed open. He stared up at the ceiling and said aloud: "Shit, I'm going to get arrested tomorrow." He threw his head back into the pillow.

Maybe not arrested, but certainly questioned. "Shit!" he said aloud again. Once the police had a chance to think about it, they were going to be very interested in the fact that Jake had gone on an overnight float trip alone, with no witnesses, and returned with a dead man's body.

6

GRAND TETON NATIONAL PARK. THE SAME EVENING.

Noelle was rolling the smooth bear tooth around in the palm of her hand. She'd been planning to drop the tooth off with Nat Passa after her patrol, but by the time she got back to the trailhead, the gate to the parking area was closed and locked.

They must be finished, she surmised.

Instead of driving into town to hand the tooth over to the police, she stopped at the Jenny Lake Lodge and, while chatting with an old friend, dropped the tooth into a hotel key card envelope and taped the flap.

I'll get it to Terrell or the bear team tomorrow.

She'd left the envelope in the truck, but that evening Noelle had the urge to retrieve it. At the kitchen table, she pulled the tooth from its envelope and held it a few inches from her eyes, studying.

It was unusual that the tooth remained whole. *Should it have broken off at the gum line?* Perhaps, but here it was, with its sharp, undamaged point and full roots.

Noelle corrected herself and laughed. *When you are investigating a bear attack in your free time, you need a hobby.*

She had an adventurous soul, though. These were the same feelings that had driven her to move to Jackson and pursue excitement via extreme sports and mountaineering. In a strange way, the current excitement was reawakening her.

Recently, Noelle had noticed that the high she once felt from these endeavors was waning. She knew she shouldn't get more involved in the bear mauling case than she already was, but she yearned for the exhilaration.

Then again, her intentions were pure. Her secret investigation wasn't hurting anyone. *Except maybe for me,* she thought. She pictured herself solving some unlikely crime—having the time of her life and being lauded as a hero. She opened her computer and double-clicked on the desktop icon for her email.

There were no new messages in her in-box. Suddenly she recalled a thought from the previous night. Noelle had an old flame—a bear expert at Montana State University. Noelle had broken off their relations suddenly and without explanation, but this seemed like a fine opportunity to get back in touch. She started drafting an email.

Keith Strang had initially pursued a PhD in fish and wildlife biology at MSU. After beginning his studies, though, he became increasingly passionate about the conservation of predatory mammals, namely bears, wolves, and mountain lions. Keith's passion wasn't fueled by a specific affection for predators themselves, but he felt that those animals that humans considered to be dangerous needed the most protection.

It was easy, Keith believed, to gain a sympathetic public opinion toward a colorful tree frog or the majestic and nationally endorsed bald eagle. Protecting animals that competed with us at the top of the food chain, on the other hand, ran counter to our instincts. It was for this very reason—the challenge of the task—that Keith decided to forgo the pursuit of his degree and work full-time as a wildlife field researcher specializing in grizzly and black bears.

His primary mission these days was to debunk the myth that certain bears became "killer" bears after they attacked once and therefore should be exterminated. Instead, Keith believed that repeat attacks could be attributed to the simple fact that certain bears inhabited areas where human interaction was more likely.

To Keith, a dangerous bear—even a repeat offender—should always be relocated. There was no reason that Keith could think of that a bear should ever be killed, and his research aimed to prove that notion.

Noelle wanted to know what Keith thought of yesterday's attack—especially the tooth. He would at least be able to tell her what species the culprit was, she figured. Maybe more. She started typing.

Dear Keith,

Hello from Jackson Hole! I hope you're well!

My apologies for the short notice, but if it is okay with you, I was thinking about stopping by tomorrow sometime. As I am sure you know, there was a bear attack down here in the Tetons. I found a tooth at the scene of the attack and I was wondering if you could take a look at it.

Thanks! I'm looking forward to seeing you tomorrow!

Warmly,

Noelle

P.S.—Don't tell anyone about this until we talk more!

Noelle left her computer open for a few minutes just in case Keith happened to be in his lab late.

Was that too flirty?

She wasn't surprised when her in-box chimed a minute later. Keith was still up.

Hey Stranger,

   I'll be here. Excited to see what you bring in for me!

                                        Peace!

                                        Keith

The email seemed a bit short, but at least he agreed to see her. She wouldn't have blamed him if he didn't respond at all.

Noelle smiled. Keith knew her quirks as well as anyone. He knew about her love for adventure ever since she had asked for his help in herding two dozen bison back into Yellowstone to protect them from hunters. That was their first date, if rounding up bison could be called a date. Under the moonlight on horseback and without the park's permission, they got all twenty-four back into their safe haven.

Tomorrow would be just like old times.

Noelle ignored the question: *Do I want old times?*

With Keith's help she could learn something from the tooth. Plus, Noelle could drive to Bozeman through Yellowstone National Park, something that she always cherished. In early summer, the park was filled with young mammals plodding along with their mothers—elk, deer, bison. It was a sight to behold.

Noelle set her alarm clock for 5 a.m. and got under the pile of old sleeping bags. The plan had energized her mind. Her thoughts wandered, trying to make sense of what was going on. Sleep was elusive, but exhaustion infected her logic. She even considered contacting a psychic in Jackson who was also a self-proclaimed expert cryptozoologist. *Maybe the attack seemed superviolent because the attacker was some yet-to-be-discovered creature! A sasquatch!* She laughed to herself.

Noelle had gone to the psychic the prior fall. The woman's prediction that Noelle would soon meet the man of her dreams was far from true, and when the woman hit and killed a bighorn sheep in a steep canyon east of Jackson, she told the authorities that a Meh-Teh, or abominable snowman, had thrown a dead carcass at her car while she drove.

In her police report, she wrote that the monster tried to kill her because she was the only human aware of its existence. Eventually the mystery of the flying carcass was resolved when the woman failed a field sobriety test and quickly admitted to smoking marijuana and drinking moonshine before driving. Noelle would stick with Keith for now.

She finally drifted off to sleep with a smirk on her face.

The next morning, Noelle woke up to her alarm and found it easy to get out of bed. She brushed her teeth, changed her clothes, grabbed the tooth, and walked to the car. She had to stop for coffee and gas at Dornan's on the way to Route 89. Again, she found herself wishing she had someone to share her morning coffee with.

You're getting soft, Noelle.

The young man working at Dornan's was a new employee with an "in-training" ribbon below his name tag. Noelle figured he was a seasonal worker who had come for the summer to fish, climb, and hike. Ninety-day wonder.

Sure enough, the man started to awkwardly make conversation with her. "Do you live here? You're up early for a tourist. Um, I . . . I just moved here last Sunday, is why I ask."

"I work over in the park." She pointed west toward the Snake River and then swept her hand north toward Mt. Moran. He smiled and nodded. She felt bad for him. She knew how hard it was to relocate to a new place without any friends or family.

He was a good-looking guy. Athletic and handsome. It wasn't that. Noelle was tempted to get his number, but she hesitated too long and made it awkward. Instead, she took advantage of the early hour and faked a yawn, making it clear to the man that she was ready to terminate the conversation as soon as possible.

He handed her the correct change for her coffee and said, "Well, I hope to see you around again. Have a nice day." Noelle forced a smile and walked away.

Her phone was ringing when she got into her truck.

"Hello?" she answered without bothering to see who it was. Noelle skimmed the park bulletin as she spoke. Mr. Passa and the others had found a bear in the area of the attack and killed it.

Dammit.

"Noelle, how are you?!" It was Anna, Noelle's sister, and she was excited about something. She rarely had time to call Noelle and it was never with the delight that her voice was now unable to hide.

"I'm great," Noelle mustered. "How're you? It's a bit early for a phone call, don't you think?" It was 5:30 a.m. Mountain Time. Anna lived in New York.

"Well, you know, there's the time change. And plus, I have exciting news for you!"

"You're getting married?" It had been a long time coming.

77

Noelle wasn't the biggest fan of the institution, but she could be happy for her younger sister.

"Dammit! You were supposed to let me break the news! What do you think?"

"It's wonderful, really. Congratulations! I can't wait to see you on your wedding day." The remark sounded contrived as it came out, but it was the best she could offer. "Who's the lucky guy?" Noelle was kidding—Anna and Steve had been dating for nearly ten years. Everyone in the family approved of him. He was a banker but had more depth to his personality than might be expected.

"Last night he proposed on the Staten Island Ferry. I was stunned," Anna said. "Oh my God! I cried! I couldn't even answer!"

"I can imagine," Noelle said, although it was a lie. "When is the big day?"

"October, here in the city. Still hoping warmish day with fall foliage. I thought you'd approve." Fall was Noelle's favorite season in New York. "And obviously I want you to be the maid of honor."

"Approved. And I'm flattered."

Fall weddings are becoming so cliché these days, she thought cynically. *And what the hell does she mean "you'd approve" of fall? Am I that drab?*

Still, Noelle was excited to see her family and she was truly happy for her sister. What she wasn't looking forward to were the comments from the family when she showed up stag.

"Hey, sis, I'm gonna go, though. I will call again soon, it's just that I have to make a zillion other calls. You are just the second to know after Mom."

"I understand. It's a busy day for you. I love you!"

Noelle sounded genuine at last.

But along with being happy for her sibling there was a tinge of sadness. Anna was years younger. Their family had always expected Noelle to get married first. For a while, she had expected it too.

Oh well. Noelle refocused on driving.

The day was warming up. As the sun rose, Noelle was even able to open the windows a bit, although she still ran the heater for her feet. She carefully glanced again at the park bulletin on the passenger seat and read the major points for the second time. Yep, they'd shot a bear yesterday at Gosling Lake. *Probably the wrong one too.*

Out of the blue Noelle started to cry, which she hadn't done in a long time. *Is it the bear, or is it Anna's engagement? Stop being so emotional.*

Noelle drove back through the northern end of Grand Teton National Park on her way to Yellowstone, without stopping at the gate to chat with the ranger. Her official vehicle granted her ingress whenever she pleased. She drove north still, past Jackson Lake Lodge and Leek's Marina. She hadn't stopped for lunch at the marina in ages. It was one of her favorite spots in the valley and she vowed to stop neglecting it. She looked forward to making the drive to the marina to eat pizza and watch the sailboats come and go.

Noelle did stop at the south entrance to Yellowstone to check that all the roads were open through the north entrance.

"Dunraven is closed, but that's it," the woman at the checkpoint responded.

Dunraven Pass led to Montana through the northeastern gate. Noelle's drive to Bozeman didn't require her to take the closed pass. It was unfortunate, in a way. That corner of the park was probably its most impressive. There, the land lacked the geothermal features that the central region boasted, but the amount and diversity of wildlife was astonishing.

On her last visit to the Lamar River Valley—the main attraction in the northeast corner of Yellowstone—Noelle observed a grizzly, two black bears, countless bison and antelope, and a few young bighorn sheep. Although she hadn't seen any wolves during her last visit, the Lamar River Valley always held that possibility as well.

Past the Lamar River Valley sat Cooke City, a tiny town tucked up into the mountains of extreme southern Montana.

The town was a single dirt road with cheap motels, taverns, and gift shops. One of the bars had a few slot machines from cowboy times. Mainly though, the town was wet and snowy and muddy, with its tiny rivulets often splitting the road into small islands.

The sun was up fully now and Noelle climbed out of Jackson Hole and onto the caldera that formed the Yellowstone Plateau. She passed the right turn for Old Faithful. In the time that Noelle had lived here, which wasn't much more than a decade, the turn had changed from a simple T intersection into its current layout—a highwaylike exit complete with entrance and exit ramps. A new visitors' center was also under construction. Progress.

Noelle spotted a herd of mother bison and their young along the Firehole River. The stumbling babies played in the green, soppy grass that was barren of snow year-round because of the river's warm springs. Birds landed on their backs and they bucked them off playfully.

She drove past the Fountain Paint Pot, through Madison Junction, and out the north entrance to the park. Just before 9:30 a.m., she arrived at her old friend's laboratory on the Montana State campus in Bozeman.

Before going in, she stopped at the student bookstore next door and purchased two cups of coffee, adding cream and artificial sweetener to her own and pocketing a few of the station's accoutrements to give Keith some options.

She took a left turn into the stairwell and went down one flight to the basement, where Keith spent most of his waking hours. When she opened the door, the man was wrestling with a large beaker that was overflowing a thick, foamy liquid.

"No! Stay back, Noelle!" he shouted. Keith's hair and beard said hippie, but his attire said scientist. The look on his face was alarming.

Noelle heeded his request, stepping backward away from the experiment.

"I've discovered something here! Something world changing!"

"Wha . . . ?" Noelle was confused. Then it occurred to her. He was playing a joke.

Keith stopped, looked up, and winked at her. "Just trying to bring back some of the old chemistry, that's all."

Chemistry. Baking soda volcano. Clever. Keith was from Chicago, and his big-city charm was still there. It stood out more up here in the middle of nowhere. Noelle kept a straight face. She wasn't here to flirt.

"Yeah, the kid that I Big Brother for wants to take me to Dads' Day at his school, and I just really want the other kids to be impressed." He sounded genuine.

"You are one of the most prominent grizzly and black bear experts in the United States, and you are going to try to impress them with cliché chemistry magic?" The stoicism left her face. She clucked her tongue in mock disapproval.

"You can't take a grizzly into a public school anymore."

He has a point, Noelle admitted. "Well, glad, and sort of surprised, to see you have the sense to know so."

He laughed with her and the two hugged. "So you have a bear tooth to show me, you say?" He gave her a puzzled look, getting down to business.

"Um, yeah." *Good,* she thought. *Keep it professional.* "I was hoping that you could take a look at it for me. The thing is that I don't really have it . . . on the record, that is; I took it from the scene of the attack without telling anyone. I guess what I'm saying is let's keep it on the down low."

"Is that supposed to surprise me, Noelle?" He laughed again.

She rolled her eyes, more at herself than him.

"This attack was really bad, Keith. I mean, it looked like the bear punctured the victims obsessively, like the animal had rabies or something."

"That would be pretty rare up here. Rabies, I mean."

"It just doesn't seem right, that's all."

"Have you ever witnessed a bear attack before?"

"Never."

Keith walked over to her and took the tooth, which she had removed from the envelope.

"This"—he held it up in front of her—"is backed by jaws strong enough to crush through the femur of an elk. Strong enough to crush a human skull. I've seen grizzlies bite through thick pine saplings. And those were just cubs playing, honing their skills."

Keith reached behind her with the tooth in hand. "It would bite here and here, upper jaw and lower jaw." The touch of the tooth was cold on her upper neck. "Get the idea?"

Keith's lips were only inches from Noelle's. She stepped back but held his gaze for a second.

Noelle cleared her throat. "But *two* victims were thoroughly mauled—and I mean *thoroughly.* And more chest damage than head and neck. Isn't that a bit unusual? Wouldn't the second victim get the idea that she was in danger and run from the scene?"

"Unless one stayed trying to protect the other. That's the most likely reason I can think of. It happens. And chest wounds some-times happen when the vic doesn't roll over onto his or her stom-ach." Keith paused. "Or maybe there were two or more bears—is that the sort of speculation you wanted to hear? That this story has a twist?" He smiled wryly.

Noelle knew he was hassling her in good fun, but she was still offended. "I'm being serious here, Keith."

"Okay, okay."

Keith took the tooth over to a black lab table and focused a large magnifying light on it. The contrast of the colors made the tooth's virgin white gloss stand out even more than it had last night.

"Mighty clean," Keith said immediately.

Noelle nodded and studied Keith, trying to gain some understand-ing of his meaning, and then eventually said: "How do you mean?"

"I mean that I can tell you right off that this tooth probably wasn't hanging out in the mouth of *any* wild animal recently."

"You're sure?" Noelle asked.

He picked it up. "It should have at least some plaque gunk up on the gum line there. Who knows? It might be fake, and if it's not fake it might have been cleaned and bleached and had some type of sealant applied." Keith walked with the tooth to another table. Noelle followed.

"I'm happy to crack it open to try and confirm it, but it's unlikely a real bear tooth would be this clean into adulthood, and the size of this canine—that's the tooth type . . . canine—tells us that it is definitely from an adult bear if it is in fact real. Even more obvi-ously, there is no gum flesh left on the roots of the tooth suggesting that it was torn or bumped out of place. This tooth is either a good fake or a great refurb. Either way, a quick chemical test can show you what I mean."

"The chemical test I can agree to, as long as the cops won't know I messed with it."

"You're gonna tell the police?" Keith smirked.

Noelle shrugged. "Still plotting my next move." It was Keith's turn to cluck his tongue.

Keith went to a drawer and picked out a large bone, from a bear's hind legs, as far as Noelle could tell. Then he grabbed a clear condiment squirt bottle filled with blue liquid and a tool that reminded Noelle of the dentist's office—chrome, sterile clean, and with a jagged, hooked end.

He squirted a tablespoon of the liquid into two small plastic cups. "The natural biological matter," he intoned as he scraped off a bit of the bone's surface, which fell into the cup in the form of a fine powder, "will dissolve easily into the solution." Sure enough, as he gave the mixture one quick swirl with the tool, the powder disappeared and left no trace. The liquid retained its transparent blue color.

"The exterior on this tooth—or this impostor—or whatever it is, will fail to dissolve in the solution. Instead, it will cloud the liquid and flakes or particles of the solid will remain visible. To dissolve this epoxy or sealant, we'd need acetone or some commercial formula designed for that very purpose."

Again, the results were exactly as Keith predicted. The coating on the tooth fell in larger, thin flakes into the solution. Despite a few vigorous stirs with a wandlike chrome tool, Keith couldn't dissolve the particles.

"So, this tooth"—he held Noelle's discovery in the air as if he were completing a magic trick—"has some epoxy, lacquer, or finish on it to preserve it and to give that shiny surface. It's likely not real, and if it is, it looks like a human got ahold of it after it was in the bear's mouth."

"What does that mean?" Noelle asked herself aloud.

"Don't know, Noelle. Above my pay grade. Your guess is as good as mine and mine's not too good."

"Humor me," Noelle instructed.

"Gosh—who knows? Everybody whitens these days . . ." He trailed off as Noelle gave him another look. *Get serious.*

"Keith, can you buy bear teeth or replicas anywhere?"

"I'm sure you can buy replicas online, hell, probably authentic ones, too. It's hard to imagine something that you can't buy online. That's where I got my Noelle Klimpton blow-up doll. Complete with uniform."

"Ew! That's not funny, Keith. From what you're saying we have something unusual on our hands." She stated this more than asked.

"Murder!" He threw his hands up in the air and laughed. "Unless you folks have been doing restorative dental work on some of the bears down there. Or it just fell out of some tourist's souvenir bag."

Noelle and Keith went to lunch and spent an hour catching up. She'd missed him to some extent, but not enough to tell him that.

Then Noelle thanked Keith, promised to write to him again soon, and put on her jacket. She went to her vehicle and entered the number into her cell phone of the man Keith recommended she call if she couldn't get any traction in convincing the police to investigate this case as a potential homicide. The man, Keith told her, could become indispensable if it turned out that the local police were unable to find any leads on the case.

Directly above the man's phone number on the piece of paper, Keith had scrawled a name: "Jake Trent."

7

WEST BANK, SNAKE RIVER. LATER THAT DAY.

Jake's cell phone buzzed in his pocket. He shuffled around in the back-seat of the cruiser so he could pry the oversized and outdated device from his jeans. It was a local number, but one Jake didn't recognize. He set the phone beside him on the bench seat rather than trying to stuff it back into his pocket. The minimal legroom in the cruiser's backseat would have made it impossible, and the car was warm and stuffy. He was sweating. Sitting in the backseat of a police cruiser when you have no alibi for a man's death wasn't particularly comfortable.

Jake had expected a visit from the police department that day. It seemed odd to him, however, that Chief Terrell had led him to the back door of the cruiser when he asked Jake to come to the station for questioning.

"Is this really necessary?" Jake's voice filtered through the wire mesh that separated him from the chief.

86

"I told you, Jake. We'll discuss it when we get to the station. You know how these things go. Better safe than sorry."

"Have you determined that the man was murdered?"

"Jake!" Terrell sighed, annoyed. "We're investigating the possibility, yeah."

The cruiser passed over the river on a single-lane bridge. Jake gazed upstream past the boat launch to look for birds and moose. In the distance, perched near the top of a tall cottonwood tree, he saw fuzzy white-black-white vertical dots stacked like a snowman and recognized them as a bald eagle.

Investigating, Jake thought, now looking downstream. He guessed the river was still several weeks away from being fishable. Snowmelt from the high country was still showing its influence.

If the police were investigating, Jake assumed that something had been brought to the chief's attention on the case. If not, why would Terrell go to the extra effort? Terrell was a good cop, but Jake doubted that the chief's deductive powers rivaled his own. Jake settled on the uncomfortable conclusion that there was evidence that the man was murdered and it pointed to him.

The chief pulled into the police station lot and parked the cruiser outside the front entrance. Jake reached for the interior handle of the car's door, but quickly realized there was none. This backseat was not designed for convenient exit.

The chief opened the door for Jake and helped him out of the car. As they walked toward the front door, the chief curled his right hand around Jake's left elbow—as if to lead him inside as an apprehended suspect. Jake shot the chief a steely glare. The chief let go.

Inside the police station, Jake was fingerprinted and seated in the interrogation room. He immediately questioned the chief—a role reversal that Terrell was not expecting:

"What's going on, Roger? May I ask why you dragged me down here rather than just chatting with me at the house?"

Terrell started to respond, but Jake cut him off. "And don't forget to read me my Miranda warning; you should have recited it in the cruiser." Jake looked toward the wall over his left shoulder and smiled slightly. Very few cops knew criminal law as well as Jake Trent.

Upon Jake's insistence, Terrell now did so. Jake interrupted him and waived his rights.

"Look, Jake, you and I have a couple of problems." The chief hesitated, not wanting to give away too much information to a suspect.

"The man you brought in yesterday didn't drown and didn't die from hypothermia or exposure. Suffocated, but there was no water in his lungs. It looks like he just had his airway cut off. Lungs stopped taking in oxygen." Terrell paused, knowing that his next sentence would sever the now tenuous relationship between the two men. "Jake, we think he was murdered."

"Wait, you mean he was strangled?" Jake interjected.

"No . . . not strangled necessarily. The coroner seems to think that something was held against his face to block the intake of oxygen to his lungs—a hand, a plastic bag, who knows . . . a pillow. There is some bruising around his mouth and nose, and his front teeth were loosened from his gums by a pretty considerable force."

The chief watched Trent, as he was trained to do, to see if his body language would give him away.

"I didn't see any signs of a struggle when I found him. Did you find lacerations or bruises on his knuckles or wrists?" These were usually evidence of the self-defense instincts that kick in when a person is attacked.

"Smith didn't mention any," Terrell responded, referring to the coroner. "But I don't know how you suffocate without struggling."

"Inebriation," Jake quickly replied, not intentionally aloud, "or the influence of certain drugs. Either could explain it. A large amount of alcohol or drugs can act as an anesthetic. The victim may not have even known that he was being suffocated."

"Hold on, Jake. There's more," he said, trying to regain control of the conversation. The chief shifted uncomfortably in his chair. "We identified the body. The guy was a young lawyer working for a litigation firm in Boise. Went missing five days ago. Left work one day and never made it home."

"You think I'm out eliminating my competition, Roger?" Jake laughed. "It's a cutthroat business, man, but not literally. I don't even practice anymore."

The chief pressed on. "That's just it, Jake. This particular lawyer happened to be doing research for a developer working on a project here in Jackson. Finding loopholes, or whatever it is that you people do." The slight was intentional. "The man was apparently trying to find an argument that would allow the developer to ignore a conservation easement, because it was not properly recorded or something."

Shit. Really?

Jake thought of the argument he was to present to the council later that night. He hoped he would be released quickly and wouldn't have to explain his absence.

"Anyway," Terrell continued, "some guys here at the station—cops, you know, also work as civil servants in other capacities . . . like you. Your name came up right away. They told me you are fighting any development of this piece of land that would violate the easement."

"Alleged easement, according to them. And so you think I killed the developer's lawyer?" Jake asked, indignant. He was starting to wonder whether he should call a lawyer to represent him. No part of Jake wanted to spend *any* time in the county jail.

Even the most experienced trial lawyers prefer to hire counsel rather than represent themselves in criminal matters. Perhaps this point speaks to the lawyer's true opinion of himself—for only the man himself knows the real limitations of his abilities.

The chief was softening a bit. "I don't really think that, Jake. What I do think is that any cop worth his wages would consider you a suspect. You can't argue with that."

"I'm not yet in a position to argue, Chief. Let's get on with the questioning. Oh, and I would like to make a phone call at some point." Jake's phone, along with the rest of his belongings, had been surrendered to the authorities at the intake desk.

"Sure . . . of course. First question is whether you knew this guy, this lawyer—name is Bryan Hawlding. Twenty-eight years old, Lewis and Clark Law School graduate is what our background check says."

Jake answered honestly, telling the chief that he knew nothing of the victim. *Lewis and Clark, though?* Jake thought. That was an unusual choice for a student who wanted to work with a real estate developer. The school had a liberal reputation and a prominent environmental law program. Jake attributed this dissonance to the ever-changing nature of the human mind—he himself had once worked in a field that he now despised.

"Next, some folks have said that this development issue has really fired you up to, uh, to an extent that they haven't seen before. What is your beef with the proposed project?"

"I don't have a *beef,* Roger. I wasn't even familiar with this specific developer until this started. I just happen to think that a decades-old covenant should be honored when there is adequate evidence to support the document's existence. Call me crazy, but I hope I'm not alone in that view."

"Hasn't the developer offered to spoil the town rotten if allowed to continue, though? That's my understanding." Terrell relaxed a little more.

Jake didn't answer the question. It was clear that Terrell was uninformed. A moment of silence passed and then Jake spoke.

"How long are you planning to keep me, Rog? I'm supposed to speak to the council tonight." Jake took this obligation seriously anytime it arose, although the council was admittedly a "small pond."

"That's up to you. Just a couple more questions, Jake, and you can make that phone call. Can you give me a verifiable alibi that you were not with Mr. Hawlding on the days leading up to when you found him?"

"I saw a buddy at the boat launch the prior day, ask him. I was on the river overnight. I went fishing alone. Guy's nickname is Caddy. I don't know his real name."

"How can we get ahold of Caddy?" Jake shrugged in response, so Terrell continued. "Where were you the night before your solo fishing trip?"

"I was at home the night before; J.P. can vouch for me. Shit, Roger. I was stewing over this development business. Now, would I reveal that to you if I had killed this guy?"

"Maybe not, but with no alibi, we've got to hold you for the time being. Now, since I am in charge around here, I'm going to return your cell phone to you and let you wait this out in here, rather than in the holding cell. Gotta lock the door, though, Jake. Call me or knock on the door if you need anything."

Chief Terrell left the room, and Jake heard the click of the lock. It was the type of dead bolt that required a key on both the inside and the outside.

A few minutes later, the chief brought Jake his cell phone. He stood in the interrogation room as if he was going to supervise Jake's phone call, but Jake made no move toward the phone sitting on the steel table and Terrell left with a shrug.

Jake reached for his phone and flipped the cover open. A missed call; no voice mail. Either that or the phone hadn't yet received the message. Service delays were common in these parts.

Jake was happy to have his phone, but he didn't have anyone to call. He decided against calling a local attorney. It would only draw attention to his situation.

Surely, accusations of murder wouldn't boost his credibility in the development dispute. Besides, he felt confident that Roger knew he was not guilty and was holding him at the station only until the circumstances of the man's murder became clearer. He was being overcautious. If Jake's name had come up with his deputies, Terrell had no choice.

Jake's first call was to J.P., who offered to come over and keep Jake company at the station. J.P. promised to pick up a six-pack. It was clear that he didn't understand the gravity of the situation, but that was fine with Jake.

The locksmith had come over in the afternoon to let him into his camper, and J.P. requested that the man remove the lock entirely rather than make a key. *Smart,* Jake thought sarcastically.

J.P. had some potential guests to call back, so he excused himself from the conversation. This early in the season, Jake wondered what the guests had planned for a trip. The alpine hiking trails were still covered with snow stained pink with watermelon algae,

Chlamydomonas nivalis, the streams and rivers high and off-color, and the ski slopes closed.

Jake briefly thought of Elspet. Perhaps if she had come with him to Wyoming, the two would be awaiting their guests at the bed-and-breakfast right now. He imagined the couple greeting the travelers: Elle engaging them in conversation after dinner about travel, local art, and music, Jake talking fishing, snow conditions, or wildlife. Her dark eyes would enthrall the male half of the visiting couple, and her furtive smile would irritate the woman.

He had a sudden, intense urge to call her, but he stopped himself. Hearing the voice mail click on and ask that he leave a message would hurt too much.

There wasn't a chance Elspet was going to answer a call from him without listening to the voice mail. Unless Jake left a message regarding a legal question or some gravely serious personal matter, she would never return his call.

His mind left the past and Jake thought about who he might call next.

Jake again thought of the unknown number that had tried to contact him while he was in the cruiser. Maybe they were involved in all this. He opened the "missed calls" directory on his phone and pressed call.

"This is Noelle," a female voice answered pleasantly. Jake was surprised.

"Hello?" She spoke again before Jake could respond. "Is this Jake Trent?"

"It is. Uh, who am I speaking with, please?"

"Noelle Klimpton," she repeated. "I work for the National Park Service. A friend of mine, Keith Strang, gave me your number."

Jake remembered Keith well. They'd met years ago on Lewis

Lake, Jake fishing and Keith tracking a bear. They used to fish together in Yellowstone—a convenient, in-between meeting place—and had plenty in common. Keith, like Jake, had fled mainstream life to pursue the things he was passionate about. If Jake remembered correctly, the only things Keith was passionate about were bears and trout.

Keith sometimes gave Jake's number to fishermen who were traveling through southwestern Montana on their way to Jackson Hole and looking for a guide. Jake appreciated the referrals. He assumed that Noelle had called for that very reason.

"Regarding what?" Jake asked. There was a twinge of irritation in his voice.

"It's a bit complicated and sort of out there . . ." Noelle started. "Um, I think it would be easiest if you and I met to discuss it."

"I would love to . . ." Jake replied honestly. He was getting frustrated at her inability to get to the point. "But I'm in police custody at the moment, so an in-person meeting wouldn't be possible."

"Um . . . well, I'm sorry. What for?" She thought this sounded rude. Keith had apparently thought very highly of Mr. Trent's crime-solving ability. *Why in the world is he in prison?* she wondered. "Never mind . . . I . . . none of my business."

Noelle started anew. "Okay, look, two days ago a French couple was mauled by a bear near the Gosling Lake overlook on the Death Canyon trail."

"I'm aware," Jake said. *Get to the point, lady*. He needed to conserve his cell phone's battery for as long as possible.

"Of course. Well, I found a bear tooth up there, at the scene of the attack. Because of a silly suspicion about the attack—you know, things just didn't add up—I took the tooth up to Keith. As you know, Keith is a bear expert."

Noelle continued, "So, Keith looks at the tooth with his naked eye and sees something wrong . . ."

"A cavity?" he deadpanned. The woman's circuitous story wasn't going anywhere, and Jake wasn't too enthusiastic to discuss anything other than how he was going to clear his name.

"No, it was a fake, or possibly a fake. It could have been a real bear tooth, Keith told me, but if it was, it had probably been preserved with a man-made epoxy or finish. A chemical test confirmed for us that whoever left the tooth behind—well, it wasn't a bear." She quoted Keith almost verbatim.

Whoa. Jake thought about what her assertion might mean. "Well, have you considered the possibility that the tourists were carrying a souvenir bear tooth?"

Noelle's heart sank. This was the same criticism Keith had of her suspicion. "But that seems odd, doesn't it? Isn't it unlikely that a park visitor would be carrying a bear tooth? I'm fairly certain we don't sell them anywhere in the park."

Jake questioned her further. "I have no idea how odd it might be. Why did you drive the whole way up to Bozeman to investigate this? And why didn't you hand the evidence over to the police?"

Noelle was concerned. As far as she knew, Jake had no authority within the police force (the man *was,* in fact, in custody), but she still hesitated to admit to him that she took the tooth without permission.

"I was curious because the damage done by the animal seemed . . . well . . . unusual. I expected to see scrapes and cuts and bruises on the victims, but instead I found puncture wounds. Keith agreed with me that this was strange for a bear attack."

Jake recalled the same details from his discussion with Chief Terrell. "Yeah, I think perhaps that was odd."

Noelle was encouraged to hear his approval. "Well . . . so I took the tooth. I shouldn't have, but I did. I think the incident should be investigated as a murder now. And Keith told me that you would be the man to ask for help in convincing the cops. Can you help?"

The wheels started turning in Jake's head again. The occurrence of three deaths in one day was unusual enough to alert the former investigator's sixth sense. Now that there was a possibility that at least two of the deaths had been murders, it was too much to ignore. He weighed his own suspicions against the possible repercussion—getting himself in deeper with Terrell. On the flip side, he might be able to exonerate himself.

"Can you come down to the police station, Noelle? Is there any chance that the chief owes you any favors? I'd like to speak with you as soon as possible."

"He doesn't owe me anything, but it's worth a shot. I can stop by in a few hours and ask to speak with you. And, Mr. Trent, why are you in custody?"

"Call me Jake. I'm in custody for murder." He hung up the phone, focusing his thoughts on what he had just been told.

8

It was getting late in the day and Jake was going to miss his opportunity to speak at the eight o'clock council meeting because of Terrell's misguided suspicion. It was all so ridiculous.

He decided to draft a memo to be handed out to each council member. If he couldn't deliver his speech, at least he could get his point across on paper. He called a fellow councilman named Nick Begaye and asked him to come by the station before the meeting; the memo would be waiting for him at the reception desk.

Jake knocked on the door of his make-do holding cell. A young officer opened the door and agreed to bring him a legal pad and pen.

When the young cop came back, Jake sat down at the interrogation table and began to write.

Dear Ladies and Gentlemen of the Council,

Because of the righteous forethought of many men and women in our history—John D. Rockefeller, Franklin Roosevelt, Horace Albright, to name a few—the United States of America is situated uniquely among developed countries with respect to its public lands.

A visit to any European nation will reveal this distinction. In the United Kingdom, for example, a pursuit as basic as fishing is reserved for the wealthy, for those who can afford to pay the substantial day fees necessary to convince the private landowner to allow others to use his or her property.

In these nations' histories, almost no land was set aside for public enjoyment, and thus their natural environments are principally private. Private owners, as we all admit, tend to cherish the private nature of their possessions, and rarely choose to share them with others.

This theme recurs in nearly every developed country that you might decide to visit. There, notions of unfettered economic competition and first-come, first-served ideology have led to what many of us believe is an undesirable situation: natural resources sitting solely in the hands of those who can afford them.

Before you consider the specific repercussions of the decision you are about to make, I would urge you to consider the following series of more general questions: If a man is not entitled to the free enjoyment of the earth onto which he was born, what is he entitled to? Are we, as a society, truly desirous of pursuing wealth and personal gain until all the natural resources are used up? Was it not the intention of the men and women who created our public lands to look out for us—to prevent us from destroying these lands despite our vicious appetite?

And most importantly—Do we not have an ongoing obligation to give this same gift to our future generations?

Of course, the question we face presently doesn't directly involve those lands set aside by the Rockefellers or by the United States government early in the last century. Rather, it involves a tract owned by a man who made his promise to future generations by attempting to ensure that their enjoyment of this beautiful landscape would not be ruined by condominiums or business. The man who formed this covenant knowingly took a substantial loss in the future value of his land the moment he created it. He acted selflessly and intended to benefit others rather than himself. Now we are faced with the same opportunity.

Because of the confusion regarding the filing of the easement, it appears as if a court of law may decide this issue in either way. We, the council, have an opportunity to first decide the issue by making a judgment from a far more meaningful source of jurisdiction. We can make judgment on this issue based on what is right and selfless, or what is greedy and self-serving. By denying the developer's zoning applications, we can both honor the wishes of the original landowner and help guarantee that future generations will be entitled to the same enjoyment of natural lands that brought many of us to this area.

There was a knock on the door. Jake assumed that it was Noelle Klimpton. He shouted, "Just a minute," and hurried the closing of his letter.

I hope you will consider this issue with the gravity it deserves. My apologies for my absence. As always, I am—

Very truly yours,
Jake Trent

Jake folded the letter into thirds and walked to the door. It was Terrell.

"You have a visitor. Noelle Klimpton," he said. "I normally wouldn't allow this, Jake, but I know you and I know Ms. Klimpton. Please don't prove my instincts wrong."

"Will do," Jake responded. "Could you please have the receptionist keep this letter on hand? A man named Nick Begaye is going to stop by and pick it up later. It's important."

Terrell took the letter from Jake's extended hand. "Okay. This isn't a four-star hotel, though, Jake," he muttered as he turned. "I'll get Noelle."

After the chief left, Jake felt a rumbling beneath him. An earthquake. The fourth today. It started small and rumbled to a slightly higher intensity. Then it stopped.

Terrell led Noelle back to the interrogation room. She and Jake shook hands. Jake was taken aback—the woman from the phone was attractive and fit. He hadn't expected that. He recognized her from somewhere, which wasn't unusual given the size of the town. Terrell shut the door.

"I'm sorry to bother you like this." Noelle quickly realized the absurdity of her statement. *What else does he have to do?* "But I wasn't sure whether to alert the police or not about Keith's findings. I didn't know if it was too trivial. Keith thought you might be a good person to discuss it with."

"First," Jake replied, "there is no reason whatsoever *not* to alert the police about the tooth. Secondly, I'm not a cop or an investigator in any sense of the word. As you can see," Jake said, motioning toward the door, "I am not even a free man at the moment. If you are planning to interfere with police business, I would urge you to reconsider."

"I just want your opinion. Keith trusts you." Noelle blushed.

"Okay." Jake glanced in her eyes. She genuinely wanted to help. He sat down and took a deep breath. "Well then, sure, my opinion is that you're probably right. That is, if everything you say is true. A bear attack occurs under somewhat suspicious circumstances at the same time as another murder, which was framed in the same way—as a natural death, and I think it makes sense to consider the possibility that it was a murder. Add in the evidence about the tooth and I think you've got a viable hunch. But then again, I'm a suspicious person by nature."

After a short silence, Noelle spoke. "So you're telling me the avalanche death has been determined to be a murder?"

"We haven't even gotten there yet. There was a third death. I found a body in the river two nights ago. At first it looked like simply a drowned fisherman—another victim to the Snake—but the coroner says he was suffocated before he ever entered the water."

"Is that why you're here? The drowning?"

"I'm here because I have no alibi—I was alone when I found the body, and therefore I'm what they call a 'preliminary suspect.'" He made air quotes to emphasize the ridiculousness of the charge. "Why are you interested in all this?"

"They really think you murdered someone?"

Jake could see the wheels turning in her head. Did he look like a murderer? Finally she gave him a look; she doubted it.

"You didn't answer me," Jake said, deflecting her question.

"I wish I could say. I just . . . something doesn't seem right."

"I see." Jake again noticed something attractive and intriguing in her while he watched her intuition work. She was a thoughtful woman. And sharp, perhaps even to the point of being cynical.

He looked at her, feeling now that he could trust her intellect and intentions. "Listen, I want you to turn the bear tooth over to the police with the information you got from Keith. Provide them with his contact information so a more formal test can be done, if necessary. If they pursue that lead, great. If they don't, I'll help you, but only under one condition."

"What's that?"

"Do the same thing with the man in the river as you did with the bear tooth—ask some questions. I want you to go into all the river businesses—fly shops, taverns, boat rentals, everything. See if you can find anyone that knows who he was with, when he went out fishing, anything like that. If you can help get me out from under the chief's suspicion, I can help you. You game for that?"

Noelle perked up. "Deal. What was the guy's name?" She took a pen and notebook from her breast pocket.

"Bryan Hawlding. About five ten, medium build. Blond hair and light eyes. Light skin. Twenty-eight years old."

"Got it." Noelle scrawled the information down and gave Jake an understanding look. She stood up, shook his hand, and left the room. Someone on the outside slid a key into the dead bolt and locked it.

Jake was alone again. He looked at his cell phone: 7:15 p.m. Nick should have come for the letter and taken it to the meeting.

He stood up and paced the room. Noelle's beauty had not gone unnoticed.

On the main floor, Noelle was nervously looking around for the chief. She thought about just leaving the tooth on a desk, but she knew the police would find out who put it there. Then she would be much worse off.

Before any more scheming thoughts leaped to mind, Noelle spied Terrell, who was making a beeline across the office. She jogged to catch up with him.

"Roger, can I talk to you for a second?"

The chief never looked up. "Walk with me."

"The thing is that . . ." She decided to fudge the truth. "When we were trying to get the female victim of the attack up to the helicopter, I found something there on the ground that now I think might be useful to you."

"What do you mean?" The chief stopped walking and gave her a serious look.

"I think our bear attack may not be what it looks like." The chief gave her a dubious look. "It'd be better just to show you." Noelle reached into her pocket and took out the envelope. She handed it to Terrell, who took it and shook its contents into his other hand.

"It's fake."

Before Terrell could respond, Noelle started pleading her case. "I was just under so much stress! I think I was in shock, and I know I should've . . ."

"You found this at the scene?"

Noelle nodded and tried to speak again. Before she could, Terrell reached out and pinched her lips together like a duck's bill, gently but forcefully. Noelle looked around, unable to talk, to see if anyone was witnessing this bizarre act.

"I must be going crazy!" the chief whispered in Noelle's ear. He was still holding her lips. She silently agreed. "Get the hell out of here before I arrest you for withholding evidence."

He finally let go of Noelle's face. He looked at his hand as if it had betrayed him. Noelle quickly shuffled out, muttering to herself. *What the hell was that about?*

*   *   *

Driving north from the station toward home, Noelle approached Broadway and the town square. A large crowd was gathered. She slowed down and pulled over onto the shoulder to take a look. The elk antler arches on the square's west corners straddled her park service vehicle; the Cowboy Bar sat on her left. The sun was just setting behind her, over Teton Pass.

It was some kind of rally or protest. Cacophonous chants filled the evening air. Clusters of people held signs and banners. The town as a whole was politically engaged, so the gathering itself didn't surprise Noelle, but she was curious.

She got out of the truck to have a better look at the crowd. She searched for familiar faces but saw none. Not a single person she recognized.

Strange.

The protesters were dressed in drab, baggy clothing, hippies. The square smelled of sweat, patchouli, stale campfire, and weed. Their chants were uncoordinated and impossible to understand, but their picket signs spoke for them. Closest to her a thin, blond man held a sign that read, "End Earth Alteration!!!" Other signs declared: "Land Use: Is it really our decision to make?" and "What did Mother Earth ever do to you?"

Noelle approached another spectator, an old man, and asked what was going on.

"I don't really know," the man responded. "Wasn't scheduled in the paper or anything." The old man seemed upset by this.

Noelle nodded. "What exactly are they protesting?"

"The council is deciding whether or not to allow the big lot across from the Southside Works to be developed. The meeting is taking place as we speak. Obviously, these guys oppose the development."

"What are they going to build down there?" Noelle asked.

"I think it's more condominiums—something like that." He seemed indifferent on the topic, more troubled by the fact that there was a gathering in his town square without public notice.

"Thanks." Noelle walked back to her vehicle.

Someone had thrown an egg against the front windshield during her short absence. "Oh, shit!" she said aloud, entering the vehicle and looking around for the culprit. When she got in, she activated the windshield wipers, spraying the egg and its shell remnants with cleaning fluid and running the wipers over the mess. The egg smeared, further hindering Noelle's visibility, but she'd deal with it later.

Noelle started north on Cache again, noticing that of the many vehicles parked along Cache, very few had Wyoming plates. Instead, she saw cars from Oregon, Colorado, California, and Utah. Even some eastern states were represented—New Hampshire, Vermont, and New Jersey.

What would bring all these protesters to Jackson? All because of a condo development?

As she drove, Noelle thought. Tomorrow, after her a.m. patrol duties, she would head south along the Snake River to see what she could find for Jake.

But before that, Noelle had another stop in mind: she would go to the hospital to speak with the French woman widowed by the bear. *If she speaks English.*

Noelle knew almost no French.

The thought of hospitals always made Noelle squirm. The smell, the lighting. And worst of all, the moans of pain and despair that echoed down the corridors. Tomorrow would be a challenge for her, but she thought the visit might shed some light on the attack.

It was dark now. The reflectors that stood atop the roadside plastic tubes shone brightly back at Noelle as she drove. She reached down toward the dark floor on the passenger side of her truck to feel around for her phone, finding food wrappers, CDs, and a pair of sandals. The truck veered intermittently across the centerline.

Finally, she found the phone and dialed.

9

JACKSON POLICE HEADQUARTERS. THE SAME EVENING.

It was 8:15 p.m. Jake was getting antsy. He was starving and thirsty as hell. Terrell hadn't checked in for quite a while and not knowing what was going on outside the interrogation room bothered him. It was getting late in the evening and he had no desire to spend the night at the station. He was starting to fume.

To this point I've behaved and cooperated. If I don't get released in a few minutes, though, that's going to change.

Jake started to brainstorm procedural arguments that might get him out of the room. It had been a while since he had used that part of his brain. He knew there were plenty of tedious rules to follow when making an arrest and Jake hoped the chief had overlooked at least one of them.

Got it! Booking procedure.

An arrestee—a suspected criminal—had a right to be "booked"

after his arrest. The booking procedures include a mug shot, a suspect lineup, and fingerprinting. When a suspect is detained by the police for an unreasonable amount of time without being booked, he has the right to request that a judge issue a writ of habeas corpus, which allows the suspect to ask a judge to determine whether his detention is proper.

What defined an "unreasonable amount of time" varied from state to state, and Jake wasn't aware of Wyoming's protocol. But he remembered that an overnight stay in a holding area without a booking almost always constituted an unreasonable amount of time in any jurisdiction. It was worth a shot.

Jake stood up, walked to the door, and knocked loudly. There was no response. He waited half a minute and knocked again, even harder this time. A moment later Terrell opened the door.

"What do you need, Jake?" the chief asked. He looked overwhelmed. There was sweat on his brow and his face was red. Jake had no idea, but he had just disturbed the chief's Internet research on "workplace stressors."

"I haven't been booked yet." The chief didn't react.

"So? You want to be photographed? Is that why you knocked on the door? You wanna be booked?!" The chief turned, shaking his head.

Jake smiled a bit. He knew he had him.

Jake shouted, "Well, I expect then that you aren't going to ask me to spend the night here? You've gotta book me if you are going to keep me detained." Jake paused. "Otherwise, I'll just get a writ tomorrow morning from the judge and the court will release me. You know you haven't got enough to keep me here in the court's eyes."

Terrell thought for a moment, his hand still on the doorknob.

Yep. Got him.

He surely knew Jake was right—it was stupid of Terrell not to simply book him on the way in, when the men at the desk had inventoried and locked away his possessions. Now the officers who usually booked prisoners were gone for the evening.

Jake figured Terrell was leaning toward allowing him his freedom, partially for convenience's sake. The questioning, if you could call it that, had yielded very little that truly justified Jake's detention. Besides, the chief was tired.

"Okay, Jake. You're free to go. Please don't embarrass me by flying the coop tomorrow. *Please*. Did you speak with Noelle about this 'hunch' that she's got?"

Jake was relieved and he let his guard down too. "I did. That's the reason she came in to see me. I assume you have the evidence now?" Jake hoped Noelle had done as he asked.

"She gave it to me before she left."

"Good." Jake was pleased. "Are you going to get a second opinion on the tooth?" he asked.

"Second opinion about what?"

"The tooth. Whether it's real."

The chief just rolled his eyes. He didn't say a word.

The two men walked through the open door that had held Jake in for the past few hours, past the desks, usually empty at this hour, and computer monitors, which were usually dark, and finally arrived at the reception desk of the small police station. A nervous energy filled the air, despite the late hour. A few cops and support staff still bustled about. They were working overtime because of the recent events; there were public statements to prepare, crime scenes to preserve, and new evidence to process.

Terrell stepped away for a moment and then reappeared with the rest of Jake's possessions. Just as Jake looked at his cell phone—

realizing that its battery had died—the chief asked him whether he could find his own way home. He told Jake he was awaiting an important phone call.

Jake told him he could find his own ride, in part because he didn't want to inconvenience the chief, but also because he didn't really like the idea of getting back into the police cruiser. Jake wasn't easily embarrassed, but he nevertheless preferred that his neighbors and friends didn't see him being released from a cop car.

The valley had adequate public transportation in the form of buses—and there was a stop nearby. Jake walked from the police station past the town square and waited at the stop that sat just north of the square. A few early season tourists were still out taking photographs of the famous elk antler arches that haloed the entrance to the square. It was chilly again. The cool air helped Jake feel human after his temporary incarceration.

He waited a few minutes and caught the bus west toward Teton Pass, requesting that the driver stop at the small town that sat at the bottom of the pass before the road started its climb over the mountains. From there, a single-lane road paralleled Trout Run to the south. He could follow it and be home in a few minutes on foot.

As he walked, anxiety regarding the council's meeting that he had missed arose again in him. He was impatient to get home and to his cell phone's charger, so he could call Begaye and, he hoped, hear some good news.

Nick Begaye was a forty-something man of Navajo descent who had moved to Jackson Hole in his twenties from Taos, New Mexico. A competitive free skier, Nick moved in search of more consistent snowfall and better sponsor exposure. He'd faded from the extreme skiing scene as his injuries, and his age, piled up, but he stuck around in Jackson. Like many, he'd discovered the extraordinary variety of activities available in the area. River sports and kayaking in particular had kept him entertained for years. Kayaking had the convenient attraction of being a comfortable sport for those with harshly used and battered legs. He had joined the town council five years ago.

Jake looked up to Nick. The two got along well and shared a common worldview. In the case of the current issue before the council—the development—Begaye agreed with Jake wholeheartedly, but Jake suspected Nick would hold his position with less tenacity. Nick Begaye took almost everything in stride. He didn't like to make a big stink.

Oh well. No use in guessing the outcome, Jake thought as he walked down the drive leading to his home. He looked around for Chayote, who was nowhere to be seen.

Back at the station, Chief Terrell was on the phone with the weeping mother of the man found in the river—the call he had been awaiting when Jake left the station.

The call wasn't as helpful as the chief hoped.

No, Bryan never got into any trouble, and no, she had no reason to believe that someone would have purposefully murdered him.

Interestingly, though, she indicated that Bryan was her closest friend—and vice versa. Apparently the man had kept in touch with just a few friends by email, but otherwise he was quite the loner. The conversation continued—the man's mother sniffling and asking for verification that it was indeed *her* son who was found in the river.

It was.

She spoke a bit more about his personal life. The only thing that

Terrell deemed worthwhile enough to scrawl down on the otherwise blank piece of tablet paper were the words "Ondine's curse," apparently a health condition the man had suffered from. Terrell knew nothing about it, but at least it was something.

After about twenty minutes, Terrell, as much as he pitied the woman, couldn't listen to her bawling monologue anymore. He was just too exhausted.

He thanked her for her time, expressed his condolences, gave her the 800 numbers for a few loss hotlines, and hung up. Then the chief decided to call it a day. He locked the front door of the police station and headed for his car. Until morning, the police force in Jackson would operate through a shared dispatch center at the hospital and just a single patrolling officer.

Home at last, Jake walked into the guesthouse and went upstairs to the loft, where he could charge his cell phone and call Begaye to get the scoop on the meeting.

Jake plugged the phone into the charger next to his bed and waited while it started up, slipping off his shoes and lying down on top of the covers. When the phone finally lit up with life, he reached over and dialed Begaye's number. He was sitting up now, too anxious to hear the news lying down.

It hadn't gone well, Begaye informed him. Yes, Jake's letter was read and everyone had genuinely appreciated his efforts. Many council members even expressed the same concerns.

"But where da hell were you, man? What happened?" Begaye kept asking, his Navajo accent struggling to convey anger over the phone. Jake deflected the question each time.

When it came down to it, the council as a whole couldn't resist the money pledged to the town by the developer. Recent years had been difficult for the tourist town—the national economy was faltering and as a result, people were stashing away their checkbooks and staying at home. Unnecessary spending such as vacation expenses was among the first to be cut from the budget of cash-pressed families. The town just wasn't collecting the lodging tax revenue that it needed to maintain its public buildings and facilities.

This reality flew in the face of Jake's philosophy in many ways, but he always felt he could reconcile the two. Of course the town needed resources for the public good. Nobody could argue with that. But to Jake there was not so fine a line between making rational compromises for the greater good and pawning off irreplaceable natural resources for cash.

Still, he wondered: *If there was no greed, if nobody came to Jackson to pay to catch fish after fish or to develop land, wouldn't our little community collapse?*

He had pondered the question before.

Begaye was still talking, but Jake wasn't listening.

This is exactly the point of the political process and the beauty of being human, though. We are supposed to be too smart to pick something and stick with it regardless of the circumstances. We're supposed to innovate and compromise.

The council, Jake felt, had fallen under the sway of the idea that all growth is good growth. They were afraid that rejecting the proposal would leave the town behind the Joneses. Aspen, Park City. They wanted to keep up, to be a destination with the best and most modern facilities.

Jake knew this plan couldn't be sustained forever.

How long would a fishery last if all the fishermen remained in the first stage of the hierarchy and always caught as many fish as they could?

Jake knew such an ecosystem would be doomed. A functioning fishery, community, or society needed participants with different ideals. It needed healthy debate. Decisions had to be made through negotiation between individual principles, not influenced by a constant pressure to get bigger, better, and faster.

The council members were principled and opinionated and Jake knew that, but they had disregarded those things in their decision. And for what?

It was a scary thought to Jake, who feared that if this continued, man would keep trying to perfect Jackson Hole until all its perfection was gone.

Jake tiredly wiped his hand over his face and tuned back in to Begaye, who nervously brought up one other point before bidding Jake good night: the council had become aware that Jake was in jail, though they didn't know why.

Great. Really helps my credibility.

Worse yet, the council always had the option to vote him off.

Insisting he wasn't the leak, Begaye finally let Jake off the phone. *It was probably someone at the police station who told another councilperson.* Gossip always annoyed Jake; it was a reckless transgression motivated only by the selfish desire to have someone pay attention to you.

Jake's mind turned for a second to the development issue again as he searched for some stowed-away knowledge regarding property law and administrative procedures, but he quickly shut that inquisitiveness down, as he could sometimes do. The day had just been too long and too frustrating. Instead, images of Noelle—her smile, her skin, her body—ushered him to sleep.

PART
TWO

10

CAMP BODHI, SIX MILES SOUTHWEST OF YELLOWSTONE
NATIONAL PARK. THE NEXT MORNING.

"This came for you, sir." The proselyte, Sam, was nervous as he approached the Shaman, who was sitting alone, looking like he was stewing over something. The Shaman didn't respond. Sam placed the envelope on the desk and slunk from the room.

The Shaman opened the letter, took a quick glance, and crumpled it, then closed his eyes for a second to calm down. Serenity eluded him. Visions of a woman were projected on his eyelids by his mind's eye. The woman was lying in a pool of her own blood, horribly mutilated, motionless. That woman was his mother.

Twenty minutes later, Sam entered the main lodge of the camp for the first time. He was ecstatic. In only a few days among the others, it had become clear to him that being invited to the lodge was quite an accolade for a proselyte.

Proselyte was the name given to new members, and the proselytes were rarely invited into the central cabin—that was an honor generally reserved for the votaries, the members closest to the Shaman. Sam had been told that from time to time, when a proselyte had shown extraordinary courage or commitment to the cause, the Shaman would invite them in, allow them to participate in the meeting, and personally thank them for their dedication.

Sam was still learning the ropes, although he had followed the Shaman's underground podcast for ten years, until it unexpectedly disappeared.

When he first heard the Shaman's voice, Sam was a small fish. Making efforts that were merely a drop in the bucket while this collection of rogue superheroes was out changing the world. If they believed that an area should remain undeveloped, they protected it themselves. They didn't waste valuable time lobbying and negotiating with big business like Sam had. They simply fought for the land that they were entitled and destined to protect.

Now, Sam was finally there, at the main community and the hub of all the action. The Shaman's cabin. Camp Bodhi. Shuffling inside with a few others, he found himself thinking that the cabin was not exactly what he'd expected. He knew the Shaman was a devout nature worshipper like the others, but there were no dream catchers or totems. The cabin looked like an old tool shed. The mostly bare walls displayed farming equipment, a few rusty machetes, two rifles, and two wooden spools, one each of barbed wire and razor wire.

The votaries sat on whatever they could find, milk crates and old wooden stools, and settled in. Having wasted a moment taking in his surroundings, Sam lost his opportunity at a seat and so he sat down on the wooden floor. The men and women in the cabin talked quietly among themselves in a way that reminded him of the pre-bell murmurings in high school. These students, however, wore long, matted hair and dirty clothes in place of prep school uniforms and tight haircuts.

It wasn't long until the Shaman stood. There was nothing particularly impressive about his appearance. The man was of average height and thin, but his frame featured long, sinewy muscle. Much like the others, he wore a hodgepodge of old, worn-out clothing. Unlike most of the men, though, his hair was clipped short and he had a clean-shaven face. His appearance suggested a man around thirty-five when in reality he was older.

He walked toward the center of the single-room cabin, causing the small crowd to turn their bodies to face him. Sam spun around on the floor and watched. The leader turned back to address the crowd. Before he began, Sam noticed his hands trembling. He was seething.

When he spoke, his voice was quiet, consistent, and calm—but with a sharp edge that belied the fire within him: "Good morning." Some in the crowd replied with their own muttered "good morning," and there were a few nods and claps, but most stayed silent, too focused on listening to formulate a response.

Sam had counted more than fifty votaries. They conformed to the Shaman's every whim.

"How many of you joined me because you were tired of useless protests?" Everyone in the cabin raised his or her hand, including the Shaman, who nodded as he did so. A few cheered or whistled.

He was playing to the crowd. Sam hadn't expected such a pep-talk tone to the meeting.

"How many of you get *really pissed off* when you think of our elected officials discarding the letters you have sent them about the fate of our irreplaceable environment?" Now more people cheered. The Shaman's voice grew louder.

"Today," he continued, directing those standing to take their seats

again by slowly lowering both of his hands, "you all have an opportunity to take action in the truest sense of the word. To our south,
near the mighty Snake River, Parrana wishes to turn preserved land
into a condominium development." Nods of affirmation. The Shaman held out his palm, extending his skinny fingers as if motioning
for someone to stop. His voice got quiet. An airy whisper. "Before I
continue, if you wish to protest gutlessly in the town square again as
some of you did last night, I request you to leave this lodge now." No
one moved toward the exit, although some shifted around uncomfortably in their seats to try to identify those who had apparently
disappointed their leader.

"Good. I'm impressed with your courage. As some of you may
know, the town of Jackson—that spineless political amoeba with
jurisdiction over this proposed development—voted last night
to allow the developer to continue unimpeded toward its goal of
destroying our wilderness.

"The time for argument and negotiation has now passed. I have
one task for all of you: I want you to do what it takes to prevent this gluttonous developer from working on, or even setting
foot on, this land. There is no time to coordinate lockouts or to
search out and disable their equipment. No, instead, I want you
to make every contractor or construction, no, *destruction* worker
think twice before he sets foot on that land. Use our supplies"—
he motioned toward the razor wire—"use whatever you can find
here. And if you need funds for this mission, please see Ryder after
we adjourn. There is no spending limit for this task." The Shaman
pointed to a man in the cabin's corner who held a backpack.

"I don't expect a coordinated sabotage—I expect you to go out
tonight and take care of this. I leave it up to your imagination as
to what types of deterrents you will use—but the message must be

clear: Mother Nature will not be raped for profit. When she cannot defend herself, we are her defenders!" The crowd cheered. The Shaman stepped out of the center of the room and walked toward the banker, Ryder.

Sam watched and listened.

"Well done, Shaman," Ryder said, setting the backpack down on the cabin's floor and unzipping it. A line of votaries had queued up.

"I trust that our new recruits have been screened for loyalty before sending them out on such an important mission?" the Shaman said quietly to Ryder.

He nodded. "Of course, sir."

The Shaman stood by while Ryder distributed the money in the backpack and the crowd started to filter out. Some of the votaries made eye contact or nodded to him, hoping to impress him, form a personal bond. Very few actually spoke to their leader. They were afraid.

As Sam passed, the Shaman smiled. Sam smiled back and nodded, too, noticing that he was the only one who had been lucky enough to elicit a friendly response. And he was just a proselyte—the only one invited to the meeting.

As Ryder handed over Sam's spending money, he spoke to Sam: "Please wait here for just a few moments. The Shaman would like to speak with you." As he moved toward the door, Sam looked over his shoulder toward his leader to see that the man was watching him.

Two others, one male and one female, remained in the cabin with Ryder and the Shaman. Sam knew them to be the high votaries—the Shaman's closest advisers. The woman quickly went to the wooden door, shut it, and locked it. Then the high votaries, the Shaman, and Ryder formed a small circle in the center of the room, the Shaman pulling over an old bar stool for the woman. She sat next to him.

"As you all know, destiny has led me down a new path," the Shaman said. Sam looked around to see the others nod. He was clueless. "I have always looked to Nature with a humble and subservient eye. I can imagine no greater purpose for any one of the earth's creatures than protecting her. When I was much younger, I formed our sister organization, EcoAmicae, to lobby government officials, to convince corporate leaders and the public to treat our earth with the respect that she deserves. These methods were effective and our voice was heard around the world. Eventually, though, I realized there was no getting through to some people, to some organizations, with dialogue and rhetoric. Big business was raping the earth and feeling no remorse. Moreover, *we* could make them feel no remorse."

The Shaman's face turned graver, his voice quieter. "At that point, I had a decision to make—either abandon the cause, something I *believed* in, or change the tactics of the organization to deal with those that carelessly destroyed the world. As a somewhat intelligent man"—the Shaman smiled at the group, rolling his eyes, a rare glimpse of spare warmth within him—"I knew that to conduct the type of missions I had in mind would erode the credibility of EcoAmicae—the credibility I had worked so hard to attain within the scientific and political communities. If EcoAmicae were perceived as an extremist rebellion, it would lose its effectiveness. You all know what happened, of course: I formed the nameless organization under which we meet today."

The four remaining members nodded knowingly, urging the Shaman to continue.

Where is this going? Sam thought.

"Now, although I am incredibly impressed with our little militia, I find that another change is necessary. As leaders, we know that we have limitations to what we can accomplish. This development, for example—we may stop it, but we cannot stop the *idea* of it by simply booby-trapping one site. No, we need to engender a realization in the public that Nature is not something we take from or use, but rather, she is a goddess to whom we should dedicate our lives to praise and protect. We need to remind the citizens of this earth that if they trespass on sacred ground—that is, if they *use* the earth rather than worship her, they will be punished by her."

The Shaman stood up from his seat and rubbed his smooth face anxiously with his hand. Sam sensed that the group, besides Ryder, didn't grasp the importance of what he was telling them. The Shaman spoke again.

"Are any of you familiar with the study of eschatology?

"Christians, for example, believe that the world will end in a Judgment Day," the Shaman continued. "They believe that at some point in time, God will descend on the earth to choose which humans have led a devout life and which humans have not, and thus will be sentenced to eternal damnation. This could be described as the Christian eschatology. Eschatology is the study of the end. That is, the study of what certain groups believe will be the end of the world.

"I am sure you are not surprised to hear, though, that modern religion—in fact, all religions since the pagans—has overcomplicated the issue. The world itself, you see, cannot end. She is eternal. The question becomes then, how are the righteous rewarded and the vile punished? The answer is easy: it happens every single day. The event—or, more accurately, a series of millions of events—occurs every time a boat is overturned in a squall or a town is destroyed by an earthquake.

"'Survival of the fittest' is often cited as a simple model for our reality. This idiom is close to getting it right—it would be on point if it were changed to 'survival of the most devout.' You see, Nature is a killer, but she kills only when she has been wronged. Those that challenge Nature and doubt her omnipotence are crushed by her. Culling events take place every day and this is *our* eschatology.

"Our most holy mission, then, is to remind the world that despite advances in industry and science—even in survival techniques and equipment—they must respect Nature. In this way alone, the groundwork will be laid for true cooperation with Nature. Human ingenuity has allowed us to trespass against Nature—a man who is snakebit can now simply be given an antivenin. This, however, is the ultimate sin. We are reversing the will of the being that created us."

The Shaman now paused for a moment. "Our job, as protectors of this earth and humble servants of Nature, is to facilitate her will. For this reason, I am hereby creating a new division of our family of soldiers." Sam had never heard the man use the word *soldier*—a word that held such solemn connotations. "I invite you, as competent and honest followers, to join the Revelators."

Moved by the Shaman's words, Sam felt anxious to fulfill his will. Still, he had questions regarding the formation of this new and seemingly violent team.

What exactly is he asking of us? How are four people supposed to change common thought about the world?

The Shaman walked toward the door, sensing their apprehension. "You don't have to decide at this moment," he said, "and there is no formal invocation. If you are interested in helping us change the world, we will proudly include you in one of our missions. Think on it."

"Thank you, Shaman," Sam said with a slight grin pulling at his lips. The opportunity to work closely with the Shaman stirred excitement within him.

The door was now open and the man and woman quickly understood that they were to leave. When Sam moved for the door, the Shaman shook his head, asking him to stay behind.

"Have a seat."

Sam did as the Shaman asked and sat down with the two men in the center of the cabin. A short time of silence prompted him to make eye contact with them, but they were looking at each other silently. Finally, the Shaman spoke.

"I've heard that you joined us from quite a ways off, Sam," he started informally. Sam nodded. "We're happy to have you and impressed with your dedication. Crossing an ocean to aid us in our mission is admirable, and I think such an act . . ." He paused for a short moment, thinking of what to say next. "It reenforces the gravity and urgency of the situation facing us. Is it true that you are living under an assumed identity here in the States?"

Sam nodded. He had arranged for it through a contact before he left London.

"Given your incredible motivation to help us—to help the whole world—I have decided to invite you to participate in an operation of great importance. This task does not require much of you. In fact, it is a simple task, but the *importance* of your success is incredibly high. If you accept my request, you will undertake to act as one of the key cogs of the most significant mission this organization, or any other organization that calls itself a friend of the earth, has ever accomplished.

"Your assignment involves the fundamental purpose of our new branch. Your job will be to help us inform the world that their abuse of Mother Nature will no longer be tolerated, that they are not and have never been the sole inhabitants of this world, and if they continue to take advantage of the being that provides for them without showing due respect, they will suffer."

When he finished this statement, the Shaman looked angry, and shades of violence showed on his face. Another moment of silence nearly prompted Sam to ask for more specifics—for some real idea of what was actually being asked of him. To ask, though, would have been considered disrespectful, so Sam was relieved when the Shaman spoke.

"What I ask that you do, Sam, is simply to observe a person. The mission, in a sense, is a reconnaissance mission. Your one and only duty will be to observe, noting all of your observations in a notebook, so that you don't forget any details. The details are very important. Every day, you will provide us with a phone report of your observations."

The Shaman paused for a second, then said: "That's it—you will not be asked or required to do any more. You will not be informed of the relevance of your task unless you wish to be so informed. You will only be provided with information equivalent to the amount of trust that we place in you. Our level of trust, of course, will be dictated by your own devotion to the cause. In the glove box of your vehicle you'll find a notebook with a few addresses. These locations are the places you must watch. Start tomorrow. For tonight, help sabotage the site if you'd like."

Sam smiled, but finally, the longer, unmistakable silence came that meant Sam was supposed to respond. He cleared his throat nervously and spoke briefly, agreeing to do as the Shaman asked. He was still not clear on the details, but Sam expected those would come soon enough. The proposition still made him uncomfortable—the Shaman's words were serious; he spoke of suffering explicitly, and even worse, he conveyed implicitly to Sam that he intended to punish those with whom he disagreed. It seemed that the Shaman was not eager to share the details of the plan with Sam, and even if he was to offer up such information, Sam wondered whether he wanted to know. He left the cabin, however, without voicing these concerns to either the Shaman or the banker. He did not want his loyalty doubted.

Shortly after Sam left, the banker was dismissed from the room. He walked out into the ramshackle camp, a spiral-shaped village of old tents and lean-tos with well-worn pathways connecting them. The cabin where the meeting was held was the largest structure, situated in the center of the spiral. Outside their homes, the team members were busy preparing to honor their leader's request, which made Ryder feel proud of himself and of the organization—they were finally becoming a real army, no longer asking for change but now compelling it.

Soon, these team members, proselytes and votaries alike, would make it impossible for the plot of land in Jackson Hole to be developed, and over time, the Revelators would coerce all developers, *all those who abused the earth . . . all people,* to pursue a more righteous path in the name of Mother Nature.

The Shaman, alone now, was suddenly struck by an ugly mood. He clenched his teeth, wiggling his upper and lower jaws firmly against each other so he could feel them move slightly at their roots from the force. The Revelators were meant to bolster his power over his contingent, but he got the feeling it left them somewhat confused.

The boy, Sam, had annoyed him, internally debating whether he should heed his new leader's requests, but too insecure to question him. This anxiety and weakness reminded the Shaman of the way he imagined others saw him as a child—bitter and full of criticism. But meek. Passive-aggressive.

The speech, the camp, and even the clothes he wore, it was all a ruse, but his followers and his power over them were real. He, their Shaman, could command them to do anything, and they would listen. The feeling was intoxicating.

The original Shaman, of course, was dead. The *new* Shaman had arranged a meeting with him in private and crudely slit his throat with an old box cutter.

It hadn't been easy, either; the real Shaman had put up quite a fight. As he lay there bleeding out with his assailant leaning over him, he still fought. All the killer felt at first was a pinch, like a bee sting. He looked down to see the dead man holding a leather pouch in his left hand and a bamboo skewer in his right.

The effects kicked in quickly and the newly crowned Shaman stumbled to his car. He wiped the blood from himself and went to the emergency room as fast as he could, but by the time he got to the reception desk he could barely stand up.

For three days he slept in the hospital, suffering hideous night terrors. When he was conscious, the doctor came in firing questions.

"Have you been in Central or South America recently? Africa? How were you poisoned?"

He fell back into unconsciousness before he could answer. When he awoke again, the doctor was still there, standing over his bed with a group of nurses wearing face masks. The bright lights burned his eyes.

"You're lucky to be alive, you know. We need to know how and where you came into contact with whatever caused this. It's extremely important."

The doctor was suspicious, and the patient, despite the lingering fog of the poison, could tell.

"Answer me!" the doctor shouted.

The new Shaman sat up in the bed. "I need a shower," he said. "Then we'll talk."

He refused assistance, assuring the group he could shower on his own. When the doctor left, he slipped out through a back stairwell. He was free.

The new Shaman returned to the crime scene and burned the body in an incinerator some two thousand miles from Jackson Hole. He slowly grew healthy, but he was sure he could still feel the effects of the poison within him. It put him on edge, made him tense and angry. Angrier than usual.

What the hell was in that dart?! Some voodoo bullshit! He fucking cursed me! Stupid hippie!

He had killed quite a few men in his life, but the effects of killing the Shaman had stuck with him like no other. After that day, everything in his life was darker. Whether it was the poison or a curse or something else, he couldn't be sure. All he knew was that while he was never a saint by any stretch of the mark, he now felt even more like a devil.

None of his followers knew anything about the murder. Not even those who had met the real Shaman before his untimely death. For a while, the real Shaman was traveling. Then he was imprisoned in France for five years. Those who knew the real Shaman best barely knew him at all and so this new leader easily took his identity. He had cut his hair and lost some weight, but this was their Shaman. They had no doubt.

||

ST. JOHN'S MEDICAL CENTER, JACKSON. THE SAME MORNING.

The wait for visitation hours seemed like an eternity. Noelle had left her cabin with plenty of time to get to the facility by 9 a.m. She sped and arrived ten minutes early. Working for the government had its perks, not the least of which was near total immunity to traffic citations. Her excitement had apparently manifested itself visibly when she got to the hospital's reception area.

"No visitors yet," the nurse retorted somewhat harshly when Noelle tried to check in.

"Oh, sorry. I thought it was visiting hours."

The woman looked at her watch. "Eight fifty-three. Morning visiting hours are nine to eleven thirty." She pointed to a plaque that said the same. "Any other questions?"

Noelle's zeal for her investigation had grown overnight. She'd tossed and turned, pondering the fake bear tooth and what it could possibly mean. Now she leafed through magazines anxiously, awaiting the opportunity to speak with the only surviving witness of the attack.

Although Noelle was excited by the prospect of the unfolding mystery, the hospital waiting room sickened her in a way that she could only barely ignore. The gravity of death couldn't be avoided in a hospital. Here, close calls and miracles were less and less likely, and death, the only *real* fact of life, often prevailed.

Noelle kept her mind focused on her task, but she still pondered the legitimacy of her self-directed mission. On one hand, she felt in control, as if she was on to something here, about to do something right. On the other, she was starting to feel a bit guilty and even embarrassed.

What the hell am I doing here, questioning a critically injured woman because I have some stupid hunch? I should leave and go back to work.

Just talking with the woman, though, a Mrs. Adelaine Giroux, according to Noelle's coworkers at the park, could do no harm. She hoped the woman was in good enough health to provide some answers. She also hoped the language barrier wouldn't prevent her from comprehending those answers.

Jake was just waking up, but he hadn't slept in because of fatigue. More because his subconscious was trying to wish away the reality of the problems he would face when he awoke.

At least I'm out of custody, was his first conscious thought. He brushed his teeth quickly and made a pot of coffee while listening to the news on KMTN, the Mountain. There was hardly any local news that day, mainly a few national stories that didn't interest Jake. They didn't sound like they would interest anybody, actually.

He'd half-expected to hear news about another mysterious death in the area. This was from his years in Philly—when his thought process was darker, more suspicious. A thought process that had reestablished itself in the last few days, much to his surprise.

Before long, as if his feet had a mind of their own, Jake was on his way to St. John's hospital. He had no idea that Noelle was already there.

To help unravel the river murder, Jake wanted to understand what really happened at the Gosling Lake bear attack. Maybe it was a long shot, but the truth about the bear attack might be enough to lead the police down a path that didn't point to Jake.

When he parked at St. John's, he saw the National Park Service truck. *Damn.*

He hoped Noelle hadn't already ruined his chances of seeing the Frenchwoman. The sight of the vehicle made him both sigh and chuckle—the surviving victim was clearly the next best step in determining what happened in the Tetons that day. Any investigator would pursue the witness's story as soon as possible. If she was badly injured, who knew if she could bite the dust at any moment. In death, her story would be lost forever.

So Noelle was sharp but not particularly tractable. From his experience, Jake knew this was the worst type of partner.

Jake had less trouble than Noelle getting through the reception area. He was better versed in the language of deception. He referenced a nonexistent division of the NPS that he made up on the spot and slid straight through. He didn't like to do this—to deceive and feign authority to get his way—but it had its uses.

He noticed the name Giroux on the tag hanging from the room number plaque. Jake had taken high school French and remembered a surprising number of words, but this wasn't exactly "How do I get to Notre Dame?" He had no idea how to say "murder" or "bear," or even "attack," *en français.*

"*Cómo está?*" Jake asked halfheartedly as he entered, a weak attempt at an already lame joke. Even worse, it came out in a more high-pitched tone than he expected. Noelle looked surprisingly attractive—vibrant—in the drab hospital room, like a blossom in the desert. This momentarily stunned Jake.

"*Bien, bien!*" Noelle replied without missing a beat. She smiled. Jake knew just enough French and Spanish to realize that this response was acceptable in either language.

She's clever.

The fifty-something Adelaine Giroux lay on the hospital bed looking frail and confused, but conscious. Her hair was somehow both frizzy and matted. It hadn't been washed since before the attack.

"How is it going?" Jake asked, pointing toward Adelaine.

"Not very well. You aren't fluent in French by chance, are you? Or is it just legalese?" Though he was already more than a little smitten with her, Jake found it surprising that she didn't apologize for breaking her promise to help exonerate him at her first chance. She didn't even mention it.

"Unfortunately not," Jake replied. "But the hospital must have a translator."

Noelle objected—"Don't you think that's a bad idea? Shouldn't we lay low?"

Obviously there was *some* means by which the woman was communicating with her caregivers. Otherwise, how would she explain her pain to them, her allergies, her needs?

"Don't worry about it." He hadn't taken this much pride in his espionage skills since the last time he came across a pretty woman. *It's strange how character flaws, like ego, reveal themselves in the presence of women.*

"Before you go up there, you should know that I told the receptionist I was Adelaine's niece . . . It was the only thing I could think of at the time."

"Um. Okay, no problem," Jake said, trying to decide just how big of a problem this would be. *Probably a significant one.* He left the room without a real plan, trusting that something would come to him before he arrived back at the reception area and had to face the skeptical nurse.

"Hello again . . . I've got a bit of a problem here . . ." Jake said in his best cop voice—smiling and with his hands folded across the counter in front of the woman, who was pretty and plump. "I came to interview the bear attack victim, the Frenchwoman, to get some specifics on the attack . . . species, etc. . . ."

"Didn't Ranger Harroup cover that yesterday afternoon? I figured you had something else to ask her. Wouldn't have let you in, she doesn't need the stress," the woman interrupted. She was bright. And protective.

Uh-oh, Jake thought. *Maybe Noelle's story isn't so stupid after all.* He had talked himself into a trap with his first sentence. He would try to work with it, though, think on his feet; he used to do that for a living.

"I know." Jake needed more time to think, but that wasn't an option. "We were just hoping to get some more complete answers this time, by having her niece ask some questions, rather than a cop. Less intimidating." He tried his most charming smile.

"Problem is, the niece—that Noelle woman—she can't even speak French. I need a translator. You must have someone here who is helping her communicate with the doctors and nurses?" Jake should have known that the park service would have investigated the incident for a myriad of reasons. *Why didn't Noelle know about this? Hell, why wasn't she the one who conducted the questioning?*

"Why wouldn't she be honest about the attack?"

Jake paused. "Wha . . . ?"

The nurse spoke again before he could.

"And of course we have someone here who can translate. How do you think the first guy you sent out here questioned her? That person is *moi. Enchanté.*"

Figures.

The nurse held out her hand. Jake took it and pretended to kiss the top, just behind her knuckles.

Great. The prying, but flirtatious, nurse was the translator, too. It would have been a hell of a lot easier if there had been some break in the chain of deception.

Now he had to carefully manage the questioning so as not to arouse her suspicion. He felt certain that the police chief wouldn't appreciate his presence here at the hospital with the victim. If things went awry, it might even get him arrested again.

He was getting ahead of himself, though. The first obstacle was avoiding a disaster immediately upon entrance. After all, Noelle had no idea about the scam he had fed to the translator. If Noelle indicated that she knew Jake at all, or that she worked for the park service, the jig was up.

"You were running late this morning?" the woman asked. "Her niece was here bright and early. About to knock down the door."

"I'm sure she was just anxious to make sure her aunt was okay."

Jesus, Jake thought, *I thought I was going to do the questioning today. One problem with small towns is the inquisitive people.*

"It's this one, isn't it?" Jake said, motioning toward the plain wood-grain door as they approached. Noelle had shut it.

"Yeah, that's it."

When Jake entered, he hoped Noelle would make eye contact with him first, giving him the opportunity to maybe convey some kind of hint about the lies he had told the nurse-turned-translator. She didn't even seem to notice him enter.

Oh well; telekinesis was a long shot anyhow.

"Hello and *bonjour,*" the nurse said with what sounded to Jake like an authentic accent. The folks who lived in Jackson never ceased to impress him. Many had lived completely separate lives before they made their move, and *all* of them had an interesting story or two.

Some of them liked to tell the stories, but most wouldn't speak a word of their past lives. Jake knew plenty of people around town who never revealed that they were successful physicians, business-men, academics, or politicians in a previous life. Sometimes Jake recognized the names, but he never brought it up. It would have embarrassed them.

The injured woman, who had pepped up noticeably, began speaking in rapid French. From her physical cues, Jake could discern that the two were exchanging pleasantries and discussing the woman's health.

Jake tried to think of all the French words he knew. *Decepage* he remembered from law school, although he had forgotten its meaning. *Something to do with the conflict of laws? Voir dire* was another one, and this one he knew well. The term referred to the jury selection process in a trial.

Not exactly helpful.

While the two women conversed, Jake and Noelle exchanged nervous looks. If the nurse mentioned Noelle or, worse yet, referred to Noelle as the injured woman's niece, their plan would fall apart.

Finally, the nurse fell silent and turned to Jake and Noelle.

"Okay. Fire away."

Jake and Noelle started to speak at the same time. The nurse's vision scanned back and forth between them, suspicious, but Jake quickly quieted himself, yielding to Noelle.

He shouldn't have stopped talking; it was clear that Noelle was unprepared to lead.

I'm supposed to be the interrogator.

He stared at her, but too obviously.

"What is *up* with you two?" interjected the nurse. "You were both strange on your own, and now that you're together, it's downright weird."

There was a pause, a long one. Too long.

The question was hanging in the air. Jake was out of practice. His instincts told him to tell the nurse the truth. Hopefully it would be enough to avoid a call to the police.

"We used to be lovers. I haven't seen him in years. This was unexpected," Noelle blurted out. "To say the least."

The hell? Jake looked at Noelle again. *What kind of explanation is that?*

"Sorry I asked." The nurse didn't seem sorry. She still eyed them with suspicion.

"Yeah, well, it's a bit awkward. I'll let Jake do the talking; he *always* wanted to be the boss."

Jake was momentarily speechless.

What a ridiculous turn.

Now he had to rescue the situation. At least the lie had worked, for the time being.

Speak slowly and cut the sarcasm.

Jake ignored her slight. "Mrs. Giroux," Jake started, "I want to first express my sympathies for your loss. I'm sorry to bother you. We will keep the questions short and to the point."

The nurse translated smoothly and quickly. Jake hoped that she had imparted the same sympathetic message that he intended to impart in English, and that she wasn't cutting corners. He did feel sympathy for the woman; she had just lost her husband in a horrific attack and now she was stuck in some hospital thousands of miles from her home and family.

Except for her niece, Jake mused to himself.

Jake was relieved that his apathy toward the victims of trauma had faded over the years. He was turning back into a human. He always shuddered when he recalled the deposition of a widow whose husband had, according to the widow's complaint, died in a hundred-foot fall at the defendant's amusement park. Jake and his client had held the position that the deceased had committed suicide and thus the widow was not entitled to any damages.

The experts all agreed based on the trajectory of the body and the way the man landed. He didn't even try to get his feet under him. Jake asked the woman if her husband had ever expressed any thoughts of suicide. The woman said no, but Jake sensed otherwise from her woeful demeanor. All he could think at that time was: *She's lying.* It was a disgusting way to think about such a tragic event. He regretted it every time it popped into his mind.

The nurse was waiting for Jake. He continued. "Just recall the attack as best you can." Jake should have brought a pad of paper. It would have been helpful for his true purpose and to sell his cover as an investigator. As it was, he just sat with his hands folded on his lap.

The nurse translated and the victim responded with a short burst of French.

"She says that she didn't really see much of the attack. It all happened very fast."

Great.

"Okay, thank you. Could you ask her to please recount the moments before the attack?"

More talking; this time the woman responded more thoroughly: "She was walking quite a distance ahead of her husband so that she could turn intermittently and take photos of him on the trail."

The translator stopped and Mrs. Giroux spoke again.

"She says twenty meters or so. When they neared the overlook, she heard a scuffling, a shuffle of feet, and then a muted groan. She asks us to keep in mind that the distance and wind was such that it was difficult to hear clearly. When she turned to see what the noise was, her husband was on his knees and blood was on his chest."

Jake asked the obvious: "She didn't see the animal?" There was another short exchange between Giroux and the nurse.

"She saw something, a shape, forcing its way into the forest behind her husband. Branches and leaves moving."

A shape?

"What happened next?"

"Her husband was looking around in a panic, bleeding and shaky. Then she was attacked herself as her husband watched."

"Could she try to recall what the attack felt like or what she saw, if anything? Could you kindly tell her that this is important to our investigation of the attack?"

"She says that she recalls being violently struck—*pummeled* would be the closest translation—and that her husband yelled, 'Stop, stop!' at the animal. She lost consciousness after that."

Jake thought for a moment and then asked: "Wait. Her husband yelled 'stop' in English or in French?"

"Hold on." The victim said only one word. "Both. First in French, then in English. He knew some limited English, she says. He was the one who made all their travel plans: got directions, got them through customs, and the like. Why do you ask?"

Jake ignored the nurse's question. "Does she remember anything else?" Jake asked this mainly to tie up the session; he was pretty sure he had the answers he needed.

"She can't remember anything else, she says. Is that *all* the questions you have for her?"

Again, Jake ignored the nurse's question. *She isn't here to inquire, she's here to translate.* "Please tell her that she has been very helpful. I appreciate her recounting such a tragic event. My condolences again."

Jake stood up first and Noelle quickly followed, smiling at the nurse. "Wait," the nurse said, stopping them. "This is her niece, you said?"

Oh shit. "Yes, that's right," said Noelle, "but we weren't very close. I only met her on this visit." Jake assumed the victim had blown their cover—asked who Noelle was or worse.

The nurse seemed a bit baffled. "Well, regardless of that, wouldn't you like to spend a few more minutes with her before you go?"

"Well, yes. Of course I would, thank you," Noelle responded, relieved. The nurse left the room, shaking her head.

The two allowed a few moments to make sure that the nurse

had moved far enough down the hall and then started to talk, both at once.

Jake said excitedly: "Look, if we're going to work together, I'm asking the questions first, okay? And *lovers*?"

Noelle seemed hurt for a second but then gave him a confident glare, a warning like a snake's rattle. That look morphed again, this time into a playful, patronizing smile. She nodded to show her sarcastic understanding of his new rule.

She was playing Jake, as beautiful women could. And it was working. He couldn't help but smile back.

"Sorry."

Noelle just laughed. "I am *so* glad you asked what language he said 'stop' in! Brilliant!"

He played it down. "It was an obvious question."

She shook her head and laughed again.

Noelle and Jake calmed down as they realized they could still reveal their ruse if they were too loud. For all they knew, the nurse could be calling the park service or even the police as they spoke. They didn't want to push their luck; their impromptu interrogation session had provided them with the information they needed. Against all odds, they hadn't been discovered as impostors yet.

"Okay, so what we learned is this," Jake began, using his recollection to Noelle as his memory's notepad, "we still have no concrete evidence that the attacker was something other than a bear, but—"

Noelle cut him short, excited, but talking in a whisper: "But we do know that for some reason, the husband, who apparently *did* get a clear view of the attacker, asked him or her to stop in their native tongue. Bears don't talk! Why would he change from speaking French to English to convey a message to a bear? It wouldn't matter either way—he could have just as well been yelling gibberish at the beast and it wouldn't stop."

Jake chuckled, a bit irked that Noelle had interrupted but intrigued again at the wit and curiosity of the woman. She was smart, no doubt. *And beautiful,* but that was neither here nor there.

Jake started again when Noelle quieted herself, realizing that she had taken the glory of their recent discovery from Jake. "Right. So, we had a man pleading for his wife's life. He wasn't simply screaming to distract a beast—he changed his pleas to a language that he thought the attacker could understand, and as you noted, Noelle, bears don't speak English."

When Jake and Noelle passed the reception desk on their way out, the nurse was on the phone. She gave them a nervous glance and spoke as quietly as she could, but they still heard her.

"Yeah, they're still here. Okay, will do. Thank you." Then she hung up and pretended to be busy at her computer. She never looked up.

Jake looked at Noelle and pointed anxiously toward the stairs.

"We've gotta go. Now."

As they ran toward the stairwell, the nurse shouted at them to stop. When they got outside, they could hear a siren in the distance, but getting closer.

"We'll talk soon!" Jake shouted to Noelle as she got in her vehicle.

She nodded. Jake and Noelle pulled out of the parking lot separately and merged with the local workday traffic. The police cruiser passed them going the other way, toward the hospital.

12

SNAKE RIVER, JACKSON HOLE. THE SAME DAY.

It was no longer ski season, and without guests, J.P. felt antsy. He had slept in and missed Jake by just a half hour.

Where is he? Fishing again?

That seemed the most logical explanation.

J.P. briefly entertained the idea of making himself a big breakfast but rejected the thought when he realized this would require grocery shopping first.

To pass the time, J.P. decided to go walking alongside Route 89 in the canyon south of town to pick up garbage. This was something he did from time to time, and though it was far from his favorite thing to do, it did keep him busy. His unofficial Adopt-a-Highway.

J.P. parked his truck partway down Swinging Bridge Road, a popular spot for summertime river-goers. Today it was empty. The lot still had some patches of snow and muddy puddles in the shade, and J.P. drove the vehicle too far into the slushy remnants of winter. He knew he'd probably have a hard time getting out of the parking spot, but he would cross that bridge when he came to it. He had all the time in the world, so he didn't mind the challenge of recovering the truck if it was stuck.

J.P. walked up the dirt road toward the main highway with his black, industrial-sized garbage bag, snagging beer cans, cigarette butts, and beef jerky wrappers along the way. He realized quickly that he was out of shape, even though ski season wasn't that long over. He wanted to light a cigarette, but off-season living—late nights, copious amounts of pale ales and whiskey, barbecue, and smoke of all varieties—had finally taken its toll. He was restless, raspy, and guilt ridden. He called it the moral hangover.

Sam was driving fast in the new car. He fiddled with its knobs and buttons and played with the stereo system. He was ecstatic that the Shaman had chosen him for such an important task, not that Sam knew exactly what the significance of his role was.

Sam was a people pleaser by nature, and he aimed to make sure the Shaman was happy with him. He wasn't frightened by the grave nature of the Shaman's requests. Instead, driving down the canyon in the new sedan with open windows, he felt empowered. He imagined himself as a racehorse just released from the start gate. He was finally in action—a man with a cause.

It was just bad coincidence that he passed the remains of an elk as he had these thoughts. *Another victim of arrogant humans. In a rush to get somewhere—get to some engagement that was trivial in the grand scheme of things—someone mowed down a beautiful animal and left it for the ravens.*

The gruesome sight enraged him and he cursed out loud.

"Fucking wankers!"

Sam's ball of rage exploded when he saw the man walking back up the highway's shoulder toward the carcass with a bag over his shoulder. *He's going back to see what he can salvage from the animal. This redneck wants the meat!* Like most of the Shaman's followers, Sam was disgusted by the thought of a human consuming any of Nature's noble beasts. This display of arrogance—destroying a native animal and then removing it from its ecosystem—appalled him.

Sam swung the car around in the entrance to a dirt road, making a quick three-point turn that threw dust into the air. The reckless turnaround probably wasn't good for the car's transmission, but Sam didn't care; it wasn't his car and the Shaman would be proud of his zeal regardless of any damage to the vehicle. He floored it back onto the highway.

Sam initially planned to frighten the man by skidding to a halt in his walking path. But a darker notion hit him, and it presented a much more appealing option:

Why not just hit the bastard?

He backed off the accelerator—he didn't necessarily want to kill the man who was now bending over and paying no attention to traffic. If he died, though, so be it.

The Shaman isn't fucking around anymore, and neither am I!

Sam decided to nudge the man with the right corner of his bumper. He didn't want to run him over and risk incapacitating the car.

Hit by a car! How apropos!

Sam wrapped his fingers firmly around the wheel so he wouldn't lose control on impact. Then he steered the sedan so that its right side was just barely over the white line. He was on the perfect path for a collision.

When Sam was within fifty yards, the man with the bag heard the engine, squared with the car, and looked through the windshield at Sam. The shared eye contact lasted but a fraction of a second. The soon-to-be victim's face expressed confusion rather than fear.

A truck was rounding the corner, coming fast toward Sam from the opposite direction.

Oh shit!

The truck driver would be able to identify the car. In a last-ditch effort, Sam tried to steer back onto the road, but the gravel was unforgiving and his sedan held its trajectory. The pedestrian started to move right and out of the way just as the car's mirror smashed into his hipbone.

Wham! The impact spun the man into a cartwheel. He landed hard on the roadside.

For a second, J.P. looked straight up at the blue sky. It was serene. Then everything went black.

One mile north on the same route, Jake and Noelle were pulling into their first stop, one of the many combination fishing shop, tavern, trailer park, and campgrounds that dotted the corridors of the great fishing rivers of the West. They had parked south of town, and both jumped into Jake's SUV to continue their quest. The business, perched above popular trout rivers, offered the one service necessary for all guides and recreational fishermen who floated in drift boats down the river—shuttle service. The necessity of the service was obvious. If a boat is put into a moving river, the boat will end up downstream from the put-in location and the angler's vehicle.

Drift boats, like kayaks and canoes, lacked motors, and rowing far upstream against a strong river current was not an option.

Hence the need for arranging for boat, angler, and vehicle to all end up in the same place at the end of the float. Amazingly, people unfamiliar with rivers foolishly challenge this unforgiving rule, floating a rental vessel downriver without making any arrangements to move their vehicle. This seemed to happen about once a summer in Jackson.

Jake and Noelle hoped to speak with someone who might have shuttled the vehicle of the dead man. Maybe that person would be able to recall where the vehicle was left for the takeout and who, if anyone, was with the man on his last day on earth. Unfortunately, there was also the possibility that the man had phoned in the request, or never even arranged for a shuttle.

"Definitely worth a shot" was what they settled on. Finding the man's vehicle and discovering the identity of any companions would be extremely useful pieces of evidence.

Jake killed the engine. "I think it would be best if you did the talking this time," he said, which made Noelle smile. Her tan face emphasized the whiteness of her teeth. The contrast made her face glow. Jake imagined how stunning she must look in a white linen shirt—the same hue as her teeth—and how the disparity between her bronzed body and the fabric would make her whole being glow.

Jake hoped Noelle's looks and charisma would help them get the answers they wanted. Pretty girls didn't exactly wander into fishing hangouts every day. He didn't want to be seen with her for fear of ruining her chances, so he fell back as Noelle approached the desk closest to the fishing and boating supplies—the counter where you could jot down your information on a yellow notepad for the shuttle service.

He looked at flies and fishing gadgets and tried hard to listen, though he couldn't hear much. Glancing over, he could see Noelle had one hand resting on the counter and was turned slightly to the side. The clerk had followed her hand with his eyes, up her arm and over her shoulder to her eyes. She had his attention.

After just a few moments, Noelle strode past Jake and back into the main room of the shop, where they sold cold drinks, cheap bait-fishing equipment, and gastronomic treats like nacho-cheese-flavored sunflower seeds.

J.P. *was* breathing, but it didn't sound right. His breath was raspy and constricted. When he got to his feet, it improved somewhat. He didn't say anything to the truck driver who was now standing beside him, looking horrified. J.P. just stood there holding his right side, wobbling.

An ambulance arrived, and the paramedics strapped him onto a backboard and loaded him in. Then J.P. finally spoke: "Shit, am I going to die?"

"You're gonna be fine." The look on the paramedic's face disagreed.

During the ride to St. John's, he hoped that Jake would show up soon. Jake always seemed to know what to do.

"What do we do now?" Jake asked. Noelle and the clerk had only made small talk. The clerk didn't know anything about a man named Hawlding.

Of course the guy wanted to chat, look at you! Jake thought.

"I bet he offered to teach you how to fish, right?" he said.

"What? Who says I don't know how to fish?" Noelle was smiling. Aside from a few disastrous experiments, she had no experience with a fly rod. She could only boast that she had hooked a friend's ear, several trees, and her own thumb.

"Never mind," Jake said. "Where to next? Should we just keep going, shop to shop?"

"Hoback River Tavern is just down the road," Noelle replied, "and I don't think I have ever met a fisherman or river rat that didn't like cold beer." She was right about that. The bar was an out-of-the-way hole-in-the wall; neither Jake nor Noelle had been inside the place in a few years.

They got back into Jake's vehicle and pulled out of the dusty parking lot toward the bar. As they did so, an ambulance whizzed by them, headed north on its way to the hospital.

"Must be another accident," Noelle said nonchalantly. Route 89, where it meandered through the Snake River Canyon, was twisty and congested with migrating wildlife. Add in the shady and sometimes icy surfaces, and the road was a recipe for disaster. Jackson didn't have many suburbs to speak of; those residents looking for tranquillity or cheaper rent were limited to living on the west side of Teton Pass, a treacherous road in its own right, or down south by Route 89. The roads were scenic, but both induced anxiety on a stormy day even for the most weathered locals.

Stormy was exactly what it looked like the afternoon was going to become, and quickly. Dark palisades of thunderheads rolled ominously toward Jake and Noelle from the south, filling up the canyon. The air was cooler and more fragrant now as well—a sure sign of an approaching storm. When they pulled into the tavern's parking lot the rain was beginning to fall in large, bulbous drops. The parking lot was so dusty and the drops so huge that each individual dollop tossed up its own dust cloud into the air.

"Well, we could use the rain," Jake said aloud as he looked up at the darkening sky, eyes half-closed in case one of the giant drops unluckily landed on him.

"Isn't that always the case?" Noelle responded. "Same deal as before? You want the hot chick to do the talking?" Noelle smiled.

"Pretty much." Jake's eyes bugged at the flirty tone, but he kept his cool. "Let's just have a seat at the bar and see where it leads."

Jake held the door for Noelle as she entered the cavelike tap-room. It wasn't an intentionally polite gesture, but one that she appreciated nonetheless. She acted as if she wasn't expecting him to hold the door and then slipped through, mouthing the words "thank you." Her lips were only a few inches from his face.

Jake felt silly—was he using this opportunity to spend a bit more time with Noelle? He fruitlessly tried to steer his mind from Noelle and his feelings for her. He'd spent too much time in the past pondering questions of romance and women. Unfortunately, he never came up with much.

Elspet had presented him with an unsolvable problem, and it had left him confused and insecure about romantic relations. She was a strong woman who needed independence but still demanded a man stronger than herself. She had high expectations, but also yearned for someone free-spirited and adventurous. She was incredibly sweet but, when crossed, horrifyingly lethal.

After much post-Elspet pondering, Jake's conclusion was that whatever he felt for her or she felt for him, it wasn't love. *Love* was a word that described the mutual feeling of respect and reliance between two people. It wasn't the attraction or lust that one felt early in a relationship. That was something else, something dangerous. It was also the close brethren of jealousy, hateful passion, and insanity. There was a reason they called it "sparks." It almost always led to a wildfire.

Now, as he and Noelle sat on the knobby pine bar stools, something occurred to Jake that seemed like a final piece of the puzzle dropping easily into an otherwise complete picture. The problem in part was his own expectations—he couldn't expect any woman to be his savior and that was exactly what he had needed during those last few years on the East Coast. Now, as he settled into the seat, he understood that he finally wanted someone to *love. Someone to care for and enjoy.* He didn't expect perfection, but could something very close to it be sitting right next to him?

"Jake?" Noelle asked, at first with a worried face and then laughing as Jake came back to reality with the same tiny daydream shudder that affects a person as he is falling asleep.

"Ah, I'm sorry—was just trying to think about the forest, but I got stuck in the trees," Jake said coolly, glancing to see if a bartender was near.

"Easy, Wordsworth. If there's a big picture here, we'll find it," Noelle responded, misunderstanding his sentiment. Jake gave her a meaningful look.

A large, tattooed bartender ambled over, and Jake motioned for Noelle to order first. She got a bottled beer, some microbrew that Jake wasn't familiar with. Jake ordered tonic water with lime.

"Can't have just one?" Noelle said.

"It's not that—just the driver." He patted the pocket of his jeans where he kept the keys. This was only partially true. He wanted to stay sharp, not just because he was keen to do some serious problem solving regarding the recent deaths, but also because he wanted to listen to Noelle and learn about her. A couple of beers and he might just talk about himself. This was something he wanted to avoid.

When the bartender returned with their drinks, Noelle asked him if he had been working the prior weekend.

"Sure was," he responded. "I work every night this time of

year." He began drying a few old, pitted pint glasses in front of them with a stained cloth.

Jake looked around the bar. It featured a handwritten sign advertising a "roll-a-day" dice game among the traditional beer mirrors and posters.

It wasn't at all uncommon around Jackson. He knew that when closing time was approaching, the bar probably turned into a dice casino. People mostly played with small bills—usually just ones or sometimes fives. There would be some hard-core players that bet twenties, but they were a small group and most folks wouldn't play with them for fear of losing their modest paychecks. For the most part, the cops turned a blind eye.

"Do you think you would happen to remember a certain patron if we could describe him to you?" Noelle asked the bartender.

"More than likely. It's been pretty empty around here. Only a few guys a night and I know most of them. Who's asking?"

Noelle glanced at Jake, giving him his cue. "Right," he said. "The guy was five ten or so, fit, blond hair. He was young." *Sounds like every guy in Jackson Hole,* Jake thought.

"Well, there were mostly locals here Saturday night—people I recognized, and most of our demo is not so young," the bartender said, keeping his eyes on Noelle as if she were the one who described the man.

"Friday night there was a couple here early—around eight p.m.—and the guy was *not* fit. Later on, three dudes came in and hit it pretty hard. I guess they were young and fit, not that I really noticed." He laughed, keeping his eyes on Noelle.

Machismo bullshit, Jake thought. *Judging by this guy's muscles and the way he keeps his hair, he pays plenty of attention to what his competition looks like.*

Noelle resumed the questioning. "What do you remember about the three guys? Were they people you know?"

"Nope, never seen 'em before in my life," the bartender responded. "Looked like it must have been the one guy's bachelor party or something. It seemed like the other two were kinda taking care of him—feeding him drinks, clapping his back—but they didn't have much to drink themselves. Bad tippers, too."

"What made you think it was a bachelor party?" Jake interjected.

The man seemed annoyed that Jake was getting involved again. He huffed quietly. "They didn't *say* it was a bachelor party, no, but I didn't ask. I just got that idea because it seemed like they were celebrating something for the guy in the middle."

"The guy who was drinking more than the others?"

"Yeah, exactly. Maybe it wasn't a bachelor party, maybe my man just broke up with his girl, how should I know? Could've been a pity party."

Jake got up and headed for the bathroom without saying anything to Noelle or the bartender. As he rounded the corner of the bar he looked back to see if the bartender was watching him. He was still focused on Noelle. Jake reached behind the bar to the keypad of the cash register and grabbed the pen that was resting there. Then he took a napkin from the disorderly stack on the bar. Jake returned shortly and smiled at the bartender, who didn't return the smile. In his absence, Noelle and the man had started making small talk. Jake set his hand on Noelle's thigh and said, "Honey, I've got to go to the car and make a phone call. Meet me there?" Jake finished his virgin beverage.

"Of course," Noelle replied smoothly, and Jake left the bar.

The bartender stepped away for a moment to tend to another

patron. Noelle looked down at her thigh, which was shielded from the bartender's view by the overlapping edge of the bar's counter. Scrawled on the napkin were the words "Get cc info. Meet at car."

Cc info? Noelle thought for a moment. Jake must have meant credit card information, but how the hell was she supposed to procure the credit card information for the men at the bachelor party, or whatever it was that caused them to celebrate that night? There was no way that the bartender would give up this information. She thought again.

The bartender was chatting with another customer. When he came to see if Noelle wanted another drink, she had figured out a solution, though she was doubtful it would work.

"The reason we asked about those men is that . . . well." Noelle feigned embarrassment.

"Well, go on," the man urged her, interested.

Noelle put on her best spoiled-housewife facade.

"My dear husband is in sales. Has been forever. His father was in sales and his father before him. They have been very successful. Selling extremely rare items. Unfortunately, my husband's little brother was never interested in the family business. He was always sort of—how shall I say—a fuckup, you know, like the black sheep?"

Where am I getting this stuff?

"He wanted to start his own business. Anyway, my husband invited him up to our place to stay and figure things out or whatever. His brother shows up, but with two friends, two guys we don't know. They don't even make it one night before they take off with all of my husband's inventory. The thing is, this stuff is valuable, old stuff, *really* old stuff, and it's worth a fortune. Our entire savings."

The bartender was listening intently. Noelle had him hooked.

"The problem is, it's not all on the books. Do you know what I mean? We can't try to recover our stuff by normal means. We can't just call the cops." Noelle looked directly at him.

"So what do you want from me?" the bartender asked. She brushed a few strands of hair from her eyes and intensified her eye contact, whispering:

"If you can, I need the names of the guys that were here. Did they happen to leave a credit card receipt, anything like that?" Noelle was cringing on the inside. This was the moment of truth.

"I can check," the man responded, as if she hadn't asked for much. As Noelle breathed a sigh of relief, the bartender pointed at her hand. "Where's your ring?"

"If you must know, we haven't been getting along so well recently." She winked at the man. "It's mainly a financial relationship these days." The bartender looked at her and nodded.

The wink and the possibility that Noelle might in fact be single had sealed the deal. He went to the cash register, grabbed a stack of receipts from under the cash drawer, and went into the back. Noelle could only hope that the men hadn't paid in cash. The fact that they had apparently heartily indulged made it more likely that a credit card was used.

"Your lucky day," the bartender said as he strode toward Noelle, now on her side of the bar. She crumpled up Jake's note in her fist. "I've got a name on the receipt."

"Wow, I can't thank you enough." Noelle took the receipt from the man and looked at the name. C. Stanford. It didn't ring a bell, but it was something to go on.

"That's perfect. Thanks so much! I'll see you around." She winked again and left the bar.

13

CAMP BODHI. THAT EVENING.

The Shaman was furious. He had just been asked—ordered, really—to abandon his followers and stay under the radar until the original task was completed. Even the Shaman had a boss.

You have to lay low at this point, his boss had told him. When they were done the Shaman would have to disappear anyway, but with his pockets fuller and his wicked thirst finally quenched by the crisp chill of due revenge.

He had agreed to do what was asked of him during their little meeting but never intended to actually follow through.

Fuck him! Who is he to tell me what to do?

He was enjoying his ploy too much to abandon it now. There was intense satisfaction in maintaining power over his contingent. To them, he was like a god. *Why throw it all away now?*

The Shaman's cell phone rang. "Yes." His tone was cold as he spoke into the mobile phone. Every phone was purchased with stolen credit card numbers and prepaid, except for one. That mobile phone was purchased on an account under the name of a real individual—Jake Trent of Jackson, Wyoming. A name the Shaman thought about often. This was the phone the Shaman primarily used.

"I hit someone . . . um, I hit someone with my car, er, *the* car, *your* car." A nervous voice threw the stream of words into the phone and they poured out of the small speaker, which added its own edge to the already annoying whine.

"Okay," the Shaman responded, being cruelly cool at first. "I have no idea *who the hell* I am talking to." His intensity escalated. "Let's start over and please stop shrieking like a woman." Only a handful of his followers knew the number to this phone and so the Shaman did in fact have an idea who it was. One of his moronic followers had screwed something up already.

"I hit someone with the car on my way to the stakeout point. I . . . I think I probably, er, definitely killed him. This guy, he had just killed an elk, hit it with his car. I saw red, thought he deserved the same. This is Sam, sir."

"Did anyone see you?" The Shaman gripped the phone tighter with anger.

"I don't know—I don't think so, there was a truck nearby but I couldn't tell whether or not he saw it—the collision, I mean. He didn't stop, I don't think."

The Shaman weighed the consequences before speaking. "And that's all?" The Shaman was calm now. This incident might not be such a bad thing after all, as long as nobody had seen Sam. *Hell, it might actually work out better if someone did see the car.*

"Um, yes . . . sir. That's all." To the Shaman, the kid seemed confused. His voice was still strained and trembling.

"Okay. What do you want from me? Why did you call?"

"I thought you should know, sir. And also . . ." His voice trailed off. "I didn't know what to do. I was afraid," he said meekly.

The Shaman sighed and sarcastically thanked Sam for calling. If he were actually depending on Sam's commitment to the cause, he would be concerned. But Sam was just a pawn, a cover. The Shaman laughed at what Sam perceived as a horrible deed.

What does this kid know about true evil? About darkness—a completely consuming nightmare rolling alongside reality in your own head? Pussy! Kid does have principles, though. Just hit a guy with a car to save a totally fucked world!

The Shaman laughed harder now. These kids were impressive in their own right—he could use more people like them in his own business.

The Shaman divided his followers into a two-part hierarchy: proselytes and votaries, and one could move up at Camp Bodhi only by completing a task deemed worthy by the Shaman himself. One of the proselytes had already sacrificed his life for the cause. He had longed to become a votary and the Shaman gave him his wish.

Too bad he died in vain. The Shaman laughed out loud again.

During his short life, the proselyte had had very little to live for. He was a sufferer of what laypersons called Ondine's curse. The loss of the subconscious instinct to breathe.

Now that is some dark shit. We could've got along, he and I.

The disease necessitated that a mechanical nerve stimulator be surgically placed in the man's neck and chest when he was an infant—the purpose of which was to stimulate breathing during sleep, when the man's body would otherwise forget to breathe.

Alcohol, as it does to any system in the human body, impaired the man's nervous system even further, rendering the stimulator inadequate.

This worked out well for the Shaman and his plan; the man had been easily killed—though not quite as easily as one might think—and the desperate, pitiful soul had died a meaningful death, in his own eyes at least. Even though the decision to die for the cause seemed easy for the man, the Shaman was impressed with the man's self-sacrifice.

But the man's willingness to die did much more to the Shaman than merely impress him. It enthralled him. The man's last struggling breath had sent shivers down his spine. It was difficult for the Shaman to keep his composure in front of Ryder in that final moment. He did his best to appear cheerless, but inside his hardened shell he felt a desire to clench his fists in front of him, push his chest upward and outward, and howl like a wolf.

He'd felt an uncontrollable desire to release the burning pleasure that built within him while he killed the boy. He imagined it a violent, sadistic orgasm, but it never came to be. He didn't want to compromise his hold over Ryder by coming off as insensitive, so he restrained himself.

While he walked back to the car, though, the energy from the act was still coursing through his veins. His muscles and ligaments were rigid. Adrenaline had taken over his entire existence. His mind and body wanted more. He looked at Ryder. The electricity shooting through him was affecting his eyesight; the man appeared to him like a thin, bloodred neon sign. *Another sacrifice wouldn't hurt the cause,* he thought, somewhat logically. *Fucking tear him apart!* a voice not his own hissed from within.

Luckily, Ryder had spoken to him at that exact moment and interrupted the spiral of violence silently spinning in his head. On the ride back to the compound, the desire came and went, assaulting his mind like waves eroding a beach.

During the rushes of violence that poured over him every few minutes, he imagined the pleasure that would come from another killing. He knew that feeling well. It was the only thing he lived for now. It was the feeling of total and complete control over another human being.

Fuck money and status, who needs it when you can play God for free?

Ryder wasn't the ideal victim, though, and the Shaman knew that. He was a committed follower of the cause, as evidenced by his actions that night. There would be other chances.

In the cabin now, the Shaman realized he was still gripping the phone. His knuckles were white and his teeth clenched again. He made a quick phone call.

"Send her in," he said, and then put the phone back in its place.

Only a few seconds later a young woman slipped through the door. She was wearing a long, loose-fitting skirt, moccasins, and a scant buckskin bikini top that she had made herself. She didn't smile at all.

The Shaman approached her. He could smell the earth and body odor on her. "You're disgusting," he said. The girl only looked down at the ground, trembling.

With the quickness of a cougar, he picked her up and dropped her onto the old table that served as his desk. He unzipped his fly and threw her skirt up over her head so he couldn't see her face. She groaned as he forced his way inside her.

* * *

When Noelle emerged from the tavern, she found Chief Terrell standing next to Jake with a sour look on his face. Terrell attempted a pity smile, intending to convey a "nice to see you, sorry about this" message without saying a word. It didn't seem genuine.

Jake wasn't wearing handcuffs, which was good, but the chief was holding the keys to Jake's vehicle in his hand. This was not good. Noelle looked over to Jake, who didn't look afraid or concerned, just moderately annoyed. His head was held high, looking straight at Noelle. Noelle looked right back and nodded, hoping he would understand that she had procured the information they needed. She got the feeling that if anyone could understand such a vague message, he could.

"What's the deal, Chief?" For the first time in front of Jake, Noelle showed a bit of attitude—a self-confident defiance almost palpable enough to make Jake cringe. He admired her courage and shared her sentiment but knew that a heavy-handed approach to cops was rarely effective.

The chief wasn't smiling anymore. "You know I can't tell you that. Now, I'm going to ask you to drive Mr. Trent's car back into town if he allows it. I'd like to transport him in the car with me to the station." Jake nodded to Noelle, indicating that she should do as the chief suggested.

Noelle knew why the chief wanted to take Jake in his cruiser, and it wasn't because he considered Jake a flight risk. Instead, the officer wanted to keep the two separate so they could not corroborate their stories and come up with a bulletproof alibi. Classic police tactic.

Noelle watched as the cruiser flung gravel as it left the lot.

What the hell is going on?

*   *   *

Meanwhile, in the backseat of the police cruiser, Jake was frantically trying to assess what kind of trouble he was in now. When Terrell asked him why he was down in the canyon that afternoon, he was surprised.

How the hell did Terrell find out we were down here?

He said the first thing that came to his mind. "We were having a drink, Roger, at the tavern. Is that illegal?"

"Don't give me a hard time, Jake. Dammit!" the chief shouted. The outburst surprised Jake, but the chief gathered himself quickly. He spoke more quietly now. "I'm trying to do my job and I'm dealing with quite a few difficult questions myself. I'd appreciate your cooperation." The chief seemed exhausted.

"We were having a drink, Roger. What more can I tell you?" Jake repeated. He wasn't trying to act defiantly but wasn't quite ready to admit that he and Noelle were snooping around the investigation until he got some more information from the chief.

"How many cars do you own?"

What on earth is he getting at?

"Just this one . . ." Jake nodded back and to the side, indicating the vehicle Noelle was driving. He realized Terrell could not see the gesture. "The silver SUV, why?"

"Do you own a recent-model Chevrolet Impala? Are you sure you only own the SUV?" The chief got to the point. "Some of the construction guys saw an unfamiliar car down at Parrana's Dairy Ranch. Said the driver was snooping around on private property. It's registered under your name."

"I wouldn't forget buying a car, Roger. Boat, yes. Rickety old Winnebago, yes. No Chevy. When did this happen? We've been here for an hour or so," Jake lied.

"The site is only twelve miles off, by my count." The Chief

ignored Jake's question and asked another of his own. "Are you aware of any other vehicles being registered in your name here in Teton County?"

"I'm not, Roger, and I find it very unlikely that a car could be registered in my name without me knowing. Wouldn't you? What's going on?" The irritation that Jake felt during his first apprehension was quickly returning with a multiplier effect.

"Okay, Jake. We'll finish this when we get to the station." The chief pulled his sunglasses down from his head and over his eyes and made an effort to appear more focused on driving back to the station. The conversation was over for now. There was excited police chatter coming over the radio, but Jake couldn't hear well enough to understand the codes.

Without warning, Terrell muttered something else and crossed two lanes of traffic. He came to a skidding halt in a turnout perched high above the river. With the car still running, he went out the driver's door and came quickly around to the back. Then he roughly pulled Jake from the cruiser.

"Hey, Roger! What the hell?" Jake yelled as he tried to regain his balance after being pushed against the rear quarter panel of the car.

Terrell's stereotypical gold-framed aviators were still sitting on his nose. The look he gave Jake suggested that the questions about Terrell's intentions were about to be answered.

Noelle continued past the police cruiser and parked Jake's car on the shoulder just as soon as she was out of view.

What are they doing?

She walked quickly south, toward Jake and Terrell, then stopped on a small rise next to the road sparsely populated with sagebrush and crouched down to watch.

The sun peeked out for a moment. What Noelle saw next shocked her. After what looked like a heated exchange, the chief was letting Jake free. He led Jake around to the far side of the car, where the duo was obscured from the view of passersby. Then, Chief Terrell wound up and struck Jake violently in the face. The blow sent Jake to the ground in a heap.

Jesus Christ!

Noelle was standing over Jake when he came to a few seconds after the punch. He looked woozy and not quite ready to stand. Despite Noelle's warning, he tried to get to his feet immediately. Jake stumbled a few steps down the roadside turnout.

Terrell had hit him square on the jaw—a clean knockout. The man knew how to throw a punch. His right fist had come up and across, nailing Jake on the lower left side of his chin. Jake's head had spun forcefully from one side to the other, and when the muscles and tendons in his neck stopped that spin, his brain continued the momentum, charging through the cerebrospinal fluid and bumping into his skull at the back of his head.

Noelle could see Jake was embarrassed and generally out of sorts from the attack.

"It's okay. Relax."

"He surprised me," Jake said in a soft, muffled voice. He spit out blood. "I wasn't expecting that at all." He laughed now, feeling a bit more stable.

"Of course, what could you have done?" Noelle replied in a seemingly forced encouraging tone.

He didn't say a word, but Noelle saw something in his eyes.

"What happened?" she asked.

Rain was falling hard on them now.

"He's losing it." Jake mustered a laugh. "I heard something about a car pursuit on the radio. He ditched me here and headed out. But not before showing his true feelings for me. Which way did he go?"

"He took off south. Quite a head of steam, too," Noelle responded.

A rare bolt of cloud-to-ground lightning hit a butte nearby. Its thunder was deafening.

14

SNAKE RIVER CANYON. A FEW MOMENTS LATER.

Just before he left Trent on the roadside, Terrell had heard the call: a 10–57 on the highway less than a mile from his location. *Hit and run.*

"10–80. In progress. Possible stolen vehicle. In pursuit." He was shouting into his radio's handset. "Does the EMT need assistance with the victim or can I pursue the perp?"

"Victim loaded and in transit to St. John's. Proceed in pursuit. Unknown condition. Perp is south of you by several miles by now."

"Local plates?"

"Registered to Jake Trent, sir. Late-model Impala."

"Shit!"

"Go again for dispatch? Did not copy."

The chief slammed the hand piece into its cradle.

What the hell?!

Terrell already regretted hitting Jake.

A Teton County search-and-rescue helicopter had been summoned to track the perpetrator's vehicle and was en route from the helipad.

The chief had to find out who was driving around hitting people in a car registered to Jake Trent.

Just need to get a visual on the suspect before he gets to the intersection.

Terrell floored it. The intersection, a T, was coming up shortly. It was a junction where the highway dead-ended and split into an east–west route, the westerly path crossing into Idaho. If neither Terrell nor the helicopter could catch sight of the car before it reached that point, the chances of a successful arrest would be cut in half.

More important, if the driver fled to Idaho, Terrell knew there would be complications. He would have to coordinate a pursuit changeover to the Idaho State Police. Depending on the location of the closest state officer, the perpetrator could have time to escape.

Jake and Noelle waved their hands in front of their mouths to try to keep the damp dust out of their lungs. They looked at each other. Although it didn't need to be said, Jake voiced his reaction in a raspy command. "Let's go." The pair got in the vehicle and Jake punched the gas, opening the throttle to the SUV's big V-8.

Before long they tore through another dust cloud that had nearly settled to the ground from the fast-moving wheels of the prior vehicle. They were making progress on the chief and whatever he was chasing.

"What do you think it is?"

Jake only shook his head to answer.

The scenery smeared past them out the windows.

"Maybe we shouldn't follow. We might be getting too involved in all this." It wasn't that Noelle was no longer curious about what was going on, but rather that she was becoming afraid. The look she noticed on Jake's face after Terrell had hit him was even more obvious now. It was resolve.

Jake spoke without moving his eyes from the road. "After what just happened, I've got to find out what's going on." His right hand left the steering wheel for just a second to rub his jaw.

"Let's just call the cops, or whoever, I mean. Internal affairs, right? You know this sort of thing. He can't just hit you like that!"

"In a town this small, there's no sense in it. They'll back him up no matter what."

With that, Jake pressed the accelerator again, coming out of an S curve. Noelle looked him over. All she saw was calm. *Resolve.*

The chief was pushing the car to its limit. These were the moments when Terrell prayed that no wildlife wandered into the road. The sun was lowering in the sky and there were countless blind curves on the highway. A swerve to avoid an elk or mule deer would send his cruiser into the river or, worse, head-on into the cliffs to his right. He rounded the most dramatic of the bends with his cruiser straddling the centerline, tires squealing. Centrifugal force was trying to peel the sedan from the road and toss it in the river.

Terrell was worn-out and far from sharp. There was so much going on in Jackson that he could barely keep up with it all. He was half-tempted to call in the state and let them handle it. His instincts wanted him to catch the perpetrator, but his body and mind were tired. He looked at his gas gauge; the tank was full. He wished that he himself were running on a full tank.

As he rounded the next corner, he saw a sedan ahead of him. He squinted and shielded his eyes from the sun to make sure. The Impala was only a hundred yards in front, moving at the speed limit but appearing to Terrell as if it was standing still. *I'm gonna get my man.*

Terrell stood on the brakes not only to avoid hitting the car but to be sure that he wouldn't spook the driver into fleeing. The driver seemed to have no idea that he was being pursued. Terrell turned on his lights and motioned with his hand for the driver to pull the Impala over, acting nonchalantly and hoping not to give himself away. He wanted it to look like a run-of-the-mill traffic stop.

The perpetrator eased the Impala onto the shoulder, making sure to leave all four wheels on the asphalt surface. Terrell approached the vehicle. His right hand was resting on his pistol. He shared a millisecond of eye contact with the driver. Something wasn't right.

The Impala took off. Gravel from its tires pelted the hood of the police car. Terrell ran back to his cruiser to continue the chase south.

"C'mon!" Terrell shouted aloud, slamming his palms against the steering wheel. He took the radio into his hand but thought again before he called the dispatcher. He had to know what was going on around Jackson.

If he handed over the pursuit to Idaho state troopers and the man driving the Impala was somehow involved in the recent events, there was a good chance the dots would never get connected. He laid the handset back in its cradle. Something sinister was going on, and he had to get to the bottom of it.

*   *   *

Ahead of him, Sam was calling the Shaman again. The road had become flat and straight. The Impala's speedometer read 88 miles per hour.

"Sam?" The Shaman's tone was aggravated.

"I'm in trouble," Sam replied. "Someone must have seen what I did. The cops are after me."

"How many?" The Shaman's tone betrayed a sudden concern.

"One so far. He came up on me with speed and then slammed on the brakes. Acted like it was a normal traffic stop, but I could tell something was up. He looked nervous—hand on his gun." Sam was starting to enjoy this.

The Shaman didn't seem impressed. "Did he see your face?!"

"I don't know—um, I don't think so." Sam hoped this was the answer the Shaman wanted to hear. He thought back to the brief moment when he made eye contact with the officer through the car's window.

"Good. You need to lose the cops—that is essential." The word *essential* came through the wire as a hiss. "Where are you?"

"South of the valley. Going west into Idaho."

This seemed to please the Shaman. "Good. Stay off the highways, head to the back roads. Get some distance on your tail . . . out of his sight, and make an abrupt turn. Try to lose him. Don't ditch the car and try to escape on foot, no matter what. We need that car. Call me when you can."

The Shaman hung up just as Sam heard the hum of the helicopter. *Shit!* Losing the chopper would be tough. Sam would have to head for thickly forested areas to obscure the pilot's view.

Sam slowed the Impala to the speed limit as he approached the

Idaho line. He had to abandon the main road and if he did it too fast, he would risk a rollover.

He crossed the border and arrived at a series of forest service roads that broke off the highway like dusty veins. Their names read like a zoological dictionary: Little Elk, Osprey, Bear Lake.

Dead ends?

Sam had to be patient. At the first road sign indicating a network of roads or a destination, he would turn. Then he could be sure he wouldn't end up cornered in the mountains.

The rolling hills, hummocks, and creek bottoms were getting greener as summer set in and they glistened from the recent rain. Sam looked out the window and time slowed down for a second. Despite the spring, his mind's eye still picked out the remnants of a long winter. The landscape made him feel abandoned.

On the side of the highway was a herd of grazing deer. They looked up when he buzzed by and then immediately resumed eating. Despite all the chaos inside and around Sam, the natural world was quietly going on as usual. He longed to be out of the car, watching from the roadside and free to carry on with his life once he got his fill of the spectacle.

A sign snapped him out of his daydream. "Small Springs Recreation Area: Saddle River Junction—1.4; Small Springs Trailhead—9.5; Victor, ID—29." Sam turned right into the network of forest service roads. He headed north.

Terrell was second-guessing his decision not to involve the Idaho police. Backup officers would be helpful if the perpetrator tried to use this web of back roads to his advantage. It would take only one intersection for him to be spread too thin.

Dispatch called again and again asking for the chief's location, but he ignored it. Next, the woman at dispatch addressed the chopper. "What is your location?" Terrell glanced into the sky around him but saw nothing.

"Idaho border near Small Springs. Returning to Jackson helipad. We are low on fuel and out of jurisdiction. Over." Terrell recognized the voice as that of his deputy chief. The rest of the department obviously hadn't overlooked the jurisdiction issue. Terrell was in charge at the station, but that didn't mean his decisions were above review. He would have to deal with this when he got back.

"Copy. Please report to us immediately upon return. The chief is incommunicado."

What am I thinking?

He was letting his curiosity about the murders and Jake Trent get the best of him.

At the mouth of Small Springs road, Noelle shouted, "Skid marks!"

"Got it."

Jake pulled a quick U-turn and followed the road north. With all-wheel drive and a beefy suspension, he was confident in his vehicle's ability to gain ground on the back roads.

Within a few moments, the three vehicles were in an unlikely traffic jam. Stream crossings and rocks had slowed the progress of the lead vehicle. Now within a fifty-meter stretch, the procession moved forward at less than twenty miles per hour.

"Who the hell is driving that car?" Jake said aloud.

Noelle had no answer, so she stayed quiet.

"What sense does it make? Is it someone from Parrana?"

"The developer?" Noelle asked.

"I don't know. It just doesn't add up to me."

"The chief knows we're here." She pointed to Terrell's cruiser, which was now only a few meters in front of them. "Maybe he's involved?"

"Maybe." He contemplated for a moment.

The slow speed sparked more conversation between Jake and Noelle. They tried to sum up the facts. Noelle recalled the woman's description of the bear attack that killed her husband. Shortly before his demise, the man had attempted to scare off the attacker. He'd used words. In both French and English. This troubled Noelle once more.

"All the death . . ." Noelle muttered, probing. "Is there a serial killer in Jackson?" She looked at Jake, trying to gauge his reaction to her question. "Maybe someone at Parrana just wants to make your life hell?"

"Impossible to say for now. Whatever it is, I bet this guy in the Impala knows something about it."

"Maybe not, though. You're just saying that 'cause it's a small town." In her mind, Noelle again confronted the possibility that Jake was the murderer. Now she was alone with him in his vehicle. In the middle of nowhere.

"Yeah, small town," Jake responded, again without turning toward her. He was distracted. Noelle frowned slightly.

Could he still be involved in all this somehow? Out of the corner of her eye, she glanced around the cabin of the SUV.

What the hell? On the floor in the backseat was a small folding hunting knife. Noelle looked at Jake, trying to get a read on him. His eyes revealed nothing.

Could he have used the knife on the Frenchwoman and her husband?

She forced the notion out of her head. Neither one spoke as they wound through miles of back roads.

*   *   *

If Sam felt penned in when he was fleeing through the open land-scape that cradled the highway in its wide valleys and rolling hills, now he was claustrophobic.

He was moving at painfully slow speeds through thick forests and creek bottoms. He had a half a tank of gas, two tails, and no real plan for his escape. At least the helicopter was gone. He tried to call the Shaman for advice but his cell had no signal.

Sam had been warned about roads like this. They left the valleys and followed rivers and streams to their headwaters in the mountains or simply ended in the middle of nowhere. Signage was unreliable. Some went on for a hundred miles before they reached anyplace of significance.

He became even more nervous and started to doubt the accuracy of the sign that promised the town of Victor was only twenty-nine miles away.

Haven't I gone that far already? What if I misread the sign? This isn't fun anymore!

Finally, Sam saw a sign that showed he was getting close to the next highway, Route 87. Four miles or so and he would be out of this entrapping corridor of foliage. Freedom. The chase had been going on for nearly two hours.

Thank God!

In the slow frog water next to the creek on his right, a large blue heron waded. In a pinch, the bird could fly off, never to be seen again by its pursuers. Sam wished he could somehow change beings with the animal, freeing himself from this mess. He swiped his hand down over his face. He was sweating.

The bird flew off.

The cars turned left onto the highway, which immediately curved right again, heading north and then slightly east. Sam accelerated, taking confidence from the intensifying hum of the engine and the open landscape, now revving to higher rpms. They were only about fifty miles south of Yellowstone. The rain had stopped and the orange afternoon was finally fading into evening's dim glow.

The others were farther behind him now.

Sam had a destination in mind. He was leading the chase back to the tent camp. *Strength in numbers.* He was unfamiliar with the region and really didn't have a choice. He figured once he got there, the Shaman and others would be able to help.

A dozen miles later, Sam exited the highway, drove along a windy secondary for a few miles, and then abruptly turned left into the entrance of the encampment. The access was inconspicuous. It was disguised as a private driveway complete with a mailbox and an eight-by-eleven No Trespassing sign.

Camp Bodhi was set up around the central cabin where the Shaman had addressed the votaries and Sam—the sole proselyte invited—earlier that day. A dirt drive circled the cabin in a quarter-mile loop. Along the outside edge of the crude road sat the tents and other structures where the followers lived, votaries on the inner circle, proselytes farther out.

There on the eastern boundary, surrounded by willows, was a creek, which the community used for water and, to some extent, ingress and egress. An old aluminum canoe rested upside down on the bank.

Sam led his pursuers around the loop slowly. His eyes searched the grounds for someone who might help. Nothing. There was nobody there. No vehicles were parked around the loop and Sam didn't see a single person among the makeshift cabins. Losing his nerve, he swerved the car into the sages in front of the Shaman's cabin.

Where the hell is everyone? His heart was racing.

"This doesn't feel right, does it?" Jake said, half to himself and half to Noelle.

"It's strange, no doubt. Sabotage?" Noelle answered. "What is this place anyway? It's like a compound."

Jake shrugged. "We're close to the park," he said, referring to Yellowstone. He dropped back from the leading vehicles, proceeding more cautiously now.

Inside the cabin, Sam could barely see. The sun was disappearing fast and the cabin had no electricity. Still, it was evident that the space was unoccupied. No candles or lanterns were lit. Everyone was gone.

Through the window, Sam could see the policeman approaching the cabin with caution, gun drawn.

I've got to get out of here!

If he stayed in the cabin, it was over for him. Worse yet, he knew it would interfere with the cause.

Suddenly, the second vehicle came to a stop next to the cruiser. He strained to think of a plan for his exit, but nothing came to him. His nerves made thinking difficult. Panic swept over him.

What the hell am I doing here? He longed for the brick row houses and manicured hedges of suburban London.

Outside, the cop was yelling and motioning to the man and woman in the car as they opened their doors. He was telling them to stay in the car.

Who are they?

Seemingly insistent on being a part of the action, the woman was trying to get out of the car. The officer jogged toward her to stop her. Sam took this opportunity to make his move. He slipped through the side door of the cabin and sprinted across the road, through the waterside hummock, and to the creek.

At the creek's side, Sam grabbed the gunwales of the camp's canoe and heaved it into the water. It splashed into the rushing snow runoff and started moving downstream. He searched the sandy bank for a paddle, but to no avail—someone must have made off with it. Without any means of propulsion besides the current, he crashed into the canoe, upper body first, causing sloshing waves to course across the width of the brook. Fortunately the high, fast water would move him quickly downstream.

Jake watched as the chief wrestled through the willows in pursuit. Game trails, likely broken by deer, followed the course of the river, providing a meager path, but the ceiling of the canopy was low and dense.

He'll never catch up.

Jake looked to his side for Noelle.

"Noelle, stop!" It was too late. She was running along the streamside trees, peeking through breaks in the cover.

Jake took off, too. "Stay back! He might be armed!"

Noelle eventually slowed to a stop, but not on account of Jake's warning. The chief had given up pursuit.

When Terrell emerged from the tree tunnel in an opening, he looked downstream for a few moments. Nothing. No sign of the canoe or the perpetrator. Huffing, he shot a glance upstream. Again nothing.

"Shit!"

Jake and Noelle heard the shout from eighty yards.

The man had escaped.

"I'm guessing that car back there"—Jake took a deep breath— "is the one registered in my name?" The chief was jogging back to get to his car's radio.

"That car"—Terrell exhaled—"almost killed a pedestrian. Hell, the guy might be dead by now, and it might've been intentional."

Terrell and Jake walked back toward the encampment exchanging quiet words while Noelle followed closely behind them. They were both shaking their heads. Jake was thinking about why someone would register a car in his name and hit someone. It didn't make sense.

"What's going on? Jake?" Noelle felt like a younger sister left out by her older brothers. "Jake?" They ignored her.

"We'll talk about it on the ride home. Get in." Jake opened the passenger door for Noelle. "That's assuming I'm free to go?" He smiled, intending this as a joke, but Terrell only nodded. Jake held his gaze on the chief's face for a second longer, hoping to discern what the stoic nod had meant. There was no indication.

15

ROUTE 89, JACKSON HOLE. THE SAME EVENING.

Jake did his best to fill Noelle in about the car's registration. He knew it all sounded absurd, but the chase, the vehicle's registration, the hit and run, and all the other pieces that fell into place in the last several hours did mean only one thing: Jake was one of the targets in whatever was going on, not that he knew what that was.

Noelle looked him over as he remained focused on the road. When he looked back at her, she spoke: "Well, we have to find that out . . ." She paused long enough that Jake gave her a puzzled look from the driver's seat. "Err, who is framing you and why, I mean."

"Thank you for your help, Ms. Klimpton."

Did I just mean to sound flirty?

They retreated to their own thoughts for the remainder of the ride home. Elk and mule deer crossed precariously in front of them from time to time and Jake deftly avoided them. He paused for a moment after each animal.

They always say where there's one there's usually more.

The moon shone brightly on the Cathedral Group by the time they got back to Noelle's cabin. It was 9:45 p.m. Jake killed the engine. They were both tired, but there were too many thoughts swirling in their heads to call it a night. Noelle asked Jake in for some coffee, though she wasn't sure she had any.

He questioned her intention in his own head. Jake hadn't been alone with a woman for some time now.

In for coffee? This sounds like a proposition. What the hell do I do?

Again he held the door for her, the rickety spring-loaded screen door that kept the bugs out on warm summer evenings. This was not such a night; the sun had abandoned the day and left the valley cold and dark. There were no clouds to insulate the earth from the unthinkable expanse of the universe. It was too cold for bugs.

Noelle smiled as she brushed by. A curious, furtive smile, Jake thought. Although Jake was still muscular in a wiry sort of way, he wished he'd kept up the fitness program he used in law enforcement.

Did I shower this morning? He looked down at his worn flannel shirt, then brushed it off with his hand.

Below an old four-paned window, the cabin's dining area consisted of a roll-a-table made for camping. There was seating only for one. Noelle went back outside and returned with a weathered green plastic patio chair for herself. She motioned for Jake to sit on the slightly more comfortable spindle-back and went to hunt for the coffee.

Noelle sorted through the almost-empty bags in her cabinet. There wasn't enough to make a pot, even in combination. Instead, she found some instant and lumped a couple of spoonfuls into two colorful, mismatched mugs. Then she filled the teakettle and turned on the burner.

"I like your place . . ." Jake trailed off when Noelle turned quickly and showed a skeptical face.

She walked toward the table and sat down, maintaining eye contact and wondering whether or not to translate his comment as sarcasm. She decided not to. Jake seemed too polite to make fun immediately upon invitation to her home.

"It's a nice life, I mean. Isn't it?" Jake continued, motioning toward the window and the pine forest standing behind it.

"It doesn't get any better." She stood and checked the water. It wasn't boiling yet. *It's getting old having it all to myself,* she thought. Checking to make sure Jake wasn't watching, she glanced at herself in the mirror and fixed her hair. He was busy fiddling with his cell phone.

"It's instant . . ." she shouted over her shoulder, probably too loud for the meager distance between them. "Uh, I hope that's okay."

"Fine with me," he replied, still looking down at his phone. The call he had just declined came through again: 307 area code. A local number. Moreover, it looked familiar. He thumbed the decline button once more. The caller didn't leave a message.

"Here's some sugar. I'm out of milk." In reality, Noelle never had any milk. She kept very little food in the cabin. It all went bad before she could get to it.

"I know very little about you, Jake, but our situation here requires a lot of trust. Why don't you tell me something?" She flashed a smile that nearly transformed into a surreptitious giggle.

"How do you mean?" Jake was feeling slightly uncomfortable. Noelle looked incredible, the cabin was romantic in a subtle, rustic way, but the timing wasn't quite right. Plus, he was curious about the phone calls.

"I mean, why get involved in all this? Why not let the police handle it? Go away for a week and let it settle out?"

His phone was ringing for the third time. He looked down. Same number. "There is something I don't quite trust about the police—the chief especially. It's not like him to assault a suspect and then let him go. Besides, I have a bit of a history in this sort of thing. I think the better question might be why you have such a keen interest in these events." He smiled at her, playing lawyer now, happy to deflect the questioning since his phone was ringing for a fourth time.

Noelle was trying to formulate a reasonable response, but Jake interrupted her thoughts as he stood up.

"I'm gonna take this," he said, holding the mobile phone up for her to see. "Whoever it is really wants to get ahold of me." Jake pushed open the ratty screen door and stepped into the cool night air.

"Hello?" Jake heard heavy breathing through the earpiece. "Hello? Who is this?"

"Hey . . ." The man coughed. "Jake, I need you, buddy. Where the hell have you been?" It was J.P., but he didn't sound like himself. He sounded sick, or hurt.

"What's wrong—where are you?" Jake's heart rate quickened.

"I'm fine. I mean, sort of fine, man. I got nailed by a car, dude, believe that? I was lucky, though, they say. Instant karma for cleaning up trash would be my guess. The doc agreed. Anyway, I need a ride from the hospital."

J.P. was the victim of the hit and run? Questions filled his head. *How does it fit? Why would they target him? He's got nothing to do with the development.*

"Are you hurt?"

"Oh, right, no. Yeah, I'm good. I was in shock or whatever, they told me. But unscathed, you could say, is that a word? Anyway, bruises, cuts, and a little concussion."

"Good. Now you're smoking again?" A smile washed over Jake's face. He chuckled at the comparative luck of his friend.

"Ha. You're good, man. Nothing gets past you." He took a long drag. "I figured I deserved it after the day I had. What's weird is that it seems like every one of these nurses smokes ciggies. They have to deal with all the shit that comes through the sick bin from lifelong smokers, but they still suck down those darts . . ."

Jake sensed his friend diverging on a tangent, so he spoke up. "Whose phone are you on?"

"Some foxy nurse's."

Jake heard a giggle in the background.

"Just kidding. It's Annette, my nurse. But she is rather foxy."

"Are you ready to go now?"

"Yeah. Hell yeah. Why do you think I've been calling you over and over? They say I shouldn't walk home." Jake's home was about sixteen miles away from the hospital, and it was now almost 10 p.m. and below freezing. The idea of walking was silly even for a healthy person.

"I'll be there in a half hour. Stay put."

"Jake." J.P. butted in before Jake could hang up. "Where you been? I was worried."

Jake fell silent for a moment.

"Don't worry. I'll be there soon and explain everything." Jake hung up the phone and put it back in his jeans pocket.

When he opened the door, he sensed that Noelle had been listening in. "My friend, he was the one who was hit by the car, but he's okay. I have to go pick him up at the hospital."

"What? What does that mean? Why him? I can come if . . . ?" Noelle said hopefully.

Jake waved off her questions. "There's no need, get some rest."

With that, he got into his vehicle and headed toward town.

Noelle sighed and got up, bussing the still full cups of coffee to the sink. She dumped them both and rinsed them. Then she slipped into bed, not bothering to strip. Her mind was still buzzing. She was both disappointed and anxious; the nervous energy from a thwarted intimacy mingled with confusion about the day's events. Her brain argued with itself.

Did I do something wrong? Is that why he left so abruptly?

His friend was nearly killed, silly. What does this mean to us? Does it clarify or complicate what is going on in Jackson?

You move too fast. Let it develop. He is a nice, attractive, solid guy. Don't ruin this.

A third voice started to ask whether she should even be involved in any of this.

Deep down, Noelle was pleased that *something* was keeping her up at night.

*　　*　　*

When Jake arrived at the hospital, J.P. was leaning on the wall outside an employee entrance smoking and surrounded by a gaggle of young, giggling nurses. When he gestured with his hands or laughed too hard, he would clasp his midsection and grimace.

Jake contemplated waiting in the car for their jovial meeting to adjourn. He knew J.P. was in his element. Instead, he parked and walked toward the group. With the arrival of an outsider, the women stubbed out their cigarettes and quickly dispersed.

"Don't look too bad to me, brother," Jake said in a good-humored tone. He gave J.P. a gentle embrace, careful not to aggravate his injuries. "I'm glad you're all right. Let's get out of here."

"Hell yeah, man, I hate hospitals. All those sick people circling the drain."

That's a rather cold way to put it, Jake thought, laughing to himself. He helped his friend into the car.

As they headed toward the West Bank, before Jake could get in a word, J.P. rushed into an elaborate description of the hit and run. What it felt like to be hit by a car: "Kind of satisfying in a weird way . . ."; what he saw when he was convinced he was going to die: "Like, my family all dressed up as old-time English judges at the gates of heaven . . ."; and how the experience had caused him to reevaluate.

When the torrent of words finally ended, Jake surprised J.P. with his own story about the day.

"No shit! Did you catch the bastard?"

"We have the car, but that's all. The guy escaped on foot. Actually, on foot, then into a canoe, believe it or not." Jake shook his head. "I would expect the police would want to talk to you. Whether you recognize the guy, stuff like that . . ."

"Stop here! Whoa!" J.P.'s cry startled Jake.

"What's wrong?" Jake asked, alarmed.

Without answering, the wounded ski bum jumped out of the still slowly moving vehicle and jogged gingerly into the small liquor store alongside the road. He emerged after a few minutes with a cheap bottle of tequila, which he opened even before buckling his seat belt. The smell wafted to Jake's nostrils and he shook his head when J.P. held the bottle in his direction.

"Wooo-eeeeee! That feels better, man! Shit!" he said, shaking his head wildly. J.P. reached into his pocket, chose some music from his iPod, and plugged it into Jake's stereo. He turned up the volume, lit a cigarette, and opened the window. Jake cracked a smile and put his foot on the gas.

J.P., crazy as he was, had some big parts of life dialed right in. He was not self-conscious, overly guilt ridden, or judgmental of others. He enjoyed his time on this planet as much as anyone Jake knew—a quality Jake envied.

Gravel murmured under the SUV's tires as Jake came to a gentle stop outside his house. It was colder yet, but J.P. insisted on sitting outside the house and sipping the tequila. He lit another cigarette and offered Jake one. He accepted. It had been a long while since his last smoke, so Jake could outrationalize the guilt. It tasted good and harsh at the same time. Calming.

They passed the bottle back and forth for nearly an hour, barely talking. The porch furniture had not yet been moved back outside for the summer, so they sat on the floor and rested their backs on the wooden beams of the structure, legs outstretched in front of them.

The air was cold, twenty-five degrees now, but there was a distinct feeling of springtime floating about. Smoke from campfires and wood-burning stoves came and went. Occasionally an owl would hoot or a coyote would yelp and the domestic dogs would bark in response. Jake wondered which one was Chayote. He assumed the loudest, and therefore the closest.

The moment broke when J.P. spoke up.

"Someone's after you, eh?" He handed the bottle to Jake, who took a short pull.

"Looks that way. I just don't know why or what they're after." He lifted the cigarette pack from the porch floor and opened it before deciding otherwise.

"I'll take 'em." J.P. grabbed the pack. "You're kidding, though, right? I know why. You're pretty dense for a PhD, man."

"JD—juris doctor."

"What? Anyway, I can help."

J.P. did sometimes have a knack for finding the obvious answer to complicated problems.

"I don't know his or her name obviously."

Jake rolled his eyes to tease J.P. "Obviously," he said.

"But I can narrow it down. You, like, pissed off a lot of dangerous people, right?"

Jake nodded. "I guess you could put it that way, sure." In reality, J.P. had no idea how true his statement was.

Dangerous. Evil. Maniacal. All of the above.

"You came out here and for a while it was like witness protection almost, you know? Nobody knew where you were and they couldn't even find out if they wanted."

Jake doubted that. Some of the men he had dealt with were savvy enough to find him, if they had the right resources. Some of them did.

"But somehow, someway, man, word got back to these thugs

back East or whatever and one of them thought, 'Well, maybe it's revenge time.' You are in trouble, my friend. These guys want you to *suffer*."

"Not bad, Sherlock. One problem: I have a hard time believing that anyone would go to such effort to kill me. Seems like a trivial undertaking. The criminals I dealt with—the ones I pissed off as you so eloquently put it—were smarter and more calculating than you might think. They were thieves and murderers and drug dealers, but smart folks. Plus, anyone with the resources to try to kill me while two thousand miles away would be sophisticated enough to know it was a waste of time. I'm out of their hair, they would know the right move is to move on and forget I ever existed."

"That's your problem, man. You're too smart! You think just because you're logical or whatever, that other people are too. You're overestimating people, Jake. People are maniacs."

"Didn't know I had a problem. Want to tell me more about it?" Jake smiled, still kidding around. "Maybe you're right, but it just doesn't add up to me. There's too much risk in chasing me around for revenge. There's gotta be something else."

"Well, I hope you're around so I can say 'told ya so.'" J.P. coughed a bit as he took another big swig of the tequila, then pushed the bottle toward Jake.

"No thanks. If I'm gonna survive the night, let alone the next couple days, I need to go to bed. *No más.*" J.P. held out an open hand as Jake stepped past him to get to the door. Jake took it and shook heartily. "Glad to have you back, buddy. Sleep in the house tonight, would you? In case you need anything."

"Thanks, man. Good night." J.P. was coughing and lighting another cigarette.

Once inside, Jake took off his jeans and watch but got into bed with his T-shirt and socks on. He didn't brush his teeth. His mouth still tasted peppery from the tequila. His mind wandered, perching momentarily on images, scents, and sounds of Noelle, rivers, Elspet, crime scenes, and courtrooms. He was drunk.

As sleep approached, his thoughts settled on Noelle. The way she looked and talked. The way she smelled. Her smile. A drunken mutter left his lips. *Don't get involved.* It wasn't Elspet's memory that caused it. He was *meant* to be alone. He could fast-forward a few months in his mind and see the aftermath. Two hurt, estranged individuals wondering what went wrong, hoping never to run into each other again. He wouldn't make that mistake twice. It was so much easier this way.

Sleep was near, but his mind posed some final questions: *What if J.P. is right? What if I am overthinking it? What if I am too far removed from the game to sense my own demise?*

16

THE HOT ROCK TRACT, MONTANA, ELEVEN MILES NORTH OF
YELLOWSTONE NATIONAL PARK. THE SAME NIGHT.

The man looked out over the Yellowstone Plateau from a large
house on a hill. The home was a modern-looking cedar structure
and it was built in a hurry. He had bought up the land and con-
tracted the build from start to finish in only six weeks. Cost was
no concern. It sat up high in a swath of trees that was surrounded
by wildfire damage, facing south so that the sun warmed it during
the day.

The room resembled a control center. A few computers, a fax
machine, two flat-panel TVs, and other various, albeit less common, electronic devices. Like the rest of the house it was cold,
unlived in.

The man stood up and rolled his neck. He had been sitting at the
computer for too many hours. Checking numbers and worrying.

Walking to the window that looked out on the national park's northern tract, he inhaled deeply and rubbed his face with his hands. He was anxious.

His name was Jan Lewis Rammel, pronounced "John" for simplicity's sake. Born in Germany, he had a huge, muscular body that stood six feet three inches tall. His cropped blond hair was just now starting to gray as he approached middle age.

A former college athlete and successful businessman, he was used to pressure, but the type of pressure he was under now was enough to make anyone crack. The unlikely possibilities were slowly turning into probabilities, and they were sickening. If the worst happened, the consequences were mind-boggling.

Horrific, really.

But the others involved in the project seemingly couldn't be bothered with that reality. They were trying to remain optimistic. "Stay positive. Do your job," they told him. But they were unrealistic and greedy. The truth of the matter was that the situation was getting out of control, and there was no stopping it.

At first he had spent what seemed like eighteen hours a day, seven days a week with them. Working to end the crisis. Save the world. He wasn't so sure they weren't destroying it.

Now everyone had left. Now, with the wheels in motion. They'd all gone back to their cities: D.C., Houston, Abu Dhabi, and New York.

They were oilmen and politicians mainly, all criminals in one way or another, but that identity was hidden behind a thick wall of respectability. A few, he didn't know what the hell they did. They operated in the shadows. Google searches revealed nothing. They treated Jan like shit.

He was the low man on the totem pole, except for Makter.

Jan's wealth was significant, but not compared to theirs. Anyway, his money had been made by endeavors more conventionally criminal: drugs, arms, and bribes. A few times, someone's life. This made Jan a less-legitimate businessperson in the eyes of the others. It also made them fear him.

In his own eyes, he wasn't hopelessly evil. Quite the contrary. He was motivated by success just like anyone else. And like most, especially those who had hired him, he was indiscriminate about the means to the end.

His career had started with legitimate businesses. It was manufacturing plants, the low cost of labor, that first drew his interest to South America and Asia. There his companies found relaxed regulations and higher profits. After a few years, the opium industry's outlandish profits convinced him to pawn off his companies and invest in poppy fields, refineries, and trafficking vessels. He expanded his operations into the Colombian cocaine industry the next year. In the 1980s, when civil unrest was tearing apart El Salvador, Guatemala, and Honduras, Jan made a killing, both literally and figuratively, in the weapons trade.

By 1999, he was completely detached from the day-to-day operations of all these endeavors. He held estates in Mexico, Costa Rica, and Florida and had a four-thousand-square-foot flat on Manhattan's Upper East Side, where he resided with his wife and their child. It appeared as if he'd escaped from the risky game unscathed. He had finally made it. It was country clubs, private schools, and five-star dining from here on out.

Then, one early morning in New Jersey, things changed.

Unbeknownst to Jan, his son, Argus, had begun operating an outfit between Miami and New York City with Makter. A drug outfit.

Makter. Uncle Mak.

Argus had become attached to Makter over the years. It wasn't really a bad thing, their relationship. Mak took care of Argus. Helped him become a man. It was just that Makter had always had something off about him. Dark. Ghoulish, even for a criminal. This frightened Jan, which was quite an accomplishment.

South of the city, in the gritty Jersey suburbs, Argus and Makter would sell their product to middleman dealers.

Jan got the call at 5:18 in the morning, and he would never forget that time. His bright, young baby boy had been shot four times and was in intensive care in Brooklyn.

When he arrived at the hospital Argus was stable, but the prognosis wasn't good. The boy had been shot three times in the chest and once in the neck. Luckily, the bullets had pierced the right side of his body and left his heart undamaged, although his right lung had collapsed. The neck wound was more significant. When the swelling came down, the doctors confirmed that the round had severely damaged his spinal cord. If Argus survived, he would never walk again.

It was the cops that did it. *Those rats.* They'd raided the transaction, guns drawn. When Argus reached for his pistol, two officers had fired on him without mercy.

The boy lived, but what kind of life? He'd lost the ability to speak and spent his days wheeling around the flat, silently. A permanent look of shock was plastered on his face—one of the many surgeries he underwent during his recovery left him with facial paresis.

Jan was distraught. He also secretly despised the hideous sight of his own progeny. A strong, cunning, and proud heir brought to his knees. Jan refused to accept his son's condition as permanent.

No cost was too high. He installed elevators and ramps in his villas. He rigged his son's favorite boat so that it could accommodate him. He bought cars and leased a private jet so that Argus would not have to endure the public humiliation and inconvenience of the airport. It all started to add up.

Then there were the medical expenses. Jan sent Argus all over the world for experimental treatments: India, California, Switzerland. Jan paid out of pocket. But none of it worked. Still, his son wheeled around silently, looking as if he had just seen a ghost.

Communication was limited to notepads and Argus's small repertoire of sign language signals. As Jan became more engaged in his son's crisis, his wife wandered: she traveled, gambled, cheated, and developed an expensive drug habit. Before long, his family's expenses had caught up with them. It was a lucky coincidence that he was called about this project before his assets were completely drained. The job had sounded so good at the time.

Jan poured himself two fingers of scotch and spent a moment smelling the golden liquor before he took his first sip. He remembered the pitch. The payoff could be in the hundreds of millions, they said. The risk was low, they said. The federal government was aware of the situation and they were turning a blind eye because they were interested in the results. The only risk was state authorities and the media. Jan hired Makter to take care of those things.

The idea was genius in many ways, and it appealed to Jan especially. He had made his first fortune by knowing what people needed, never bothering with what they wanted. Wants could be ignored. So he'd sold drugs for their addictions and guns for their survival. Rehab from heroin was extremely rare, especially outside of the developed world. Civil unrest rarely resolved itself without guns in undeveloped nations.

In Jan's mind, this experiment was based on similar assumptions. He was disappointed that he hadn't made the connection earlier, for he could have been a much richer man by less risky means. "Energy," he said aloud for the umpteenth time in recent weeks. He shook his head and chortled as he walked back to his desk to watch the numbers.

Now he knew the payoff wouldn't be quite as much as expected. They had conveniently shared that news with him yesterday. Still, if the experiment proved unsuccessful and the major payoff never occurred, they guaranteed ten million dollars and a clean police record. "As long as the drills get deep enough," they told him. Not a bad take for one job. Nonetheless, the idea of working for politicians made the seasoned criminal wary. The only real upside was the immunity.

The men in charge were shortsighted, Jan thought. Even a criminal like him could understand that this project needed more planning and research. Nobody had really understood until now how bad it could get; they were too caught up in its potential.

And it all started with those fucking cops shooting down Argus. My boy in the wheelchair with the hideous face.

And Jake fucking Trent.

17

WEST BANK, SNAKE RIVER. THE NEXT MORNING.

Jake woke up with a start. His head felt like a pressure cooker ready to explode. To remedy this, he started the coffee, downed a glass of water, and got in the shower. When he finished, he poured the coffee, black, into a plastic to-go mug, grabbed two ibuprofens from the cabinet, and headed for the door.

His stomach grumbled as he pulled off the road to fill up on gas. It occurred to Jake that he had neglected dinner, which surely didn't help the hangover. While the gas was pumping, he jogged inside to the convenience store to find a bite to eat. He bought a handful of granola bars and two bottles of water. On the way out the door he also picked up the local freebie newspaper.

Glancing at the paper, which he had laid on the hood of the vehicle, a headline leaped to his eye: "Development Site Vandalized." Jake read quickly.

Police are interested in "any and all leads" from the public,
Jackson Police Chief Roger Terrell said last evening, stressing
that the force is treating the vandalism as an act of "aggres-
sion and terror, rather than meaningless destruction."

When asked what factors went into his determination of
the nature of the vandalism, Terrell refused to elaborate, cit-
ing the ongoing investigation.

Jake read on. The construction site had been thoroughly sabo-
taged—replete with booby traps made of barbed wire and threats
scrawled into the yellow paint of its back-end loaders and bulldoz-
ers. Someone had even burned out the interior of a pickup truck.

It still didn't quite add up to Jake. It was clear that someone
wanted the building at the milk ranch to stop. Someone had it in
for the Parrana family.

But who? And what the hell does it have to do with me? And
J.P.?

He thought briefly of Noelle—thought of calling her but decided
against it. There were more important things to do. Besides, Jake
knew he would never forgive himself if he put her in danger.

The tank was full. Jake started the long drive back to the camp
near Yellowstone to investigate for himself. He hoped the chief
and the police had already come and gone.

The Shaman was long gone from Camp Bodhi by now. He'd left
immediately after Sam called. He didn't fill his followers in totally,
but he told them a raid was coming. They knew what to do, this
scenario had been practiced. They dispersed randomly, mostly
north. The Shaman went south, toward Jackson; he still had busi-

ness to do. He'd registered at a cheap motel under a fake name, and that was where he sat now, perched on the bed's edge. The TV was on but he ignored it.

The Shaman's name was Makter, but even that was somewhat of a farce.

He'd assumed his middle name as his first name a few decades back to avoid some enemies. He'd been messing around with a dancer from the Phillies' Club. A girl from a connected family. One night he beat her up pretty good and she went crying to Daddy. That was all it took—the wrath of an overprotective Sicilian patriarch became focused on one thing: killing the asshole who hurt his baby girl.

Makter had wanted to kill the whole family, but the risk was just too high. Someone would ultimately find him and make him pay, and he knew it. He changed his name but vowed to go back for the father and daughter eventually.

I want the fat fuck to watch his daughter die.

Thinking on it now excited him. He closed his eyes and pictured the scene. Like his mother lying in his dreams, a woman was motionless in a pool of her own blood.

When I get out of this fucking wilderness, I'll take care of it.

His fists were numb from being clenched, and the pinprick tingling brought him back to reality. Earlier that day, Makter had heard the reports about the sabotage efforts in Jackson. He was disappointed that the attack was so weakly executed—more aesthetic than damaging—but it didn't matter much.

What mattered more was that his spy, Sam, was out of the picture. This would make things a little more difficult. *Who would keep tabs on Trent?* The police had seized the Impala the night before and Sam was God knows where.

To make matters worse, the police now knew that Jake wasn't the culprit behind the hit and run. That didn't matter much to Makter, but Jan would be furious.

Makter and Jan had seen eye to eye at first. They both wanted Jake out of their hair, now and forever. Since he was poisoned, though, the thought of Jake's imprisonment didn't satisfy Makter. That poison, *whatever the hell it was,* had planted a rage inside him. He wanted blood.

Of course, Jan said that wasn't necessary.

Weak, frightened Jan. A little boy in a man's body.

Noelle was awake early that morning, too. She cringed as she recalled the prior night.

What did I even want from him? It wasn't like her to be so bold.

She thought of calling him, clearing things up, but changed her mind. If he needed her he would call. Besides, she wanted to go to the morgue to look at the Frenchman's body.

Before she left, she called the hospital and asked to be transferred downstairs to the morgue. Smith answered.

"Hello?" he said in a hurried voice.

"This is Noelle Klimpton from the NPS. I'd like to come in and look at your bear attack victim if I could."

"Yeah, uhhh, fine. Hurry though. The body is leaving with the family this afternoon. You'll have to let yourself in through reception; I'm leaving for Pinedale. Suicide. Sad, sad. Real messy."

Noelle thanked him and let him off the phone. *Weirdo.* She got dressed and drove toward town. As she did, a gentle quake shook the car.

The women at the reception desk were expecting Noelle. One of them led her down the stairs to the cool basement and waved her through the doors before turning back. Noelle opened the push doors to the morgue and walked inside. The room reeked of chemicals.

Something moved in a dark corner of the space. Noelle froze. The bright lights elsewhere in the lab made it difficult for her eyes to adjust to the dark place that delivered the noise. She couldn't see a thing. She sensed a large, human-sized shape there but couldn't be sure. Suddenly a bright LED ray shined directly into her eyes. The beam of light blinded her. Panic gripped her.

"Holy . . ." The man's voice faded to calm. "Whoa, you scared me there, miss! I thought Smith left. Should you be down here? Excuse my language." The man hadn't even let an expletive escape his lips.

Noelle hoped her own fear wasn't quite as apparent as she took a deep breath. "Er . . . yeah. It's okay. I spoke with Smith earlier; he gave me permission to take a look at a body. What are *you* doing down here?"

The man switched off his headlamp and stepped into the light. He was in his late sixties. "Working on these halogens. Whole row has been out for two weeks. I can't figure it out. It's not the bulbs or the power source . . ."

Noelle looked up at the steel fixtures with their chrome reflectors, understanding now. Before she could speak again the man glanced at his watch and excused himself for a coffee break.

"Be back in a few."

She shook off the remaining chills and moved farther into the room. Approaching the wall of drawers, she checked for the red name tag that meant there was a body inside. Empty, empty, empty. Only one compartment was in use.

Noelle grabbed the cold chrome handle on the drawer and pulled it open to find a black zippered bag. Before opening it, she put on a pair of latex gloves that she grabbed from Smith's desk. She took a deep breath and slid the zipper down.

The sight and smells weren't as grotesque as she expected. The man looked like one of those plastic corpses from a science exhibit and the only scent was that of the chemicals. Noelle took the top part of the bag that was still obscuring her view of the body and tucked it under in a few spots, under his head, his shoulders, and his heels.

There was a long Y-shaped cut starting at either shoulder, converging at the sternum, and ending shortly below and left of the belly button. The incision had not yet been stitched shut. Noelle could see that the victim's organs were inside, but contained in a plastic bag. Reinserted for burial, she assumed.

Noelle looked closely at the puncture wounds. No signs of scratching or tearing, just pencil-girthed holes punched into the chest cavity. Turning the body on its side, Noelle felt around the man's back for wounds but found none. That probably ruled out a bite. She was rethinking the possibilities when the broken light flickered for a second and then came on brightly.

"What the hell?" Noelle was a little startled. Her nerves still hadn't settled since her surprise run-in with the hospital's engineer. On the exam table directly under the recently repaired light was the engineer's tool belt.

"No way," Noelle said in a whisper. She walked over to the tools, grabbed one, and then went back to the desk for another glove. She slid the shaft of the screwdriver into the forefinger compartment of the glove to keep it sterile. Plus, it seemed disrespectful not to. Then she lined up the screwdriver with one of the puncture wounds. The shank slid through with just a little force.

Noelle checked the other wounds too. "No way," she said again, aloud.

She set down the tool and looked closer at the penetration points. Around the wounds were halos of bruised skin, three-quarters of an inch, perhaps. She placed the screwdriver in the wound again. The hard plastic lip where the shaft met the handle perfectly matched the size of the bruise.

The bruising must have increased slowly after the man's death! she thought. *There's no other way the coroner could have missed this.*

Noelle zipped the bag and quickly closed the drawer. She put the screwdriver back in its place and tossed the rubber gloves on the way out. As she went up the stairs, taking two at a time, she passed the engineer.

"Light's fixed!" she said between breaths.

"I figured—they just told me that last fixture was on a different fuse. Hey, why are you in such a hurry?"

Noelle didn't say anything. She ran to the car, started the engine, and picked up her mobile. She had to call Jake.

To her dismay, his phone rang without answer. Noelle couldn't leave a message; the news was just too big. She sped north.

The camp was still a ghost town like it had been the day before. Jake surveyed the cabins, lean-tos, and old canvas tents. No sign of anyone. The Impala was gone, likely towed back to Jackson. Jake stayed still and observed for a moment, as if just breathing the air and looking around might yield some clue. The cool wind lent an extra dose of loneliness.

Strange, really. Like a commune or something.

His tactic yielded nothing else, so Jake started looking around inside the structures. After scrounging around in three empty tents and the main cabin, a lean-to gave him some hope.

Bingo.

Stuffed into the nook between two lodgepole supports, Jake found a thin book. He pushed aside some of the smaller branches making up the wind stop and pulled it out. The shoddy wall fell outward as he did so.

The book was ratty and faded from the elements but the title was easy to read. It said, *Avalanches: Causes, Prevention, and Rescue.* Jake leafed through it, looking for anything that might provide him with more information on the camp and its deserters. The receipt for the book, purchased at the Montana State University bookstore, was folded into the middle of chapter 7, which was titled "Wet-Slab Avalanches."

His heartbeat increased and he looked around the camp. Still deserted. Jake sat down on a worn log that must have been used as a bench by the previous occupants.

Back to the book. Jake flipped to the beginning of the marked chapter and started there. On some pages he found highlighted words, and on others notes scrawled in the margins. The focus of the reader was clearly on the triggers of wet-slab avalanches rather than prevention and rescue: "occur in spring during rainy and/or warm periods," "unlikely to be triggered by skiers," "except in periods of high rainfall, occur most often in the afternoon on sun-exposed aspects," and "slow-moving but extremely destructive."

"Shit!" Jake closed the book and jogged to his vehicle with it in his hand. The book hadn't revealed everything—why or how the Maelstrom avalanche had been started, for example—but it revealed enough. Jake was almost certain now: the avalanche on Maelstrom wasn't an accident at all.

He knew what he had to do next. He had to try to get in contact with Mr. Ricker, the survivor of the Maelstrom slide. Jake had a gut feeling that Ricker wouldn't be easy to find.

He got in the car and checked his phone. A missed call from Noelle. He had spotty reception there in the woods and was too excited to pursue his new lead to return her call at the moment anyway. When the reception improved, he dialed the Jackson station and asked to speak with the chief.

"Roger, it's Jake." He held the phone with his shoulder as he used both hands to make a right turn back toward Jackson Hole. "I need another favor, if I might."

"I'll see what the favor is first, if *I* might."

Jake sensed some hostility in Terrell's voice.

"Of course. I need the contact info for that Ricker guy that survived the avy up on Maelstrom. I think he's involved in all this, but I'm not sure how. I'll give you my evidence if you let me talk to him first. *These guys are after me, Roger.*"

The chief laughed. It sounded manic to Jake. "We already got his statement, he was clean. If there's new evidence, we need it *now*. You talk to him first, he'll disappear before we even have a chance. If he does stick around, he'll know he's been found out. What the hell do you think he did wrong anyway? He might have been stupid, but he didn't do anything illegal. You're not a cop, Jake. Never were and certainly aren't now."

"I have evidence, Roger," Jake pleaded. "I just need to have him alone. I'm convinced this doesn't end with him. If your guys arrest him, he doesn't talk and we lose our trail. I—"

"I said no, Jake. Anything else?"

Jake hung up the phone without answering him. *Dammit.* Until the last couple days, he always thought Terrell respected him. Now he wasn't so sure.

What the hell is going on around here?

He had no real chance of getting to Ricker now. Jake wondered if he was better off just giving up the information to Terrell and the cops, but what if the cops botched the investigation, deliberately or accidentally?

True, Jake wasn't a cop; he was much more than that. Jake knew that if Ricker was a pawn in a scheme to destroy him like J.P. suggested, he wouldn't give up any names to the cops with such weak evidence against him. There was no reason to; he would know that the cops couldn't build a case.

Shit!

Now closer to town, Jake returned Noelle's call.

"We need to meet up," Jake said hastily.

"Agreed. My place. Twenty minutes."

Both vehicles pulled into Noelle's driveway at the same time. Jake got out and walked quickly over to Noelle's door to open it, but she scrambled out before he could get there.

"They killed him with a screwdriver! The bear did, that is. The impostor bear!" Jake followed Noelle's hasty path to the porch, but not her line of reasoning.

"Slow down. What?" Jake's news would have to wait. They stopped at the front door.

"Sorry, come in." She opened the screen. "The couple that everyone thought was attacked by a bear. You and I, though, we knew something was off about it! We were right! They didn't run into a bear up there at the lake, they ran into a killer with a screwdriver. He was definitely murdered, Jake. No doubt about it."

"How do you know?"

"I went to see the body at the morgue. The guy's body. And it didn't look right, you know? From the beginning, we heard 'puncture wounds,' and guess what? The wounds, I examined them closely and it looked like someone just stabbed him with a screwdriver. No slicing or cutting, Jake. Just straight through." Noelle neglected to mention the lucky sighting of the tool.

She continued. "So I went and I got a screwdriver. Just a regular Phillips head like this one. Short shaft." Noelle held up the implement she'd borrowed from the park. "And I checked it. And it fits perfectly in each wound. There is even a mark where each thrust came to its end when the handle hit flesh. I bet that screwdriver is up there somewhere, Jake. We have to go look."

"Hold on. Just because a certain object fits into this guy's wounds doesn't rule out everything else."

Noelle had overlooked this in her excitement. "Well, I know that. I mean, it was just perfect, though. Halos, Jake! There were little circular bruises from the handle hitting the skin." She walked to Jake and showed him the part of the plastic handle that she was talking about, pointing emphatically.

"Okay. Maybe you're right. If you are, I think you'll want to hold off on calling the police until you hear me out . . ." Jake tried to butt in with his own news.

Noelle was offended. "I didn't mean I would call the police, I thought we could—"

"Just listen for a minute. Relax." Jake hesitated. "I'm not sure we can trust Terrell."

"What?" This surprised Noelle, though she had found the chief's recent behavior a bit odd.

"I'm not sure why. I just get the feeling he wants to ruin me for some reason. Jealousy? I don't know." Jake realized this sounded cocky. "But look, I found something up at that camp too. Something that I think proves that the avalanche wasn't an accident. I think the survivor of the slide was the one who killed the victim. And on the way back, I realized a few things. Why wasn't there anyone at that camp when we got there? Somebody must have tipped them off. And how did Terrell even end up so close to an accident that almost killed J.P.? In a car registered in my name no less. Who would have easier access to change the title than the chief of police?"

Noelle looked astonished. "I don't know, Jake. Now *you* need to slow down. Sounds like a stretch, doesn't it? And think about it—Terrell could have already killed or arrested you . . . or whatever his intentions were. Why wouldn't he have done it by now?"

"That's the thing I don't understand," Jake admitted. "Maybe he's toying with me—maybe he just wants me to leave town."

"What did you find up there, anyway?"

"A book. A guide to avalanche safety. There was the avalanche on Maelstrom and—"

Noelle interrupted. "Yeah, but think about where we are, Jake. Everybody has that book, or one like it. I've got one right there." Noelle pointed to a small bookshelf that hosted *Surviving Avalanches* among others.

"No. No, it wasn't just the book that made me think, it was what the reader was interested in. Whoever owned the book took a really keen interest in how wet-slab avalanches start. They highlighted almost every other word in that section. Notes too."

"You're thinking a single person is responsible for all this?"

"No, not a single person. How could one person do it all? Plus, we found a *camp*. Gotta be more than one person involved. I'm certain that everything is connected now. An organized group."

Jake was drawing conclusions and playing out the rest of the script in his head as he spoke.

It dawned on him now that whether it was vengeful criminals

from his past or Terrell or someone else, he knew he would have to involve the federal authorities at some point. It was too risky to reach out to the town police for help with Terrell in charge. Jake had plenty of friends in the business: CIA and FBI.

Noelle didn't let the silence last too long. "Okay. Either way, what do we do next?" Jake snapped out of his inner monologue.

"We don't have enough information to go to Terrell or his police force. Even if he isn't involved, he won't believe us. We need to talk to that kid who survived the avalanche. J.P. knows him—they're at least acquaintances."

"Who is he?" Noelle asked as Jake dialed J.P.

He'd better answer.

"Don't know much about him, really." Second ring. "He's been involved with some protests and things in the past. Arrested actually, during one of them." Rings three and four.

"You think he's still in town?"

"Don't know." The call rang one final time and went to J.P.'s voice mail.

"Shit!"

"What's wrong?"

"J.P., he's just impossible to get ahold of sometimes." Jake was grabbing for the doorknob.

"Where are you going?"

"I'll run into town and try to find J.P. Any better ideas?"

Noelle gave him a quizzical look. "Uh, the Internet—do a search for him, social networks, whatever. It'll take a second. If we don't find anything, I'll help you find J.P."

Noelle's idea was obvious, but Jake had overlooked it. Noelle went to her bedside and picked up her laptop. As she plunked it down on the table, Jake went outside to get the other chair.

They huddled next to each other on one side of the table, and Noelle turned the machine on. When the search engine came up she asked Jake for the name.

"Graham Ricker," Jake said. "I think his first name was Graham."

The results came in. A Facebook profile. "Looks like it's spelled Graem. Must be him. Location is Jackson, Wyoming. Let me log in."

"You're a member?" Jake asked.

"Yeah, sure. Just to keep track of old friends and stuff. People from school." She was a little embarrassed, even though she was younger and more computer savvy than Jake.

"*Everybody* is. It's not like I'm e-dating or anything."

The comment lingered awkwardly in the air.

"Wait—I think I've actually skied with this guy before," Noelle said as she examined his profile and pictures. "I met him in a carpool group for skiers. I can send him a message through the site. What should I say?"

Jake thought. J.P. was the more obvious route. At least J.P. and Ricker seemed to have a connection.

Damn. The hit and run. If Ricker was involved, hearing from J.P. might spook him. He'd likely leave town before I even got a chance. Even if J.P. asked around about where Ricker lived, word might get back to him through the grapevine.

"Just ask him for it," Jake finally said.

"Huh?"

"Just ask him. If you can send him a message, send one and ask for his number. It's the least suspicious thing you can do."

"You think that will really work?" Noelle was skeptical. It was too barefaced. Too direct. "Hold on, I think it might. I always get these messages from people on this site that say they lost their phone or got a new one. They want their old phone's contact information back. I usually send my number, even if I'm not sure who the person is or how they got my number in the first place."

Jake nodded at her when she looked up from the computer screen, even though he didn't quite grasp the laws of social networking.

"Okay. I'm gonna send it." She typed, "Hey Graem, lost my phone. Could I have ur number?"

"Now what?" she asked Jake.

"Now we wait. I'm going home. See if J.P. has any info on Ricker. Call me right away if you hear back." Jake let his hand slide across her shoulders as he excused himself past her and out the door.

He was on his way home when another stray thunderstorm hit the valley. He thought he felt a slight quake, but it could've been the thunder. He clicked on the wipers and slowed down.

Murder, deception, and who knows what else?

The rain had a sentimental effect on Jake. He thought about Philadelphia. His past life. In some sense, he missed the excitement and danger of it all, the challenge of outsmarting the bad guys and cracking the case. Putting his life on the line for the greater good. His investigations had always begun with those feelings, though.

But at some point, the excitement and thrill always morphed into tangible peril. That part he didn't miss. He could feel it when the change occurred. It was as if a far-off war being played out on television news and radio came crashing into your hometown. Maybe it was the rain and darkness, but Jake sensed that moment was coming soon.

18

GRAND TETON NATIONAL PARK. THE NEXT DAY.

It was early Monday morning. A new workweek. Noelle was up and about, checking her messages for a response from Graem Ricker. After four or five times looking at an empty in-box, her enthusiasm wore off and she felt tired, so she walked over to her kitchenette and fixed some instant coffee. Now she was out of both sugar and milk. The brew was bitter without accoutrements, but it got the job done.

Noelle looked at her watch and remembered that she had to be at work at eight thirty. *An hour and a half.* She still had a real life to tend to. Before she left for her patrol, she checked her work email. Her supervisor at the park had emailed her and asked that she check on the trail crews throughout the park to make sure they were on course to complete their work before the tourist season began.

The trail crews were responsible for maintaining the park's many hiking paths. They removed downed trees that crossed the trail, diverted snow runoff that interfered with the route, and monitored erosion. If a section of trail became damaged due to overuse, they were also responsible for rerouting the trail and closing the area.

The crews were mostly composed of locals in their early twenties who considered the job a pretty good gig. They were left alone for days on end, camping in the wilderness and working at their own pace. Unfortunately for Noelle and her superiors, this sometimes meant they slacked off. Noelle's random inspections were aimed to remedy this.

If she wanted to fit a run in, she would have to go now. She closed her computer, tied her shoes, and bounced down the stairs. The cold, dry air wafted easily through her synthetic mesh T-shirt. It chilled her completely, so she picked up the pace. She would make one loop around the camping area that was adjacent to her cabin and then grab her shower stuff. After her shower, she planned to start her random checkups around Gosling Lake.

Monday mornings meant less to Jake since his retirement, but he woke up early nonetheless. He checked his cell phone for a call from Noelle. Nothing yet.

He then checked the reservations system on the desktop computer downstairs. There weren't any bookings for the next two weeks. Big surprise. The unpredictable weather in the early summer could deter visitors, but he wondered whether news of the unsolved crimes or the earthquakes could be to blame.

There had been several articles on the crimes in the local paper, but nobody had cause yet to link the incidents together and paint the frightening picture that Jake and Noelle were starting to see.

The major national news websites didn't give the accidents much coverage either. There were a few mentions of the avalanche and the bear attack in the various travel sections, but nothing else. None of the articles made any connection between the incidents.

This didn't surprise Jake. He knew that the police department was almost entirely responsible for press releases in the valley. If Terrell didn't want to reveal too much, it might not reach the outside media for some time.

The earthquakes were a different story. Their continuing occurrence was now starting to attract national media attention. Snippets from the Jackson Hole paper were turning up on all the major news websites.

Grabbing his mug and a handful of granola from the kitchen, Jake headed out to the garage. On the way, he stopped and poked his head into J.P.'s trailer, but it was empty. Jake didn't hear him come in last night, which worried him only slightly. If there was a party somewhere, it was a good bet that J.P. had found it. He called J.P.'s cell but there was no answer.

Still sleeping, probably. Damn. Jake had wanted to talk to him about Ricker. *Oh well.* He let the trailer door close behind him and headed to his vehicle.

In the garage, Jake unscrewed the top from the glossy green tube that held his favorite creek rod. A custom-made eight-foot-four weight. Fiberglass. Outdated now, since everything was graphite. But it had more soul than its graphite counterparts.

The fiberglass eight footer wasn't built for winging flies seventy feet to the far bank. That's what stealth was for. If you couldn't get closer than that, you were probably more of a caster than an angler anyway.

No, the eight footer was a fishing machine. A tool. With a heavy fish on the end of the line, it absorbed runs and headshakes with its flex, protecting the light tippet. It bent but never broke.

Fish were feeding everywhere along the banks and in the bubble lines, clueless as to the earthquakes and murders. Above the gentle current, pale morning duns flitted and flirted, preparing to mate.

Jake finished his meager breakfast, put his mug down in the grass, and rigged up the rod. He tied a size 18 spinner to the end of the leader. Pale yellow, like the insects above him. The spinner represented the final stage of the insect, the fragile, ethereal, and lifeless form that fell to the water's surface after it had mated.

On his first cast, a trout lazily drifted toward the fly and inhaled it, but the hook didn't hold. Jake brought in the rig to dry off the small fly.

As he did so, Jake pondered what to do with the evidence at hand. He wanted to build his case more, but if he came up empty-handed he needed a backup plan to protect himself. He trusted the friends that he made during his years as a Philadelphia special investigator; federal prosecutors, FBI agents, and state cops would believe him.

The FBI in particular would be interested in looking into any allegations of a corrupt and criminal police force, but he still felt it was too soon. He had no doubt he could get a team to fly in from the East Coast and investigate, but he was worried that it might put their jobs on the line. If Jake was wrong, his friends would take the brunt of it from the head honchos. The federal government wasn't keen on wasting public funds on domestic crime hunches these days. At the most, he might consider calling on his friends for a bit of investigative research. They had access to databases that the normal civilian couldn't imagine.

Jake made another cast. This time, he brought the yellow-bellied trout to hand after two strong runs into the current. He released the fish carefully and washed his hands in the creek.

When they were dry, he reached into his pocket for his cell phone and called Noelle.

"Jake? Is everything okay?"

He cleared his throat. "Fine, yeah. Was just calling to see if you've heard anything back from that site—from Graem Ricker, I mean." Jake picked up his coffee and sat himself down on a stump, listening attentively. The sun was starting to dry the long grass near the creek of its morning dew. It needed to be mowed.

"Oh. No, I haven't, I would have called. I won't be near my computer for a few hours, though. I'm working. Probably be back at one or two."

"Okay. Listen, can I check your computer while you're gone? I've got nothing going on today, and I think we need to chat with Ricker as soon as possible."

Noelle felt the earth shiver for a second and looked down at the dirt around her feet. A small rock had hopped up from the ground and squarely onto the toe of her shoe. She kicked it off.

"Yeah, that'd be fine. The key is under the rock to the right of the second step. My computer is by the bed. I'm logged in, so all you need to do is open it up and click refresh to check my messages." She hoped there weren't any embarrassing messages in her in-box. "I'll try to hurry back."

Jake finished his coffee and went back inside to get dressed and brush his teeth. The feeding trout would have to wait.

The weather was getting warmer by the day and Jake was able to drive at highway speeds with the windows open, although he still wore a light jacket. He arrived at the cabin, and the key was where Noelle told him. He felt somewhat awkward going into the cabin without Noelle—it was small and there wasn't room for any of it to be free of her personal belongings. There were dirty clothes in a pile next to the bed and hand-washed bras hanging above the kitchen sink.

He smiled and looked around. It was nice to be around a woman again.

Is that why I drove up here? He shrugged the question off.

Jake opened the computer and moved his fingers on the touch sensor mouse to wake it up. He clicked the refresh button on the top left of the browser screen. The page reloaded but no new messages appeared. He walked outside and wasted a few minutes wandering around, then came back in and clicked the button again. Nothing. Back outside again. He got a bottle of water from his truck and drank it. It was cold, almost frozen, from the night. He thought about how silly it was to sit here expecting the message to arrive any minute. There was no reason to think the man would ever reply, let alone right now as Jake waited expectantly.

He thought about Noelle as he paced on the porch. Beautiful, clever, and charming. The more time he spent with her, the more he liked her. He was beginning to feel that it was his duty to protect her from whatever it was that was happening in the valley.

Back inside again. Click. Nothing. He was only staying for one more try.

This is a waste of time.

He should be doing something else, hiking up to Maelstrom to see the avalanche path and looking for clues or going back up to the camp. Any number of things would probably pan out better than this. He went back to the computer.

A message had been received. Jake clicked on the category on the left margin titled "Messages." The only message there had the subject line "sure." He opened it. The message stated the coveted info straight up; it simply read "sure" and then a local phone number. From: Graem Ricker. The long shot had panned out.

Jake couldn't believe his luck. Assuming the man was involved with the crimes, he had given up a vital bit of information. Jake could use the phone number to get an address.

Although he was eager to get moving, Jake decided to wait for Noelle before making a move on Ricker. He thought she would be a valuable asset if the man was hostile. Rather than just showing up at the man's house himself, he hoped that Noelle could get Ricker to meet them in public somewhere.

If Jake fooled him using Noelle's account, he would flee the second he saw Jake. Or he would never answer the door in the first place. In public, Jake could be assured the interaction would be safe. He wasn't willing to drag Noelle into a dangerous situation. Surprising a criminal at his house was the definition of dangerous.

Jake looked at the alarm clock on Noelle's bed stand. He had plenty of time to kill before she got back from work. With too much energy to sit around and wait, he decided to go up to the top of Maelstrom Couloir.

He also wanted to talk to his contact at the FBI, but it was lunchtime on the East Coast. Lunch break was one of the few things the government did on time every time.

I'll call when I get back.

Jake felt like they were on the threshold of discovering something important. He knew this probably meant things were coming to a head on the other end of the equation too, so he would have to be cautious. He had no idea what the end game was for whatever dark force was working against him.

He stood up from the table and scrawled a note for Noelle saying he would be back around 1:30 p.m.

For now, checking out Maelstrom was his best bet for making progress. He jumped in his SUV and headed toward the ski area, windows down again and ignoring the speed limit. He paid the fee to park close to the base area and went to the ticket office. "One ticket, please." It was possible to hike up to the couloir, but the trail was about seven miles in length and nearly a vertical mile up. Instead, he chose to ride the tram. From the top, it was only a mile of level walking outside the resort boundaries to Maelstrom. There would be some snow left, but the harsh Wyoming wind kept the trail across the ridge mostly bare. It was only an hour round-trip. By then Noelle would be done with work.

Jake boarded the tram with a group of tourists and a few diehard skiers who were using the lift to access the high alpine terrain, just like Jake. The visitors, from all parts of the world, took pictures of the valley, the mountain, and each other. They gasped with fright each time the tram swung slightly in the wind.

When the tram landed at the summit, Jake moved through the crowd and started on his way, heading south along the rocky ridge. The wind was strong, as always, and blowing from the west. The temperature was easily twenty-five degrees cooler than at the valley floor. With no equipment, Jake was able to keep a big lead on the skiers who were headed in the same direction. This was fine with him; he had no idea who was involved with the efforts against him and he didn't want to be seen snooping around up there.

Jake scrambled across the craggy granite ridgeline and passed the entrances to many popular backcountry runs: Regret-a-Bowl, Just Chute Me, Paradise, Veni, Vedi, and Vici. The runs plummeted off to his left at varying degrees of steepness. Unlike Maelstrom Couloir, these chutes faced directly east. Before he came upon it, the ridge that Jake was on made an abrupt westerly turn, revealing Maelstrom, which faced due south.

Jake stepped as close to the precipitous drop as his sensibility allowed. He looked down. This was where the avalanche was born. Below him, he could see where the snow slab had started its journey down the hill. Only a dozen feet past the entrance, there was a sheer cut in the snow—what avalanche experts called a crown—at a ninety-degree angle from the pitch of the slope. This was where the snow had torn free from the material beneath it, beginning its deadly slide.

The crown was somewhat affected by the sun now; its edges were softened and decayed. Farther down, the debris pile showed the terminus of the avalanche. Somewhere in that pile was where the rescuers had found the victim, suffocated to death by snow.

Jake thought about how it might have happened: the south-facing slope would have absorbed the early summer sun, causing moisture to drip through the snowpack from the surface and run downhill along a lower layer of snow or even along the ground. When the underwater flow weakened the supporting snow enough, the surface slab would break free.

Although this type of avalanche moved slowly, it would be quick enough to overtake a skier on a slope as steep as Maelstrom. Once it caught up with you, the soggy snow would be so dense that it would be impossible to escape its grasp. *A horrible death, no doubt.* Jake started his walk back to the tram.

He didn't make it very far. A sense of vertigo washed over him. He stopped walking, thinking he must be getting ill, but the feeling didn't cease when he stopped. Jake looked down at his feet and noticed a few pebbles nervously bouncing around like popcorn on the granite. Then more.

There was a tremble from deep within the earth. Some heavier stones were moving now, breaking away from the larger mass that had held them from the beginning of time. Jake looked to his right, down the chutes. A tumble down any one of them would likely result in death. He felt the earth rumble beneath him again, intensifying every moment.

Slabs of snow were losing their anchor to the steeper slopes and cascading downward toward the flats below. Jake checked his footing. Rocks, larger yet, were bouncing into the accumulating flow of snow, granite, and debris going down the mountain. He backed up several feet and got low to the ground. Like a climber on a hazardous face, he grabbed the rock and held on.

19

SOUTH BOUNDARY, JACKSON HOLE MOUNTAIN RESORT

As abruptly as it started, the earth made one final shiver—the strongest yet—and stopped. The debris flow continued for a few moments longer and then silence fell over the mountain. Jake took stock of his surroundings. The damage was significant, but not catastrophic. The ridgeline trail remained mostly intact. The largest boulders were still in place above the slope, but several pieces of granite approaching the size of golf carts had been shaken loose. They now rested at the bottom of the steep chutes.

Jake's breathing and heart rate slowly began to return to normal. *That was close.* His mind turned to the avalanche—*Maybe the book was a coincidence? Maybe a quake started the slide?*

Deep in thought, he made his way along the trail, reminding himself to stay focused, be careful. Another seismic event or even his own footfall could trigger a dangerous rockslide. He kept his eyes open for injured skiers and hikers but didn't notice anyone.

When he made it back to the tram dock at the top of the resort's main peak, the lift wasn't running. The woman at the top told him they had recorded a major quake. It didn't likely damage the tram, she said, but the engineers needed to have a look. Just to be sure. The lift would be down for at least an hour.

As dazed tourists congregated at the top to chatter about the quake, Jake decided to walk the maintenance roads to his vehicle. He had to get back to Noelle's cabin. He noted the damage on the way down. Below cliff faces and steep rocky slopes, there was evidence of more rockfall. As Jake lost altitude and the terrain became less steep, though, the signs of the quake mostly disappeared.

The hike to the bottom of the mountain took longer than it looked, more than an hour.

Noelle was waiting on her cabin's porch. She ran to the driver's door and opened it for him.

"Are you okay? Did you feel the quake?" She looked him over. He seemed fine, at least physically.

"I felt it all right." They walked inside. Jake put his keys down on the table, shaking his head. "Could I have a glass of water?" Noelle filled a glass. The normally calm man was rattled, which caught Noelle's attention. She tilted her head with curiosity as she handed him the drink.

Jake continued after his first sip. "It felt like the mountain was coming down up there. Rocks falling, little avalanches and cornices breaking off. I thought I was gonna get swept off the peak too. A 5.1, they said? Pretty rare around here, huh?"

"Hold on. Where *were* you?" She held up her hands, palms out.

"Top of Maelstrom. I know, I know. I just wanted to put my eyes on the scene before we talked to Ricker. I was up top there when I felt the quake. It really moved some stuff around. Rockfalls, the whole nine yards." Jake drank more water.

"Was anyone hurt? What did you find?"

"Not a thing."

Noelle paused. "Well, I looked around this morning near the Gosling site. I thought maybe I would find the screwdriver, or anything that would help—a shoe print, who knows? Nada. There's too much land to cover. If someone wanted to dispose of a body it'd never be found, never mind a six-inch screwdriver. I talked to the trail crew too. Nobody had seen or heard anything about the attack other than from the newspapers."

Jake nodded. "I've got good news. You got a message. Graem Ricker actually gave us his phone—"

Noelle cut in. "I know." She brought her computer to the table. Jake held out his hand for it and Noelle obliged.

"If I can send an email from your computer, I can get his billing address. I know a guy . . ." Jake trailed off. "It should only take a few minutes."

With his email open, Jake glanced up at Noelle, who was standing behind him, watching. She got the idea. Privacy.

She sat down across from Jake and the computer. He knew that Noelle wouldn't recognize any of the FBI domains used for covert communication—@hammerco.com, @magazinepub.com, @20sumthingdate.com, and so on—but it was easier to avoid questioning. Jake got to the point quickly:

Daniel:

Long time no see, friend. Let's fix that sometime.

Need a physical address for the following name and mobile number, no PO box.

Jake typed the name and number and clicked send. Before he could finish telling Noelle that it shouldn't take long a new email arrived.

Jake:

Will do. Gimme 10. Walking back from cafeteria.

Sent from my iPhone

"Ten minutes," Jake said. "Think you can wait that long?" He smiled.

"Pretty resourceful buddy."

"He spends all day sitting in a cubicle." This much was true. "I'm sure he's loving the excitement." The latter part wasn't true. Daniel spent his days doing work that was far more meaningful and stimulating than hacking an address for an old friend. Still, he owed Jake a few favors.

Ping. The reply was as succinct as the request:

722 Ranch St., Basement Apt, Jackson.

Agreed on the get-together. East or west?

Dan

Jake was entering the address into his phone's notes. "It's on Ranch Street. I don't want to surprise him at home, though, unless that's our last option. Try to arrange for a meeting somewhere. If not, I'll head into town and check his apartment, but I'd like to do this out in public in case he's dangerous."

"How do I do that? He may be dumb enough to give out his cell number, but if I ask him to hang out, don't you think he'll find it strange? I don't know him that well. It's been years since I saw him last."

"Ask him on a date. What man could say no to that?" He cracked a smile.

"Are you serious?" Noelle asked. The look on Jake's face insisted he was.

Noelle sighed and typed.

Graem, long time no see. Want to grab a beer sometime soon?
:) *Noelle*

Jake stayed at Noelle's for a few hours. They chatted, waiting to hear from Ricker, but nothing came through. At five thirty, he excused himself and drove home. Noelle promised to call the minute she heard anything.

Jake prepared dinner for himself and J.P., who evidently had just woken up. The game freezer was still nearly full from last hunting season, so the pair agreed on elk T-bones and a Caesar salad. Neither Jake nor J.P. hunted, but friends did.

It wasn't that either morally objected to it. They were meat eaters and knew it was a fact of life. But for both men, there had been moments in their past that inexorably linked gunfire—the sound, the recoil's punch, the smoking barrel—to something far more disturbing than taking an animal for food.

Still, every fall, they would each help a few buddies carry out their kills. They were always rewarded with meat. Last fall had been cold and snowy, bringing more animals than usual into the valleys, where they were accessible to hunters. It seemed like everyone who ventured out was bagging big cow elk and mule deer.

J.P.'s assistance consisted mostly of drinking beer while standing in the kitchen. And he was in charge of the grilling, of course. "The only manly thing about cooking," he liked to say.

"The secret with game," J.P. preached for the millionth time, "is to either cook it way long, like in a Crock-Pot or a stew, or barely cook it all." Jake generally liked his meat medium rare, but he would rather eat a bloody steak than insult his friend's grilling prowess. It was one of the few things J.P. took seriously.

"Grab a beer, man! What're you doing empty-handed out here?" J.P. pointed toward the handmade wooden steps leading to his trailer's front door. Beside them sat a blue tub with a few beers cooling in water from the creek.

"I'm gonna pass, thanks. I might have something to do tonight that requires a clear head."

"Aw, shit. Suit yourself, then." J.P. laid the thawed steaks on the grill. There was a pause. "Well, c'mon. Whaddya have going on later that's so important?" He was waving smoke from the burning remnants of past meals away from his face.

"I want to try to talk to that Ricker kid. See what he knows about all this stuff. It may be nothing, but I'd be willing to bet he doesn't let me down." Jake was looking at the art on J.P.'s beer bottle, a microbrew from Washington State. J.P. motioned for Jake to hand it over and took a chug.

"Really? You think that dumbass is the one after you?" Another swig.

"I don't think so, no. I just think he's involved with whatever *is* going on around here—"

CRACK!

What the . . . ?

At first the noise didn't make sense to Jake. Then he felt the rushing air and the sudden warmth. The last sense to contribute was sight, and it confirmed what the other senses suggested—fire, light, heat. An explosion.

The propane tank below the grill had burst and was spewing flames from a hole in its side. J.P. was still stunned, standing close enough to the grill that flames were licking at his forearms, his horrified face lit up by pyrotechnics.

20

Jake lunged for J.P. as he tried to beat back the inferno with his hands.

They fell off the porch together and onto a soft pad of dead pine needles. Jake stood up, grabbed J.P. by the shirt, and pulled him away from the inferno. At about thirty yards out, Jake looked J.P. over for injuries.

His friend seemed okay. They both glanced back at the burning grill, speechless, expecting a massive explosion, but it never came. The flames fizzled out in a few moments, and the men cautiously returned to the porch. Smoldering ashes littered the wood panels, but the house was safe. J.P. went inside and returned with a pitcher to douse the remaining flames. After a few trips with the water, J.P. sat down in the wet mess and lit a cigarette.

"I guess we're eating out tonight, my friend," he said between puffs.

"Guess so." Jake grabbed his keys and the men loaded up. Before he started the vehicle, Jake turned to J.P. "You still like grilling?"

J.P. smiled. "Bug off, man. Your grill is faulty! Let's sue the mamma jammas who made that death trap." He turned up the radio and put his window down.

As he approached the end of the driveway, a hundred yards from the grill, Jake stopped, clicked off the music, and put the SUV in park. "Sonofabitch!" He practically flew out the door and jogged to a stand of pine trees along the main road, only twenty-five feet from the intersection with the drive. He bent and picked up a shiny object. Twirled it in his fingers and looked around. He walked back to the car.

"What's up, man?"

Between his forefinger and thumb, Jake held the brass shell of a seven-millimeter rifle round. He was careful to touch only the firing ring. It was still hot and could be dusted for prints. J.P. brought his hand up and covered his mouth in disbelief. "Shit, let's get outta here, man."

Jake looked around in the darkness but couldn't see a thing. He floored it out of the driveway.

Two hundred yards to the west, hidden in the pines, Makter laughed out loud. He took the rifle apart and put it in his backpack, then walked back toward the road.

Jake and J.P. ate their barbecue in a deserted diner in town. One or the other would look around every so often. Neither could finish his meal. Paranoid, maybe, but someone had just tried to kill them. Or at least Jake. If he were J.P., he would've left Jake for his own safety, but Jake knew that would never cross his friend's mind. He was too loyal.

J.P. flipped through a newspaper, shaking his head.

"Everybody wants to be in control, man," he said with his face still buried in the pages.

"What?" Jake had been wrapped in his own tangled thoughts.

"In nature and stuff. Just, like, look at the news any day. Elk population is too big, elk population is too small, wolves should be eliminated, wolves should be protected, we should put out wild-fires, we should let them burn—"

"What are you getting at?" Jake interrupted.

"Like, do you think any of it makes any difference? Do you think we as humans can make the world a better or worse place? Is that even possible?"

Jake thought for a moment. "Sure, civil rights for example."

"No, man, like in the natural world. Can we make it what we want? Can we improve upon Mother Nature? It seems like every time we try, we end up worse off."

"Don't know, really. Seems to be a popular ambition. Since the beginning of time."

"Yeah, man." J.P. was deep in thought again.

"I don't know, J.P. Not something I'm really focused on right now." Jake immediately regretted sounding harsh, but his friend didn't seem to take offense to the dismissal.

"Right on." J.P. looked around anxiously, thinking about what to talk about next. "So, this is all gotta be connected to your past, right? I know you were a criminal lawyer or whatever, but you never really told me much about it."

"Yeah, sort of. I worked at a prosecutor's office for a while." He hated having this conversation, even with close friends.

"Well, like, how did you know that shell back at the house was a seven millimeter?"

The question caught Jake off guard. "Oh, well . . ." *Shit. Because they're almost the same rounds used by military Special Forces and police marksmen, the same rounds my snipers used in raids.* Then it occurred to him. "It says right there on the shell."

"Oh, ha. Duh!" J.P. seemed satisfied with the answer and went back to his paper.

Phew.

Jake was always careful not to reveal too much. It could get him and those around him in a whole lot of trouble.

It seemed like a different world now. One that Jake only occasionally missed. *The Big Office.* That's what they'd called the federal Office of Special Investigations. The umbrella organization, the DOJ, called it the "other office," referring initially to its secrecy and eventually its irrelevance.

Chasing Nemo. That was the code name. No coincidence *nemo* meant "no one"—the targets were often elusive, shadows in the fog. *I have to go to Portugal to chase Nemo.* Nazis. War criminals. Terrorists. The deepest and darkest evil that has ever existed on this earth. Eradicate them, that was the main job of the Big Office. The Big Office punished those who committed crimes against humanity.

Then there was the Philly Office. Totally unrelated to the Big Office, except for the fact that so many of the officers moved to smaller offices around the country once the slime from World War II, Bosnia, Serbia, Darfur, and Rwanda had been prosecuted or killed.

Philly, New York, L.A., Houston. Not every city had a special investigations unit, but those were the big ones. The targets of the Big

Office were dying off, so the talent from the Big Office had flooded those markets when it downsized. Jake had been one of the transfers.

The focus at the Philly Office was totally different from the fed deal. It was all about TCP, threat investigation and control (local), crimes (major), and police affairs.

Low-level shit, relatively speaking. It hadn't particularly interested Jake, but he found it preferable to sitting in an office.

The work itself varied, but it always came back to TCP.

TCP. The acronym that had defined Jake's life for three years. *Everything* was TCP. If it wasn't, it got handed down to the local or state cops. If it wasn't, it meant nothing to Jake.

The office was occasionally commissioned by police departments for internal affairs matters, but most often major crimes investigations and terrorist threat evaluation came from the feds. Sometimes the office's own sources found information that merited investigation.

The office, along with a couple of other city departments, was in Tier One, which meant they had first access to the big guns—SWAT, police negotiators, and heavy artillery and equipment. Jake had hated when it came to that.

The secrecy surrounding the office had more to do with containment than anything else. Rumblings of terroristic threats and major crimes caused chaos. Fear. Internal investigations of public officers or whole departments made people doubt their public servants. More fear, more chaos.

"Buddy, you're buzzing." J.P. snapped Jake out of it.

It was Noelle. She sounded anxious.

"He's in town tonight. He wants to meet around seven in the

square. It's a friend's birthday; they're going dancing, and he said I could join them."

"Perfect. Stay put and I'll pick you up. Well done, Noelle."

Jake asked for the bill. When they got in the car, J.P. wanted to know what was going on. "I can help, man, I swear."

"There's no reason to," Jake replied dryly. "You're still dealing with your injuries. Plus, if you come along, it will only hurt our chances. I just want it to be me and Noelle. I'm going to drive you into town. I want you to stay at a friend's house. Our place isn't safe."

"I'll second that," J.P. said, chortling. "If you need me, call me. I'll probably end up at Ted's house."

For the rest of the ride into town, Jake thought about his strategy. He wanted to confront Ricker in public, but away from the group. He also needed a reason to be there. He thought of presenting himself as a cop, but quickly discarded that idea. Jackson was too small. Ricker may very well know all the police on the force, especially given his run-ins with them. He settled on a newspaper reporter. Jake would bluff, telling Ricker he had enough information to get him arrested. If Ricker revealed more of the story, he could walk away without being implicated. It wasn't a perfect plan, but it was the best he had.

In town, J.P. hopped out. Jake continued north toward Noelle's cabin. It was a beautiful evening, but almost too nice. Like the eye of a hurricane. Elk were beginning to leave the safety of the trees and feeding on the margins between sagebrush flats and pine forests. The coyotes were out looking for field mice and carcasses.

The SUV came to an abrupt stop outside Noelle's cabin. She was waiting on the porch. It was 6:35 p.m. Jake didn't bother to get out. Noelle jumped right in. Her attire surprised Jake; she was dressed to the nines, ready to go out dancing as her invitation suggested. She looked beautiful in the angular light of the early evening. As Jake searched for words to compliment her, she spoke.

"We've gotta hurry, Jake." He nodded at her and put the car in reverse.

Jake sensed their mutual nervousness as they drove back to town. Noelle, he knew, wasn't versed in the art of deception. And he was rusty himself.

"What do I say to him?" she asked.

"If it goes as planned, you won't have to say much. I just want you to say hi, a couple minutes of small talk. I'll confront him as soon as he seems to buy into it enough that he won't immediately run."

Jake explained the reporter guise. She seemed to think it would work.

"Do I stay there with you after?" Noelle's tone suggested that she wanted to.

"No. Absolutely not. You go back to the car. Just walk away." Jake neglected to tell her about the explosion and the seven-millimeter shell. No need to frighten her. He considered for a moment that he was using her, putting her in danger. Maybe he should call the whole thing off. *No.* He needed to know what was going on before it was too late. If she walked away like they discussed, the danger was minimized.

"Okay." Noelle nodded, holding eye contact a second longer than usual, like she was looking for some hidden meaning in his eyes.

Jake parked in the town square's public lot. It was getting chillier now as the sun dropped lower in the sky. Noelle pulled on the white, open-meshed cotton sweater that she had clutched in her hands during the ride. She tucked some errant strands of hair behind her ears.

She looked at her watch. It was already seven. "Let's go."

Noelle walked along the east sidewalk of Broadway, while Jake crossed over and took the west, so that they wouldn't be seen together. From a block away, she noticed a group of seven or eight gathered near the elk antler arch on the southwest corner of the square. Locals, no doubt. None of them were taking pictures of the arch. The men wore jeans or Carhartts and stylish western button-downs with fleeces over them. It had to be them.

She could hear them as she approached. "What are we waiting for again, Graem? I need a beer like crazy, dude. Long day . . ."

"Some *girl*," one of the females said. A short, skinny man with a tan face and sandals on looked embarrassed. *Ricker.* He was wearing ratty, old cargo shorts and a hooded sweatshirt with a ski logo on it. His face matched the picture on the website and her memory. That was her mark.

"Seriously?" the first man retorted. "We're waiting out here so Ricker can get laid? Do it on your own time!"

"C'mon, guys, take it easy," Ricker urged.

"Graem?" Noelle said, smiling, as she approached the circle. She was now about twenty feet away. Jake heard her speak and took notice. He was ready to cross the street as soon as the traffic light changed.

"Noelle?" Her looks caught everyone by surprise. "How are you? Been too long!" They hugged for a second.

"Right?" Noelle smacked him playfully on the chest. "You rip around pretty good on the slopes, if I remember right. Didn't know you were still in town."

Jake was walking fast across the crosswalk with his head down. While Ricker was trying to come up with something witty to say, Jake interrupted with a stern voice.

"Mr. Ricker? Graem Ricker?" Jake's face was under the shadow of the ball cap he put on as he crossed. "I need to talk with you in private, right now."

Without missing a beat, Noelle crossed the street the way Jake had come. Ricker spun to see her leave, a look of utter confusion on his face.

"What's your problem, man?" one of the men in the group yelled.

"Stay out of it and there won't be any problem," Jake said calmly.

"Lucky I'm on parole, man. I'd fuck your shit up!"

The crowd started to disperse, laughing and hooting.

"You need to come with me." Jake turned to face Ricker again.

"What the hell, man? Who are you?" Anger and confusion washed over Ricker's face.

"I'm a reporter, Graem, *Salt Lake Sun*." Jake flashed his wallet as though it had credentials. "And I need to talk to you about the avalanche." Jake stared him down. Suddenly, the man's furious look morphed into a sinister smile.

"Bullshit! I call bullshit!" Ricker looked around as if someone was there to be impressed. "I know who you are, you sonofabitch! You're Trent, man!"

Jake had to reformulate his plan quickly. Thinking on his feet, he remained calm, but his intensity increased. "Wow, you're a real genius, kid. It doesn't matter, though. I need to talk to you about this avalanche and I think you'll wanna talk to me, too, once you realize the stakes."

Ricker laughed. "Fuck you, asshole." He turned and started to walk away.

Jake was too quick for him. He grabbed Ricker's shoulder firmly from behind and whispered in his ear. "I know you staged that slide up on Maelstrom. I know you waited around for the sun to toast the snow, begging to slide. Sure, an earthquake started it, but you were gonna do it anyway. I can put you in jail, Graem, or worse."

The skinny man stopped walking and cursed. "You don't know shit! I didn't kill anybody, man!" He was still facing ahead with Jake's hand on his shoulder.

"I think you know something about who or what is killing people in Jackson, Graem."

When Ricker started to laugh, Jake dug his fore- and middle fingers into the sensitive tissue beneath his clavicle, just as he was taught.

"Aaaaarrghh!" Ricker buckled to his knees in pain. Jake let off to avoid attracting the attention of passersby.

Ricker sat for a moment on his knees and considered his options. "Shit. Shit. Shit! Okay, follow me to my car but stay back a ways. Don't make it obvious." Jake helped him to his feet.

Ricker, twenty yards in front of Jake, looked around and got into the driver's seat of an old, white Subaru wagon. As Jake approached, he looked around, fearing a trap. It looked safe, not too quiet and nothing suspicious. Jake entered the passenger side.

"Okay." Ricker turned on the radio, presumably in case Jake was wearing a wire. *Not as dumb as he looks.*

"I told you what I want. It's your show now." Jake watched Ricker, hoping for some clue that he wouldn't give away verbally.

"I don't know shit. I was set up, man!"

"Set up for what?" Jake growled. He was growing impatient.

"I don't know."

Jake brought his left hand slowly to his face and stroked his scruff for a moment. He could sense Ricker's apprehension. They made eye contact for a moment. Ricker was breathing heavily.

Will he break? Jake wondered. *Only one way to find out.*

With lightning speed, Jake reached behind Ricker's head and slammed it forward, breaking the man's nose on the steering wheel.

"What the hell, man?! Shit!" Blood was pouring onto Ricker's lap.

Jake calmly looked around to make sure no one had seen them and then reached down to the cluttered floor of the Subaru, grabbed a dirty T-shirt, and handed it to Ricker, who held it against his bleeding face. He was panting now. Spitting blood from his mouth between fast, shallow breaths.

"This isn't a game you want to play with me, Graem."

Ricker let out a low whimper, then looked around the empty street, wishing there was someone to help him.

"Shit, shit, shit. Shit! Okay, it's not who, it's more like what."

Jake wrung out his hands, causing his knuckles to crack. Exactly the effect he wanted.

Ricker looked at Jake's hands and then spoke again. "I-I-It's like a group—a cult or something. Nobody really knows what the other members are doing. And to set the record straight, I didn't kill that kid up there. I would never do that, no matter what. I didn't know how crazy these people were before I got involved."

Jake gave Ricker a thorough look. "Then what happened?"

"Shit went bad, that's what happened. As far as I knew, we were up there just to try to start a slide. When we got near the top, he was . . . Marcus was his name . . . Marcus was talking about who we were gonna push the slide onto. You see what I'm saying? He was talking about starting a slide that would hit hikers or skiers below us."

"Why?"

"Marcus was nuts. I had just met him that morning, but he was clearly not sane. When nobody walked beneath Maelstrom for a few hours, he went out onto the slope and started jumping up and down, chanting and stuff. When I asked him what he was doing he told me he was begging Mother Earth to take him."

"Then what?"

"You know the rest, basically. I got my skis on and slid out there to try to stop him. Pull him off the slope. He was being so loud, I was scared he would attract attention and get us in trouble. When I was about thirty feet away, a damn quake hit and the slope broke free. That was that. I guess his prayers came true."

"Why were you even up there? Why would anyone start an avalanche on purpose?" Jake's mind was working quickly to answer his own question as he asked it.

"Are you serious? You, man. You're why."

"What?"

"You. Everything you and other people like you stand for. That's what this is all about, you know."

Jake gave him a quizzical look. "And what is it that I stand for exactly, Graem?" He was getting angry. *What the hell is this guy talking about? He doesn't even know a thing about me.*

The kid seemed a little nervous. He was sensing Jake's frustration and didn't want him to boil over. "You know, like people who . . . umm . . . don't care about the future, don't care about the earth. That development—the one south of town. Some people don't care for your support of it."

Jake had to laugh. "What would you say if I told you I've spent the last two months opposing that project?"

"Wait, what?"

"Who told you I was to blame for the approval of that project?"

Ricker shifted in the driver's seat. "Well, I told you it's not that easy. It's a bunch of people and there is no leader or anything, it's just—"

"Bullshit."

Sighing, Ricker checked his nose, which was still bleeding. "Okay . . . okay. Have you heard of EcoAmicae? Well, they . . . this guy . . . their leader . . . he also runs other organizations, underground. Ones that do their work in the shadows."

"Eco-terrorists?" Jake asked.

"Kind of, yeah. He gave us our assignments. He recruited us, told us about what was happening here and how we could stop it. And I don't mean protests."

"He wants you to kill me because he thinks I'm involved in the development?"

"Not me," the man said quickly. "And I don't think he cares whether you die or not, really. I think he just wants you to get the message, like everyone else."

"And what's that message?"

"Well, in layman's terms, I guess it's that if you mess with Mother Earth, you will be struck down by her. Like the avalanche."

"And you buy into this bullshit? But you intended to start the avalanche," Jake said, pressing him. "It wasn't going to be Mother Nature by any stretch. It was coincidence, the way it happened.

You intended to hurt someone and someone else got hurt. You are still accountable. Cops and lawyers call it transferred intent."

"Yeah. Well, I don't know anything about that, man. Pretty weird coincidence, though, don't you think?"

Jake gave him a look that shut him up for a moment, then he continued.

"Anyway, yeah . . . so that's it. We were never aware of any of the other projects, the missions. It was kept that way, I think, so that we couldn't be arrested for conspiracy or something. . . ." Jake had no doubt any court in the land could and would find a conspiracy here.

"So the other murders—the man in the river and the bear attack. You know nothing about them. That's what you're saying?"

"Nothing, I swear to God. But I don't doubt the Shaman would do that." He paled, realizing the name had slipped even before Jake did.

"The *Shaman*?" Jake asked. "Who the hell is that?"

"I don't know, man, really." He squirmed. "Listen, my buddies are going to start looking for me if I take any longer . . ."

"Name?" Jake raised his voice.

"Dude, look . . . I'm sorry. I don't know. I swear it."

He's being honest again.

"What's next? Are more going to die?" Jake's voice was a growl again.

"No, it's over. Word came around this morning, we're done."

"Done?" Jake doubted that, thinking about the shooting at his house. "If you hear anything else, contact me. Do you understand?" Jake handed him a card from his bed-and-breakfast.

"I am not a person you want to lie to." Jake pointed casually at Ricker's broken nose. "And one last thing, do you know whether this organization or the Shaman have any connection to the police here in Jackson?"

"Wouldn't surprise me. The Shaman seems to have friends in high places."

Jake got out of the car. In a way, Jake felt a bit sorry for Ricker—he was just a lonely guy who finally found something to be a part of. The Shaman and his crew took him in and made him feel important. Wanted. This was the danger with such groups.

Jake turned back. "Oh, and, Graem? Don't you dare try to follow me." He took out a buck knife and jammed the blade into Ricker's rear tire.

Back in the parking lot, Noelle was leaning against the side fender of Jake's vehicle, looking down and nervously shifting her weight from foot to foot. "Where the hell have you been?" she shouted when she finally looked up and noticed him. "I was scared to death, Jake. I don't want to do anything like that ever again."

Jake consoled her. "You're fine and so am I. I just had a bit of an extended chat with Graem. He became rather helpful after I mentioned jail time."

"Really? You have enough evidence to put him away?" Noelle looked like a child, and Jake regretted frightening her.

"Something like that. Let's get out of here. I need a place to stay tonight, if it's okay. I got shot at earlier outside my house." He let out a burdened sigh.

"What? Jesus, Jake! Weren't gonna mention that?"

Jake put his palms up toward her, apologizing. She shivered and shook her head as he opened the passenger door for her. On the way home, Jake told her about the gunshot and the propane explosion. The story made her gasp. Jake tried to calm her by telling her that if the man had intended to kill him, he would have shot for his chest rather than the tank. Noelle wasn't convinced.

It was nearly 9 p.m. when they got back to Noelle's cabin. The remnant glow of the sun was barely hanging over the valley. In the distance, coyotes were yipping and barking. The few early-bird tourists in the adjacent campground had started fires for warmth and comfort, and the smoky pine scent was wafting to the cabin. It was almost summer. Soon the valley would be buzzing with visitors—*potential victims,* Jake thought.

As they entered the cabin, Noelle spoke. "I've got a gun—like, a shotgun, you know. We should bring that out, I think. Uh, I don't have anywhere for you to sleep, though. Obviously no spare bedroom." She was talking fast. Jumpy. Jake couldn't blame her, given the circumstances. He slowly sat down in an attempt to downplay the situation.

"We don't need the shotgun, Noelle. Nobody knows I'm here." Jake laughed. "And I can sleep on the floor, no problem. I have a feeling I wouldn't get any rest no matter where I slept tonight."

Ignoring Jake's comment about the gun, Noelle thought for a moment and then kicked down on one of the floorboards, causing its far end to jut diagonally into the air. She reached down and brought out a dusty over-under shotgun and a box of shells.

"Wow, has anyone shot that thing since Antietam?" Jake gave the weapon a dubious look.

"Ha. Well, maybe not. My grandfather gave it to me when I moved here. I haven't shot it since he showed me how it works." She was trying to load two shells into the chamber backward. Her hands trembled a bit.

"Whoa. Let's leave it unloaded, Noelle." Jake got up and held out his hands, in which she rested the gun. He checked that the

chamber was empty and clicked the safety on, then leaned the barrel against the cabin's wall. "Fear and loaded weapons are not a
good combo."

Noelle seemed to be looking for something to do. "These two
sleeping bags will serve as a pretty good bed." She took the bags
and laid them on the floor. "One on top and one on bottom." Then
she threw a pillow from her own bed on top of the pile. *Is she
nervous 'cause I'm here?*

"No, no, what will you use for a blanket?" Jake asked.

"I've got this." She held up the corner of a light cotton throw.
"It hasn't been very cold in here the last few nights," she lied.

The two stayed awake for a long time in the dark, talking about
the day's events, but also sharing bits of their own personal histories. At a quarter after ten, they each slid into their separate beds
and bade each other good night. A few minutes later, Jake heard
Noelle get out of bed. Then she lay down and positioned her body
firmly against his. She whispered in his ear, "I was worried about
you today."

By the dull yellow light from the porch lamp, Jake could see that
she was wearing a light blue tank top that was just loose enough so
that it draped freely over her body, begging the question of what
lay beneath. It didn't cover her well-defined stomach. She looked
gorgeous. He pulled aside the top bag and allowed her to come
into the warmth. Her legs were smooth against his, and he put his
hand on her bare hip. "You were just cold." She pulled herself up
on top of him and began kissing his lips and neck.

Jake slid his hands up beneath the tank top. His hands were
cold but Noelle didn't notice. His touch felt wonderful. He held
her there on top of him with his hands on her rib cage while she
continued kissing him. She pushed herself down against his sup-

port, wanting to kiss him deeper and harder. She playfully bit at his lower lip. "Don't get yourself killed, Jake. Please."

He didn't say a word, instead sliding his hands around her breasts and taking the soft weight of them into his hands. She stopped kissing him and sighed smoothly through a wide smile. Then she sat up, still on top of him, and pulled the tank top off. He couldn't help but smile too.

She took a hair tie from her wrist and flipped her hair into a ponytail. Then she lowered her face to his and began to kiss him again while unbuttoning his shirt.

21

GRAND TETON NATIONAL PARK. THE NEXT MORNING.

Jake woke at sunrise with Noelle in his arms. At some point during the night, they had migrated from the cold floor up to the bed. He pulled himself out from under her and slipped on his jeans and walked over to the small kitchen. Coffee. The thick glass jar that held the instant mix was nearly empty. Not even enough for one cup.

He looked at Noelle on the bed. She was sleeping peacefully. Her presence was especially ethereal when she slept. It was the most at ease that Jake had ever seen her. Her hair lay in wispy curves on the white pillow. Jake smiled.

He decided to head into town to retrieve some coffee. He hoped Noelle would appreciate the gesture. The air was brisk, barely forty degrees. He shivered and hurried to the SUV. He opened the tailgate first and grabbed a thick fleece, pulled it on, and jumped in.

Starting the engine, he turned off the heater fan so that it wouldn't blast cold air on his already cold feet.

Jake stopped at the first breakfast spot coming into town, the Cowboy Café. There was a line in front of the to-go counter. Mainly locals with their plastic carryout mugs ready for the morning fill, but a few tourists were perusing the volumes of brochures conveniently set within view of the queue. Jake grabbed a ten-dollar bill and the tattered punch card for the diner from his wallet. The line moved along quickly.

"Two mediums, please."

The woman asked if he'd brought his mug.

Typical Jackson.

"Not today. Give the family tree my condolences." She didn't laugh.

"It's three twenty-five," she said, sliding the steaming paper cups across the counter.

The change in his hand, Jake wandered back into the cool air, thinking about his night with Noelle. He drank from the coffee in his right hand and looked meaningfully at the paper cup in his left.

It's been a long time since I did this.

The sun felt good on his shoulders and he felt a strange, unexpected serenity.

He knew he shouldn't get involved, but here he was. Spending the night, bringing her coffee. He couldn't help but think about how it would all end—broken hearts and estrangement.

It's probably nothing, anyway. I'm overthinking it like always.

He took one more sip, squinted to look up at the bluebird sky, and headed back to the car.

As he walked, something caught his eye. A man was leaving the diner, wearing khakis and a down sweater. Familiar, though he couldn't say who. Thin, harsh face.

Someone from a long time ago.

Jake took a few steps, south along Cache Street, to get a closer look. He stopped in his tracks when he saw the man pause fifteen feet in front of him. He was reading the paper. Jake turned his back so he wouldn't be recognized. A moment later the target started walking along Cache again, still reading the paper.

Jake watched with his peripheral vision so he wouldn't lose track of his target and then followed, still going south. When the man stopped to cross the street, he looked back north. Jake got a second-long glance at his face, and it finally clicked.

Holy shit!

The man got in a truck and pulled a U-turn, headed north. After he passed, Jake jogged back to his vehicle, the hot coffee sloshing in his hands. He got in and peeled out. There were now four or five cars between him and the truck. Jake wiped the hot liquid from his hands onto his pants.

There was no easy way to pass until the extra lane by the airport, another four miles. Until then, Jake could only hope the man didn't turn. The traffic was spread out and he couldn't see the truck anymore.

It occurred to him that this was the moment he had been fearing.

The moment when the war comes crashing into your living room.

There was no way out now. They were really after him. They had been after him all along, but now that notion slapped him in the face. As he approached the airport, he was struck with the irony; there was no easy escape for Jake Trent.

The sun was heating up the SUV. Jake removed his fleece and turned off the heat.

When the two-lane stretch began, Jake gunned the engine. He

passed one car, then the next and the next. He could see the truck again. There was only one vehicle between them. It followed the truck closely—too close for Jake to squeeze between it and his target.

What the hell is he doing here?

It was Jake's worst nightmare—seeing the man who had vowed to kill him, alive and well in Jackson Hole, Wyoming.

But how does it fit with Parrana? With the Dairy Ranch Development? The camp? The car and J.P.?

The passing lane was coming to an end. The space between the vehicles lengthened slightly. He could probably make the pass, but it would require him to pull up on the truck's rear bumper with a lot of speed, which would let his target know he was in pursuit.

For all Jake knew, his target might even know his vehicle. He decided to hang back and use the car between them as a buffer. They passed the park entrance that led to Noelle's cabin. *So much for nice gestures.*

For the next forty-five miles, Jake stayed within visual range of the truck. At that point, there was a T in the road. A right turn went east toward the old cowboy town of Cody. Make a left and you were headed to Yellowstone. The truck went left.

At the entrance gate, the pickup stopped and the man showed his pass. Jake pulled up a moment later and did the same, but in that brief pause an RV squeezed its way between them from another lane. The caravan continued on deeper into Yellowstone country. They went up and over the first plateau and along the deep canyon scribed by the Lewis River.

Behind the slow RV, Jake soon lost sight of the truck. He was relying on the fact that this portion of the road had very few turn-offs. Most of the intersecting roads were service roads for park staff. There *were* a few turnouts for views of the canyon and its waterfalls and rapids, but the truck would still be in sight from the road. He hadn't seen the truck, so his target was still ahead of him somewhere.

Is he going to the camp where the Impala ended up? This is a roundabout way to get there.

It didn't add up.

What kind of connection could there possibly be between me and these eco-nuts?

On the right, Jake passed the first geyser basin from the south entrance. The pickup, now leading a line several cars beyond Jake's, was observing the speed limit.

Signs for Old Faithful came and went. They were ninety-some miles from Jackson now.

Where the hell is he going?

Wherever he was headed, it was a long commute for a cup of coffee.

Jake knew the pursuit was about to get more complicated. In just a dozen more miles, the road network would get convoluted. Roads left the main artery and went to geyser basins, paint pots, and other attractions. Then more roads intersected from all directions, coming from Cody, West Yellowstone, and Montana. If Jake wasn't careful, he would lose his mark.

Jake was trying to formulate a guess on the destination of the man. West Yellowstone was most likely, he thought. It had the most businesses—hotels, restaurants. There wasn't much at the north entrance in Montana, and if the man wanted to go toward Cody, he would have turned before entering the park.

It turned out to be a moot point. Ten miles past Old Faithful, traffic came to a stop. The wide body of the RV totally obscured Jake's view. After two minutes or so, Jake put his SUV in park and killed the engine. He got out to look. A few hundred yards ahead a dozen bison were standing in the road, blocking both lanes of traffic.

Then, squealing tires. Bison hustled out of the way as the pickup floored it through the herd. Jake ran back to his vehicle and swung it around the RV. Dust from the disturbed herd filled the air. When it cleared, the gap made by the pickup had filled with more animals.

Shit!

Jake laid on the horn, but the behemoths didn't budge. He slammed his fist on the dash and turned around.

Jake tried to send a text message to Noelle: "Something came up early this morning—are you still home?" But he didn't have cell reception. He felt guilty leaving her in the cabin, but there was no choice, the coincidence was just too much to be ignored. The man in the truck had to be involved.

Jake ignored the speed limit on his way back. The temperature had climbed to the point that he could put the windows down, even up in the Yellowstone high country. He checked his phone while driving, something he hated to do, but there was still no reception.

Why in the world is he here?

He wasn't even sure whether the man was due to be out of prison yet. *How many years has it been?*

They pressed for a more severe sentence, the prosecutors, and they should have gotten it. The defendant was extremely dangerous.

Jake and everybody else in the Philly Office knew that.

They hadn't even been after Makter in the beginning; they

were after Jan, and they had been for many years. Jan was the big fish.

In the end, they couldn't get any charges to stick to Jan. *All because of the damn informant.* He was the one who told Jake that some of Jan's runners were out selling in their free time; that they were trying to break free and start their own gig; that they would be willing to talk, just to put Jan and his boys out of business.

The informant was dead wrong.

The team got into position and waited for the transaction to take place. They'd been instructed to move in immediately after the money changed hands and arrest the dealers. Supposedly low-level street dealers. They were expecting an easy night.

When the two vehicles arrived, Jake recognized Argus and Makter immediately as they got out of the first car. He knew their faces well from his research.

"Shit! Don't move in! Back off!"

Jake knew if they took Argus into custody, it would only serve to spook Jan, force him even deeper into the shadows.

It was too late. The team was moving on the transaction, the radio call overpowered by their own short breath and beating hearts. Argus pulled his weapon first. He was immediately mowed down by the officers' automatic gunfire. Makter went for his pistol too but was tackled before he could fire. The buyer sped off into the night.

Jake ran from his car, down the hill, and onto the scene. Argus was down, bleeding everywhere.

"Goddammit! Listen to your fucking radios, people!"

Jake tried to get a response, but the boy was already unconscious. He looked over to Makter, who was writhing under the constraints of two officers and screaming, his hate-filled eyes focused on Jake.

"He was like a fucking son to me! I'm going to kill you!"

Thunder crashed, and the muggy Jersey air was cut by pouring rain.

Jake silenced Makter with a quick blow to the jaw.

Makter repeated the threat throughout the entire questioning process at the station. Among all the other threats Jake had received over the years, it seemed more visceral and the most real.

When Jake and his team gave up on Makter, who was elusive and indignant, they met to assess the situation.

"We have nothing," Jake told the officers with a stern face, pacing back and forth on the tile in the office. Without testimony, there was no way to make Jan's charges stick. "We hoped for some rats, some information on our guy, and instead we almost killed his son. How does that help us? Why the hell didn't anybody hear my radio call?"

Nobody said a word. "Does anyone in here think that we're gonna get this asshole's son, who may be dead by the morning, to rat out his own dad? If you think this raid was a success, get the fuck out right now! Nobody?"

It was one of the few times that Jake lost his composure in front of his own team. But it wasn't entirely their fault. The informant had been a complete whack job looking to get in the office's favor. They were back at square one; Jan would lay low, hiding after the botched raid.

Part of Jake's anger that night had also stemmed from fear; there was something about the look in Makter's eyes, the way he screamed when he threatened him, that chilled Jake.

Makter wouldn't talk. Jake asked the prosecutor to charge him with whatever he could. During the trial, Makter lashed out at Jake to the point that he had to be restrained and muzzled. Eventually, Jake was asked to leave the room so that the proceedings could go on without interruption.

The sentence wasn't as long as Jake had wanted. Sixteen years. Less if Makter behaved. Apparently he'd behaved. That was only eleven years ago.

As time went on and Jake headed West, he put Makter and the threat behind him. But now the threat seemed more real than ever. And now Noelle and J.P. were at risk too.

22

GRAND TETON NATIONAL PARK. THE SAME MORNING.

Back in the cabin, Noelle was starting to worry. She called Jake. Straight to voice mail.

Where the hell is he?

She wondered if whoever was out there knew where she lived. To be safe, she locked the door and drew all the blinds. She grabbed the shotgun. If anyone pulled into her driveway, she would hear them coming. She sat down with the gun and her phone.

Tourist traffic was slowing Jake down. He was still in Yellowstone, headed south on the park road, replaying the past and trying to connect the dots. There was a lot to work with, but he couldn't put the puzzle together. Had Makter really come here simply to exact revenge like he'd promised so many years ago? How did that connect with the events of the last week?

For the first time in many years, Jake was starting to panic. He sensed that whatever crescendo was approaching, it was coming soon.

He wanted his life back. He wanted to be out on the river. Better yet, he imagined himself wading some tropical shoal, casting to shadows that gave away the presence of a bonefish or permit. It would be nice to get out of Jackson for a little while after all this. He pictured Noelle, bikini-clad and leaning against a coconut palm, her portrait backlit by the setting sun.

Still daydreaming, Jake came around a bend to an excited crowd on the side of the road. At first it seemed like some people were gathered looking at wildlife. A dozen folks, two. But then Jake realized something was wrong; people were waving frantically and shouting as he approached. Then a man covered in blood. Some were injured—grasping their arms or legs in pain, wailing. Others were writhing in the gravel. Jake could hear their screams through his open windows.

What in the world?

Jake jumped on the brakes and stopped the car. He got out and ran toward the group, looking from person to person, trying to assess what had happened. He had been the first responder on his share of crime scenes. His training kicked in.

Stay calm. Figure out who needs help first. Prioritize.

Before he could do so, he was interrupted. "Hey! Do you have a cell phone or walkie-talkie?!" A young man was yelling from the boundary of the basin. Jake snatched his phone out of his pocket. He looked at the screen. *No service. Shit.*

The area was low-lying and geothermally active, like a prehistoric marsh. Sage and a few burned pines were the only vegetation. Boardwalks installed by the park kept the tourists off the soft, boiling earth.

Jake ran through the crowd and found the man who'd shouted for him. A park employee, brown sweater, brown slacks. He looked frantic.

"I need your help, follow me! Hurry! Everyone ran!" Jake followed the man down the gravel entrance and to the geyser viewing area. They stepped up onto the wooden boardwalk, only a foot above the smoldering ground. "It's over here!"

Jake's mind was reeling. *Another attack? Makter?*

"Grab his arms! Help!" The man was waving Jake over.

The scene was otherworldly. Near the signpost for a geyser, a long section of boardwalk had collapsed into the geyser basin below.

Pieces of two-by-four were bobbing in the boiling water. Other fragments lay on the moonlike crust around the water, smoldering. Jake saw a middle-aged man only a few inches from the break in the walkway. He was up past his waist in steaming water. His arms were stretched above him for help and a look of utter terror was plastered on his face. He looked too afraid to scream. The only signs of life were in his shocked eyes, which darted frantically from side to side.

The park ranger grabbed the man's left arm and Jake got his right. They pulled, but the man was heavy. In the background, Jake could hear pieces of the walkway splintering off into the boiling water. There wasn't much time.

Jake and the ranger counted to three and pulled with everything they had. This time, the man came out of the water. They backed up, but as they did so, the man's lower body slid across the rough edge of the wood, peeling large chunks of flesh from his burned legs.

Nausea washed over Jake.

They dragged the man to safety, seventy yards from the collapsed boardwalk. Bits of flesh pulled away from his legs every step of the way.

Jake told him it was okay. That help was coming. That he would be fine. The man didn't respond. His wounds were so catastrophic that Jake didn't know where to start. The man closed his eyes and let out a few more strained breaths. Then he was silent.

His legs had very little skin or muscle left on them. The flesh that remained had the dark purplish-brown color of cooked meat. The smell was overwhelming. He had been burned alive.

23

YELLOWSTONE NATIONAL PARK. THE SAME DAY.

"What the hell happened here?" Jake shouted to the ranger when he had gathered himself.

"I . . . I don't really know." He was nearly hysterical. "Like an explosion. It . . . it came out of the ground. All of a sudden there was this hollow boom, then steam everywhere and water, even rock was high up in the air—a hundred feet, I bet . . . the boardwalk collapsed. People ran. Some of them were burned." He nodded toward the group congregated on the road's shoulder. "But I don't think anyone else was like this." The ranger looked over again at the lifeless man and had to put his hand over his mouth.

"Where's your radio?" Jake was looking at the man's empty chest holster.

"I dropped it. It's on the ground over there, but I can't walk over. The ground's not safe."

Jake looked where the man pointed. About eight feet from the boardwalk, the radio was lying on the ground. Jake lifted a heavy rock. Still warm. Almost too hot to touch. He threw it hard at the ground near the radio. The earth broke and steam escaped in a small puff. The rock was gone, sucked into the boiling water below.

Jesus.

Dismayed, Jake gave up on the radio, and he and the ranger jogged to the crowd on the side of the road. The more capable victims had already loaded into their cars and gone for help. To Jake it looked like the survivors had suffered only minor injuries. Nothing life threatening.

Jake walked among them asking if anyone had a cell phone that worked. Nobody spoke up. Abruptly, a young girl stood up and walked over behind a sage bush and vomited. She held her head in her hands as she walked back.

Jake watched her carefully: *She's in shock.*

Then another person left the gathered group. This time it was a grown man. He grabbed for his mouth, but was too late. He vomited on the road's shoulder. A few people were clutching at their throats. Jake took a deep inhale through his nose, smelling the air. Something wasn't right. *The air.* The newly formed cracks and fumaroles were releasing poisonous gasses. Jake had read stories of cave explorers who had been killed by this very phenomenon in Yellowstone.

Shit.

"Let's go! Now!" Jake checked the wind direction. "This way!" He motioned to the west. "Fast! Let's go!" The young girl who first became ill was struggling. Jake ran over and picked her up. "Hurry!" He chased the group across the road and a hundred yards west to the top of a small hill.

"What the hell was that about?" the ranger asked Jake pointedly when he caught his breath from the run.

"Sulfur dioxide, I think. We shouldn't be down there." The ranger glanced back at the geyser basin. It was still steaming.

"Sorry. I should've known."

"It's okay." Jake waved off the apology.

Jake went back to the girl he had carried from the road and asked how she was doing. She still felt woozy, she said, but it was getting better.

"Where's your family?"

"I don't know. I just came with my daddy. He was taking pictures of the geyser when everybody ran." She looked up at Jake. "Is he okay?"

"I'm sure." He tousled her hair, and then he had to walk away. When he was out of earshot, Jake cursed out loud. Tears nearly came to his eyes. The group wasn't so big that she wouldn't have found her father; there were only eight or ten remaining. He was the man they had tried to rescue. The man burned alive. Jake went back to the child and sat with her.

The ranger approached them.

"Go for help. I will wait here." Jake couldn't stand to leave the girl. The ranger jogged to his vehicle and took off north.

Within the hour, paramedics came and set up a battlefield-like triage there in the sage. Park rangers took statements. Jake stayed on and lent a hand to the medics. After a couple of hours, the supervising ranger approached Jake.

"You're set to go whenever you'd like, Mr. Trent."

Jake looked up at the paramedic. He was sitting with the young girl again. "Can I talk with you for a minute in private?"

The paramedic nodded and they stepped away.

"Where will she go?"

"The girl? Oh, she'll be okay. We've made a phone call. Her mother will be over in West Yellowstone by midnight. Coming in from Massachusetts. We'll have a sheriff with her until then. She lives with her mom, just on vacation with Dad."

Jake wondered how the man thought this made any difference. "Have you told her yet? About her dad?"

The man shook his head. "Nah, we usually find it better to let the family inform the kid when they're that young. We told her we're still looking for him." He walked away.

"Thanks again."

The girl sat alone. Considering the circumstances, she looked like she was doing rather well. Jake knelt down next to her. He put his hand on her back. "Did you find my dad?" she asked him.

"No. We haven't." Jake changed the subject. "Listen, your mother is coming in to see you. You're gonna be okay." The girl's expression made Jake shudder.

"One more thing," the ranger shouted back toward Jake. "Just so you know, they closed the park because of all this business, so you'll find the gate shut. Just give the ranger station there a knock on your way out and someone will come open it for you."

Jake stood up, nodded at him, and went to the car. He shook off another wave of nausea, started the car, and headed south.

Jake checked his watch; he'd been gone for well over three hours. When he got within range of a cellular tower, he called Noelle. She sounded anxious, and he reassured her that he was okay and asked if they could meet in town. She agreed.

*   *   *

Jake and Noelle met in the town square. She hugged him, feeling around for injuries as if there might actually be holes in his body.

"What the hell happened?"

Jake told her about the man he followed but kept it vague. She wasn't ready for the whole story. Not yet.

Noelle put her hand to her mouth when Jake told her about the man plunging into the boiling water and the young girl. When Jake finished, they both fell silent for a moment, until Noelle suddenly spoke.

"I almost forgot!" Noelle walked quickly across the street to a newspaper stand and grabbed one. She came back waving the paper at him. "Did you see this, Jake? Have you seen this?"

Jake hadn't yet read the paper. "No, what is it?"

"You said they closed the park, right? Look at this!" Noelle held the paper up. Jake took it into his hands so he could read it.

The headline read: "Old? Sure; But Not So Faithful."

Below the headline was a picture of a park seismologist at a podium. The caption explained further:

Yellowstone park scientist Jarl Hughes explains the reasons for a possible park closure. The proposed shutdown would be temporary until scientists determine what is causing the seismic changes in the region and deem the area safe.

Jake skimmed the remainder of the article. Geothermal features throughout the park were betraying their schedules and habits. Some, like Old Faithful, were not erupting at all. The seismologist quoted in the article attributed this to "a change in the underground anatomy of the geyser."

263

Other geysers had grown more intense. In some places, small releases of steam and water, miniature geysers, had seemingly sprouted overnight. The temperatures had changed drastically in many of the park's hot springs and pools. Sulfur dioxide readings were at an all-time high in the region, and fresh elk and bison carcasses indicated extremely high levels of noxious gases in certain localized areas. And of course there were still the earthquakes. There'd been sixty-one documented quakes in the last two days in the Yellowstone area. Ranging from 1.2 to 3.4, most were too subtle to feel.

Jake flipped to the second page. Accompanying the remainder of the article was a small photo of Old Faithful, complete with its crowd of international tourists. The geyser was completely quiet. The caption read: "11:55 a.m. yesterday. The eruption was expected to start at 11:30."

"Jesus." Jake looked up at Noelle for a second, and then buried his face in the paper again.

A second article ran below the lead story: "End of Days?" An opinion piece by a staff writer for the *Daily*. The article contained nothing new to Jake. Yes, Yellowstone was a supervolcano. Yes, a complete eruption could send the world into an ice age. Sure, it could be a similar event to that which killed the dinosaurs. Compelling stuff, but it provided no new information that might explain why this all was happening now.

It was all just speculation. Jake knew that it was many times more likely that small change was occurring rather than an impending big eruption. Still, it wasn't every day that the local newspaper predicted the end of the world with your town as the epicenter.

"This is crazy. And printed before this morning's fiasco. They must have made the final call right before or after the boardwalk failed." Jake handed the paper back to Noelle. "Have you heard anything through the park service grapevine?"

"Not really. Except to be ready for a big crowd in case Yellowstone closes. Guess I've gotta 'be ready.' They're expecting a lot of refugee campers in the Tetons if they close Yellowstone. They even designated some temporary campsites."

"Don't you need to get back up there?" Jake asked.

"No."

Jake didn't believe her.

"They'll give me a call if they need me," she reasoned.

"What do we do now?"

"Do you have the license number for the car you followed that we could run?"

"Nope. Never got close enough. I think without that, we just wait and see what happens next." That thought made both of them uneasy.

Jake put his arm around Noelle. "Let's get something to eat, I'm starving."

Inside the café, the barista was playing R.E.M.'s "It's the End of the World as We Know It."

24

THE HOT ROCK TRACT. NOON.

The sun was bright and warm when Makter arrived, bringing a deceitful aura of tranquillity to the structure and its surroundings.

On the way out of the north entrance, the ranger had informed him that the park was going to be shut down for at least a few days. He had to go back now to get his camping supplies if he had been camping in the park.

"Just driving through, thank you," he told the man in the booth. Makter tried to smile genuinely. Somehow he despised the man in the booth, even though he'd interacted with him for just a moment.

You're losing it, Mak.

Another voice retorted, *You never had it, Mak.* He did his best to block out both.

After a few miles, Makter pulled into the driveway, got out, and rang the bell. Nobody answered. Makter tried again but with the same result. This wasn't unusual. It was a big house and Jan was usually focused on his work upstairs in the office. Makter tried the doorknob. It was open. He let himself in.

The relationship between Makter and Jan went back more than forty years now. They'd played together as kids and they'd learned to be men together. Both from German families living in Hoboken, their kin got along naturally. Both were raised in broken homes, and this cemented their fate together.

Neither could even remember when they had first met, it was so long ago. In the beginning their respect and adoration for each other was mutual. They were equals in every way—school, sports, popularity. Both outsiders in school at first, they shared an envy and hatred toward the ruling class.

They were inseparable.

But during their freshman year in high school, Jan began to move up in the social strata of Washington and Jefferson High. He still spent time with Makter, but mostly when they were hanging out in the neighborhood. In school, it seemed like Jan wanted nothing to do with him.

Makter was a troublemaker. Family life had led him to become violent and destructive. When he was fourteen he nearly beat a classmate to death with a bat after school, because of a trivial insult. The boy recovered but was too afraid to rat Makter out. The event was empowering. He never forgot that feeling.

As the years passed, Makter saw Jan less and less. At fifteen, he was selling weed to his classmates. By their junior year, it became commonplace for Makter and his gang to drive into the cities, New York or Philadelphia, to buy cocaine and acid to sell in their hometown. Makter bought a car, and this helped him gain some popularity back in school, but he still felt neglected. He didn't care about the money he made selling drugs, and he spent it freely. He had learned to crave power, respect, and fear.

Meanwhile, Jan was succeeding in a more traditional sense. He was the offensive captain of the football team, a star receiver. His grades were among the best in the class. In the fall of his junior year, he was already talking to Harvard, Princeton, and the University of Virginia. Things came easily for him.

Then he got injured. It was a late-season home game, and they were up by fourteen in the third quarter. The play was a fluke; Jan wasn't even injured by an opposing player. His own tight end fell against his knee, tearing his ACL and MCL. He missed the remainder of the season. As he recovered, Jan also spent a lot of time at home. It was his right leg, so even if he could have borrowed his mom's car, he couldn't drive anywhere.

His friendship with Makter was reestablished. Mak's house had become quite the hangout for those from the wrong side of the tracks. His mother was working two jobs and even if she was home, she didn't bother herself with disciplining her only child. She mostly sat upstairs in her bedroom, watched TV, and drank vodka chased with cheap beer.

At that time, Jan didn't want to be too involved with nefarious characters. He would smoke pot with them, watch a movie, and then limp home on his crutches. The idea stuck in his mind, though: *Sixteen- and seventeen-year-old kids making as much money as their parents make working twenty hours a week. Dumb kids, too. I could make a killing if I were them . . .*

After Jan recovered, those thoughts went dormant. He set records in his senior year and went on to Harvard on scholarship. He didn't excel there, but he did better than average. After Jan graduated with a degree in economics, his good looks and charisma made him a natural in commercial real estate. Entrepreneurial endeavors followed. He always stayed in touch with Makter, who was doing surprisingly well in admittedly darker circles. Jan traveled far and often, but when he was in the area, he always made time for his old friend.

"Jan? Hello?" Makter shouted into the cavernous two-story entryway. There was no response. He tried one more time and then climbed the stairway to the top floor. No sign of life.

Makter turned in to the office with the big picture windows. The monitors were lit up and beeping. There was a half-empty glass of water on the desk and a bottle of scotch with two old-fashioned-style glasses on a serving cart.

Someone left in a hurry. Makter looked around and then took out his cell phone. *Where is everyone?*

Footsteps. The clicking sound of expensive leather soles echoed in the mostly unfurnished building. *A cop? Sounds like a fucking cop.* Makter looked around, but there was nowhere to go, nowhere to hide. *Dammit.*

The man spoke before he entered the room. "Do you know why you're here, Mak?" His voice betrayed his disappointment.

It's just Jan.

Makter was relieved it wasn't the cops but not too eager for the conversation, judging by his old friend's tone. Just like in high school, Jan had naturally risen to the top. Although Makter had helped him gain connections in the criminal world, Jan was now his superior.

How can he know Trent tried to follow me?

"Jesus, Jan. I came up to . . ." Makter was trying to come up with an answer. He had come to give Jan a piece of his mind, but Jan's aggression was derailing him. He was on the defensive.

"I asked you a question, do you know why you're here?"

"To get rid of Jake Trent."

"Wrong." Jan's voice got louder. "You're here to keep me safe and worry free. You're here so that I can do what I have to without interruption. Do you know the other important part of your job? Maybe nobody mentioned this to you." Jan had a crooked smile on his face.

"Don't try to intimidate me." Makter's eyes were fixated on Jan's.

Jan ignored the stare. "To take the fall if things get really bad. You and that little cult of hippies you've collected go to jail while we finish our tests and move on. You know damn well that the people I work for can't have their names mixed up in this."

"So you say." Makter spoke defiantly now.

"So now that you know who is going to take the fall if this thing goes wrong, why don't you tell me what your progress is with Trent?"

"Everything is going fine."

Jan opened his eyes wider and looked at Mak with doubt. "So you've got nothing to tell me about today. Nothing?" He laid the sarcasm on heavy.

"I didn't do *anything* today except drive here, *sir*." Makter was trying to be respectful, but the violence in him surfaced through this sarcastic remark. He had bashed men's brains in for disrespecting him like this.

"Let me show you something." Jan led Makter over to an open map on the desk. He pointed to the location where the house sat. "We're here. Jake Trent lives down here. Mr. Trent, as we both know, is a legendary crime solver . . ."

Makter laughed out loud thinking it a joke, but quieted himself because of Jan's glare.

"Am I wrong, Mak? Do you think I'm stupid?" Jan's anger was hitting a peak. He started to shout. "So if Trent lives down here, and we're trying to keep him in the dark about what's going on up here"—Jan again jammed his finger at the location of the house; his voice turned into a strained shout and his face was red—"why the fuck would we allow him to follow us up to here?" Jan's thumb was now on the road in Yellowstone, about where the bison had crossed. He was spanning the distance between his thumb and forefinger. "Fifty miles south of here! You brought a criminal investigator fifty fucking miles south of me!!"

Makter raised his voice in response. "What? Nobody followed me anywhere! And Trent's retired! If I *was* followed, how the hell would you know? I told you to give me space to operate, you sonofabitch!"

There were dissonant voices in Makter's head. In some ways, he still feared and respected Jan. Mostly, though, he wanted to slit his throat. Watch him bleed out.

"How would I know? Despite my confidence in you—my now rapidly fading confidence—I took some of my own measures to ensure my safety."

"You put a fucking tracker on my car? His too? I'm not a fucking child, Jan!"

"I did indeed. And rightfully so, as it turns out." Jan's temper was flaring. "You out of your mind, Mak? What did I ask you to do?" He didn't leave time for the man to answer.

"I asked you, no, I *told* you, to stay near Trent and watch him. Watch him! I told you if and when I needed more, I would instruct you further. I told you we needed to make sure that he didn't come snooping around, that nothing caught his attention.

"And what did you do?" Jan was shouting now. "You came up with some sick fucking fantasy world! You let your own twisted desires put our work at risk! Start a cult? That's what you gleaned from my instructions?! That you should dream up a goddamn cult to 'distract' Trent, that just so happens to satisfy your sick mind? We only needed three months! Your 'distraction' is going to ruin us!"

Jan was pacing in front of Makter now, the veins in his head and neck bulging with boiling blood.

"I mean, fucking murdering people, Mak? Really? You're a sick fuck! I used to think it was a good trait, to be merciless and demented like you. You would do anything, no matter the consequences. Now I know you're just a demented little child!"

This was too much for Makter's mind to digest. He wanted to pounce, to end Jan's life. But again, something held him back.

Argus was like a fucking son to me!

Another voice: *Fucking kill Jan, you pussy!*

Then another: *Keep it together. He'll get his!*

Makter's eyelids twitched. Instead of addressing Jan's insults, he dissociated totally and readdressed the previous topic. His voice was friendly.

"Well, shit, don't you think that would have been helpful for me down there? The trackers? Sonofabitch, Jan! How the hell did Trent follow me anyway?"

"I've got no idea." Jan's voice was calmer, resigned. "I'm guessing he recognized you, you *idiot*. Have you even figured out what I am in charge of up here, Mak?"

Makter ignored the insult. "No. *Hell* no. I don't give a shit. I just wanna do my job, make my money, and get back at that bastard for what he did. For both of us."

"I share your sentiment on Jake Trent. But don't you think his death would attract some unwanted attention? If you'll recall, he's still got some pretty important fed friends. Someone could come looking around. Someone not on our payroll."

"You've paid off the feds? What for?"

"Feds, a few locals. Everybody we could. Some of the low-level authorities were too principled and shortsighted to hear me out." Jan paused. "It's time you understand what's going on here."

Makter wasn't listening. *He's soft! Kill him!* The voices came out of nowhere again, louder now.

"I need a glass of water," Makter said. His scalp and face were itching and burning. He felt hot.

"I'll do you one better." Jan walked over to the serving cart and poured Makter a scotch.

Jan started talking again. "Do you know what a barrel of petroleum costs right now?"

25

THE HOT ROCK TRACT. THE SAME DAY.

The question caught Makter by surprise. "It's high, I know . . . a
hundred dollars?"

"It's one sixty, and that's an all-time record high. Do you know
where we get energy in this country?" Jan asked. Makter shook his
head rather than guessing again. He could feel the scotch coursing
through him. It relaxed him slightly.

"Coal, natural gas, nuclear power, and the rest? What do you
know about nuclear reactors?"

"Nothing really. I don't wanna live near one; coal's dirty—pollution and shit." Makter shrugged, still not seeing the point.

"Right. Nobody wants a nuclear plant in his or her backyard.
And with this eco-generation"—Jan practically spit the phrase
out—"moving us all toward sustainability and eco-friendliness,

nobody can stomach the thought of black smoke billowing into the air anymore, right?"

Jan is always interested in the dumbest shit. What the hell is he talking about? I thought he wanted Trent's head?

"Mak, what if I told you that what we are working on here could someday contribute as much energy as both of those sources combined?"

Makter was confused. "Are you fucking with me?"

"I'm a businessman, you know that. I don't give a shit about the environment one way or another. I go where the money is, and I get no real thrill from committing petty crimes." He gestured at Makter, who took it as a compliment.

"The people who came to me with this job, they can't afford to be held accountable if things should go wrong. My reputation isn't quite as spotless as theirs. So like you, I'm a liaison, a link in the chain. I watch over the day-to-day operation of the project. It wasn't complicated really."

Makter glanced around. The instruments, monitors, and litera-ture in the office seemed complicated, despite what Jan said, but Mak learned long ago never to doubt Jan's intellect.

"It took a few days for me to get a grasp on everything. Any-thing gets out of my control, I just call my contact and they take care of it. In two more weeks, our project is over; it's really just a test, you see, and we all go home."

"Except for Trent?" Mak asked hopefully.

Jan looked frustrated. "Do whatever the hell you want with Trent. Just don't lead him here. And cut the cult bullshit. Then you can use your imagination, if it's feasible."

"Feasible? Trent is responsible for what happened to your

son. . . . They could've killed us! I want you there to watch him suffer and die! I went to fucking prison, Jan. Six years! How can you be so fucking soft? He deserves worse than death. Your son—"

"Don't tell me about my son!" Jan's voice rose again, and then settled quickly. "I'm getting too old for this bullshit. If I finish this job, I go home to my family with my money. If I go chasing after Jake Trent, I risk it all. There's a time for vengeance, Mak. For me, that time has passed. I bid you luck in your endeavor against him."

Makter stood up. "You're being a pussy, Jan, and you know it." He slammed his fist down on a desk. He was crossing the line, but the words had already left his mouth. His old friend responded in a surprisingly calm tone.

"Is there anything else?"

"No." Makter caught his breath.

"Okay, then one last thing."

Makter sat back down, trying to remain cool. "Okay, what is it?"

"Do you know why I hired you? Why I always hire you?"

"Because I'm good at what I do."

"Because I didn't want to take the risk. I hired you back then and now because I wasn't willing to go to jail, and I had money. You needed money and were willing to take the risk. That's business."

"What's your point?"

"My point is that our government learned of this project, gave it the green light, and gave responsibility to some private security brain farm who hired the tech people, who hired some scientists. This went on and on until I got the call. I'm the project manager, the man on the ground, the fixer, but I needed help. The men at the top of the chain have no idea who I am, and my boss has no idea who you are. That's the way everyone wants it."

Makter looked confused.

Jan sighed. "Do you know why our criminal justice system works? Because everyone can deny accountability for the awful punishments they hand out. The judge makes the call but doesn't have to witness the execution. The executioner takes a life, but he feels no remorse because it was at the judge's orders. You are the executioner."

More confusion. "What are you getting at, Jan?"

"Just do your part. No more, no less. And then collect your money."

After Makter left, Jan poured himself a drink. He stepped out onto the deck and looked over the rolling hills and buttes of northern Yellowstone. For a second he thought he felt the earth move again. He hoped it was just the booze.

He hadn't mentioned the quakes to Makter. Hadn't told his old friend everything.

If I'm going down out here in the middle of nowhere, Makter is going down with me.

Jan finished his scotch in one gulp.

Noelle thought she felt a tremor, but it could have been her nerves. Jake looked at her, confirming that she had. It lasted only a few seconds. They were at Noelle's cabin doing some research on EcoAmicae. Jake's bed-and-breakfast was still unsafe.

They'd settled on leaving the police out of the equation from now on. Even if the cops weren't in on it, Terrell and his crew had been useless to this point. There was no reason to believe they could help now.

The research was yielding very little. EcoAmicae had been fingered for a few acts of questionable legality—trespassing, chaining themselves to trees, and otherwise interfering with development. But for the most part, they seemed to get positive press. An Internet search yielded message boards that coordinated rallies and fund-raisers. Their website sold T-shirts, vegan cookbooks, and green living manuals.

"I don't really see any reason to think these guys are out to kill you," Noelle said over her shoulder.

"Can I have a look?" Noelle agreed, and handed the laptop over to Jake.

Jake scrolled through the search results, clicking on a few links. Noelle was right. There wasn't anything incriminating to be found. Jake opened one of the message boards. There wasn't much besides a few random rants and old meeting info.

One user name stuck out: WYldlife111. Based on the username, the person was a local. The *WY* likely referred to Wyoming, and the number of environmentalists seemed to drop off precipitously once you left Teton County. WYldlife111 *had* to be here.

Jake searched for all posts by that name. He or she had contributed quite a bit to the forum. From the posts, Jake could confirm that WYldlife111 was in fact in Jackson; there were plenty of references to Teton County. He copied the username and pasted it into the search engine.

Noelle watched him. "Got something?" Jake didn't answer. Noelle paced the cabin, thinking.

Most of the results were garbage, site squatters trying to sell their domain names. The seventh one down—www.theonlycause. com—seemed promising, so Jake clicked on it and navigated to its message board.

Jake waved Noelle over but kept his eyes on the screen. "Look at this." Jake pointed to a thread started by someone under the username WYld111. "It looks like this person posts on both the EcoAmicae board and this one. They live here in Jackson."

"Check it out, click on it."

The post was dated only ten days ago. It was a call to action for the very protest Noelle had witnessed in the square. This was enough to get Jake's attention, and he carefully read each post on the thread.

"Holy shit!" Noelle pointed at the middle of the screen. Her heart stopped.

#12 Re: . . . "town square protest . . ." BondurantJOE says: fingers crossed for appearance by THE Mr. S!!! (finally!)

"I remember this! There was a bunch of people there in the square protesting. Some asshole smashed an egg on my car. The Shaman was there?"

"Maybe." *THE Mr. S? The Shaman?*

Jake searched all posts referencing "Mr. S" and then tried the entire web. There were occasional mentions but nothing really stood out. No history of violence; quite the contrary.

"Seems more like a hippie than a terrorist."

Noelle considered the statement. "Maybe something sent him over the edge?"

Noelle was walking around the cabin, bouncing an old tennis

ball nervously on the wooden floor. Occasionally a noise from outside would startle her, and she would look out the window.

Jake eventually noticed this. "I think we're safe, Noelle. I don't think anybody knows we're here. Besides, nobody is after you."

Noelle wasn't so sure. "How do you know? Did I tell you a bear tried to get in here the other night? When I found the couple up there? Walked right over to my window, huffing and puffing, like it was trying to scare me." Noelle was pinching her brow between her thumb and forefinger, clearly anxious. *Almost forgot about the bear . . .*

Jake stood up and walked over to her. "Noelle, think about where you live. Look outside." Noelle looked through the window into the dense pine forest.

"I'm guessing you've seen bears up here before?" Jake was giving her a comforting smile, and just wry enough to show her how silly her suspicion was.

"Well, yeah."

"Look, maybe you should take a little break from all this." Jake closed the laptop. "It's for the best really, it might get dangerous, you know?" He walked back over to her and put his hand on her shoulder.

The sexism implied in his statement irritated Noelle. She stepped back, away from his reach. "No way. I'm fine. You know I'm actually a federal law enforcement agent, right, Mr. Big-Time Lawyer? Let's just go get some fresh air. I haven't had exercise in way too long."

Noelle set the pace high, a power walk bordering on a jog. From the cabin they headed due west toward the Tetons. It was late afternoon, but the sun was high and bright. Evening's chill was still an hour away.

It's only Tuesday? Jesus. A lot has happened in the last couple days. She looked at Jake. *Including that.* A smile crept onto her face.

She skipped up and over the rocks on the trail. She knew the route well. In half a mile, they reached a series of shallow lakes and marshes. The Cathedral Group—the range's highest peaks—loomed over the water and were reflected back up from its glassy surface.

Noelle stopped.

"Never gets old, does it?" Jake said aloud.

"The view? No, it sure doesn't." Noelle felt a momentary wave of serenity.

They started moving again, but at a slower pace, walking alongside the water. It was still early in the summer, but some of the birds had returned for the season. A bald eagle was stoically perched atop a lodgepole pine across the pond from them, looking for fish. In the mud, Jake pointed out the tracks of moose, elk, and coyote.

While they walked, Noelle thought:

All this chaos, and no sign of it here. Nature plugs along as if nothing is happening.

After fifteen minutes walking along the shore, Noelle spoke.

"Wanna run back?" She had a devilish smile on her face.

Jake looked down at his attire, corduroy pants and a button-down flannel shirt. Stiff leather boots.

"Oh, c'mon!" Noelle pleaded before Jake could even speak. "I'll take it easy on you. Follow me!"

Noelle pranced off directly into the woods, taking a different route from the one they used to get there. Jake tried his best to keep up. The trail was not as well used as the first. It looked to Jake like it was just a game trail, something used by the elk and moose to get to the water in the evening. The willows and underbrush kept it isolated from the sky and the rest of the world. Time after time, Jake had to slow his jog to a walk to squeeze through small openings in the vegetation. This was a perfect place to surprise a bear or moose.

Apparently she's not so frightened anymore, Jake thought as he strained to keep up.

Up ahead, Noelle was gaining more ground, her fitness and familiarity with the trail giving her a clear advantage. After what seemed like an eternity to Jake, the trail finally tunneled through one last thicket and into a pine forest. Just ahead was Noelle's cabin.

He slowed to a walk and caught his breath as he approached the back of the cabin. There was no sign of Noelle.

When Jake was breathing normally, he shouted, "Remind me never to go jogging with you again." He waited for a response. "Noelle?"

Suddenly alarmed, Jake slowly came around the corner of the house. He slowed his breathing. The front door was open. He picked up a sturdy stick from the ground and tested its strength, should he have to use it as a weapon. It held against his pressure; it would do.

He walked along the front of the cabin, ducking down so that the porch obscured him from the view of anyone within. Jake couldn't see anything; the cabin looked empty.

Quietly, he walked up the front steps and onto the porch. The wood creaked slightly under his weight. With the make-do club drawn back and ready to strike, he slid in through the door.

Kssshhhhhh! The sound of glass shattering. Noelle yelped, but Jake didn't see her. The ruckus came from the right, near the sink.

He quickly spun and finally saw her, standing alone, hands in the air, with a shocked look on her face.

"Jake?! What the *hell*?"

"Jesus!" Jake said aloud, tilting his head back and sighing with relief. He tossed the stick through the open door and onto the gravel driveway.

"I thought something had happened. I thought someone was in here with you."

Noelle was stooped over picking up shards of glass from the floor, breathing heavily.

"I appreciate your vigilance, but I was just having a glass of water."

They both laughed. Jake walked over to her and helped her clean up the mess.

26

JACKSON. LATER THAT DAY.

Makter drove back to Jackson, trying to decipher the message Jan had just given him. *It's all gibberish. He's getting philosophical now?! He thinks he's so much better than me.*

He had to take the long way back to the motel—through Idaho, crossing the Henrys Fork and climbing over Teton Pass into Jackson Hole. He checked his phone messages when he got there. Nothing on the room phone. His cell phone had quite a few messages, eleven to be exact, but he deleted them after listening to the first three. Everyone was looking for the Shaman. Each caller reported that they had done as he asked and that the development site was ruined. Makter knew this wasn't true—they probably had delayed the development by only a few days, not that it mattered. For all they'd done to annoy him, he would miss his followers. Miss the power. But Jan had given him an ultimatum: continue and get removed from the job. If he was fired, Makter knew this also meant that Jan would have him killed.

But is that the only way?

He had worked so hard to achieve something, and now it had been taken away. Jan couldn't understand it. Makter *needed* the power. He needed his followers.

There had to be some way that both he and Jan could get what they wanted.

If not, kill the asshole! Makter ignored the voice as best he could.

He called the front desk for a massage.

"Yes. A *female* massage therapist, please."

Meanwhile, on the deck of the big cedar house, Jan was desperately trying to get ahold of his wife. He hadn't spoken to her in weeks. For all he knew, she had left Argus with the caregiver and wandered off to Vegas or Rio. It wasn't really her he was worried about, though.

After the fourth attempt at her cell phone, he left a message: "Hi, we need to talk. Something came up. Do not come West no matter what you do. Call me as soon as you can. Good-bye." He hadn't told her he loved her in years.

Should he warn Makter of the danger?

It's too early. If things got worse, he could still warn him. For now, the risk of disclosure didn't outweigh the benefits.

Who knows what he might do? Kill me? Ruin the whole experiment?

Both possibilities were equally undesirable to Jan. The machines had only a half mile to go and then ten million dollars would be his, maybe more. Legal and tax free. He would be able to care for Argus again—regain some pride in his life.

In Jackson, another quake was rocking Makter's bed. *I swear these fucking things are getting stronger.* The TV went out momentarily, only to come back on a bit fuzzier. *Jesus,* Makter thought. *If I'm gonna deal with this shit I wanna be in California, where it's warm.*

27

GRAND TETON NATIONAL PARK. THAT EVENING.

It was dark outside. Noelle poured boiling water over the noodles in the Styrofoam cup, walked over, and handed Jake his dinner.

"I know it's not gourmet."

"It's perfect. Thank you." Jake was back at the laptop now, his shirt still sweaty from the run. Noelle was pacing again.

"It just doesn't make sense," she said. "This old enemy of yours is around, doing who knows what. Then there's this development project, which you oppose, I mean we all do, and a group of conservationists are after you because they think you support it? What are we missing? How would they get that idea? You really think this is all related?"

"I don't know, probably. It doesn't make sense to me either, but sometimes it's hard to understand things when you can't relate to the person behind it all."

"You mean like 'seeing things through the eyes of a madman' kind of thing?"

"Something like that."

Noelle went back to her thoughts again. Now walking the inside perimeter of the cabin, still occasionally looking out the window.

"Holy *shit,*" Jake whispered. Noelle scrambled over to the table where Jake sat.

"What?!"

"One of the members of this site—Cursed1—his quote says 'Save the Willamette—NO MORE DAMS!'"

"So?"

Jake spoke fast. "The Willamette River. It's a short ways from Lewis and Clark Law School. The anadromous fish, steelhead and salmon, their spawning runs have been demolished by dams on the river. And under education, it says JD."

"What do fish have to do with this?"

"Nothing. The dead lawyer I found in the river. He went to Lewis and Clark."

"Didn't a lot of people?"

"Sure, but this guy lives here. He must, he responded to the protest invitation. Said he couldn't make it."

Noelle looked at the screen. He was registering as a member.

"Thank you! Your username and password will arrive shortly!"

Jake opened his email. From www.theonlycause.com, a username and temporary password were already in his in-box. He went back to the page, entered the information, and clicked the log-on button.

"Maybe I can get more information this way." He searched by member for Hawlding. Cursed1 had chosen not to enter his or her real name.

"Shit!" Jake's fingers hovered over the keyboard, unsure where to go next.

"Try C. Stanford. The name from the receipt."

Jake nodded and entered the name. There was a long list of posts and messages that contained both "C." and "Stanford." Jake scrolled through the first page of results and then opened the second, then the third.

"I don't see anything."

"Stop! Middle of the page."

Jake looked where she pointed.

CarlofNature (posts to)>Cursed1, re: celebration: r u nervous or excited or both?

"There's no response."

"Click on his username."

Jake did as Noelle asked. "CarlofNature went to Stanford." Jake looked up at Noelle in disbelief. "It's a fake name. C. Stanford is CarlofNature."

Noelle finished his thought. "And Cursed1 is Hawlding. Open the rest of his profile."

Jake looked at the "About Me" section—"cursed like Palemon," he read to himself. It didn't ring a bell immediately. Jake handed the laptop to Noelle. "You'll be faster."

Jake gave the name some thought. *Palemon. Greek mythology?* He couldn't pin down the source of his memory. *Palemon, palemon. A painting? An opera?*

"Do you know the name Palemon? I mean, does it sound familiar?" Jake asked Noelle.

She shook her head. "The only place I've heard of it is in that ballet."

Jake paused and looked up at her. "*What* ballet?"

"*Ondine* or *Undine*. I'm not sure which it is. One was a book and the other was the ballet."

Jake took a moment to think. "That's it. I *knew* it sounded familiar. The story of Ondine, do you remember what it was?"

"Not really, no. I was young when I saw it. I was just interested in the costumes."

"I don't remember all the details, but Ondine was some type of water nymph. Palemon fell in love with her. At the end of the story, Ondine finds out that he has been unfaithful and she gives him one final, fatal kiss and then returns to the sea."

"Wow. Impressive knowledge of ballet, Jake. You're a real man's man." She laughed. "How does it help us?"

"Look here, under 'About Me,' Hawlding wrote 'Cursed like Palemon' . . ."

"Yeah, so what? He had his heart broken and wrote something cheesy on the Internet to express himself."

"I don't think so. There's a medical condition called Ondine's curse."

Noelle smiled at him, shaking her head in disbelief.

"I did a medical malpractice case for a sufferer of Ondine's curse once. The automatic reflex related to breathing is nonexistent. The person has to breathe consciously. Depending on the severity, they may have to have a pacemaker-like device surgically installed. It tells their body when to breathe while they're asleep."

"So this guy had this disease? What does that mean for us?"

"I think he was a human sacrifice. They mention a celebration; it must have been that night at the tavern. A farewell party of sorts."

Noelle was speechless for a second.

"Why would he sacrifice himself? How does it help their cause?"

"He felt he had nothing to live for. Ricker mentioned that one of the group's aims was to show others that to ignore Mother Nature's dangers could be a fatal mistake. That if you didn't respect her you would be struck down. Hawlding didn't want to fight his disease with modern medicine; it was against his belief system. His death also served the purpose of furthering the cause. They feel our land is overused, abused. Death in nature would certainly put a damper on tourism and spread their message. If you're a maniac, those are some pretty good reasons to die."

The ground shook hard under them. "A bunch of earthquakes coming from the world's largest volcanically active region would sure put a damper on tourism. And spread a message too."

A jar of rice fell from a shelf and crashed loudly to the floor.

"They're still getting stronger, Jake."

"Feels that way. Might be in our heads, though." Jake thought of the serenity they had just witnessed on their walk.

He paused for a bit to think. "You can't just start an earthquake, Noelle. You're overestimating the ability of man."

"I don't know," Noelle said. "But I know where we might be able to find out. Keith's got friends in the geology department up at MSU. We should check out Yellowstone on the way: the camp was near the park, the geyser basin death, your car chase—"

"Noelle, that's silly," Jake interrupted. "Plus, it's dangerous; we'd be driving through the hotbed of all this activity. It's insane."

Noelle ignored Jake. "You have a better way to figure this out? We'll leave first thing in the morning."

PART THREE

PART
THREE

28

It was sweltering in the nation's capital. Cherry blossom season was long gone. There was only heat and humidity to look forward to until September.

Five men were spaced evenly at one end of a large, rectangular table. They all wore dark suits, except for one, who wore an army uniform. They kept their voices low, and each man had a laptop in front of him.

At the opposite end of the table, a screen unfurled from the ceiling, stretching nearly to the floor. After a few seconds of blank blue, a figure appeared and the men quieted down.

The man was skinny and relatively young, in his early forties. He looked nervous, adjusting his eyeglasses as the men in the room acknowledged him.

"We need you to come back to the States," the army man said. "We need you to go out there and tell us exactly what's going on."

The other men in the room nodded.

"I'm swamped here." The man spoke with a British accent. "Besides, I have access to all the same information here that I would if I were there." His voice cracked ever so slightly.

One of the men in a suit stood up, raising his voice: "We're not making a suggestion, Jules! We need to know what the hell is happening out there!"

The man to his left calmed him down, and then he spoke. "Look, Jules, what's your most recent prediction, given the current data?"

The man called Jules looked anxious. "Despite the news, Jim, my prediction remains the same. I've told you this a million times. Nothing has changed. There's no way to know exactly what is going on down there."

"Then what are we paying you for?" another man said in an icy staccato.

Jules took a deep breath. "You're paying me for the best advice there is. And remember that I *never* recommended this way forward. I said it was too unpredictable. Now, here we are."

The second man snapped, "Is this your project, Jules? Did you fund it? Who pays your salary?"

Jules shook his head silently.

"You're a fucking *scientist*. Do your job."

"You let us know immediately if anything changes. And if you don't return our calls, know that we will find you."

The screen went blank. The man who had last spoken slammed his computer shut and stood up to leave. The others filed out behind him.

29

GRAND TETON NATIONAL PARK. THE SAME MORNING.

Jake and Noelle were in Noelle's ranger truck and headed toward Yellowstone. Noelle had called off work, citing a family obligation. It was first light. "Remind me, how is Keith gonna help?" Jake asked. She had just picked up her cell phone to make a call. She gave him the universal hand signal for "just a minute."

"Keith? It's Noelle." She'd woken him. "Listen, Jake and I are headed up to Bozeman to see you." She paused. "Yeah, right now. Both of us. We need your help with something. We need to talk to a seismologist, someone we can trust. And we might need access to their lab." She was silent for a few seconds and then hung up the phone.

"Seismology lab?" Jake asked.

When they reached the south entrance to Yellowstone, the ranger booths were empty. Jake knocked on the office door, but that was abandoned as well. The entrance gates were chained and locked.

"Shit. We'll have to go around, through Idaho," Jake said after taking one last look around.

"No way, that's gonna take too long. Watch out." Noelle grabbed a thick-tined digging rake from the back of her truck and headed to the closest gate. She jammed a tine inside one of the chain links on the lock mechanism.

"Cover your eyes. Stay back," she told Jake. Noelle started twisting the rake clockwise by its wooden handle, and the chain began to creak. After four or five turns, it was twisted and coiled onto itself in quite a mess. She couldn't turn the rake anymore. Jake walked up to help. Using all their strength, they tried one last turn to break the chain free. Jake planted his feet and pushed, holding the rake at the terminus to generate the most leverage. After a few seconds, the chain couldn't take any more. It popped and clattered to the ground in a heap. Jake stumbled, and Noelle fell over from the instant lack of resistance.

"How do you think your boss would feel about that?" Jake asked as Noelle threw the chain into the weeds and opened the gate.

"Let's go" was her only response.

They got in the vehicle and sped through the park. There were no rangers, no speed limits. Near Norris Geyser Basin a group of scientists was huddled around the geothermal feature. They thought nothing of another park service truck speeding by.

Jake and Noelle kept their eyes open but saw nothing out of the ordinary, aside from the unusually intense activity in the geyser basins. No Makter. No protesters, no bodies. The park was deserted.

In less than two hours, Jake and Noelle were crossing the Montana border. To exit the park, they simply drove around the gate on the remnants of a construction entrance. Again, the ranger station was unoccupied. Jake was relieved not to have to cause more property damage.

They got to Keith's lab at Montana State by quarter after nine. He greeted them as they entered. "Noelle, wonderful to see you! Have a seat." He hugged Noelle and shook Jake's hand.

"Keith. Nice to see you," Noelle said.

Keith turned to Jake. "Glad to see she roped you into this mess! It's been too long. How's the fishing?" Jake pronated his hand to say "so-so."

"Did y'all feel that quake an hour ago? Shook enough to rattle my stuff around." Keith swept his hand across the vials, tools, and cameras on his shelves.

"So you're feeling them here, too?" Keith's observation invited Noelle to get right to the point. "We were in the car; we wouldn't have felt that last one. But there've been plenty of them. That's why we came."

Keith looked confused. "Feeling them? Hell, they think they're centered not too far from here. Northwestern part of the park, they say. Probably equidistant from Jackson and Bozeman. What do you mean you came because of the earthquakes?"

"Well, sort of. We wanted to hear from an expert, you know, someone in that field first. We think . . . er, I think there's a chance that someone is causing the quakes."

There was silence in the lab while Keith processed the statement. Then he spoke nonchalantly. There was no real sense of surprise in his tone.

"And how do you want me to help you?"

Noelle answered first. "MSU has a big seismology department, right? We just want to talk to someone who can tell us if this is possible. We thought you might have a friend or—"

"It would probably be silly to ask if you have involved the authorities, right?" Keith interrupted, grimacing. Neither of them responded.

"Okay. Didn't think so. Then, I suppose we need someone we can really trust?"

Jake spoke up. "Afraid so, yeah. We actually think the police could be involved. And obviously we don't want word to get out and cause a panic. You know what all these earthquakes could mean as well as anyone. Part of me hopes they *are* caused by humans."

"Right. Okay, I'll send some emails; it's usually the fastest way to get ahold of folks on campus."

Keith didn't bother sitting down at the desk. He leaned over his keyboard and entered a few email addresses. Then he typed a short message and stood. "Done. I guess we wait now. It shouldn't be long. Can I get anyone a coffee or tea?"

Jake declined, but Noelle accepted the offer, asking for tea. Keith left the lab and walked down the hall to the employee lounge area. Noelle and Jake were left sitting in the lab alone looking at each other. The wait made them feel idle and anxious.

Finally Noelle broke the silence. "Do you think anyone will help?"

"I don't know."

As Jake spoke, things on the shelves began to clink and clang. The ground shook for the next several seconds. Jake and Noelle looked at each other but didn't utter a word.

Again, Jake could the see the fear in Noelle's eyes that had surfaced only a few times since he'd known her. The intensity of the quake increased and she grabbed onto an epoxy-resin lab table to stabilize herself. A large glass jar slid off its perch and smashed on the floor. An organ of some kind flopped out. The smell of preservatives filled the air. It reminded Jake of the morgue.

Keith came skidding around the corner and through the lab door just as the tremors subsided. "Whooooaaa! That was wild! Another one! Bad news about your tea . . ." He held up a clear mug filled with opaque brown fluid.

"What *is* that?" Noelle asked. Her voice was shaky.

"It's what came from the tap. Quakes must have broken a waterline. It's contaminated." He smelled and shook his head. "Smells like sulfur."

Sulfur. Jake thought. *Just like the geyser basin.*

The computer made a dull beeping noise. "Email! Nice to know something still works." Keith hustled over to the machine. On his way, he noticed the spilled jar. "Yuck, sorry about that, guys. Just a grizzly liver."

This time, Keith sat down before opening his email. "Nice! Dr. Stevenson wants us to come over and chat with him."

"Uh, might wanna clean that up first . . ." Noelle pointed at the liver. Her hands crossed over her chest, holding herself.

"Oh, shoot, right." Keith cleaned up the liver and replanted it in a new jar. "We test them for all sorts of stuff, deformities, illness, probably the most important is the presence of pollution or chemicals. This one hasn't been dissected yet. It's from a big bear, though, I can tell you that from the size of it."

When he was finished, Keith led them across campus. They left the main sidewalk for a path that crossed the big lawn in the center of the quad. As they did, a shudder again rolled through the ground at their feet. It lasted only a short moment, but it was enough to get the attention of the students on the lawn. They looked around with fretful faces.

Jake looked around as well. The earthquakes seemed more real to him here. Just a few minutes prior when they got out of the truck, the campus had felt friendly and safe. Being out of Jackson Hole was a relief. Now it occurred to Jake that there was no easy escape from his troubles. Here, the lawn was manicured, there were more buildings and people, but there was still no sense of control or order.

Could Noelle be right about the quakes? Is it actually possible that they tie into all this somehow? If she's right, this is no minor disturbance where the deer go on grazing. Not a fly left stuck in a streamside bush. This is meddling with a force that no one can predict or understand.

Jake hoped that Keith's friend might be able to answer those questions. This was a matter far beyond his realm of knowledge. Another shudder in the earth. He turned to see Noelle and Keith a ways ahead of him, so he jogged to catch up.

In another basement laboratory, they found Dr. Stevenson. He was tall and skinny and of Asian-American descent. His hair was well groomed and he wore expensive eyeglasses, but there was a childlike quality about him. They shook hands all around.

"So what can I do for you? There's a lot of exciting stuff going on right now!" He sounded giddy.

To Jake, his enthusiasm was off-putting. Despite how interesting the quakes might be from a scientific standpoint, they were destructive already and bound to get worse.

Noelle was on the same page. She inquired into his meaning. "What do you mean, exciting?"

"The earthquakes of course, and the changes in geology, especially in the park—"

"Right. Sorry to stop you, but changes in geology?" Jake asked. "As in, the earth is moving?"

"Yes, of course. Something like this hasn't happened since 1959—the Hebgen Lake quake. It's pretty remarkable."

"What exactly is changing? Geologically, I mean?" Despite his eccentric bedside manner, it seemed to Jake that Stevenson knew what he was talking about.

"Everything. Well, the earth always moves when there is an earthquake. Around here we have extremely sensitive geothermal features. Any slight movement underground can change them— creating new geysers, eliminating old ones . . ."

"Like Old Faithful?" Noelle asked, thinking of the newspaper article.

"Exactly! In 1959, it was a 7.5 that did it. That quake delayed Old Faithful's eruption time by nearly nine minutes! This time, it seems as if these smaller quakes have had the same effect."

"But the geyser isn't erupting at all right now."

"Right! And it may never erupt again. There's a complicated network of tubes and ducts down there, naturally formed, of course. If some get blocked and others open up, it changes the location and intensity of the geyser. It might never return to the state it was in before the quakes."

The explanation got Keith's attention. "So, if Old Faithful isn't erupting now, does that mean that the energy—the heat—is being stored somewhere and might cause a more massive eruption?"

Stevenson laughed. "No, not at all. The water and steam would likely be escaping elsewhere, through cracks and springs and the formation of new geysers. Another close-by geyser might get bigger or more regular, who knows? Anyway, I don't mean to overwhelm you with my excitement. You were saying, Ms. . . . ?"

"Noelle, please. Our question is a little out there, but we were wondering whether there is any way for a person to start an earthquake?" She paused for a second and then spoke again. "Well, I guess a series of earthquakes."

Stevenson gave Noelle a grave look. Then he started to laugh. "Sounds like a Superman movie or something." He looked at Jake and Keith for a laugh but didn't get one. "I mean, no. Impossible. Not on this scale."

Noelle felt silly and so she fell silent, but Jake spoke. "You say not on this scale, what do you mean by that?"

"I didn't mean to offend you, ma'am," he said, turning to Noelle. "All I mean is that yes, it is *technically* possible to cause an earthquake, or at least increase the chances of one. That being said, it could never have been done across such a huge area."

"Has this ever been attempted before?"

"Not attempted, no. It has arguably happened before, but accidentally, of course." He took a big sip from an oversized soda.

"How? And how would it be done?"

"Just a simple change of conditions. You shift stuff around deep in the earth, and you just might cause some instability that could lead to an occurrence."

"How do you cause instability?"

"You could do it quite a few ways, really. Explosives would work, I suppose, if you had enough of them."

"So in theory someone with bad intentions could make this happen?"

"No way. You would need the explosives inventory of a large country and hundreds of millions of dollars of drilling equipment. The operation would be huge."

"But you said it has happened before, right, just not with explosives?"

"There's a lot of evidence it's happened before, yes. Especially in one specific event in Switzerland. Government experiments caused it. Nothing malicious. Just some miscalculations."

"What happened?"

"Well, the exact way the quakes were caused never really got out to the public. It's likely only a couple of drilling companies and the Swiss government know exactly how it went down. They would have to be involved to pull something like this off."

"Could that happen here?"

"Not possible, at least not with these quakes. Again, the scope is too big. If it was even attempted, we'd know about it by now. You couldn't do it on federal land without somebody noticing."

Noelle raised her hands in defeat. Jake spoke. "I think that's all we've got. I guess we are barking up the wrong tree. Thank you for your time, Doctor."

Noelle exchanged "thank yous" and "nice to meet yous" with Stevenson. Keith shook his hand and asked one last question.

"Hey, should we be worried about this stuff? All the activity, I mean . . . everybody knows Yellowstone is a supervolcano, does this mean it's getting ready to erupt?"

Stevenson patted Keith on the back. "Nothing to worry about. This sort of activity just comes along from time to time. Nobody really knows why it happens, but there's no reason to think it's an indication that the whole thing is going to blow. Of course someday it will, but we'll never see it coming."

A lovely thought.

Keith nodded at him and shook his hand again. Jake and Noelle exchanged dubious looks.

The trio walked back to Noelle's truck. It was just after noon.

"Y'all are welcome to stay and hang out. It's a long ride back, and I know a place that makes a mean green-chili stew," Keith told them as he walked them to the car. "Jake, man, we can BS about fishing, like the good old days."

Jake and Noelle looked at each other. "Maybe just a quick lunch, then we'd better get back."

Lunch took longer than Jake or Noelle would've liked. In the two hours they spent at Rio's Café, six small quakes interrupted Keith's animated stories of bears, trout, and general adventure.

As Keith walked them back to the truck, he looked from Noelle to Jake. "Wait, are you guys like . . . you know . . . ?" His voice trailed off into an embarrassed laugh.

"Are we what?" Noelle asked.

"Like an item or whatever, you know, a couple?"

The question made Noelle uncomfortable. Her short fling with Keith was a long time ago, but romance was still a topic she didn't want to discuss with the present company.

Noelle finally responded. "Why would you think that?"

"No reason." He hugged Noelle and firmly shook Jake's hand, promising to come down to Jackson for some fishing "if the world doesn't end." He was kidding, but the joke failed in the face of the looming uncertainty.

They got in the truck, Jake in the driver's seat, and waved to Keith. As they headed south, neither of them said a word about Keith's question. Both wondered if a conversation on the matter was really necessary. If it was, this wasn't the time or place to do it. They sat in silence.

Meanwhile, just a mile from the north entrance, a female grizzly bear was digging furiously at an embankment. Every thirty seconds or so the sow would stick her dish-shaped face into the dirt, huffing, trying to smell for any signs of life. Then she resumed digging more frantically after each break.

Her hackles were up, making her already huge shoulders look all the more impressive. The pile of dirt and rocks behind her was nearly three feet tall already—this is what the animals were built for, using their powerful shoulders and long claws to scrounge for food when conditions were tough.

This mother's urgency stemmed from another primal urge, and when she lowered her heavy head to sniff the earth one last time, she had hope. A small black nose was protruding from the wreckage of the collapsed den.

She started digging again. More carefully this time and only around the outside of the dusty form she had discovered. When all the dirt was cleared away, she grabbed her cub by the scruff of his neck and dragged him a few feet away from their collapsed home.

The cub lay motionless for a moment. Its mother was distraught. Then, without warning, the cub stood up and shook off. The elated mom licked away the remaining dust and dirt from his fur. She curled her lips and huffed at the collapsed den. Then she turned and sauntered off with the cub in tow, looking for safer ground.

*   *   *

Noelle was pumping gas into the truck at a station twenty miles south of Bozeman. It was three fifteen. "Do you want to go through the park or around the long way?"

"Was thinking the long way," Jake answered. "Unless you have a preference. We're not in a hurry, are we? No reason to risk it."

"I'm not," Noelle said, but she was disappointed in his decision. She paused, then spoke again. "Let's just go through the park. If someone stops us, I'll just fess up. It can't be *that* big of a deal."

He laughed. "Okay, Ranger Klimpton."

"You mind driving for a bit?"

When they got to the next intersection, Jake turned the vehicle left toward the north entrance of Yellowstone.

Fifteen miles north of the park, another bison jam held them up.

"Weird to see them this far out of the park," Noelle said.

"Wonder what they're doing?"

"Fleeing, maybe." The implications of Noelle's statement made them both stay silent for a few minutes. The line of animals crossing the road stretched on for a few hundred yards. They moved at a deliberate pace.

"Still want to go through the park?" Jake gave her a concerned look. He lowered the windows and killed the engine to let the bison pass.

She nodded.

They were about ten miles from the north entrance of Yellowstone when they felt another shiver in the earth. This time the car shook hard, jostling its passengers in their seat belts. CDs fell from the overhead compartment. The tall evergreens that made up the forest swayed at their pinnacles.

Noelle was afraid. She fidgeted with her seat belt, which had become uncomfortably tight.

The quake stopped abruptly like all the others. Noelle bent to pick up her CD collection from the floor of the truck.

Jake looked at her. "You're sure you still wanna go through the park?" he asked one last time.

"We're committed now." The herd had continued moving in behind the truck after they'd passed. "I don't want to wait for the bison again."

She shoved the albums back into their storage compartment. Outside, the pine needles and leaves knocked from their roosts were still floating in the wind, descending slowly and playfully.

They went on a few more miles in silence. Small quakes occasionally broke through the landscape's facade of serenity.

Jake was thinking about their visit with the seismologist, trying to decide whether or not there was anything of value in his assessment. "What do you think he meant by government experiments, exactly?"

"Who, Dr. Stevenson? No idea."

The truck bucked like a bronco and Jake fell silent. He slowed the vehicle to a crawl. Then another bump. Jake cocked his head, trying to feel for the source of the bump.

Is the truck breaking down?

There was a pause in the chaos before the earth roared back to life. It was the strongest one yet. Noelle braced herself by pushing her palms against the roof of the truck. Jake held the steering wheel tight, trying to keep the vehicle on the road.

The earth groaned louder. Jake feared the worst. *The eruption.* Scrambled thoughts cycled through his mind. *I'll never see Noelle again. We were so close to figuring it all out. I'll never know what could have been.*

Jake slammed the truck to a complete stop as folds of asphalt were heaved up in front of them. Noelle could see that Jake was afraid, and that frightened her more. She reached over and held his hand on the steering wheel.

Tree branches were falling from the forest. Birds left their perches and hovered in the air, looking for solace. Squirrels scrambled down the tree trunks to the ground.

A hard knock threatened to roll the truck over. Noelle screamed.

"Hold on!" Jake shouted back.

The roadway bucked, releasing steam and water. The tremors intensified. All around them, the earth buckled, hazy smoke pouring forth.

Noelle yelled through the chaos, her voice trembling. "I'm guessing that's not a water main?" She was pointing to a jet of water shooting forty feet in the air.

"Don't think so!"

The shaking was making them dizzy, affecting their vision. Everything was a blur.

Holy shit!

Whole trees fell. First the smaller Engelmann spruce. Then a handful of lodgepoles flopped to the ground, many that had proudly stood seventy-five feet tall. Their branches slapped the earth as they fell and sent clouds of dust up and out.

The steam bursting from the road increased, and the temperature was rising fast in the truck. Noelle yelled at Jake over the rumbling earth and hissing steam. "Get out or stay in?!" Her face was panicked.

"Stay in!" Jake yelled back, and pressed down the automatic door lock.

It was getting hotter in the car, and fast. *Probably ninety degrees.*

Now around a hundred. Jake looked at Noelle. They were both sweating. He was rethinking his decision to stay in the vehicle.

The chaos was still carrying on outside. *One hundred and five.* They heard a crack below the truck's transmission and the body tilted backward. The road was literally crumbling beneath them. Steam flowed around the cabin. *One hundred and ten degrees.*

"Shit! We're parked on a steam vent!" Noelle shouted.

Jake and Noelle exchanged a horrified look. They held each other as tight as they could.

The singular thought in each of their heads was identical.

This is it.

30

One hundred and twenty-five degrees.

Jake threw the transmission into reverse and floored it. With a thud, the truck slid off the ramped slab and back onto the flat road. Jake reached across and opened Noelle's door and then his own. The heat poured out of the passenger cabin like smoke out of a burning oven.

The quake stopped. Jake took stock of the damage. It looked like a tornado and wildfire had swept through the woods at the same time. *But we're still here.* Yellowstone hadn't erupted, but the quakes were intensifying.

They got out of the truck to cool off. It was still outside now. After a few minutes, Noelle stuck her head back in, looked around, and found a bottle of water on the floor. Its plastic had melted slightly from the heat. But it was still full. Jake insisted that she take a drink first. It was warm but still tasted good. She handed the bottle to Jake.

"Well," he said after taking a gulp. "It would be nice to say we could turn around. But it looks to me like we're going through the park no matter what."

Noelle followed Jake's glance back up the road. About fifty yards away, an enormous pine rested on the road. There was no way through the mess that they could see. The tree extended sixty feet past either shoulder of the road. On one end, the dirt-packed ball of roots sat heavily, soil still falling from its gangling tentacles. On the other end, the wispy upper limbs hung in the air.

"Shit!" Noelle was visibly shaken. She brought her trembling hands to her head. She was losing it.

Jake had to keep her sharp if they wanted to survive. "How could you know? Let's get out of here." He put his arm around Noelle's shoulders and led her to the car, embrace more protective than romantic. When they got in, the evening breeze had cooled down the vehicle's cabin significantly.

Ahead of them, the right lane of the road was damaged to the point that travel would be impossible. Although the earth's tremors had ceased for the time being, there were still steam vents and miniature geysers dotting the roadside. It was an unearthly atmosphere.

"We'll get through the park as quickly as we can." Jake skidded out, turned into the left lane, and drove as fast as possible until they came to the north entrance.

"No!" Jake put the truck in park and killed the engine. They exited the car. The small ranger station booth was in ruins. Two of the four walls had fallen outward, leaving the interior of the building exposed. A medium-sized pine rested menacingly against one of the remaining walls. Worse yet, another tall pine lay suspended across the road to their south. Four feet in the air, its tip resting on the upturned roots of another fallen tree. There was no way to go under or over with the truck.

"Now what?" Noelle asked him as she dropped her hands to her sides. "I'm sorry—" Jake stopped her. As he did, the earth groaned again. They braced for another thrashing, but it never came. Instead, the noisy grumble faded back into the silence that normally came with the isolation of the park.

"Don't be sorry. We're fine. I'm going to see if the phone in the booth still works. I'll be right back."

Noelle looked around nervously. It was starting to get dark. Her fears of the wild—bears, mountain lions, and storms—had long faded after years of living in the mountains. Now, though, there was a new set of threats. The deserted woodlands had transformed into a nightmarish landscape.

Inside the remains of the booth, Jake was fiddling with the phone. No dial tone.

He looked around for another means of communication. The fax machine had suffered the same fate as the phone. On the floor below it, though, Jake saw a facsimile. He picked up the paper. It was dated only a few hours before. It looked to be the product of some automated disaster alert system. It contained information on the series of quakes in the last few days; "nothing to worry about," it said. Park employees should do their best to keep the public calm during evacuation.

On the bottom of the page was a simple map of Yellowstone, really just a rectangle with a few markers for the obvious points of interest. Tiny asterisks showed where the most recent geological activity had been. It was hard to say from such a rudimentary map, but it looked as if they were centered in the area that Keith was referring to as the epicenter of the quakes, in the northwest corner of the park. If not there, somewhere damn close.

Jake and Noelle were near the epicenter, and he got the feeling it wasn't coincidence. He had never believed in fate, but he couldn't shake the thought that they were there for a reason.

He ran out of the booth and headed toward Noelle.

"Noelle!" Jake called for her as he left the booth. "Look at this!"

Noelle had wandered a short distance into the woods. She came jogging back. "Did you find a phone?"

"Yeah, but it's dead. I found this, though. It gives us the locations of all the tremors in the last forty-eight hours." He passed her the fax.

She looked it over. "Not too far from here. What's your plan?"

Jake paused for a second, trying to think how to best phrase what he was about to propose. "We're never gonna get around this tree. I'd say we try going back north. I think there might be a big enough gap at the end of that tree to get through. You have four-wheel drive, right?"

"Of course. But what're we going to do when we get past the tree? There could be more roadblocks. It could be worse up there closer to the epicenter."

"Well, we have a map now; we could drive up there and take a look around." He felt a tinge of guilt at his proposition. The idea would only put Noelle in more danger. His instinct, however, told him that this was a lead that needed to be followed. "I have a feeling this isn't going to stop unless we stop it."

"Go to the epicenter, you mean?" She looked at Jake dubiously.

"It sounds worse when you say it. I don't think we're going to be safe until we find out exactly what's causing these quakes."

She looked for confidence and determination in his eyes and found it.

"I'm in." In a fraction of a second, she was back in the car.

31

YELLOWSTONE NATIONAL PARK

Jake was in the driver's seat again and going fast. He deftly maneuvered around potholes on the freshly pocked road, fallen trees,
and newly formed geothermal features. They arrived back at the
roadblock in less time than their original opposing journey.

He pulled the park service vehicle over to the shoulder—an
unnecessary move because of the seclusion of the road. There was
no way another vehicle would cross their path; the precaution was
a habit, a remnant of their world that had just been turned upside
down.

"I'm going to walk around the end here." He pointed to the
tree's upper terminus. The root ball on the other end created a
much bigger obstacle. "Stay in the car. It's hard to tell how solid
the ground will be out there." The gruesome scene he'd witnessed
at the geyser basin flashed in his mind.

Jake walked on the tree trunk as long as possible to avoid the steaming ground. When the trunk narrowed to the point that using it was impossible, he stayed on miniature hummocks of high ground and rocks.

Back on the road, Noelle ignored his request and was looking around the scene, trying to formulate her own idea for a way out.

Looks like Jake is right, she thought as she looked at the opposite end of the tree. There around the root ball, dense trees made passage impossible.

She went back to the truck, which now had a few sinewy clouds of sulfurous steam twisting around it. The road was warming and small fractures were silently forming. The earth shivered ever so slightly.

Night was just around the corner. The evening light was a cool blue, and the mangled trees were silhouetted in black against it. Noelle got in the truck and threw on the headlights to illuminate Jake's path back to her. The cylindrical beams of light cast an even more peculiar mood on the scene. Although the evening mountain air was crisp, the emerging gasses lent their share of humidity and heat.

Jake looked around and squinted through the dusk when he reached the end of the pine. It would be tough going; the ground was already soft from spring moisture, and again, it was hard to tell how deep and strong the earth was at any given point. There was no way to know whether it could support the weight of a person, let alone that of a large vehicle. At any time, the truck could get bogged down in mud or worse—the mass of the vehicle might break through the earth's crust, exposing Jake and Noelle to God knows what lay beneath.

Boiling water and steam or two-thousand-degree lava.

There was a path, though—a small swath through the still standing pines that would barely accommodate the width of the pickup. Assuming the ground there was firm, Noelle's four-wheel drive would have no trouble navigating the route. It was their only option.

He hopscotched on the rocks and walked back down the tree's trunk to the road. Jake shielded his eyes from the headlights and approached the truck.

"I think we've got a chance getting around that way," he said. "It's hard to say how much weight this crust can hold, though. If we get stuck and have to leave the car, we could be in trouble."

"In a few minutes, we're gonna be in trouble *here*." Noelle pointed to the scatter of now-widening steam vents and crevices in the road. Again the earth shivered and the asphalt belched out steam.

"Okay." Jake thought for a second. "I want you to walk over, though. There's no reason for us both to put ourselves at risk. I'll see you on the other side."

Before Jake could put the transmission into drive, Noelle clamped her hand over the keys where they rested in the ignition. "No way. If we're gonna try this, I'm driving."

"No. I don't think—"

She interrupted before he could finish. "It's my truck, Jake. I'm more familiar with it. I'm driving the damn thing." The look on her face told Jake that it wasn't worth arguing over.

"Fine. But I'm going with you."

Jake and Noelle exited the car and switched positions, Noelle getting in the driver's seat. Jake had no idea what he could do to help if the car started to bog, but he wanted to be there to try. The thought of standing idle while Noelle struggled—maybe to her death—to get the car through the steaming swamp was too much for him to handle.

"I'd go in with some speed," Jake told her as she put the car in drive and cranked the wheel to the left, toward their way out. "You know, I mean, momentum is your friend. The faster we can go through this junk, the better."

"Are we in driver's ed?"

"Sorry, can't help it."

Jake grabbed the molded plastic handle on the ceiling of the cab and held on. Noelle pulled up to the gap in the trees and scoped out her planned route. She reversed the truck a short ways to put a runway between the truck and the unstable ground ahead.

Dropping the truck into drive, Noelle accelerated deliberately toward the opening in the trees. She turned the dial on the dash to "4wd-hi." Then with a quick pull on the wheel, the truck bounced off the road's man-made plateau and down a few inches onto the forest floor. Jake and Noelle looked at each other for a moment as the truck cruised through the first short stretch of the route with ease.

Around them, vents in the earth released more and more steam, and small, bubbling hot springs were showing up in the low-lying hummocks. Every so often one of these springs would spout a fountain of steam and water a few feet into the air. The rumbles coming from the earth were becoming constant. As Stevenson predicted, the energy fueling the newly lifeless geysers to the south was finding new ways to run its course. The area around Jake and Noelle was becoming a new geyser basin.

Pace is good. Traction is good. Keep moving.

Noelle kept her eyes well ahead, focused on potential obstacles forty feet or more in front of the car. She wanted to anticipate any blocks early so she could avoid them without losing too much speed. The truck was fast approaching the tree, where its delicate upper branches were shaking slightly with the earth's trembles.

Just like Jake said, there wasn't much space for the truck; the limbs, some as much as five inches in diameter, reached out over the most viable portion of the morass. She could go far left to avoid them, but the terrain was even more treacherous there.

Noelle decided to force the vehicle through the mass of branches. She accelerated toward them, hoping the extra momentum would help her break through. Jake was startled at her choice—the direction and acceleration—but he gave her one quick look and realized her intentions. He gripped the interior handle more firmly in preparation for impact.

The first few branches bent under the force of the big engine rather easily. The tree was still green, so rather than snapping, the limbs folded as they smeared across the windshield before flinging back to life behind the truck. As they ran across the roof, they screeched and scratched like fingernails on a chalkboard. If they lived, Noelle was going to get flak for the damage to the paint job.

The branches were becoming thicker and thicker as the vehicle worked its way to the center of the organism. No longer just scraping, the wood met the metal with dull thumps. The truck began bucking as its engine struggled to push through the resistance.

With their thicker diameters, the bigger branches tore and cracked when they were overwhelmed by force. With a dull thud, a particularly large branch smacked the windshield, causing a spiderweb crack to appear. *Damn.*

Jake was trying to think of escape options should they stall out. The branches nearby were not strong enough to support their individual weights. If they were forced to leave the truck stuck in the boiling bog, they wouldn't likely be able to get to the main trunk without touching the ground. The very ground that was seizing and steaming and bubbling with heat below them.

The truck was slowing despite Noelle's best efforts. She wondered if the tires could take it. Noelle wanted to punch it, push the engine to its max, and hope for the best, but she knew this might make the wheels lose traction or, worse yet, cause a flat. Instead, she accelerated deliberately through the mess.

Wham! Another thick branch slammed into the passenger side of the car, swatting the side-view mirror away from its moorings like a papier-mâché replica. Jake looked back to see the mirror flying through the air as if weightless.

Then, without warning, the truck stopped, engine still running but going nowhere. Noelle stood up as much as she could in the cabin to look past the hood and see what obstacle had blocked them. She couldn't see anything. The limb that had swept the mirror off the truck was now behind them, its damage done. She tried the gas pedal again. The engine revved and whined, but to no avail.

"What is it? Why aren't we moving?!" Noelle shouted. She was trying to look out the closed window to see what the obstacle was.

"Hold on." Jake opened the passenger side, letting in a rush of hot air and steam. He poked his head and shoulders through the now open door, but carefully left his feet on the floor of the cabin. He planted his hand on the roof to steady himself. The metal was warm enough to cook on. It burned him. He pulled his sleeve down to act as a barrier between his hand and the hot steel. After just a short moment, Jake pulled himself back into the truck and closed the door.

He was panting from the heat. "It's getting hot out there." He shook the burning sensation out of his left hand. "There's a rock ledge just in front of your tires. Fourteen, maybe sixteen inches high. Almost up to the bumper. No way around it."

"Well, we'll have to keep trying to get over it, then." Noelle put the transmission in reverse and backed up a few feet. Looking over her right shoulder, she continued until a tree branch impeded her progress. She stopped and put the truck into drive.

"Here we go, cowboy." Noelle pressed hard on the gas, pinning it to the floor. The truck jumped forward. When it reached the ledge, its front bumper scraped against the surface of the rock. The front wheels hit the corner of the ledge, the force strong enough that the air between the tires' rubber and the wheels compressed. Jake and Noelle felt the wheels themselves slam the rock. Noelle backed off the accelerator at precisely the wrong moment and the truck rolled backward off the rock. Their efforts had displaced the earth and dug them deeper into the trough below the rock.

"We've got two more chances, Noelle, tops. When you get the front tires up there on the ledge, keep on the gas. They'll catch traction and pull us up. Be careful not to pop the tires on impact."

"Okay." *Easier said than done.* Noelle was already looking through the rear windshield, gaining as much ground as she could for a run-up.

Before putting her car into gear, Noelle closed her eyes for a short moment and said nothing. This was as close to prayer as she had ever ventured.

Shaking all other thoughts from her mind, she dropped the car down past drive and into first gear. This time, Noelle approached at a slightly slower pace, but accelerated to get the vehicle to climb up on the rock. The bumper scraped again, more harshly than the first time.

Somehow, the truck kept moving forward. It bounced hard when its wheels hit the corner of the rock. Noelle punched it. The front wheels slipped for a second on the smooth top of the rock, then they engaged, pulling the truck up and over. The car bucked just slightly as the unweighted rear wheels bounced over the ledge.

The truck crashed through the last few branches. Noelle steered it over and around the remaining rocks and then up the short, steep grade and back onto the road. She stood on the brakes and the truck skidded to a stop on the dust. They both took a deep breath.

Then the relief of the moment overwhelmed Noelle. She laughed as she put the gearshift back into park. "Okay, you can drive the rest of the way." Noelle held her hands out in front of her and Jake could see them shaking. They switched seats again and headed north.

It was dark now. In the forest on either side of the road, Noelle saw the occasional smoldering fire. Each one illuminated its own surroundings: pine boughs, branches, and ascending smoke. The fires looked like campfires, as if the park were filled with cheerful campers. In reality the area was closed and nobody was there. Noelle longed for normalcy.

Jake drove on, toward the epicenter.

32

CONTROL ROOM, THE HOT ROCK TRACT. THE SAME AFTERNOON.

Jan was pacing back and forth. Intermittent tremors caused him to stop, tense up, and look fearfully out the windows. Then he inevitably would return to his pacing. The men had promised him that they would get the group together and have a conference call. That was over an hour ago.

Why haven't they called? Are they abandoning me out here?

His nerves made it necessary to evacuate his bladder more often than normal, and he walked toward the door to head to the bathroom. When he stepped out into the hallway, the phone finally rang. Jan rushed back to the desk and answered.

"Hello?"

"Jan, it's me." A deep voice. "Everybody is here with me. I want you to explain the situation just like you did to me earlier. We are all short on time, so make it quick."

Make it quick? Jesus! Fuck you!

They were hearing him out only to humor him. Jan was incensed at the comment, but not really surprised. Here he was, in the middle of a catastrophe, and the guys in Washington, sitting safely in a plush office, were telling him to make it quick?

"Yeah, well, obviously the earthquakes have increased—"

"We've heard. Throughout the region," another voice said, interrupting Jan. "Nothing too damaging, I guess, but it can't be a good thing."

"There's no reason to think that it's even related," a third voice broke in.

Jan picked up where he left off. He was infuriated. *Nothing too damaging?!* Still, he stayed on point.

"The readings from the gauges have fluctuated wildly. Some of the receptors aren't even reporting anymore. Damaged, and it's not just the quakes. They closed Yellowstone. Somebody was killed near the geysers, things are *changing* here."

The third voice spoke again. "Right, but, Jan, like I said before, there's no reason to think that any of this means anything. Those readings have always fluctuated, ever since we started monitoring them ten years ago. These things come in swarms. Even you know that. Besides, we planned for a modest amount of collateral damage. We chose you because you said you could deal with that."

Silence. Jan tried a couple of deep breaths, but it didn't help.

They think you're stupid. That you can't see this for what it is.

Jan slammed his fist on the desk hard enough that they could hear it over the wire. "I'm not talking about fucking collateral damage, Michael! I'm talking about destruction and chaos greater than anything we ever imagined. Data can only tell you so much. What you're not taking into account is the experience, just *being here*—the ground out there is boiling!" He looked out the picture windows and down on the park. "There's steam shooting from the ground! Shit, the earthquakes are the least of our worries. The ground out here looks like it could turn inside out, swallow itself, and suck the whole country into a pool of lava."

Jan paused to let it sink in. The men were silent, so he continued. "That's assuming the whole fucking thing doesn't erupt!" If it were up to Jan, he would have pulled the plug earlier. However, the men in Washington had taken that decision out of his hands.

Jan could sense the effect on the room through the wire. He could hear their nervous chatter. They were trying to reassure themselves. "He's a lunatic," he heard one say. "Been up in that house alone too long."

Finally, the crowd quieted down and a single voice spoke. "Jan, I know that you are under pressure out there. You can't cry wolf at the slightest bump in the road—"

"Cry wolf? This is the same . . . no, *worse* than Switzerland. And they were smart enough to shut that down!"

"A different time, a different place. Different technology. There's no reason to think it's the same. We were told you could deal with this type of situation. Stay calm and wait for more instructions. That's all for now."

Fucking imbeciles!

Jan slammed the phone down onto its base. The plastic cradle cracked from the force and the handset rolled off onto the desk. A faint dial tone came from the earpiece. He yanked the cord out to stop the noise. Then he walked quickly over to his personal laptop on the far end of the desk. It was already open. He banged the space key to awaken it. The Internet browser was open and on the screen was an article from the *BaselPress*.

Jan had found the article a few weeks earlier in the archives section of the website. Conveniently enough, nobody on the project had ever mentioned Switzerland to him.

Although it only made him more anxious, he kept finding himself rereading the piece. Mostly, he wanted to double-check the details. Make sure he wasn't missing something that might distinguish the two events. He might have only one more chance to stop the project.

This time, Jan closed the article without as much as a skim. He shut the laptop and brought his hands up to his face. He exhaled, not realizing he'd been holding his breath for the last minute or so.

There was no need to read the article again because he knew all the facts: 3.1s and up. Nothing really major, but they were in clusters. A series of quakes just like the one that was plaguing the greater Yellowstone area now. The cause was identical, too. The Swiss project intended to harvest energy from deep within the earth. They were looking for hot dry rock, or HDR. The same type that was currently under Jan's feet.

The Swiss had drilled five thousand meters into the rock below the earth's surface. Then cold water was poured in the holes and pumped back up. The water, after flowing over and through 400°F granite, returned to the surface as steam. The steam was fed into generators and voilà: electricity. The scientists had found a way to create energy with almost no by-products. It was a miracle.

The problem in Switzerland was that Basel was a historic hot spot for earthquakes and geological instability in general. Almost seven hundred years before the Swiss project, a 6.5 rocked the region. It was the worst quake in European history. Because of the region's geological volatility, the fracturing and cracking in the deep rock that was necessary to the project's success caused unforeseen activity. When the media started making references to the catastrophic 1356 quake, everyone demanded the project be shut down.

The Hot Rock Experiment was taking place in a similar hot spot, but a more dynamic one, and that was exactly why it was chosen. According to the project's scientists, nowhere on earth could produce the amount of energy that Yellowstone could.

This much at stake and Jan considered himself the only reasonable person on earth who was aware of what was going on. *At least in Switzerland they had the scrutiny of the public.* The brains behind this operation were too biased to make reasonable decisions. Jan was the only voice of reason. There would be no protests or *60 Minutes* specials on the dangers of the project. The men had gone to great pains to keep everything covert. Various federal law enforcement officials were trained in construction, rigging, and drilling. Government engineers supervised the work. These men knew how to control.

The most horrifying difference between the Swiss project and the Hot Rock Experiment was the underlying geology. Basel was on a fault, sure, but Yellowstone floated atop the largest magma pool in the world. Not only were earthquakes likely, but any shifts in the underground vents and ducts could potentially trigger the biggest and most dangerous volcano in the world. The results were hard to predict but predictably dire: ash clouds, dramatic climate change, even a new ice age. Not to mention the direct effects of the lava explosion.

Jan went to the bathroom and washed his face. He was hungry and tired of thinking about drilling, fracking, earthquakes, and volcanoes. He needed a break. He jogged down the stairs to the kitchen, knowing there wasn't any food there but opening the fridge out of habit.

It held only a few beers and a bottle of tomato juice. He slammed the door shut and hurried toward the stairs to the garage, grabbing his keys and jacket on the way. The closest place to find food at this hour was up in West Yellowstone, about fifteen miles of back roads away. At least it would get him out of the house.

Jan backed out of the garage and plugged his cell phone into its charger. He didn't expect a call, but he wanted to be sure he could receive the orders to abandon ship if they came. Jan floored it down the long driveway. The vehicle rumbled over the ruts and potholes in the dirt. It was freeing to get out of the house.

"What's that humming noise?" Noelle asked.

"Sounds like a generator nearby. Construction maybe?"

"This late in the day?" It was a quarter after eight. The sun was set. It was getting dark.

Jake shrugged. "Household generator?"

"Kinda spooky," Noelle said.

Jake continued driving. He occasionally checked the fax to see their position relative to the epicenter.

"We should be getting close," he said. The humming was growing more intense. It was all around them, more like they were inside a machine than near one.

"Stop!" Noelle shouted. Her voice filled the cabin of the truck. "Turn your lights off. There's someone coming." The truck shook hard with another brief quake as Jake applied the brakes. Noelle gasped.

"It's okay." Jake put his hand on her forearm.

In the distance a set of headlights looked like they were coming toward them down a slope in the road. There were no streetlights and the darkness gave the illusion that the vehicle was slowly descending from space like a UFO.

"What should we do?" Noelle asked.

"Nothing. Turn the lights back on and keep going. We don't even know who it is. They won't think anything of it, another car passing them."

Noelle wasn't so sure, given the remoteness of the area. Jake flipped the lights on, but before he could start moving, the lights in the distance angled off suddenly, a turn. Now only the red tail-lights were visible.

"He turned. Where was he coming from? It looks like he just drove down that hillside." She looked at the facsimile. They were at the epicenter. She showed Jake.

"There must be another road up there." Jake looked to the hill where the car had come from. "Or a driveway—an entrance or something. Come on. Let's go."

A half mile down the road there was an opening in the brush that revealed a narrow uphill drive. Jake looked in both directions and turned up the drive. A few hundred feet in, he turned off the truck's lights again and navigated the path by the remnant glow of the just-set sun.

As they made their way up the hill, they began to see the dim outline of a structure. Jake slowed the truck to allow the vehicle to travel with minimum noise. A house. Cedar siding and expansive lodgepole decks adorned the exterior. The humming was coming from within.

Jake switched off the engine and got out. Noelle followed him. A single interior light was on, but the rest of the house was dark and lifeless. Noelle cautiously peered in through a window to see if anyone was inside. Nothing.

Noelle glanced back to find Jake, but he had already moved to the side door and found it unlocked. He waved her in. The home's interior suggested vacancy. No furniture, no dishes in the sink, no shoes by the door. When Noelle caught up with Jake he held his palms out to her. *Stop!* She stopped in her tracks. He had already endangered her enough; before he would let her go any farther he wanted to check the garage for cars.

Jake found himself wishing he were armed. In general he hated guns—they complicated things unnecessarily, and they always put the bad guys on edge. The Argus incident wasn't the only time in his career that a gunshot had completely ruined years of investigation. Still, there were times he wished he had the advantage of a pistol. This was one of those times. Noelle's presence had a lot to do with his sentiment. He had to protect her at all costs.

Jake walked across the kitchen and down the stairwell that, he assumed, accessed the garage. The space was empty, but it smelled faintly of exhaust. There was no doubt that car had come from the house.

Another strong quake. Creaking and crashing noises overshadowed the humming for a moment.

He returned to the kitchen and spoke aloud for the first time since they entered the house. "No cars in the garage. I think we're safe to look around for a minute. Just a quick walk-through, though, okay? Check upstairs. Be safe." He gave her a stern look.

Noelle nodded and headed up the stairs. Jake continued the search on the first floor. After only a few minutes, Noelle's voice startled him.

"Jake!" she shouted, before remembering to keep it down. "I think you'd better get up here!"

Jake ran up the stairs and found Noelle standing in the middle of a large room. Around the perimeter of the space were computer monitors and unidentifiable electronics. The room looked like something from NASA or NORAD, but here it was, secretly tucked away just outside of a national park.

Noelle spoke first. "What the hell *is this*?" She was sorting through stacks of dot-matrix printouts on a desk, looking for a clue that might answer her own question. They were graphs of some sort—dates on the *x* axis and unusual acronyms and numbers on the *y*. A tremor made Noelle jump. Jake jogged toward her, hoping to protect her, but backed off when the shaking stopped. *A small one.*

"Don't know. Looks like a lab of some kind. I'd bet it's a seismology lab, based on the circumstances." Jake gave her a meaningful look. "Did you try the computers?"

Noelle left her stack of paper and walked over to one of the keyboards. She pressed the return key and the screen lit up. A window popped up asking her to log in.

"No luck. Wants a password." Jake and Noelle quickly checked the other computers in the room, but all of them required a username and password.

Jake looked around the room again, thinking and repeating Noelle's sentiment under his breath.

"What the hell is this?"

His mind searched for the answer. He thought of the eco-terrorists, Ricker and the mysterious Shaman character.

It still doesn't add up. What am I missing? Jake looked around. *It all looks so sophisticated.* He wasn't familiar with the equipment in the room, but it was easy to guess the cost would be in the tens or hundreds of thousands. *Too much for some grassroots environmental campaign.*

Jake was more than curious to snoop around, but the elegance and refinement of the lab troubled him. He couldn't put Noelle at risk any longer. "Another sixty seconds and we're getting out of here. This is too dangerous. Whatever is going on is way beyond our comprehension. We need to go to a safe place and get ahold of my contact in the FBI."

Jake thought back on past searches gone wrong. How every time, the person you didn't want to see come back always showed up before they were expected to.

Before you could get the information you came for. Before you could get out.

With Ricker, Jake had known better than to surprise a potentially dangerous suspect in a private place. That's why he had arranged the meeting in public.

I need to exercise the same caution now, he thought. Although he sensed they were tantalizingly close to the answers they wanted.

"Sixty seconds," he said again. Another tremor.

Jake starting rifling through the stacks of papers, and then the filing cabinets below the desk. It was all gibberish, readouts in units that Jake wasn't familiar with and more graphs that documented unknowable variables. Finally he came across a blue folder labeled "Phase One/Hot Rock Experiment."

Experiment? What is this place?

Jake opened the file and took it to the surface of the desk where the light was better. Noelle joined him there. In the middle of the file, among more cryptic graphs and readouts, was finally something they could read. Jake unfolded the large sheet. It was a blueprint of some kind.

"Looks like landscaping plans." Noelle sounded nervous. The sketch showed what appeared to be large spruce trees spaced evenly throughout an area that the key said was about ten square miles. Weaving through the space and connecting each tree was what looked like an irrigation line. Something about the plans seemed oddly technical; again, acronyms and data were interspersed among the tree graphics. The main irrigation line led to another structure on the land.

"Why plant full-sized trees? Look at these trees. If they are shown to scale this plan shows them to measure out at about forty-five feet."

"Revegetation, maybe? There could've been a fire or beetle kill and the park is trying to restore the landscape."

"The park doesn't revegetate when there's a fire, do they?" Jake looked puzzled. "Think of the fire in the eighties. They let nature take its course. And still, why would you plant full-grown trees?"

"And even if they did, those trees surely wouldn't need irrigation up here. This is their natural habitat."

"Something's funny about the piping too." Jake glanced at the key and did some quick calculations in his head. "These irrigation lines are four and a half meters in diameter." He looked up at her.

"That's big enough to drive a small car through. What kind of plant could possibly need that amount of water?"

"Shit!" There was a splash of dim light out the window. "Someone's here!"

Noelle grabbed the blueprint and ran with Jake to the front of the house, where they could see down the driveway. Somebody had just turned in and was headed up the hill.

"Get the lights," Jake whispered. Noelle ran back to the control room and flipped the switch. When she got downstairs, Jake was at the side door, holding it open. "Back to the truck! Hurry!"

The car was getting close. It was less than a hundred yards away and closing, but because of the hill, the headlights and the driver's line of sight were pointed up into the night sky. *They can't see us yet.* At that distance the noise of the ignition would alert the driver to their presence, so Jake improvised. Without starting the engine, Jake put the transmission into neutral. He had a slight slope to his advantage.

"Put your seat belt on! Hold on!" he whispered to Noelle, who, out of confusion, had opened the passenger door, thinking they were going to run for it. Jake centered himself on the rear bumper and pushed as hard as he could. The truck crept forward. The downhill slope increased its momentum and Jake ran to the driver's side and jumped in. The front wheels left the driveway and started bouncing down the sagebrush slope behind the house. The beam of the headlights was now projecting only a few feet above the roof of the truck. The car was closing in on them. They had only a few seconds before the headlights and the driver's field of view would be right on them.

The rear wheels rolled over the edge and the truck was moving fast. Too fast. It bounced and bucked as it rolled without resistance over rocks and miniature arroyos. Jake buckled his seat belt and clutched the handle above the door with his left hand. His right hand left the steering wheel to hold Noelle down in her seat. The violent bumps were bouncing both passengers around. Their heads were nearly reaching the ceiling.

After the thrashing came to a crescendo, the slope leveled to flat ground, and Jake pulled the parking brake. The truck gave them a few more jolts and then came to a lurching halt. Afraid to move, Jake and Noelle stayed still for a few moments.

"Did he see us?" Noelle whispered.

"I don't know." Jake was watching the top of the hill in the mirror.

The driver never came down over the hill. Safe, for now. Jake looked over at Noelle to see if she was hurt. She looked okay.

He checked himself for injury. Everything was intact. Noelle shook her left hand in pain so Jake asked to have a look.

"It's fine, really, just bruised, I think. I bumped it on something." Maybe not broken, but more than a bump. Her hand was swelling quickly.

"Look!" Noelle pointed through the windshield with her right hand. "The trees!"

Jake followed her gesture and immediately noticed what she was talking about. The truck had rolled into the flat that was cultivated according to the plans they found in the house. Around them, large, evenly spaced pines stood barely visible in the night. They could hear the sound of rushing water emanating from the ground beneath them.

Humming.

What the hell?

33

THE HOT ROCK TRACT. THE SAME EVENING.

Jan took the plastic bag of snacks up to the control room to eat. He'd decided to stop at a gas station rather than drive to West Yellowstone. He was worried his phone wouldn't get reception on the way and he would miss an important call. The call that might end all the chaos.

As he ate, he felt calmer, if not resigned. If he died up here, so be it. It didn't matter, as long as his son was safe. His family would get the payout if anything went wrong. He had lived a long and prosperous life, considering the risks he had taken. What more could he ask for?

Jan headed upstairs and into the control room to check the house phone and computer for messages. Before he got to the phone, he noticed something amiss right away. The blue folder. *What the hell is it doing out on the desk?*

He picked it up and paged through the file. Pages were missing. He cursed aloud and stuffed the remaining pages of the file into the paper shredder.

Someone was in the house! Jan panicked for a moment and then collected himself. He crept over to the desk and opened the top drawer, where he lifted his Glock subcompact out of its case and crammed a magazine into the sleeve inside the grip. Then he put the two extra magazines in his jacket pocket, slipped off his shoes for stealth, and started walking.

He quietly approached each bedroom and spun inside with his gun aimed at chest level. The top floor was empty. He walked down the stairs, listening for the noise of an intruder. He heard something that made him pause.

Just another tremor.

At the bottom of the stairs he turned right toward the kitchen. Nobody. Whoever it was must have fled the house right before he got back—he was gone for less than an hour.

Jan turned on some lights in the house and jogged back upstairs to the control room. He logged on to one of the computers and checked for Makter's location. He watched for a moment. His old friend was close to the house, but it looked like his vehicle was heading toward him, not away.

What the hell is he doing?

He dialed the phone and laced up a pair of shoes while it rang. Makter didn't pick up and the call went to voice mail. "Dammit!"

What is he doing here and why is he coming back? If it isn't Mak, who the hell could it be? Jan picked up the Glock again and headed outside.

*   *   *

Jake and Noelle left the car and walked toward the nearest tree. The starlight illuminated the terrain just enough to see where they were going. They could hear the hiss from the pumping water in the irrigation system. It was getting louder and louder as they approached.

"Can you feel that?" Jake abruptly stopped walking. "The ground is shaking."

Noelle stopped. "What is it? A quake?"

Jake shook his head.

Noelle was afraid now. Horrified, really.

What the hell am I doing up here? How did I let myself get in so deep? For the first time in quite a while, she longed to be back in her lonely cabin.

Curiosity killed the cat.

"The irrigation line, probably. There would be a ton of water coursing through those lines; maybe that would be enough to shake the ground. Let's keep moving."

Now a quake roared, clearly detectable despite the humming below them. The tree in front of them threatened to fall, but the shaking stopped just in time, leaving the tree pointing to the sky at an unnatural angle.

It stood like a sentinel in the night air. It was wider at its base than any pine Jake or Noelle had ever seen. The whir of unknown man-made mechanisms was loud enough now that they strained to hear each other speak.

Noelle placed her hand on the tree. It was warm to the touch and quivering intensely. Confused, she reached up and grabbed the lowest bough, running her fingers through the needles. It felt strange. She tried to pluck some of the needles from the limb, but they wouldn't come free.

It's fake?

34

TWENTY MILES SOUTHWEST OF JAN'S COMPOUND.
THE SAME EVENING.

Makter was speeding north. Since the park was closed, he had to drive the whole way around through eastern Idaho. *Shitty timing for a road closure.* He was anxious to see Jan so he could appeal the decision on Jake Trent. The urge to kill Trent had grown within him since the day before, in part because of Jan's scolding. If Jan objected again, he would just have to kill them both.

He turned east toward West Yellowstone.

Jan had a small flashlight in his pocket. He didn't want to attract any attention so he left it there for now. Besides, once his eyes adjusted, he knew he'd be able to see well enough. That way, he could use the shadow of darkness to his advantage rather than announcing his presence to whoever might be lurking in the night.

He walked the perimeter of the house first, gun at the ready. No sign of the intruder. When he got back to the side door near the garage, his eyes were well adjusted to the lack of light. At the top of the slope there was a quick flash of movement.

He gripped the pistol firmly, ready to fire. Another movement. *Come out, you sonofabitch!*

Jan's breath was hastening. He hadn't done this in a while. He reset his grip and put his finger on the trigger.

In a blur of speed, a coyote spooked from the edge of the driveway and ran down the slope behind the house. Jan took a slow, deep breath, lowered his weapon, and walked toward the door.

Fucking coyotes! He longed to be back in civilization.

As he was opening the door, something unexpected happened. The frightened coyote came flying back up the hill and ran down the driveway in the opposite direction. It was out of sight in a matter of seconds.

Jan connected the dots quickly: *Someone or something had spooked it back up the hill.*

"What was that?" The look of fear was apparent on Noelle's face despite the darkness. All of a sudden, her breaths were coming quickly as she turned to face the source of the noise.

"Just a coyote. I'm gonna walk over to that one to see if it's the same as this." He pointed toward a tree a hundred feet to his left. "You go check out the next closest tree on the other side. Let's meet back here in a few minutes. Make it quick. Be careful."

Noelle nodded and started off toward the next tree. Something didn't feel right to her. They shouldn't be separated in this darkness. If something happened it was always better to be together.

What if that animal is the owner's guard dog and alerted them to our presence?

She tried to remind herself to stay cool. Panicking wouldn't help her any.

She looked up to the top of the hill again. Above it, clouds were moving in and blocking the limited light from the sky. She looked back for Jake but he was already out of sight. *Shit!* She glanced up again at the darkening sky, afraid that she might not even find it back to the first tree. *Stay calm.*

Noelle hurried to the second tree. The whirring noise was the same as the first. Although she already knew what she would find, she put her hands on the trunk of the tree. It was warm and vibrating. *Another fake.*

What was that? She spun around quickly, but nothing was behind her. She focused her attention back on the tree. She must be hearing things.

She had seen something similar only once: a cell phone tower in the national park that was built to look like a tree so it wouldn't be an eyesore to visitors. These couldn't be cell towers. They were too close together.

What in the world? Some kind of observatory?

A sense of dread washed over her. Whatever it was, she had to get Jake and get out of there as soon as possible. Noelle turned and started walking quickly in the direction of their meeting point.

Before she made it back, there was a flash of light near the base of the hill to her right. In the second or so that the flashlight was illuminated, she saw the profile of a man approaching another man from behind. Noelle held her hand over her mouth to stop the scream that welled inside her. She heard the dull noise of a short scuffle and then the piercing bang of a gunshot.

Noelle fell to the earth with a thud to stay out of view, should the man with the light look around for other intruders. Sure enough, a beam wandered in a 360-degree search pattern over the flats. It passed over her without pause.

Thank God!

The beam settled on the hill up toward the direction of the house. Noelle did her best army crawl to see what was going on.

Her heart was beating out of her chest. Behind a small, scrubby sage bush, she stopped and peered through the thin branches. A man was holding a small flashlight with his teeth and dragging another man's body by his feet. She couldn't tell which one was Jake.

She moved a bit closer and blinked a few times to help her blurry vision in the dry, night air. She looked up at the man, who had stopped to adjust his grip on the body. It wasn't Jake in front. This man was much larger.

Jake's dead.

Noelle was too panicked to process the thought at that moment. Her mind frantically searched for a way to get to her vehicle and out on the open road. She had to go get help.

Jan took Jake through the side door and into the garage. He opened the garage's wood-paneled door and then walked out to drag him inside. The automatic light from the door opener illuminated the body ever so slightly.

"Jake *fucking* Trent." He pulled the body into the garage, took one final look around outside, and closed the door.

*   *   *

343

Back in the darkness, Noelle crept toward her truck. She'd left her phone on the passenger seat, but the chances of finding reception in these hills were slim. If she could get reception, she would call the cops first. If not, she'd try to start the truck and get as far across the flat and away from the house as she could. It would draw attention, but it was better than trying to sneak back down the driveway. She couldn't know for sure if the man was waiting outside for her.

It wasn't long before her plans changed. The phone wasn't on the passenger seat where she'd left it. She searched the floor of the vehicle, under the seats, and on the ground alongside the doors.

Noelle walked around the front of the car to the driver's side. She sat down and reached for the ignition. The keys were gone. She looked around the cabin. Nothing. The man must have found the truck and taken the keys and her phone. Worse yet, if he found both her phone and Jake's, he would know that there was another person somewhere out on the dark sage flat. He would come for her next.

A strong quake rattled the truck. The panic inside Noelle was growing exponentially. She searched for Jake's phone or anything that might come in handy, stopping to look outside in case the man was approaching the car. After a few minutes, she stopped and sat back in the driver's seat.

Not knowing what to do next, she banged both fists on the steering wheel. *Jake is gone and I have no way to get help.* Her only option was to climb the hill to the house and try to get to a phone or a vehicle without being detected.

You can do this, Noelle. She tried to summon courage in herself. Her mind played pictures of her childhood, her mother, Jake Trent.

Let's go.

Before she started up the hill, she grabbed the tire iron from the spare tire kit in case she had to defend herself. Then she opened the glove box for the small pocketknife she kept there. Beside it was Jake's phone.

Thank God.

Noelle grabbed the device, turned off the interior lights, and closed the door.

Makter was speeding along the curvy back road toward the house. In the backseat were a twelve-gauge shotgun and a nine-millimeter pistol, both under an old sleeping bag. He had to get it done tonight: convince Jan to be a part of it and head back down to Jackson to kill Trent. He had no idea of the surprise that awaited him in the house's garage.

Jan was still in the garage dealing with his unexpected visitor. He froze when he heard the knock.

Makter? Or does Trent have backup coming?

More knocking. Rather than going to the side door, Jan pulled the Glock from his waistband and walked quietly to the front door. He opened it without a sound and crept around the corner of the house to ambush his visitor. When the end of the driveway came into view he could see a vehicle, though it was impossible to identify in the night. A figure stood at the side door, also veiled in darkness.

"Don't fucking move! Don't turn around; don't do anything!" Jan was a dozen yards from the intruder. His Glock was aimed right between the man's shoulder blades.

"It's just me! It's Mak!" He glanced over his shoulder. "Put the fucking gun down, Jan! Jesus!"

Jan walked over to Makter and grabbed him by the shoulder. He violently spun him around so his back was against the door and he could see his face "What the fuck, Mak? You're lucky I didn't blow your head off. What the hell are you doing up here?"

"I came to talk, all right? I came to talk!" His hands were up in the air in the surrender position.

"Get inside." Jan pushed him through the door and into the house. "I've got something to show you."

When Makter saw what the garage contained, he couldn't believe it. He let out a high-pitched, jackal-like howl.

Jake Trent was bound to an oak kitchen chair. Duct tape held his ankles to the legs of the chair, and his hands were tied behind him. He was conscious, but there was duct tape over his mouth and blood oozing down over his right eye and onto his cheek.

"Is he hit?" Makter checked Jake's physical condition.

"Just a bump on the head."

Makter giggled, anxious at the thought of torturing Jake Trent.

"Don't fucking laugh!" Makter immediately fell silent as his old friend demanded. "How do you think he got up here?"

"How should I know?" Mak's voice revealed anger. He was sick of playing second fiddle, and the sight of Trent bleeding made him see red. "I *did* my job! I told you we needed to kill him!"

"You *didn't* do your job, obviously. If you had, Trent wouldn't have been snooping around the house tonight!"

"What was he doing up here?" Makter asked, repeating Jan's question, looking closely at the gash on Jake's head. Jake stared straight ahead.

"I don't know, you *idiot*! You must have led him here!" Makter fell silent.

Jan spoke again. "It doesn't matter anymore. You fucked up! *You* pay the price! I'm getting in my car and I'm driving to the airport. Then I'm flying somewhere far away before this place blows. You do what you want to Trent, but you stay in this damn house until that phone rings and someone tells you otherwise. Or you don't get paid."

"What if he told someone about this place?" Makter gestured toward Jake. "Then what? What if the cops come?"

"Then you deal with them. I'll see you around, Mak. Thanks for the shitty work." With that, Jan walked out of the garage, through the short hallway, and out into the night air.

"Shit!" Makter looked at Jake for a second, and then ran after Jan.

A deep, trembling earthquake shook the house. The tremor precariously skittered Jake's chair a foot to the right.

Outside, Makter was screaming. "What happened to you, Jan? I used to look up to you! Now you're so weak, it's *disgusting*! You're no better than me!" Makter stood near the garage door and shouted at Jan, who was approaching the car.

"Bullshit, Mak. I'm the same as always. Maybe I *was* no better than you, but you've lost your fucking mind! I always knew you were a little batshit, but this is a whole 'nother level! I asked you to do one simple thing for me, and you created this fantasy, this sick fucking world where you play with people like they're your pawns. You slaughtered innocent people down there for the sport of it—only a lunatic would think what you did was necessary! You need help, Mak. See a fucking therapist, I'm gone."

"Take another step and I'll kill you." Makter had his own pistol drawn.

There was silence for a moment, and then Makter spoke again.

"The days of you telling me what to do are over."

* * *

Jake looked around at his surroundings. Sweat beaded on his brow. His head was pounding from the blow. He looked to his right—two more feet and he would be close enough to the garage door track that he might be able to use its metal edge to fray the rope that was binding his hands. *Keep arguing; give me a few more minutes.* The only other thought on Jake's mind was finding Noelle and making sure she was safe.

Now it was Jan shouting outside. "Listen, you maniac, I'm leaving *now*. You play out whatever sick fantasy you want with Trent. By the time you're done, this whole mess will be over. You'll get paid. I'll get paid. We'll both be richer men."

Jan's message sounded surprisingly like a plea.

"You're not going anywhere." The resolve in Makter's voice was disconcerting. "You're gonna die with Trent, you prick. I've spent my whole fucking life in your shadow. But you were always weak. You think you can control everything, understand everything, by being rational?"

Makter laughed loudly again.

"You wanna know where the control is? It's right here in my hand, Jan. If you want control, you take it, you don't ask for it. You don't reason your way into it."

The earth was belting out a coincidental harmony to Makter's rage. Jake was six inches away from the track now—the quakes sliding him closer and closer. He used his core to hop the chair the rest of the way. The bouncing made his agonizing headache much worse. When he got there, he spun around so the vertical rail was perpendicular to the rope binding his hands. He made small sawing motions to wear away at the rope. Because the edge was rather smooth, it was tedious work. He took breaks every thirty seconds or so to catch his breath.

"Who's in control now, Jan?" Makter cocked the gun and pushed it hard into Jan's cheek.

"Listen, Mak, if we both get in the car right now and get out of here, we'll be safe. This thing is gonna blow."

"You can't talk your way out this time, Jan. Get inside."

Instead of following Makter's orders, Jan lunged for the gun. They wrestled to the ground.

Jake heard two gunshots, then the sound of a car spewing gravel against the garage door.

Jake worked harder yet to free himself, but before he could do so the side door opened. Jake froze. It was Makter. He spoke in an uneven tone. *Adrenaline. Rage.* "Trying to escape, huh?" He pulled the chair to the center of the garage. "Not gonna happen, asshole. It's just you and me now. Jan will bleed out before the end of the driveway."

Jake remained quiet, his mouth still taped shut. Makter was breathing hard. There was blood on his shirt. He had both guns now, the nine millimeter from his own backseat and Jan's Glock. After checking the magazine of the Glock, he put it on another chair that was sitting nearby and continued to hold the nine millimeter in his right hand.

He ripped the tape from Jake's mouth forcefully. "I'd like to hear you scream before you die." There was a crooked smile on his face.

Jake had once feared Jan much more than Makter, if only because of the scope of Jan's criminal network. Now, Makter's insanity was much more horrifying.

Jake's training was guiding him. *Don't bother talking to him;*

you'll only make it worse. Stay quiet and wait for your opportunity to disarm him.

He felt around with his fingers. There were only a few strands of rope intact. *Be patient.*

Pressed against the hillside, Noelle heard a car leave, so she crept up and surveyed the scene from behind some brush. There was one car remaining, but nobody was outside. She crept in closer and looked in through the window. The house still seemed empty.

Noelle ran in a hunched position to the far side of the sedan. Once there, she dropped down to the ground again, where the car concealed her from the view of anyone who might be left in the house.

She tried the handle on the passenger side but it was locked. With no idea whatsoever about the intricacies of a car's ignition system, she couldn't possibly hot-wire it. Even if she could, breaking the window would probably trigger an alarm.

She started to make her way back over the hill. She needed to rethink her escape. Suddenly, she stopped. A scuffle from inside the garage. An unfamiliar voice was shouting. She moved closer to the garage door so she could hear.

The moment Noelle's ear touched the door, she heard something terrifying: "Not gonna talk, huh? That's fine. Let's go outside. We don't want to leave too much evidence, but of course you know that. Then some worm like you might track me down."

Jake? Her heart pounded wildly.

The garage door began to climb. Noelle ran, but it was too late. The killer saw her feet dart from the door and around to the other side of the car parked outside. He cocked the nine millimeter and cautiously moved out of the garage.

"Come out, come out, whoever you are!" Noelle held her breath. Makter's tone changed from playful to matter-of-fact. "Okay, well, if you don't come out with your hands up, I'll put a bullet in the gas tank! How does that sound? Ever seen anyone burn to death?" Makter again waited for a response. Noelle remained quiet, holding her hands over her mouth to stifle her own heavy breathing.

The madman changed his tone again. He was shouting now. "Okay, well, how about this? I'm guessing you know a guy named Jake Trent. If you don't show yourself, I'll put a fucking bullet in his head!"

Noelle paused. "Okay! Okay!" she shouted back. "I'm coming out!"

Makter couldn't believe he had heard a woman's voice.

"What a pleasant surprise!" he hissed as she walked out from behind the car.

35

THE HOT ROCK TRACT

Noelle walked around the front of the car with her hands up, just like the man demanded. Makter followed her in and closed the garage door behind them.

She tried her best to keep her hands from shaking, but the pistol aimed squarely at her chest didn't help any. Squinting to recognize the man bound to the chair, she could barely tell it was Jake. He was bruised and swollen. Blood glistened on his face in the dim light.

"A sexy one, too! Damn, I sure wasn't expecting that." Makter had an evil grin on his face. "Get over here, now!" He led her into the garage and sat her down on the cement floor ten yards from Jake. Rifling through a bin near the door, he found the roll of duct tape. "Perfect." He tapped her playfully on the forehead with the roll.

Makter started with her ankles, wrapping them tightly and thoroughly. While he did so, she could sense the evil in the man. It wasn't just the anger and fear of a criminal interrupted; it was the noxious aura of a man with horrifying intentions. Whether they were aimed at her or Jake or both, she couldn't tell.

He moved to her wrists, which he bound with several more layers of tape. There was no way she was going to wiggle free from her restraints without help.

"Now we have a party!" Makter said with a malicious grin. "Tell me, Jake, is this your lady friend? She's pretty, you know." Makter ran his fingers through Noelle's hair. She yanked her head to the left to escape his touch, but he pulled her hair sharply so that her head was against his crotch.

Jake finally spoke. "We're okay, Noelle." There was calm in his voice. In response, a riotous laughter spewed from Makter's mouth.

"You most certainly are not okay." He laughed again and approached Jake. "You are going to die, Trent. So that's not okay. Is it? The girl, what's her name?" Jake said nothing. "Anyway, I can assure you she's not going to be okay either."

With his captor's face only inches away from his own, Jake finally addressed him. "What are you doing here, Makter? You came across the country to have your revenge on me for doing my job? Pitiful and stupid, but not surprising, I guess. Let the girl go, she has nothing to do with our history."

The confidence in Jake's voice was surprising to Noelle. *He's been in this situation before.*

"The girl obviously has something to do with you, Trent. Otherwise, what would you care what happened to her? Let me ask one more time, is this pretty little thing your girlfriend?"

Jake chose to respond this time. "She's a national park employee, you idiot. An agent of the federal government. You want her murder on your rap sheet? I barely know her. She was showing me around Yellowstone today."

"Ha! The park's closed, asshole."

"She has special privileges and she shared them with me."

"I bet she did!" He glanced over at Noelle, who was trying to hold back her sobs now. An overwhelming feeling of regret again—she hadn't bargained for this.

"Listen, I know both of you were snooping around up here. Don't lie to me." Makter had taken a seat on a tool station.

"You were setting me up, you and Jan? Framing me, I mean?" Jake looked straight at Makter.

He's trying to get information. To gain leverage. Noelle watched Jake work.

"Of course. That's part of it. Also I just wanted to kill you, still do. Have a little fun, you know? Jan doesn't know how to have fun, unfortunately, which is why I shot him."

"What's the rest? Why the fake trees?"

Makter looked confused. He took a moment to respond. "I am not going to share that with you."

Jake went on. "Why not? You're going to kill me, right?"

He's trying to get in his head. Buy some time.

Before Noelle could finish her thought, the captor had come up behind her. He grabbed her hair again, pulling her head back so she was looking right into his eyes.

She could smell him. His breath was awful, and his body odor was worse. He reeked of sweat and soil. His hands were dirty and calloused. The blood on his shirt made her squirm.

Soon my blood will be there too.

"I may not kill little Miss Park Ranger, though. Maybe I'll take her along with me."

His tone changed. "You know what?" Makter jammed the barrel of the gun against her lips. She could taste blood.

"I had the most wonderful massage yesterday. I think that's where I'd like to start with you. I'm stressed, you know? It's a good release for me. Can you give a good rubdown? What happens next is up to you. Yesterday didn't turn out so well for the masseuse. She made quite a bit of noise."

Noelle was quivering.

"Do you know where she is now!?" he growled.

Jake spoke calmly. "We're okay, Noelle." Makter ignored him.

Noelle still said nothing.

"Answer me!" he screamed, putting his hand behind her head and forcing her mouth over the barrel. When her mouth opened, blood poured down her face. The barrel had knocked out a molar.

She shook her head emphatically.

"She's in the fucking trunk!" He pointed through the garage door. "I'll show you later." He winked at her.

36

THE HOT ROCK TRACT

Makter was pacing, screaming and threatening and intermittently cursing Jan.

"Doesn't matter! He's fucking dead by now!"

"Still, he tried to abandon you. He left you to do the dirty work."

Jake was trying to steer Makter into a rage aimed anywhere other than at himself and Noelle. He was also trying to discern more information, but making very little progress. As had been the criminals' modus operandi during past operations, Makter, Jake was beginning to sense, was really just the muscle.

There was a knock at the door that led to the main house. It startled Makter.

"Fuck! Don't move." He gave his prisoners a "hush" signal with his finger over an evil grin. With his gun at the ready, Makter went to the door.

"Jan?"

A grunt came from the other side of the door.

"Is that you? Shit. We'll get you help." He spoke nervously. Mak's habit of deference was still there.

Another grunt in reply.

Makter started to turn the knob. "You're just in time, I've got Trent primed and ready for the big show!"

Schwaaap, schwaap! Makter's knees buckled and he fell immediately to the concrete. Inky blood pooled around his head. At the door was a tall man wearing black work pants and a dark gray sweater. A black cotton face mask covered his facial features. Without saying a word, the man knelt down and took Makter's pulse. Apparently pleased with the lack of heartbeat, he stood up. Rivulets of blood were headed toward the drain centered in the garage.

Jake released a sigh. *The maniac is dead.*

Noelle was sobbing and squirming uncontrollably now. The man took a large folding knife from his waistband and walked toward her purposefully. She closed her eyes and turned away.

The man first grabbed her legs below the calf. Noelle squirmed and tried to kick him to no avail. He coolly held her down and used the blade to cut the tape from her ankles. She tried to get to her feet immediately—her flight instinct had taken over. He held her down for a moment more as he freed her hands. When he was done she got up and ran to the door he had come from. There she stood frozen, still unsure of the man's intentions. The man looked back at Noelle and removed his mask. He had chiseled facial features and short-cropped hair.

"You hurt, Trent?"

"Daniel?" Jake said, surprised. "How the hell did you know we were here? I'm fine, just a bump on the head."

The agent smiled at his old friend and freed him from his restraints.

"It was Makter and Jan, Dan. What the hell were they doing out here? What the hell are *you* doing out here?"

"I know." Daniel nodded. "When you emailed me that name and phone number, I did some investigating of my own. Turns out the Denver office had an ongoing investigation involving that Ricker kid you mentioned. He was just a pawn, but the search led to Jan and Makter."

"What kind of investigation?"

"Eco-freaks, I guess. I don't know all the details exactly. Sabotaging construction sites. Maybe worse."

"Murder?" Jake asked.

"I can't really go into it." Daniel looked over at Noelle.

"She's a federal agent too, Dan. A park ranger."

"Still, I can't tell you any more, you know that."

"What's going on, Jake?" Noelle's voice was shaky.

Jake walked over to her. "Doesn't matter. We're safe now."

Confused, Jake probed his friend further. "Why didn't you just call the Denver office? How did you even find this house?"

Daniel paused for a moment. "Some of that I can't share, and we'll get to the rest. C'mon, let's get you two out of here." He headed to the door and waited for Jake and Noelle to follow.

Something didn't feel right.

"Don't you need to investigate the scene?" Jake didn't move toward the door.

The agent paused again. "Denver is coming up to do it."

"You should look out back, over the hill. There's some weird stuff back there. Something industrial. Huge, fake trees with water running to them. I don't know what it . . ." Jake stopped talking. Daniel's gaze had fallen to the ground for a second and then he reached for the door, closed it, and clicked the lock. When he looked back up, there was a saddened expression on his face.

"*Fuck* me. Are you kidding?" Daniel said quietly. He was shaking his head with a look of despair on his face. "Why did you look back there, Jake? Why do you always snoop around when you aren't welcome? This nut job really blew our cover, huh?" He nudged Makter's lifeless body with his boot, then checked the rounds in his pistol.

Jake tried to decipher Daniel's face.

"Sit back down, Jake." His gun was pointed at Noelle. "You too." He motioned for Noelle to join Jake on the opposite side of the garage. She sat on the floor, her eyes wide like those of a doe on the highway.

"Danny, I didn't . . . How did you get here?"

"I was sent here, Jake." He put his mask back on.

Daniel aimed at Noelle first. In a soft, morose tone he said, "Would it be easier for you to go first, Jake?" Jake couldn't answer that question. He cared about Noelle too much.

Would it be better for her to face death first? Otherwise, she would have to watch me die—a horrifying sight. Probably not worth it for a few extra seconds of life.

She was looking at him, afraid and expecting him to save her. He had no more tricks up his sleeve. He looked at the ground, embarrassed. He had failed her.

Daniel cocked his gun. As Jake was contemplating life's last moments, a shadow underneath the door caught his eye. Jake's mind left thoughts of the existential and focused on survival.

"What is it? Back there, I mean? What's going on?" Jake knew there was no reason for Daniel to share this information, but he hoped the agent might talk, if only to delay the horrible act he was about to commit against someone he had once called a friend. He was playing to the only weakness he could sense in Daniel.

"Really? That's your last request?" Daniel chuckled. "Still trying to solve the crime on your deathbed?"

Jake maintained his eye contact, and Daniel started to talk.

"We can't all just leave the business like you, Jake. Some of us get more deeply involved. These jobs have their perks—and they pay a hell of a lot more than eighty grand a year."

A quake violently shook the house. Drywall cracked on the near wall. The garage door was almost shaken from its track.

Jake looked quizzically at Daniel, who began to speak again.

"Fuck it, you're dead anyway. We all are." The gun was at his side now. "Some years back, there was an effort in Switzerland to harvest electricity from the earth. Endless possibilities. They used heat from the earth's mantle to boil water, sent it through a steam turbine that made electricity.

"Then it went wrong. They were forced to shut the experiment down. It was too dangerous. So that concept was never realized.

"Our own government had played with geothermal power for decades. When the U.S. military heard about the Switzerland experiment, they were enthralled. A bright, young navy scientist came up with the idea of using tectonic manipulation in warfare. The problem was that we needed an in—a way to disrupt the earth below an enemy target. It couldn't be done remotely, so we needed geothermal rigs placed throughout foreign countries.

"What we came up with was a pretty basic deception plan. Since many of our enemy countries have unreliable electricity sources, it made sense to offer to build them these electricity plants as an aid project. A nice gesture, you know? Good foreign policy.

"Most of the countries we approached agreed. Turns out, people like the idea of free power. Things were moving ahead. The last step in the experimental phase was to determine the sensitivity of the trigger—see what amount of drilling causes what result. Yellowstone was the perfect testing ground."

"What about all the people? The government has no regard for its own citizens? And the land?"

"We closed the park. Our team had a pretty good idea of how much water can be pumped before something disastrous is triggered."

After seeing the park a few hours ago, Jake wasn't so sure about that.

"And Jan? Makter? What's their involvement?"

"Merely coincidental, really. Our Manhattan office was throwing some pretty serious charges at Jan. Narcotics, conspiracy. This was his plea deal. We gave him some temporary work. He handpicked Makter. Bad idea. We lost control."

"So those two coordinated the bear attack, the avalanche, the drowning, all of it?"

"Not coordinated, no. It was just Makter. Before we could get rid of him, the experiment was in jeopardy. Plus, Jan kept assuring us that he could handle it."

"Why involve criminals? Why not keep it all under wraps—a government secret?"

"Plausible deniability, Jake. If the public got suspicious, we could peg it all on Jan. Paint him as a criminal mastermind working for some foreign government. Use part of the truth to lie. People would buy it."

Jake was angry now. *How could they do this?*

"You put a madman in charge of public relations. Now innocent people are dead."

"No, Jake. Plausible deniability, remember? Jan put a madman in charge." Daniel raised his gun again and prepared to fire.

37

THE HOT ROCK TRACT

Jake saw the shadow under the door again. Daniel cocked his handgun.

I don't know who you are, but for God's sake, move now!!

Noelle was weeping. Jake wanted to comfort her one last time, but he had no idea what to say.

Better to die, he thought. *I would never forgive myself for this.* He closed his eyes.

The door came crashing down. Dust flew into the air, obscuring the intruder for a few seconds. Daniel aimed steadily in the center of the ghostlike cloud.

"Put your gun down, Officer!" Daniel shouted.

"You first!" Chief Terrell yelled back. "I heard it all. You'll kill us either way!"

The stare-down went on for a few seconds in silence. Suddenly,

Daniel backed down. "Here's the deal, we put down our weapons at the same time and kick them to the corner there. Then we figure out a way to resolve this without anybody getting hurt."

The chief sized him up. "Fine. Agreed. Put it down slowly." The two men bent toward the floor with their eyes still focused on each other. For a split second, the chief glanced over at Jake, who nodded almost imperceptibly.

The agent's gun hit the floor first and Jake lunged from the chair, slid toward Daniel, and kicked the gun into the corner. The chief stood up and trained his pistol on the unarmed agent.

"Don't fucking move," Terrell said.

"Nice of you to join us." Jake smiled at the chief and then grabbed the pistol from the floor. "We need to stop the drilling and pumping before this thing blows. Noelle, go upstairs and look for a way to shut it down."

She nodded. The chief forced Daniel into the chair that had held Jake just a few minutes earlier.

Noelle came back empty-handed.

There were violent rumbles almost constantly now. The furniture in the house was bouncing around rowdily, and it was getting difficult to stand. Looking out into the night air toward the park, they could see that geothermal activity was putting on a natural pyrotechnics show.

"I didn't see anything. No switches or anything like that. The computers all require passwords. I don't even know what we would do if we could access them."

"Okay." Jake thought for a moment. "Let's all go upstairs." He grabbed Daniel by his wrists; they were now bound behind him with duct tape.

On the way up, Daniel became talkative again. He was starting to plead. "This is a mistake, Jake. You can't just interfere with this high-level shit. This is progress, Jake! I can assure you it would be used only in emergency situations, if it's ever even employed. Hell, this might be the last we ever see of the stupid idea!"

"I'm not even thinking that far into the future yet, Daniel. I'm trying to stop something that is happening *now*. I was in the park. We need to shut it down immediately." He pulled Daniel up the last few stairs against his will.

"Every new idea requires some sacrifice, old friend. The park is cleared! If the thing does blow, casualties will be minimal."

Jake stopped and gave him a dubious look. "You want me to sacrifice our lives and allow you to destroy one of the most unique places in the world, and in the name of what? This has to stop, Dan, *now*."

Daniel fell quiet again. When they got into the control room, the chief took over. He sat Daniel down in a chair in front of one of the computers, removed the duct tape, and held the gun to his head. "Log in."

Daniel started punching keys. The computer screen showed an operating system that was unfamiliar to all three of them.

"There's no way to shut it down." As he spoke, Daniel was toppled from his chair by a tremor. The lights overhead pulsed. Sparks flew from the electrical sockets. Noelle grabbed Jake's shoulder to steady herself.

Terrell pulled Daniel up by his shirt and dropped him down into the chair.

"Shut it all down now!" This time, Daniel didn't move.

"I can't do that. I'm sorry. I don't even know how."

The chief pushed the barrel of the gun hard into the soft spot at the top of Daniel's neck, but he didn't flinch. The computer screen blinked out. Drywall cracked and fell in the control room.

"Now!" The computer screen lit back up.

Backup Power Initiated.

Daniel repeated himself, shaking his head. "I can't do that."

Without warning, the chief moved the gun so its barrel was pointed directly down onto the agent's bent knee. He cocked the weapon.

"Don't be stupid! I'm a federal agent!"

The bullet traveled through Daniel's kneecap and tunneled into his fibula. Noelle screamed and jumped back.

Daniel let out a yelp. Blood was pooling around his shoes. Terrell moved the gun to his left knee.

"Shut it down." This time, the chief said it more calmly. No response. The chief fired again, blowing apart the agent's left knee.

Daniel screamed again, followed by a series of soft whimpers. The chief put the barrel of the gun against Daniel's shoulder. "I'm sick of you hotshots bossing me around in my own town." He looked at Jake for a moment. "You think you're such hot shit, coming in here from back East?"

Jake and Noelle exchanged looks. The chief seemed to be losing his cool. Daniel could sense it too. His shoulders dropped in surrender.

"I'm going to ask you one more time, *boy*. Shut the system down, or I'll blow your shoulder up like I did your knees. Then you've got one more shoulder before I use your big fed head as a bargaining chip." Terrell dug the barrel into the wound on Daniel's right knee. Daniel hissed through his teeth, trying to hold in a scream. He was breathing hard. Nearly in shock.

Terrell cocked the gun and pushed its barrel hard into Daniel's right shoulder. The agent was losing significant blood. He tried to collect himself.

There was an uneasy silence for a moment before Daniel started typing. After forty-five seconds of entering some series of codes and swearing under his breath, he spoke aloud. "It's done. You're going to regret this, Jake." He groaned in pain. The chief rapped the pistol's grip hard against Daniel's temple, knocking him unconscious.

A window popped up:

EMERGENCY OVERRIDE: Drilling is incomplete. Do you wish to abort the Hot Rock Experiment?

The chief hit enter.

The hum filling the house came to a sudden stop. Only the noise of the quakes remained. Groaning and rumbling. The house was collapsing.

"Let's go."

Terrell handed his pistol to Jake and walked down the stairs, out the door, and down the driveway. Jake and Noelle followed after him, dragging Daniel down the crumbling stairway.

"What the hell is with Terrell?" Noelle exclaimed when they got outside. Her voice was still shaky. Jake only shook his head.

"Guy's had a hell of a week."

Jake checked Daniel's injuries. The chief had done an extraordinary job of missing central veins and arteries. Daniel would be in extreme pain when he woke up, but he wouldn't bleed out.

Jake yelled to Terrell.

"We need medevac, Chief."

It was the first time Jake had addressed him so respectfully.

"On its way."

Suddenly the windows of the house blew out. Inside, crumbling walls threw dust out the voids, giving the impression that the house was breathing its last breaths.

"How did you find us?"

The chief laughed. "Turned out one of our own was involved. He confessed after hearing about J.P. We threw a tracker on the Shaman's car."

Makter was the Shaman.

Jake pulled Daniel farther from the structure. Then he walked to Noelle, put his arm around her, and pulled her close. They watched the house fall under the starlight.

EPILOGUE

GRAND TETON NATIONAL PARK. TWO WEEKS LATER.

It was evening. Jake and Noelle stood behind Noelle's cabin, looking toward the Tetons.

"J.P. asked me a funny question the other day. He wanted to know if I thought mankind could continue to manipulate the earth—you know, to use it, without screwing things up. Like, would nature carry on no matter what?"

"'Nature will find a way' kind of thing? Rather prescient line of questioning, don't you think?" Noelle smiled.

"He can be pretty sharp."

"And what did you say?"

A stiff but warmish breeze pushed sage and pine past their nostrils, comforting them immensely.

"I didn't really have an answer at the time."

"And now?"

"I think nature *will* find a way to some extent, but there's a line. I think you and I were lucky enough to stop this thing right before it crossed that line."

"How do you mean?"

"Despite everything that happened out there, the geysers will continue to erupt, the elk and bison will graze, all of those things will find a way to carry on. But it was damn close."

"And if we didn't stop it?"

"I don't think there's any question that it would have been the end of the Northern Rockies as we know them."

Noelle playfully tousled Jake's hair. "At least. Well done, counsel. Did you hear Yellowstone reopens tomorrow? And the development? The Old Breast Milk Ranch?" She laughed.

"Nixed. Thank God. Their financiers backed out."

"The Hot Rock project?"

"The feds will explain it away, like they always do."

They looked around at the black silhouettes of the pines against the granite-gray mountains, taking it all in.

"Feel like going into town?" Jake asked.

Noelle and Jake talked a bit on the drive to Jackson, but they mainly just held hands and enjoyed each other's company. The sense of relief was palpable.

When they got to Airport Junction, they found traffic.

"What's this?" Noelle asked.

"Big flight must've come in. It's summer now, remember? Three months of traffic, lines, and general insanity."

"Ugh. What do they say? 'If they call it tourist season how come you can't shoot 'em?'"

"Maybe not apropos given what we just went through." Jake smiled at her. She squeezed his hand and laughed.

The line of rental cars in front of them lit up the highway all the way from the airport down past the normally pitch-black elk refuge and into town, where the tourists dispersed in different directions looking for their hotels.

It was comforting to Jake in a way; it represented a return to normalcy. In a contrary sense, it troubled him. *So many people.* He hated to think like one of the Shaman's crazed followers, but he wondered to himself how sustainable this situation was, not only in Jackson but throughout the whole world.

"Whatcha thinking about? You look upset."

Jake snapped out of it. "Nothing, I'm great. Where to for dinner?"

Noelle leaned over and gave him a long, hard kiss on the cheek. "Can't we just go back to your place?"

When they pulled into the bed-and-breakfast, the SUV's headlights lit up two eyes on the perimeter of the driveway. It was Chayote. He cautiously trotted to meet them where they parked. When they opened the front door, he hopped up on the porch, sat down, and cocked his head.

Jake tried for what seemed like the umpteenth time. "C'mon, Chayote! Come on!" He slapped his hands on his knees to try to create some excitement. The dog only cocked his head farther to the side and wagged his tail ever so slightly.

"What's *his* deal?" Noelle asked.

"Shy, I guess."

"He's yours?"

"Not really."

Noelle knelt down and hit on the magic words. "You *hungry,* buddy? You *hungry*?" This word he knew.

In a fraction of a second, the dog bounded to the door, rearing up playfully on his way. Noelle held out her arms to receive him, but he turned and skidded past them into the house.

Jake and Noelle heard crashing from inside as he frantically tried to find a feeding bowl.

"Great," Jake said sarcastically.

"Oh, c'mon, it'll be fun!"

Jake smiled uneasily as Noelle went through the door searching for the dog. He looked around for a moment at the wilderness spreading out into the night. Then he walked inside.

Noelle was unbuttoning her shirt and shaking off her pants at the bottom of the stairs. Jake smiled and walked toward her.

"Easy, your hands are freezing!"

"Sorry."

Noelle shrugged. "I'll get over it." She started to lead him up the stairs.

From the front door, a jovial shout: "Hey-yoooooooo!" It startled them. Noelle ran back down the stairs and tried to cover up, but it was too late.

"That kinda party?" J.P. asked, staring at Noelle. "I'm into it." He started pulling off his hoodie. An attractive woman in nurse's scrubs stood next to him, a bemused smile on her face. He turned to her. "Just kidding."

Noelle gave J.P. a puzzled look.

"Ongoing treatment is all. Doc said I might need physical therapy."

The nurse laughed and smacked J.P. playfully on his shoulder.

"All right! Get your clothes, the night is young. I've got beer for the dudes and champagne for the ladies!"

*　　*　　*

EPILOGUE

Thirty miles upriver, a small fire burned on a sandy west bank of the Snake. A spruce bough shelter was hidden in the tree line. Inside Sam chewed on the inner stalk of a marsh reed, wondering what his next mission would be.

ACKNOWLEDGMENTS

Several people lent a helping hand with feedback and research: Matt Kessler, Pat Cooper, Bob Peters, Lara Bertsch, Joshua Siebert, and last but far from least, my super-agent Margaret Riley and editor extraordinaire Paul Whitlatch. Also at Scribner, a huge thank-you to Stephanie Evans, Ben Holmes, Leah Sikora, and Nan Graham.

A special thanks to my friends in Jackson for, among many other things, sharing with me the experiences that helped create Jake Trent's world: Allen Riley, Charlie Senn, Sam Allen, Karl Koch, Mark Rector, Spencer Van Schaack, and Silas Collins, just to name a few. Let's go fishing soon.